Frederick Marryat

Valerie, an Autobiography

SALZWASSER
VERLAG

Frederick Marryat

Valerie, an Autobiography

Reprint of the original, first published in 1865.

1st Edition 2022 | ISBN: 978-3-75259-085-2

Verlag (Publisher): Salzwasser Verlag GmbH, Zeilweg 44, 60439 Frankfurt, Deutschland
Vertretungsberechtigt (Authorized to represent): E. Roepke, Zeilweg 44, 60439 Frankfurt, Deutschland
Druck (Print): Books on Demand GmbH, In de Tarpen 42, 22848 Norderstedt, Deutschland

VALERIE,

AN AUTOBIOGRAPHY.

BY

CAPTAIN MARRYAT, R.N.

AUTHOR OF "PETER SIMPLE," "JACOB FAITHFUL,"
ETC. ETC.

NEW EDITION.

LONDON

1865.

VALERIE.

CHAPTER I.

I HAVE titled these pages with nothing more than my baptismal name. If the reader finds sufficient interest in them to read to the end, he will discover the position that I am in, after an eventful life. I shall, however, not trespass upon his time by making many introductory remarks; but commence at once with my birth, parentage, and education. This is necessary, as although the two first are, perhaps, of little comparative consequence, still the latter is of importance, as it will prepare the reader for many events in my after-life. I may add, that much depends upon birth and parentage; at all events, it is necessary to complete a perfect picture. Let me, therefore, begin at the beginning.

I was born in France. My father, who was of the *ancienne noblesse* of France, by a younger branch of the best blood, and was a most splendid specimen of the outward man, was the son of an old officer, and an officer himself in the army of Napoleon. In the conquest of Italy he had served in the ranks, and continuing to follow Napoleon through all his campaigns, had arrived to the grade of captain of cavalry. He had distinguished himself on many occasions, was a favourite of the Emperor's, wore the cross of the Legion of Honour, and was considered in a fair way to rapid promotion, when he committed a great error. During the time that his squadron was occupying a small German town, situated on the river Erbach, called Deux Ponts, he saw my mother, fell desperately in love, and married. There was some excuse for him, for a more beautiful woman than my mother I never beheld; moreover, she was highly talented, and a most perfect musician; of a good family, and with a dower by no means contemptible.

The reader may say that, in marrying such a woman,

my father could hardly be said to have committed a very great error. This is true, the error was not in marrying, but in allowing his wife's influence over him to stop his future advancement. He wished to leave her with her father and mother until the campaign was over. She refused to be left, and he yielded to her wishes. Now, Napoleon had no objection to his officers being married, but a very great dislike to their wives accompanying the army; and this was the fault which my father committed, and which lost him the favour of his general. My mother was too beautiful a woman not to be noticed, and immediately inquired about, and the knowledge soon came to Napoleon's ears, and militated against my father's future advancement.

During the first year of their marriage, my eldest brother, Auguste, was born, and shortly afterwards my mother promised an increase to the family, which was the occasion of great satisfaction to my father, who, now that he had been married more than a year, would at times look at my mother, and, beautiful as she was, calculate in his mind whether the possession of her was indemnification sufficient for the loss of the brigade which she had cost him.

To account for my father's satisfaction, I must acquaint the reader with circumstances which are not very well known. As I before observed, Napoleon had no objection to marriage, because he required men for his army; and because he required men, and not women, he thought very poorly of a married couple who produced a plurality of girls. If, on the contrary, a woman presented her husband with six or seven boys, if he was an officer in the army, he was certain of a pension for life. Now, as my mother had commenced with a boy, and it is well known that there is every chance of a woman continuing to produce the sex which first makes its appearance, she was much complimented and congratulated by the officers when she so soon gave signs of an increase, and they prophesied that she would, by her fruitfulness, in a few years obtain a pension for her husband. My father hoped so, and thought that if he had lost the brigade, he would be indemnified by the pension. My mother was certain of it; and declared it was a boy.

But prophesies, hopes, and declarations, were all falsified

and overthrown by my unfortunate appearance. The disappointment of my father was great; but he bore it like a man. My mother was not only disappointed, but indignant. She felt mortified, after all her declarations, that I should have appeared and disproved them. She was a woman of violent temper, a discovery which my father made too late. To me, as the cause of her humiliation and disappointment, she took an aversion, which only increased as I grew up, and which, as will be hereafter shown, was the mainspring of all my vicissitudes in after-life.

Surely, there is an error in asserting that there is no feeling so strong as maternal love. How often do we witness instances like mine, in which disappointed vanity, ambition, or interest, have changed this love into deadly hate!

My father, who felt the inconvenience of my mother accompanying him on forced marches, and who, perhaps, being disappointed in his hopes of a pension, thought that he might as well recover the Emperor's favour, and look for the brigade, now proposed that my mother should return with her two children to her parents, This my mother, who had always gained the upper hand, positively refused to accede to. She did, however, allow me and my brother Auguste to be sent to her parents' care at Deux Ponts, and there we remained while my father followed the fortunes of the Emperor, and my mother followed the fortunes of my father. I have little or no recollection of my maternal grandfather and grandmother, I remember that I lived with them, as I remained there with my brother, till I was seven years old, at which period my paternal grandmother offered to receive my brother and me and take charge of our education. This offer was accepted, and we both went to Luneville, where she resided.

I have said that my paternal grandmother offered to receive us, and not my paternal grandfather, who was still alive. Such was the case; as, could he have had his own way, he would not have allowed us to come to Luneville, for he had a great dislike to children; but my grandmother had property of her own, independent of her husband, and she insisted upon our coming. Very often, after we had been received into her house, I would hear remonstrance on his part relative to the expense of keeping us, and the reply of my grandmother, which would be,

"*Eh bien, Monsieur Chatenœuf, c'est mon argent que je dépense.*" I must describe Monsieur Chatenœuf. As I before stated, he had been an officer in the French army; but had now retired upon his pension, with the rank of major, and decorated with the Legion of Honour. At the time that I first saw him, he was a tall, elegant old man, with hair as white as silver. I heard it said, that when young, he was considered one of the bravest and handsomest officers in the French army. He was very quiet in his manners, spoke very little, and took a large quantity of snuff. He was egotistic to excess, attending wholly to himself and his own comforts; and it was because the noise of children interfered with his comfort that he disliked them so much. We saw little of him, and cared less. If I came into his room when he was alone, he promised me a good whipping, I therefore avoided him as much as I could: the association was not pleasant.

Luneville is a beautiful town in the department of Meurthe. The castle, or rather palace, is a very splendid and spacious building, in which formerly the dukes of Lorraine held their court. It was afterwards inhabited by King Stanislaus, who founded a military school, a library, and an hospital. The palace was a square building, with a handsome façade facing the town, and in front of it there was a fountain. There was a large square in the centre of the palace, and behind it an extensive garden, which was well kept up and carefully attended to. One side of the palace was occupied by the officers of the regiments quartered in Luneville; the opposite side, by the soldiery; and the remainder of the building was appropriated to the reception of old retired officers who had been pensioned. It was in this beautiful building that my grandfather and grandmother were established for the remainder of their lives. Except the Tuileries, I know of no palace in France equal to that of Luneville. Here it was that, at seven years old, I took up my quarters; and it is from that period that I have always dated my existence.

I have described my grandfather and my residence, but now I must introduce my grandmother; my dear, excellent grandmother, whom I loved so much when she was living, and whose memory I shall ever revere. In person she was rather diminutive, but although sixty years of age, she still retained her figure, which was remarkably pretty, and she was as straight as an arrow. Never had age pressed more lightly upon the human frame; for, strange to say, her hair was black as jet, and fell down to her knees. It was considered a great curiosity, and she was not a little proud of it, for there was not a gray hair to be seen. Although she had lost many of her teeth, her skin was not wrinkled, but had a freshness most remarkable in a person so advanced in years. Her mind was as young as her body; she was very witty and coquettish, and the officers living in the palace were continually in her apartments, preferring her company to that of younger women. Partial to children, she would join in all our sports, and sit down to play "hunt the slipper" with us and our young companions. But with all her vivacity, she was a strictly moral and religious woman. She could be lenient to indiscretion and carelessness, but any deviation from truth and honesty, on the part of my brother or myself, was certain to be visited with severe punishment. She argued, that there could be no virtue, where there was deceit, which she considered as the hotbed from which every vice would spring out spontaneously; that truth was the basis of all that was good and noble, and that every other branch of education was, comparatively speaking, of no importance, and, without truth, of no value. She was right.

My brother and I were both sent to day-schools. The maid Catherine always took me to school after breakfast, and came to fetch me home about four o'clock in the afternoon. Those were happy times. With what joy I used to return to the palace, bounding into my grandmother's apartment on the ground-floor, sometimes to frighten her, leaping in at the window and dropping at her feet, the old lady scolding and laughing at the same time. My grandmother was, as I observed, religious, but she was not a devotee. The great object was to instil into me a love of truth, and in this she was indefatigable. When I did wrong, it was not the fault I had committed which caused her concern, it was the fear that I should deny it which worried and alarmed her. To prevent this, the old lady had a curious method—she dreamed for my benefit. If I had done wrong, and she suspected me, she would not accuse me until she had made such inquiries as convinced her that I was the guilty person; and then, perhaps, the next morning, she would say, as I stood by her side: "Valerie, I had a dream last night; I can't get it out of my head. I dreamt that my little girl had forgotten her promise to me, and when she went to the storeroom had eaten a large piece of the cake."

She would fix her eyes upon me as she narrated the events of her dream, and, as she proceeded, my face would be covered with blushes, and my eyes cast down in confusion; I dared not look at her, and by the time that she had finished, I was down on my knees, with my face buried in her lap. If my offence was great, I had to say my prayers, and implore the Divine forgiveness, and was sent to prison, that is, locked up for a few hours in my bedroom. Catherine, the maid, had been many years with my grandmother, and was, to a certain degree, a privileged person; at all events, she considered herself warranted in giving her opinion, and grumbling as much as she pleased, and such was invariably the case whenever I was locked up. "*Toujours en prison, cette pauvre petite.* It is too bad, madam; you must let her out." My grandmother would quietly reply, "Catherine, you are a good woman, but you understand nothing about the education of children." Sometimes, however, she obtained the key from my grandmother, and I was released sooner than was originally intended.

The fact is, that being put in prison was a very heavy punishment, as it invariably took place in the evenings, after my return from school, so that I lost my play-hours. There were a great many officers with their wives located in the palace, and, of course, no want of playmates. The girls used to go to the *bosquet*, which adjoined the gardens of the palace, collect flowers, and make a garland, which they hung on a rope stretched across the courtyard of the palace. As the day closed in, the party from each house, or apartments rather, brought out a lantern, and having thus illuminated our ballroom by subscription, the boys and girls danced the *rondé*, and other games, until it was bedtime. As the window of my bedroom looked out upon the court, whenever I was put into prison, I had the mortification of witnessing all these joyous games without being permitted to join in them.

To prove the effect of my grandmother's system of dreaming upon me, I will narrate a circumstance which occurred. My grandfather had a landed property about four miles from Luneville. A portion of this land was let to a farmer, and the remainder he farmed on his own account, and the produce was consumed in the housekeeping. From this farm we received milk, butter, cheese, all kinds of fruit, and indeed everything which a farm produces. In that part of France they have a method of melting down and clarifying butter for winter use, instead of salting it. This not only preserves it, but, to most people, makes it more palatable; at all events, I can answer for myself, for I was inordinately fond of it. There were eighteen or twenty jars of it in the storeroom, which were used up in rotation. I dared not take any out of the jar in use, as I should be certain to be discovered; so I went to the last jar, and by my repeated assaults upon it, it was nearly empty before my grandmother discovered it. As usual, she had a dream. She commenced with counting over the number of jars of butter; and how she opened such a one, and it was full; and then the next, and it was full; but before her dream was half over, and she was still a long way from the jar which I had despoiled, I was on my knees, telling her the end of the dream, of my own accord, for I could not bear the suspense of having all the jars examined. From that time, I generally made a full confession before the dream was ended.

But when I was about nine years old I was guilty of a very heavy offence, which I shall narrate, on account of the peculiar punishment which I received, and which might be advantageously pursued by the parents of the present day, who may happen to cast their eyes over these memoirs. It was the custom for the children of the officers who lived in the palace, that is, the girls, to club together occasionally, that they might have a little *fête* in the garden of the palace. It was a sort of picnic, to which every one contributed: some would bring cakes, some fruit; some would bring money (a few sous) to purchase bon-bons, or anything else which might be agreed upon.

On those occasions, my grandmother invariably gave me fruit, a very liberal allowance of apples and pears, from the storeroom; for we had plenty from the orchard of the farm. But one day, one of the elder girls told me that they had plenty of fruit, and that I must bring some money. I asked my grandmother, but she refused me; and then this girl proposed that I should steal some from my grandfather. I objected; but she ridiculed my objections, and pressed me until she overcame my scruples, and I consented. But when I left her, after she had obtained my promise, I was in a sad state. I knew it was wicked to steal, and the girl had taken care to point out to me how wicked it was to break a promise. I did not know what to do: all that evening I was in such a state of feverish excitement, that my grandmother was quite astonished. The fact was, that I was ashamed to retract my promise, and yet I trembled at the deed that I was about to do. I went into my room and got into bed. I remained awake; and about midnight I got up, and creeping softly into my grandfather's room, I went to his clothes, which were on a chair, and rifled his pockets of—two sous!

Having effected my purpose, I retired stealthily, and gained my own room. What my feelings were when I was again in bed, I cannot well describe—they were horrible—I could not shut my eyes for the remainder of the night, and the next morning I made my appearance, haggard, pale, and trembling. It proved, however, that my grandfather, who was awake, had witnessed the theft in silence, and informed my grandmother of it. Before I went to school, my grandmother called me in to her, for I had avoided her.

"Come here, Valerie," said she; "I have had a dream—a most dreadful dream—it was about a little girl, who, in the middle of the night, crept into her grandfather's room——"

I could bear no more. I threw myself on the floor, and, in agony, screamed out—

"Yes, grandmamma, and stole two sous."

A paroxysm of tears followed the confession, and for more than an hour I remained on the floor, hiding my face and sobbing. My grandmother allowed me to remain there—she was very much annoyed—I had committed a crime of the first magnitude—my punishment was severe. I was locked up in my room for ten days: but this was the smallest portion of the punishment: every visitor that came in, I was sent for, and on my making my appearance, my grandmother would take me by the hand, and leading me up, would formally present me to the visitors.

"Permettez, madame (ou monsieur), que je vous présente Mademoiselle Valerie, qui est enfermée dans sa chambre pour avoir volé deux sous de son grand-père."

Oh! the shame, the mortification that I felt. This would take place at least ten times a day; and each succeeding presentation was followed by a burst of tears, as I was again led back to my chamber. Severe as this punishment was, the effect of it was excellent. I would have endured martyrdom, after what I had gone through, before I would have taken what was not my own. It was a painful, but a judicious, and most radical cure.

For five years I remained under the care of this most estimable woman, and, under her guidance, had become a truthful and religious girl; and I may conscientiously add, that I was as innocent as a lamb—but a change was at hand. The Emperor had been hurled from his throne, and was shut up on a barren rock, and soon great alterations were made in the French army. My father's regiment of hussars had been disbanded, and he was now appointed to a dragoon regiment, which was ordered to Luneville. He arrived with my mother and a numerous family, she having presented him with seven more children; so that, with Auguste and me, he had now nine children. I may as well here observe that my mother continued to add yearly to the family, till she had fourteen in all, and out of these there were seven boys; so that, had the Emperor remained on the throne of France, my father would certainly have secured the pension.

The arrival of my family was a source both of pleasure and pain to me. I was most anxious to see all my brothers and sisters, and my heart yearned towards my father and mother, although I had no recollection of them; but I was fearful that I should be removed from my grandmother's care, and she was equally alarmed at the chance of our separation. Unfortunately for me, it turned out as we had anticipated. My mother was anything but gracious to my grandmother, notwithstanding the obligations she was under to her, and very soon took an opportunity of quarrelling with her. The cause of the quarrel was very absurd, and proved that it was predetermined on the part of my mother. My grandmother had some curious old carved furniture, which my mother coveted, and requested my grandmother to let her have it. This my grandmother would not consent to, and my mother took offence at her refusal. I and my brother were immediately ordered home, my mother asserting that we had been both very badly brought up; and this was all the thanks that my grandmother received for her kindness to us, and defraying all our expenses for five years.

I had not been at home more than a week when my father's regiment was ordered to Nanci; but, during this short period, I had sufficient to convince me that I should be very miserable. My mother's dislike to me, which I have referred to before, now assumed the character of positive hatred, and I was very ill treated. I was employed as a servant, and as nurse to the younger children; and hardly a day passed without my feeling the weight of her hand. We set off for Nanci, and I thought my heart would break as I quitted the arms of my grandmother, who wept over me. My father was very willing to leave me with my grandmother, who promised to leave her property to me; but this offer in my favour enraged my mother still more; she declared that I should not remain; and my father had long succumbed to her termagant disposition, and yielded implicit obedience to her authority. It was lamentable to see such a fine soldierlike man afraid even to speak before this woman; but he was completely under her thraldom, and never dared to contradict.

As soon as we were settled in the barracks at Nanci my mother commenced her system of persecution in downright earnest. I had to make all the beds, wash the children, carry out the baby, and do every menial office for my brothers and sisters, who were encouraged to order me about. I had very good clothes, which had been provided me by my grandmother; they were all taken away, and altered for my younger sisters; but what was still more mortifying, all my sisters had lessons in music, dancing, and other accomplishments, from various masters, whose instructions I was not permitted to take advantage of, although there would have been no addition to the expense.

"Oh! my father," cried I, "why is this?—what have I done?—am not I your daughter—your eldest daughter?"

"I will speak to your mother," replied he.

And he did venture to do so; but, by so doing, he raised up such a tempest, that he was glad to drop the subject, and apologize for an act of justice. Poor man! he could do no more than pity me.

I well remember my feelings at that time. I felt that I could love my mother, love her dearly, if she would have allowed me so to do. I had tried to obtain her goodwill, but I received nothing in return but blows, and at last I became so alarmed when in her presence, that I almost lost my reason. My ears were boxed till I could not recollect where I was, and I became stupified with fear. All I thought of, all my anxiety, at last, was to get out of the room where my mother was. My terror was so great that her voice made me tremble, and at the sight of her I caught my breath and gasped from alarm. My brother Auguste was very nearly as much an object of dislike to my mother as I was, chiefly because he had been brought up by my grandmother, and, moreover, because he would take my part.

The great favourite of my mother was my second brother, Nicolas; he was a wonderful musician, could play upon any instrument, and the most difficult music at sight. This talent endeared him to my mother, who was herself a first-rate musician. He was permitted to order me about just as he pleased, and if I did not please him, to beat me without mercy, and very often my mother would fly at me and assist him. But Auguste took my part, and Nicolas received very severe chastisement from him, but this did not help me; on the contrary, if Auguste interfered in my behalf, my mother would pounce upon me, and I may say that I was stunned with her blows. Auguste appealed to his father, but he dared not interfere. He was coward enough to sit by and see his daughter treated in this way without remonstrance; and, in a short time, I was fast approaching to what my mother declared me to be—a perfect idiot.

I trust that my own sex will not think me a renegade when I say, that if ever there was a proof that woman was intended by the Creator to be subject to man, it is, that once place power in the hands of woman, and there is not one out of a hundred who will not abuse it. We hear much of the rights of woman, and their wrongs; but this is certain, that in a family, as in a State, there can be no divided rule—no equality. One must be master, and no family is so badly managed, or so badly brought up, as where the law of nature is reversed, and we contemplate that most despicable of all *lusi naturæ*—a hen-pecked husband. To proceed, the consequence of my mother's treatment was to undermine in me all the precepts of my worthy grandmother. I was a slave; and a slave under the continual influence of fear cannot be honest. The fear of punishment produced deceit to avoid it. Even my brother Auguste, from his regard and pity for me, would fall into the same error. "Valerie," he would say, running out to me as I was coming home with my little brother in my arms, "your mother will beat you on your return. You must say so and so." This so and so was, of course, an untruth; and, in consequence, my fibs were so awkward, and accompanied by so much hesitation and blushing, that I was invariably found out, and then punished for what I did not deserve to be; and when my mother obtained such triumphant proof against me, she did not fail to make the most of it with my father, who, by degrees, began to consider that my treatment was merited, and that I was a bad and deceitful child.

My only happiness was to be out in the open air, away from my mother's presence, and this was only to be obtained when I was ordered out with my little brother Pierre, whom I had to carry as soon as I had done the household work. If Pierre was fractious, my mother would order me out of the house with him immediately. This I knew, and I used to pinch the poor child to make him cry, that I might gain my object, and be sent away; so that to duplicity I added cruelty. Six months before this, had any one told me that I ever would be guilty of such a thing, with what indignation I should have denied it!

Although my mother flattered herself that it was only in her own domestic circle that her unnatural conduct towards me was known, such was not the case, and the treatment which I received from her was the occasion of much sympathy on the part of the officers and their wives, who were quartered in the barracks. Some of them ventured to remonstrate with my father for his consenting to it; but although he was cowed by a woman, he had no fear of men, and as he told them candidly that any future interference in his domestic concerns must be answered by the sword, no more was said to him on the subject. Strange, that a man should risk his life with such indifference, rather than remedy an evil, and yet be under such thraldom to a woman!—that one who was always distinguished in action as the most forward and the most brave, should be a trembling coward before an imperious wife! But this is a world of sad contradictions.

There was a lady in the barracks, wife to one of the superior officers, who was very partial to me. She had a daughter, a very sweet girl, who was also named Valerie. When I could escape from the house, I used to be constantly with them; and when I saw my namesake caressing and caressed, in the arms of her mother, as I was sitting by on a stool, the tears would run down at the thoughts that such pleasure was debarred from me.

"Why do you cry, Valerie?"

"Oh! madam, why have I not a mother like your Valerie? Why am I to be beat instead of being caressed and fondled like her? What have I done?—But she is not my mother—I'm sure she cannot be—I never will believe it."

And such had really become my conviction, and in consequence I never would address her by the title of mother. This my mother perceived, and it only added to her ill-will. Only permit any one feeling or passion to master you—allow it to increase by never being in the slightest degree checked, and it is horrible to what an excess it will carry you. About this time, my mother proved the truth of the above observation by saying to me, as she struck me to the ground,—

"I'll kill you," cried she; and then, catching her breath, said in a low determined tone, "Oh! I only wish that I dared."

CHAPTER II.

One day, a short time after this, I was walking out as usual with my little brother Pierre in my arms; I was deep in thought; in imagination I was at Luneville with my dear grandmother, when my foot slipped, and I fell. In trying to save my brother, I hurt myself very much, and he, poor child, was unfortunately very much hurt, as well as myself. He cried and moaned piteously, and I did all that I could to console him, but he was in too much pain to be comforted. I remained out for an hour or two, not daring to go home, but the evening was closing in, and I returned at last. The child, who could not yet speak, still moaned and cried, and I told the truth as to the cause of it. My mother flew at me, and I received such chastisement that I could be patient no longer, and I pushed my mother from me; I was felled to the ground, and left there bleeding profusely.

After a time I rose up and crawled to bed. I reflected upon all I had suffered, and made up my mind that I would no longer remain under my father's roof. At daybreak I dressed myself, hastened out of the barracks, and set off for Luneville, which was fifteen miles distant. I had gained about half the way when I was met by a soldier of the regiment, who had once been our servant. I tried to avoid him, but he recognised me. I then begged him not to interfere with me, and told him that I was running away to my grandmother's. Jacques, for that was his name, replied that I was right, and that he would say nothing about it.

"But, mademoiselle," continued he, "you will be tired before you get to Luneville, and may have a chance of a conveyance if you have money to pay for it."

He then slipped a five-franc piece into my hand, and left me to pursue my way. I continued my journey, and at last arrived at the farm belonging to my grandfather, which I have before mentioned as being about four miles from the town. I was afraid to go direct to Luneville, on account of my grandfather, who, I knew, from motives of parsimony, would be unwilling to receive me. I told my history to the farmer's wife, showing her my face covered with bruises and scars, and entreated her to go to my grandmother's and tell her where I was. She put me to bed, and the next morning set off for Luneville, and acquainted my grandmother with the circumstances. The old lady immediately ordered her *char-à-banc* and drove out for me. There was proof positive of my mother's cruelty, and the good old woman shed tears over me when she had pulled off the humble blue cotton dress which I wore and examined my wounds and bruises. When we arrived at Luneville, we met with much opposition from my grandfather, but my grandmother was resolute.

"Since you object to my receiving her in the house," said she, "at all events you cannot prevent my doing my duty towards her, and doing as I please with my own money. I shall therefore send her to school, and pay her expenses."

As soon as new clothes could be made for me, I was sent to the best *pension* in Luneville. Shortly afterwards my father arrived; he had been despatched by my mother to reclaim me and bring me back with him; but he found the tide too strong against him, and my grandmother threatened to appeal to the authorities and make an exposure; this he knew would be a serious injury to his character, and he was therefore compelled to go back without me, and I remained a year and a half at the *pension*, very happy, and improving very fast in my education and my personal appearance.

But I was not destined to be so happy long. True it was, that during this year and a half of tranquillity and happiness, the feelings created by my mother's treatment had softened down, and all animosity had long been discarded, but I was too happy to want to return home again. At the expiration of this year and a half, my father's regiment was again ordered to shift their quarters to a small town, the name of which I now forget; but Luneville lay in their route. My mother had for some time ceased to importune my father about my return. The fact was, that she had been so coldly treated by the other ladies at Nanci, in consequence of her behaviour to me, that she did not think it advisable; but now that they were about to remove, she insisted upon my father taking me with him, promising that I should be well treated, and have the same instruction as my sisters; in fact, she promised everything; acknowledging to my grandmother that she had been too hasty to me, and was very sorry for it. Even my brother Auguste thought that she was now sincere, and my father, my brother, and even my dear grandmother, persuaded me to consent. My mother was now very kind and affectionate towards me, and as I really wanted to love her, I left the *pension* and accompanied the family to their new quarters.

But this was all treachery on the part of my mother. Regardless of my advantage, as she had shown herself on every occasion, she had played her part that she might have an opportunity of discharging an accumulated debt of revenge, which had been heaped up in consequence of the slights she had received from other people on account of her treatment of me. We had hardly been settled in our new abode, before my mother burst out with a virulence again which exceeded all her former cruelty. But I was no longer the frightened victim that I had been; I complained to my father, and insisted upon justice; but that was useless. My brother Auguste now took my part in defiance of his father, and it was one scene of continual family discord. I had made many friends, and used to remain at their houses all day. As for doing household work, notwithstanding her blows, I refused it. One morning my mother was chastising me severely, when my brother Auguste, who was dressed in his hussar uniform, came in and hastened to my assistance, interposing himself between us. My mother's rage was beyond all bounds.

"Wretch," cried she, "would you strike your mother?"

"No," replied he, "but I will protect my sister. You barbarous woman, why do you not kill her at once? it would be a kindness."

It was after this scene that I resolved that I would again return to Luneville. I did not confide my intentions to any one, not even to Auguste. There was a great difficulty in getting out of the front door without being perceived, and my bundle would have created suspicion; by the back of the house the only exit was through a barred window. I was then fourteen years old, but very slight in figure. I tried if my head would pass through the bars, and succeeding, I soon forced my body through, and seizing my bundle, made all haste to the diligence office. I found that it was about to start for Luneville, which was more than half a day's journey distant. I got in very quickly, and the *conducteur*, knowing me, thought that all was right, and the diligence drove off.

There were two people in the *coupé* with me, an officer and his wife; before we had proceeded far, they asked me where I was going; I replied, to my grandmother's at Luneville. Thinking it, however, strange that I should be unaccompanied, they questioned, until they extracted the whole history from me. The lady wished me to come to her on a visit, but the husband, more prudent, said that I was better under the care of my grandmother.

About mid-day we stopped to change horses at an

auberge called the Louis d'Or, about a quarter of a mile from Luneville. Here I alighted without offering any explanation to the *conducteur;* but as he knew me and my grandmother well, that was of no consequence. My reason for alighting was, that the diligence would have put me down at the front of the palace, where I was certain to meet my grandfather, who passed the major portion of the day there, basking on one of the seats; and I was afraid to see him until I had communicated with my grandmother. I had an uncle in the town, and I had been very intimate with my cousin Marie, who was a pretty, kind-hearted girl, and I resolved that I would go there, and beg her to go to my grandmother. The difficulty was, how to get to the house without passing the front of the palace, or even the bridge across the river. At last I decided that I would walk down by the river side until I was opposite to the *bosquet,* which adjoined the garden of the palace, and there wait till it was low water, when I knew that the river could be forded, as I had often seen others do so.

When I arrived opposite to the *bosquet* I sat down on my bundle, by the banks of the river for two or three hours, watching the long feathery weeds at the bottom, which moved gently from one side to the other with the current of the stream. As soon as it was low water I pulled off my shoes and stockings, put them into my bundle, and raising my petticoats, I gained the opposite shore without difficulty. I then replaced my shoes and stockings, crossed the *bosquet,* and gained my uncle's house. My uncle was not at home, but I told my story and showed my bruises to Marie, who immediately put on her bonnet and went to my grandmother. That night I was again installed in my own little bedroom, and most gratefully did I pray before I went to sleep.

This time my grandmother took more decided steps. She went to the commandant of the town, taking me with her, pointing out the treatment which I had received, and claiming his protection; she stated that she had educated me and brought me up, and that she had a claim upon me. My mother's treatment of me was so notorious, that the commandant immediately decided that my grandmother had a right to detain me; and when my father came a day or two after to take me back, he was ordered home by the commandant, with a severe rebuke, and the assurance that I should not return to a father who could permit such cruelty and injustice.

I was now once more happy; but as I remained in the house, my grandfather was continually vexing my grandmother on my account; nevertheless, I remained there more than a year, during which I learnt a great deal, particularly lace-work and fine embroidery, at which I became very expert. But now there was another opposition raised, which was on the part of my uncle, who joined my grandfather in annoying the old lady. The fact was, that when I was not there, my grandmother was very kind and generous to my cousin Marie, who certainly deserved it; but now that I was again with her, all her presents and expenses were lavished upon me, and poor Marie was neglected.

My uncle was not pleased at this; he joined my grandfather, and they pointed out that I was now more than fifteen, and my mother dare not beat me, and as my father was continually writing for me to return, it was her duty not to oppose. Between the two, my poor grandmother was so annoyed and perplexed that she hardly knew what to do. They made her miserable, and at last they worried her into consenting that I should return to my family, which had now removed to Colmar. I did not know this. It was my grandmother's birthday. I had worked for her a beautiful sachet in lace and embroidery, which, with a large bouquet, I brought to her as a present. The old lady folded me in her arms and burst into tears. She then told me that we must part, and that I must return to my father's. Had a dagger been thrust to my heart, I could not have received more anguish.

"Yes, dear Valerie," continued she, "you must leave me to-morrow; I can no longer prevent it. I have not the health and spirits that I had. I am growing old—very old."

I did not remonstrate or try to make her alter her decision. I knew how much she had been annoyed and worried for my sake, and I felt that I would bear everything for hers. I cried bitterly. The next morning my father made his appearance and embraced me with great affection. He was much pleased with my personal improvement. I was now fast budding into womanhood, although I had the feelings of a mere child. I bade farewell to my grandmother, and also to my grandfather, whom I never saw again, as he died three months after I quitted Luneville.

I trust my readers will not think that I dwell too long upon this portion of my life. I do it because I consider it is necessary they should know in what manner I was brought up, and also the cause of my leaving my family, as I afterwards did. If I had stated merely that I could not agree with my mother, who treated me cruelly, they might have imagined that I was not warranted, in a moment of irritation, in taking such a decided step; but when they learn that my persecutions were renewed the moment that I was again in my mother's power, and that nothing could conquer her inveteracy against me, neither time, nor absence, nor submission on my part, nor remonstrance from others, not even a regard for her own character, nor the loss of her friends and acquaintances, they will then acknowledge that I could have done no otherwise, unless I preferred being in daily risk of my life. On my arrival at Colmar, my mother received me graciously, but her politeness did not last long. I now gave a new cause of offence—one that a woman, proud of her beauty and jealous of its decay, does not easily forgive. I was admired and paid great attention to by the officers,—much more attention than she received herself.

" M. Chatenœuf," the officers would say, " you have begotten a daughter much handsomer than yourself." My mother considered this as a polite way to avoid saying that I was much handsomer than she was. If she thought so, she did herself a great injustice, for I could not be compared to what she was when she was of my age. She was even then a most splendid matron. But I had youth in my favour, which is more than half the battle. At all events, the remarks and attentions of the officers aroused my mother's spleen, and she was more harsh in language than ever, although I admit that it was but seldom that she resorted to blows.

I recollect that one day, when I was not supposed to be in hearing, one of the officers said to another, " *Ma foi, elle est jolie—elle a besoin de deux ans, et elle sera parfaite.*" So childish and innocent was I at that time, that I could not imagine what they meant.

"Why was I to be two years older?" I thought and puzzled over it till I fell fast asleep. The attentions of the officers, and the flattery he received from them on my account, appeared to have more effect on my father than I could have imagined. Perhaps he felt that I was somebody to be proud of, and his vanity gave him that courage to oppose my mother which his paternal feelings had not roused. I recollect one instance particularly. There was a great ceremony to be performed in the church, no less than the christening of the two new bells, previous to their being hoisted up in the belfry. The officers told my father that I must be present, and on his return home he stated to my mother his intention of taking me with him on the following day to see the ceremony.

"She can't go—she has no clothes fit to wear," cried my mother.

"Why has she not, madam?" replied my father, sternly. "Let her have some ready for to-morrow, and without fail."

My mother perceived that my father was not to be trifled with, and therefore thought proper to acquiesce. Pity it was that he did not use his authority a little more, after he had discovered that he could regain it if he pleased.

On the following day I accompanied my father, who was one of the officers on duty in the interior of the church, and as he stood in advance of his men, I remained at his side, and of course had a very complete view of the whole ceremony. I was very neatly dressed, and my father received many compliments upon my appearance. At last the ceremony began. The church was lined with troops to keep back the crowd, and the procession entered the church, the bishop walking under a canopy, attended by the priests, then the banners, and pretty children, dressed as angels, tossing frankincense from silver censers. The two bells were in the centre of the church, both of them dressed in white petticoats, which covered them completely, ornamented with ribands, and a garland of flowers upon the head of each—if I may so designate their tops. The godmothers, dressed in white as on baptismal ceremonies, and the godfathers in court suits, stood on each side. They had been selected from the *élite* of the families in the town. The organ and the military band relieved each other until the service commenced. The bishop read the formula; the godmothers and godfathers gave the customary security; the holy water was sprinkled over the bells, and thus were they regularly baptized. One was named Eulalie and the other Lucile. It was a very pretty ceremony, and I should have liked to have been present at their "*première communion*" if it ever took place.

My English readers may consider this as a piece of mummery. At the time I did not. As a good Catholic, which I was at that time, and a pretty Frenchwoman, I thought that nothing could be more correct than the *décoration des belles.* I believe that it has always been the custom to name bells—to consecrate them, most certainly—and if we call to mind what an important part they perform in our religion, I do not wonder at it. By being consecrated, they receive the rites of the church. Why, therefore, should they not receive the same rites in baptism? But why baptize them? Because they speak to us in many ways, and with their loud tongues express the feelings, and make known the duties imposed upon us. Is there cause for the nation to rejoice, their merry notes proclaim it from afar; in solemn tones they summon us to the house of prayer, to the lifting of the Host, and to the blessing of the priest; and it is their mournful notes which announce to us that one of our generation has been summoned away, and has quitted this transitory abode. Their offices are Christian offices, and therefore are they received into the church.

CHAPTER III.

An elder sister of my mother's resided at Colmar, and I passed most of my time with her during our stay. When my father's regiment was ordered to Paris, this lady requested that I might remain with her; but my mother refused, telling her sister that she could not, conscientiously as a mother, allow any of her daughters to quit her care for any worldly advantage. That this was mere hypocrisy, the reader will imagine; indeed, it was fully proved so to be in two hours afterwards, by my mother telling my father that if her sister had offered to take Clara, my second sister, she would have consented.

The fact was, that the old lady had promised to dower me very handsomely (for she was rich), and my mother could not bear any good fortune to come to me.

We passed through Luneville on our road to Paris, and I saw my dear grandmother for the last time. She requested that I might be left with her, making the same offer as she did before, of leaving me all her property at her death; but my mother would not listen to any solicitation. Now, as our family was now fourteen in number, she surely might, in either of the above instances, have well spared me, and it would have been a relief to my father; but this is certain, she would not spare me, although she never disguised her dislike, and would, if she had dared, have treated me as she had formerly done. I was very anxious to stay with my dear grandmother. She had altered very much since my grandfather's death, and was evidently breaking up fast; but my mother was inexorable. We continued our route, and arrived at Paris, where we took up our quarters in the barracks close to the Boulevards.

My mother was as harsh as ever, and now recommenced her boxes of the ear—which during the time we were at Colmar had but seldom been applied. In all my troubles I never was without friends. I now made an acquaintance with the wife of the colonel of the regiment, who joined us at Paris. She had no children. I imparted all my troubles to her, and she used to console me. She was a very religious woman, and as I had been brought up in the same way by my grandmother, she was pleased to find piety in one so young, and became much attached to me. She had a sister, a widow of large fortune, who lived in the Rue St. Honoré, a very pleasant, lively woman, but very sarcastic when she pleased, and not caring what she said if her feelings prompted her. I constantly met her at the colonel's house, and she invited me to come and see her at her own; but I knew that my mother would not permit me, so I did not ask. As the colonel was my father's superior officer, all attempts to break off my intimacy with her, which my mother made, were unavailing, and I passed as usual all my time in any other house except my home.

I have now to record but two more beatings. The reader may think that I have recorded enough already;

but as these were the two last, and they were peculiar, I must beg him to allow me so to do. The first beating was given me for the following cause:—A very gentlemanlike young officer in the regiment was very particular in his attentions to me. I liked his company, but my thoughts had never been directed towards marriage, for I was too childish and innocent. One morning it appeared that he proposed to my father, who immediately gave his consent, provided that I was agreeable, and this he ventured to do without consulting my mother. Perhaps he thought it a good opportunity to remove me from my mother's persecution. At all events, when he made known to her what he had done, and requested her to sound me on the subject, she was in no pleasant humour. When she did so, my reply was (he being a very dark-complexioned man, although well-featured), "*Non, maman, je ne veux pas. Il est trop noir.*"

To my astonishment, my mother flew at me, and I received such an avalanche of boxes on the ears for this reply, that I was glad to make my escape as fast as I could, and locked myself up in my own room. Now I really believe that I was almost a single instance of a young lady having her ears well boxed for refusing to marry a man that she did not care for—but such was my fate.

The treatment I received in this instance got wind in the barracks, and my cause was warmly taken up by every one. Finding myself thus supported, I one day ventured to refuse to do a very menial and unpleasant office, and for this refusal I received the second beating. It was the last certainly, but it was the most severe; for my mother caught up a hearth-brush, and struck me for several minutes such a succession of severe blows, that my face was so disfigured that I was hardly to be recognised, my head cut open in several places, and the blood pouring down me in every direction. At last she left me for dead on the floor. After a time I recovered my recollection, and when I did so, I sprang away from the servants who had been supporting me, and with my hair flying in the wind, and my face and dress streaming with blood, I ran across the barrack-yard to the colonel's house, and entering the room in which she was sitting with her sister, sank at her feet, choking with the blood which poured out of my mouth.

"Who is it?" exclaimed she, springing up in horror and amazement.

"Valerie—*pauvre* Valerie," moaned I, with my face on the floor.

They raised me up, sent for the servants, took me into a bedroom, and sent for the surgeon of the regiment, who lived in the barracks. As soon as I was somewhat recovered, I told them that it was my mother's treatment; and I became so excited, that as soon as the surgeon had left the house, I cried,

"Never, madam, will I again enter my father's house; never while I live—if you do not protect me—or if nobody else will—if you send me back again, I will throw myself in the Seine. I swear it as I kneel."

"What is to be done, sister?" said the colonel's wife.

"I will see. At all events, Valerie, I will keep you here a few days till something can be arranged. It is now quite dark, and you shall stay here, and sleep on this bed."

"Or the bed of the river," replied I; "I care not if it were that, for I should not rise up to misery. I have made a vow, and I repeat, that I never will enter my father's house again."

"My dear Valerie," said the colonel's wife, in a soothing tone.

"Leave her to me, sister," said the other, who was busy arranging my hair, now that my wounds had stopped bleeding, "I will talk to her. The colonel will be home directly, and you must receive him."

Madame Allarde, for that was the colonel's wife's name, left the room. As soon as she was gone, Madame d'Albret, her sister, said to me, "Valerie, I fear that what you have said you will adhere to, and you will throw yourself into the river."

"Yes, if I am taken back again," replied I. "I hope God will forgive me; but I feel I shall, for my mind is overthrown, and I am not sane at times."

"My poor child, you may go back again to your father's house, because my sister and her husband, in their position, cannot prevent it, but believe me, you shall not remain there. As long as I have a home to offer, you shall never want one; but you must listen to me. I wish to serve you and to punish your unnatural mother, and I will do so; but Valerie, you must well weigh circumstances before you decide; I say that I can offer you a home, but recollect life is uncertain, and if it pleases God to summon me, you will have a home no longer. What will you do then?—for you will never be able to return to your father's house."

"You are very kind, madam," replied I, "but my resolution is formed, and I will work for my daily bread in any way that I can, rather than return. Put me but in the way of doing that, and I will for ever bless you."

"You shall never work for your bread while I live, Valerie; but if I die, you will have to do something for your own support, and recollect how friendless you will be, and so young."

"Can I be more friendless than I am at home, madam?" said I, shaking my head mournfully.

"Your father deserves punishment for his want of moral courage, as well as your mother," replied Madame d'Albret. "You had better go to bed now, and to-morrow give me your decision."

"To-morrow will make no change, madam," answered I, "but I fear that there is no chance of my escape. To-morrow my father will arrive for me as usual, and—but I have said it. You may preserve my life, madam, but how I know not;" and I threw myself down on the bed in despair.

CHAPTER IV.

About an hour afterwards Madame d'Albret, who had left me on the bed while she went down to her sister, came up again, and spoke to me; but from weakness, occasioned by the loss of blood and from excitement, I talked for many minutes in the most incoherent manner, and Madame d'Albret was seriously alarmed. In the mean time the colonel had come home, and his wife explained what had happened. She led him up to my room just at the time that I was raving. He took the candle, and looked at my swelled features, and said,

"I should not have recognised the poor girl. *Mort de ma vie!* but this is infamous, and Monsieur de Chatenœuf is a contemptible coward. I will see him to-morrow morning."

The colonel and his wife then left the room. By this time I had recovered from my paroxysm. Madame d'Albret came to me, and putting her face close to mine said, "Valerie."

"Yes, madam," replied I.

"Are you more composed now? Do you think that you could listen to me?"

"Yes, madam, and thankfully," replied I.

"Well, then, my plan is this. I am sure that the colonel will take you home to-morrow. Let him do so; in the morning I will tell you how to behave. To-morrow night you shall escape, and I will be with a *fiacre* at the corner of the street ready to receive you. I will take you to my house, and no one, not even my sister, shall know that you are with me. They will believe that you have thrown yourself into the Seine, and as the regiment is ordered to Lyons, and will leave in ten days or a fortnight, there will be no chance, if you are concealed till their departure, of their knowing that you are alive."

"Thank you, thank you, madam, you know not how happy you have made me," replied I, pressing my hand to my heart, which throbbed painfully with joy. "God bless you, Madame d'Albret. Oh, how I shall pray for you, kind Madame d'Albret!"

Madame d'Albret shed tears over me after I had done speaking, and then, wishing me good night, told me that she would see me in the morning, and let me know what was going on, and then give me further directions for my conduct. She then left me, and I tried to go to sleep; but I was in too much pain. Once I did slumber, and dreamt that my mother was beating me again. I screamed with the pain that the blows gave me, and awoke. I slept no more that night. At daylight I rose, and, as may be supposed, the first thing that I did was to look into the glass. I was terrified; my face was swelled so that my features were hardly distinguishable; one eye was closed up, and the blood had oozed out through the handkerchief which had been tied round my head by the surgeon. I was, indeed, an object. The servant brought me up some coffee, which I drank, and then remained till the colonel's wife came up to me.

It was the first and only time that I ever beheld that good woman angry. She called from the top of the stairs for her husband to come up; he did so, looked at me, said nothing, but went down again. About half an hour afterwards Madame d'Albret and the surgeon came up together. The latter was interrogated by her as to the effects of the injuries I had received, and after examination, he replied, that although it would take some days for the inflammation and marks of the blows to go away, yet he did not consider that eventually I should be in any way disfigured. This gave me great pleasure, as I suspect it would have done any other pretty girl in my situation. Madame d'Albret waited till the surgeon was gone, and then gave me some further instructions, which I obeyed to the letter. She also brought me a black veil, in case I had not one of my own. She then left me, saying, that the colonel had sent for my father, and that she wished to be present at the interview.

My father came, and the colonel, after stating the treatment which I had received, loaded him with reproaches; told him his conduct was that of a coward, to allow his wife to be guilty of such cruelty towards his child. Then he sent Madame d'Albret to bring me down; when I entered, my father started back with surprise; he had answered the colonel haughtily, but when he beheld the condition I was in, he said,

"Colonel, you are right; I deserve all you have said, and even more; but now do me the favour to accompany me home. Come, Valerie, my poor child, your father begs your pardon."

As my father took my hand to lead me away, Madame d'Albret said to the colonel,

"My dear Allarde, do you not incur a heavy responsibility in allowing that girl to go back again? You know what she said yesterday."

"Yes, *ma chère*, I have been told by your sister, but it was said in a state of excitement, and I have no doubt that kindness will remove all such ideas. Monsieur de Chatenœuf, I am at your orders."

I never said a word during all this interview. Madame d'Albret tied the black veil round my head and let it fall, to conceal my features, and I was led home by my father, accompanied by the colonel. We went into the room where my mother was sitting. My father lifted the veil from my face

"Madam," said my father, in a severe tone, "do you see the condition to which your barbarity has reduced this poor girl? I have brought Monsieur Allarde here to tell you, before him, that your conduct has been infamous, and that mine has been unpardonable in not having protected her from your cruelty; but I now tell you, that you have bent the bow till it has broken, and your power in this house is ended for ever."

My mother was so much astonished at this severe rebuke before witnesses, that she remained with her mouth open and her eyes staring. At last she gave a sort of chuckling laugh.

"Madam, I am in earnest," continued my father, "and you shall find that in future I command here. To your room, madame, immediately!"

The last word was pronounced in a voice of thunder. My mother rose, and as she retired, burst into a passionate flood of tears. The colonel then took his leave, saying to my father,

"Tenez-vous là."

My father remained a quarter of an hour with me, consoling me and blaming himself, and promising that in future he would see me done justice to. I heard him without reply. The tears started in my eyes at his kind expressions, but I felt there was no security for his adhering to all he promised, and I trembled as I thought so. He left me and went out. My mother, who had been watching, as soon as she saw that he had left the house, hastened down stairs from her room, and came into the one where I was sitting alone.

"So, mademoiselle," said she, panting, and apparently striving to contain herself, "my power in this house is gone for ever, and all through you. Ha, ha, ha! we shall see, we shall see. D'ye hear me, creature?" continued she, with her clenched hand close to my face. "No, not yet," said she, after a pause, and then she left the room.

If my father's kindness had somewhat staggered my resolution, this conduct of my mother's confirmed it. I felt that she was right in what she said, and that in a month she would regain her sway, and drive me to desperation. During the whole of that day I made no reply to anything that was said to me by my brothers and sisters, who came in by stealth to see me. In this I followed the advice of

Madame d'Albret, and at the same time my own feelings and inclinations. The servants who offered me dinner, and coaxed me to take some nourishment, could not get any answer from me, and at last one of them, who was a kind-hearted girl, burst out into tears, crying that mademoiselle was *folle.* My father did not come home to dinner; my mother remained in her room till he came in the evening, and then he went up to her. It wanted but half an hour of the time that I had agreed to meet Madame d'Albret. I waited that time, during which I heard sounds of high altercation above stairs. I was quite alone, for my mother had prevented the children coming to me, and as the clock struck, I dropped my veil over my face, and quietly walking out of the house, made for the rendezvous agreed.

I found the *fiacre* with Madame d'Albret waiting for me, and stepping into it, I was in a few minutes safely lodged in her splendid, comfortable apartments. Madame d'Albret put me in a little cabinet inside of her own room, so that no one, except one servant whom she could trust, knew of my being on the premises. There I was left to recover from my bruises, and regain, if possible, my good looks. On the following day she repaired to the barracks, and remained with her sister till the evening, when she returned, and came up to me.

"All has happened as I wished," said she, as she took off her bonnet; "you are nowhere to be found, and they have not the least suspicion that you are here. When you were first missed, they thought you had returned to the colonel's, and your father did not think it advisable to make inquiry until the next morning, when to his surprise he learnt that you had never been there. The dismounted hussar, who was sentry during the evening, was then examined; and he replied, that about half-past eight o'clock, a young person, who by her figure he presumed to be Mademoiselle Chatenœuf, had gone out of the gates, but that she had a thick veil over her face, and he could not see it. When your father and the colonel had interrogated the man and dismissed him, my poor sister burst into tears and said, 'Alas! alas! then she has kept her word, and has thrown herself into the Seine. Oh, Monsieur Allarde, my sister said you would incur a heavy responsibility by sending that poor girl back, and now it has proved but too true: poor dear Valerie!' Your father and the colonel were almost as much distressed as my sister, and it was just at that time that I came in.

"'Sister,' cried Madame Allarde to me, 'Valerie has left the barracks.'

"'What!' exclaimed I, 'When? oh my fear was too true!' said I, clasping my hands; and then taking out my handkerchief, I covered my face and sobbed. I tell you, Valerie, that nothing but my affection for you would have induced me to be so deceitful; but under the circumstances I hope I was justified. My assumed grief and distress quite removed any suspicion of your being here, and shortly afterwards the colonel made a sign to your father, and they both left the barracks; I have no doubt they went down to the Morgue, to ascertain if their fears had already been proved correct."

"What is the Morgue, madam?" said I.

"Do you not know, my child? It is a small building by the side of the Seine, where all bodies which are found in the river are laid out for the examination of the friends of those who are missing. Below the bridges there is a large strong net laid across, which receives all the bodies as they are swept away by the tide; that is, it receives many, if not most of them; but some are never found again."

Madame Allarde did not fail to return to the barracks on the next day, and found that a general excitement prevailed, not only among the officers but the men. My supposed suicide had been made known. My father had visited the Morgue a second time, and the police had been on the search without success. My mother dared not even show herself at the window of her apartments, and found herself avoided even by her own children. As for my father, he was half-mad, and never met her but to load her with reproaches, and to curse his own folly in having so long submitted to her imperious will.

"At all events, one good has arisen from your supposed death, Valerie," said Madame d'Albret, "which is, that your father has completely resumed his authority, and I do not think will ever yield it up again."

"My poor father," replied I, shedding tears, "I feel for him."

"He is certainly to be pitied," replied Madame

d'Albret; "but it is his own conscience which must be his greatest tormentor. He was selfish enough not to feel for you during your years of persecution, and rather than have his own comforts invaded by domestic brawls for a short period, he allowed you to be sacrificed. But observe, Valerie, if you have still a wish to return to your parents, it is not too late. The regiment does not leave Paris till next Thursday."

"Oh, no, no," cried I, "my mother would kill me; don't mention that again, madam," continued I, trembling.

"I will not, my child; for to tell you the truth, you would not appear in so favourable a light, if you were now to return. You have caused much grief to my sister and husband, and they would not receive you with cordiality after having thus trifled with their feelings. It would also be a victory for your mother; and I doubt not but that in a short time she would again recover that power which for the present she has lost. You never can be happy in your family after what has passed, and I think that what has been done is for the best. Your father can well spare one child out of fourteen, having little more than a long sword for their support. Your supposed death will be the cause of your father retaining his lawful authority, and preventing any of the remaining children receiving such injustice as you have done; and remorse will check, if it does not humanize, your mother, and I trust that the latter will be the case. I had well weighed all this in my mind, my dear Valerie, before I made the proposal, and I consider still that for your sake and for the sake of others, it is better that you should be the sacrifice. Nevertheless, I repeat, consult your own feelings, and if you repent the step which you have taken, there is yet time for you to return."

"My dear madam, return I never will, unless I am taken by force. All I feel is, that I should like that my father's bitter anguish was assuaged by his knowledge of my being still in existence."

"And so should I, Valerie, were it possible that the communication could be made, and the same happy results be arrived at; but that cannot be, unless it should please Heaven to summon your mother, and then you might safely inform your father of your existence."

"You are right, madam."

"Yes, I think I am, Valerie; for, after all, your father duly deserves his severe penance, which is, to visit the Morgue every day; but painful as is the remedy, it is necessary for the cure."

"Yes, madam," replied I, sobbing, "all you say is true; but still I cannot help weeping and pitying my poor father; not that it alters my determination, but I cannot command my feelings."

"Your feelings do you honour, Valerie, and I do not blame you for your grief. Do not, however, indulge it to excess, for that is turning a virtue into a failing."

There were still three days remaining previous to the departure of the regiment for Lyons. I was sorely distressed during this time. I pictured to myself my father's remorse, and would gladly have hastened to the barracks and thrown myself into his arms; but my mother's image rose before me, and her last words, "We shall see if my power is gone for ever," rung in my ears; her clenched hand was apparently close to my face, and then my resolution remained fixed. The swelling of my features had now subsided, and I had in some degree recovered my good looks; still my eye and cheeks were tinged black and yellow in various places, and the cuts on my head not quite healed. However, I was satisfied that the surgeon of the regiment was correct in his assertion that I should not be the least disfigured by the treatment which I had received.

"I have news for you," said Madame d'Albret, as she returned from the barracks, where she had been to see her sister off on her journey. "Your brother Auguste, who you know has been away, has returned to rejoin his regiment, but has since obtained his rank in another, which is stationed at Brest."

"Why has he done so, madam? do you know? have you seen him?"

"Yes; he was at the colonel's; he stated that he could not remain in the regiment if his mother continued with his father; that he should never be able, after what had happened, to treat his mother with common courtesy, still less with the duty of a son, and therefore he preferred leaving the regiment."

"And my father, madam?"

"Your father allows him to act as he pleases; indeed, he feels the force of what your brother says, and so does my brother-in-law, who has given his assent, as commanding officer, to your brother's exchange. Auguste laments you very much, and the poor fellow looks very ill. I think he has done right, although it is a severe blow to your mother; but for her I have no compassion."

"My mother never liked Auguste, madam."

"No, I believe that; but what annoys her is the cause of his leaving his regiment, as it is open condemnation of her conduct."

"Yes, I can understand that feeling on her part," replied I.

"Well, Valerie, I did not return until the regiment was gone, and the barracks cleared. You know the commandant always goes the last. I saw my sister safe off, and now I am here to tell you that you are no longer a prisoner, but may make yourself comfortable by roving through my apartments. But the first affair which we must take in hand is your wardrobe. I am rich enough to furnish you, so that shall be seen to immediately. And, Valerie dear, let me now say, once for all, what I do not intend to repeat in words, but I hope to prove by my actions. Look upon me as your mother, for I have not taken you away from your family without the resolution of supplying, as far as I can, not the mother you have lost, but the mother which in your dreams you have fancied. I love you, my child, for you are deserving of love. Treat me, therefore, with that unlimited confidence and affection which your young and pure heart yearns to pour out."

"Bless you, madam, bless you," cried I, bursting into tears, and burying my face in her lap; "I feel that now I have a mother."

CHAPTER V.

For several days I remained quiet in the little antechamber, during which Madame d'Albret had been busy every morning driving in her carriage, and ordering me a wardrobe; and as the various articles came in, I was as much surprised as I was pleased at the taste which had been shown, and the expense which must have been incurred.

"My dear madam," cried I, as each parcel was opened, "these are much too good for me; recollect I am but a poor soldier's daughter."

"You were so," replied Madame d'Albret; "but you forget," continued she, kissing my forehead, "that the poor soldier's daughter was drowned in the Seine, and you are now the *protégée* of Madame d'Albret. I have already mentioned to all my friends that I expect a young cousin from Gascony, whom I have adopted, having no children of my own. Your own name is noble, and you may safely retain it, as there are no want of Chatenœufs in Gascony, and there have been former alliances between them and the d'Albrets. I have no doubt that if I were to refer back to family records, that I could prove you to be a cousin, some three hundred times removed, and that is quite enough. As soon as you are quite well, and I think in a week all vestiges of your ill treatment will be effaced, we will go down to my chateau for a few months, and we will return to Paris in the season. Has Madame Paon been here?"

"Yes, my dear madam, she has, and has taken my measure for the dresses; but don't scold me. I must cry a little, for I am so happy and so grateful. My heart will burst if I do not. Bless you, bless you, dear madam; little did I think before I saw you, that I should ever cry for joy."

Madame d'Albret embraced me with much affection, and allowed me to give vent to my feelings, which I did, bedewing her hands with my tears. A week afterwards, everything was ready, and we set off for the chateau in Brittany, travelling in Madame d'Albret's post-chariot, with an *avant courrier*, and without regard to expense.

And now I must make the reader somewhat better acquainted with my kind protectress. I little thought at the time that she offered me her protection, that she was a personage of such consequence; but the fact was, that her sister having made a very inferior match to her own, she, out of delicacy, while the colonel and his wife were at Paris, avoided anything like state in paying them a visit, and I supposed that she was much in the same rank and society as they were; but such was not the case.

Madame d'Albret had married into one of the highest and most noble families of France. Her husband had died three years after their marriage, and having no children, had left her a large revenue entirely at her own disposal during her life, and wishing her to marry again, had the property entailed upon her children, if she had any, if not, after her death, it was to go to a distant branch of the d'Albret family. I was informed that her income amounted to 60,000 livres per annum, besides her chateau in the country, and the hotel in the Rue St. Honoré, which belonged to her, although she only occupied a portion of it. Her husband had now been dead more than ten years, and Madame d'Albret had not been persuaded by her numerous suitors to marry again. She was still handsome, about thirty-four years of age, and I hardly need say, was in the very best society in Paris. Such was the person who came to the barracks in so unassuming a manner, and whose protection I was so fortunate as to obtain.

I could dwell long upon the happy days that I passed at the chateau. There was no want of society, and the *réunions* were charming; and being in the country, I was allowed to join them, having been formally introduced by Madame d'Albret to all her visitors as her cousin. My time was fully occupied. Madame d'Albret, perceiving that I had great talent for music, and a fine voice, had procured me good masters, and wishing to prove my gratitude by attention, I was indefatigable, and made so rapid a progress, that my masters were surprised. Music and embroidery, at which I have before mentioned I was very expert, were my only occupations—and on the latter my talents were exerted to please Madame d'Albret, by offering her each piece as they were successively taken from the frame. So far from wishing to return to Paris, I was unhappy at the idea of leaving the chateau. Indeed, if the reader will recall what I have narrated of my former life, he will at once perceive that I could but be in a state of perfect happiness.

Until I was received by Madame d'Albret, I had lived a life of persecution, and had not known kindness. Fear was the passion which had been acted upon, and which, I may say, had crushed both mind and body: now all was kindness and love. Praise, which I had never before received, was now lavished upon me, and I felt my energies and talents roused, and developing themselves in a way that astonished myself. I had not known what I was, or what I was capable of. I had had no confidence in myself, and I had believed myself to be almost as incapable as my mother would have persuaded me and every body else. This sudden change of treatment had a most surprising effect. In the course of a few months I had grown nearly three inches taller, and not only my figure, but my features, had become so improved, that, although not vain, it was impossible for me not to believe what every one said, and what my glass told me, that I was very handsome, and that I should make a great sensation when I was introduced at Paris. But although I believed this, I felt no desire. I was too happy as I was, and would not have exchanged the kindness of Madame d'Albret for the best husband that France could produce; and when anything was mentioned by ladies who visited Madame d'Albret, to that effect, and they talked about my future establishment, my reply invariably was, "*Je ne veux pas.*" I had always expressed my regrets that we should be obliged to go to Paris for the season, and Madame d'Albret, who of course had no wish to part with me so soon, and who felt that I was still young enough to remain for some years single, made me very happy by telling me that she did not intend to stay long in the capital, and that although I should appear at her parties, she did not intend that I should be much at public places. And so it proved; we went to Paris, and the best masters were procured for me; but I did not go out with Madame d'Albret, except occasionally, in her morning drives, and once or twice to the opera and theatres. My music occupied the major portion of my time, and having expressed a wish to learn English, I had a good master; but I had another resource from an intimacy having arisen between me and Madame Paon, whom, I believe, I have before mentioned as the first milliner in Paris.

This intimacy was brought about in the following manner. Being very clever with my needle, and having a great taste for dress, I used to amuse myself at the chateau with inventing something new, not for myself, but for Madame d'Albret, and very often surprised and pleased her by making alterations or additions to her dresses, which were always admired, and declared to be in the best taste. On our arrival at Paris, Madame Paon was visited, of course, that the new fashions might be ascertained, and she immediately remarked and admired my little inventions. I was therefore consulted whenever a new dress was to be made for Madame d'Albret, and as Madame Paon was a very ladylike and superior person, of a decayed, but good family, we soon became very intimate. We had been at Paris about two months, when one morning Madame Paon observed to Madame d'Albret that, as I was learning English, it would not be a bad plan if Madame d'Albret was to drop me at her establishment when she took her morning airing, as she had two highly respectable English *modistes* in her employ, who she found were necessary for her English customers, and that I should learn more English by an hour's conversation with them than a master could supply. Madame d'Albret agreed with her, I was pleased at the idea, and consequently three or four mornings in the week were passed at Madame Paon's.

But the reader must be introduced to the establishment of Madame Paon, or he may imagine that it was too condescending for a young lady in my position to visit at a milliner's. Madame Paon was the first milliner at Paris, and, as is generally the case, was on the most intimate terms with all the ladies. She made for the court, and, indeed, for every lady to whom she could dedicate her time, as it was almost a favour to be permitted to be one of her customers. Her establishment was in the Rue St. Honoré,—I forget the name of the hotel, but it was one of the largest.

The suite of apartments were magnificent. You passed from one room to another, each displaying every variety of rich and graceful costume. In every room were demoiselles well dressed to attend to the customers, and everything bespoke a degree of taste and elegance quite unparalleled. At last you arrived at the reception-room of madame, which was spacious and most superbly furnished. There were no men in the establishment except in one room, called the *Comptoir,* in which were six clerks at their desks. When I add that Madame Paon was elegant in her manners, and handsome in her person, very tall and majestic; that she was rich, kept several servants, a handsome carriage, and had a *maison de campagne,* to which she retired every Saturday afternoon, the reader may acknowledge that she was a person whom Madame d'Albret might permit me to visit.

This intimacy soon became very great. There was a

certain degree of *éclat* at my being so constantly in the house, and, moreover, as I had a decided taste for dress, I often brought forward some new invention which was not only approved of, but a source of profit to Madame Paon. Everything was submitted to my judgment, as Madame Paon more than once observed, "What a first-rate *modiste* you would make, mademoiselle; but, unfortunately for the fashions, there is no chance of your being so employed."

At last the Paris season was nearly over, and truly glad was I when Madame d'Albret mentioned the day of our departure. I had very much improved in my music and my English during our residence at Paris. I had not been out, except to small parties, and had no wish whatever to go out at all. I was satisfied with Madame d'Albret's company, and had no wish to leave her. I may say that I was truly happy, and my countenance was radiant, and proved that I was so. My thoughts would occasionally revert to my father and my brother Auguste, and make me melancholy for the time; but I felt that all was for the best, and I built castles, in which I imagined my suddenly breaking in upon them, throwing myself in my father's arms, and requesting to share the wealth and luxury with which I fancied myself to be endowed.

I was now nearly eighteen years old. I had been one year under the protection of Madame d'Albret, and the old dowagers who visited us at the chateau were incessantly pointing out to Madame d'Albret that it was time to look out for an establishment for me. Madame d'Albret was, to a certain degree, of their opinion; but she did not wish to part with me, and I was resolute in my determination not to leave her. I had no wish to be married; I had reflected much upon the subject; the few married lives I had witnessed were not to my taste. I had seen my kind-hearted, amiable grandmother thwarted by a penurious husband; I had witnessed my father under the control of a revengeful woman; and when I beheld, as I did every day, the peace and happiness in the establishment of Madame d'Albret, as a single woman, I felt certain that marriage was a lottery in which there were thousands of blanks to one prize. When, therefore, any of Madame d'Albret's acquaintances brought up the subject, when they left the room I earnestly implored Madame d'Albret not to be influenced by their remarks, as I had made up my mind to remain single, and that all I asked was to remain with her and prove my gratitude.

"I believe you, Valerie," replied Madame d'Albret, "but I should not be doing my duty if I permitted you to act upon your own feelings. A girl like you was not intended by Heaven to pine away in celibacy, but to adorn the station in life in which she is placed. At the same time, I will not press the matter; but if an advantageous offer were to be made, I shall then consider it my duty to exert my influence with you to make you change your mind; but, at the same time, I will never use anything more than persuasion. I am too happy with you as a companion to wish to part with you, but, at the same time, I should be very selfish if I did not give you up when your own interest told me that such was my duty."

"Well, madam, I thank heaven that I have no fortune, and that will, I trust, be a bar to any proposals from the interested gentlemen of the present day."

"That may not save you, Valerie," replied Madame d'Albret, laughing; "gentlemen may be satisfied with expectancies; nay, it is possible that one may be found who may be satisfied with your own pretty self, and ask no more."

"I rather think not, madam," replied I. "You have too good an opinion of me, and must not expect others to view me with your partial eyes; all I can say is, that if such a gentleman could be found, his disinterestedness would make me think more highly of him than I do of the sex at present, although not sufficiently well to wish me to change my present condition."

"Well, well; we shall see," replied Madame d'Albret, "the carriage is at the door, so bring me my bonnet and cashmere."

A few weeks after our return to the chateau, a Monsieur de G——, of an old family in Brittany, who had been for the last two years in England, returned to his father's house, and called upon Madame d'Albret. She had known him from childhood, and received him most cordially. I must describe him fully, as he played no small part in my little drama. He was, I should think, nearly thirty years of age, small in person but elegantly made, with a very handsome but rather effeminate face His address and manners were perfect. He was very witty, and apparently very amiable. His deportment towards our sex was certainly most fascinating—so tender and so respectful. I certainly never had before seen so polished a man. He sang well, and played upon several instruments; drew, caricatured—indeed, he did everything well that he attempted to do; I hardly need say, that with such qualifications, and being so old a friend, that he was gladly welcomed by Madame d'Albret, and became a daily visitor at the chateau. I was soon intimate with him and partial to his company, but nothing more; indeed, his attentions to Madame d'Albret were quite as great as to me, and there was nothing to permit any one to suppose that he was paying his court either to her or to me. Madame d'Albret thought otherwise, because we sang together, and because he talked to me in English; and she as well as others rallied me in consequence.

After two months had passed away, Monsieur de G—— was supposed to be paying his attentions more particularly to me, and I thought so myself; Madame d'Albret certainly did, and gave him every opportunity. He was the heir to a large property, and did not require money with his wife. About this time, an English lady of the name of Bathurst, who was travelling with a niece, a little girl about fourteen years old, had accepted an invitation from Monsieur de G——'s father to pass a week with them at their chateau, which was about five miles from that of Madame d'Albret, and this lady was introduced. She was apparently very amiable, and certainly very *distinguée* in her manners, and we saw a great deal of her, as she was a great favourite with Madame d'Albret.

A few weeks after the introduction of this English lady, I was one day on the terrace alone, when I was accosted by Monsieur de G——. After a remark or two upon the beauty of the autumnal flowers, he observed,

"How different are the customs of two great nations, with but a few leagues of water between them—I refer to the French and the English. You would be surprised to see how great they are, if you were ever to go to England—in none, perhaps, more so than in the affairs of the heart. In France we do not consult the wishes or the feelings of the young lady; we apply to her parents, and if the match is considered equally advantageous, the young lady is told to prepare herself for changing her condition. In England the very reverse is the case; we apply to the young lady, gain her affections, and when certain of them, we then request the sanction of those who are her guardians. Which do you think is the most natural and satisfactory, Mademoiselle de Chatenœuf?"

"I have been brought up in France, Monsieur de G——, and I prefer the mode of France; our parents and our guardians are the people most able to decide upon the propriety of a match, and I think that, until that point is ascertained, no affections should be engaged, as, should the marriage not be considered advisable, much pain and disappointment will be prevented."

"In some instances, I grant that such may be the case," replied he; "but still, is it not treating your sex like slaves to permit no love before marriage? and is it agreeable for ours, that we lead to the altar a person who may consent from a sense of duty, without having the least regard for her husband; nay, perhaps feeling an aversion?"

"I do not think that any kind parents would force their child to marry a man for whom she felt an aversion," replied I; "and if there is not much love before marriage, there may be a great deal after; but the fact is, it is a subject upon which I am not able, nor do I wish, to give my opinion."

"As you disagree with me, Mademoiselle de Chatenœuf," replied he, "I fear you will not be pleased at my courting you in the English fashion; and previous to addressing myself to Madame d'Albret, making known to you my sincere regard for you, and my humble hopes that I am not indifferent to you."

"I will answer you very plainly, Monsieur de G——; and perhaps it is as well you have taken this unusual step, as it will save you the trouble of making any application to Madame d'Albret. Flattered as I am by your compliment, I beg to decline the honour you propose, and now that you know my feelings, you will of course not be so ungenerous as to make any application to Madame d'Albret."

"Certainly, mademoiselle," replied, he, with great pique, "but on one condition, which is, that you will promise me that you will not mention to Madame d'Albret what has now passed between us."

"That I willingly promise, Monsieur de G——, as I may consider it as your secret."

"And I trust," continued he, "that you will not discard me from your friendship, but receive me as before."

"I shall always be happy to receive the friends of Madame d'Albret," replied I, "and now I wish you a good morning."

I went to my own room and reflected upon what had passed. I was angry with Monsieur de G—— for what I considered the unwarrantable liberty he had taken, the greater, as he must have known my utter dependence upon Madame d'Albret, and how unlikely it was that I would form any such engagement without her knowledge and sanction. That I had no love for Monsieur de G—— was certain, although I was pleased with his company and conversation. I was sorry on reflection that I had given my promise not to mention what had passed; but having made the promise, although hastily, I resolved to adhere to it.

I took it for granted that he would gradually withdraw himself, and that we should see little more of him; but in this I was mistaken; he was as frequent in his visits as before, dividing his attentions between Madame d'Albret and me. This annoyed me, and I avoided him as much as I could, and the consequence was, that he was oftener with Madame d'Albret than with me. At first, when Madame d'Albret perceived this, she appeared to be vexed, as she had evidently set her mind upon the match, and expected daily to receive a formal proposal from him in my behalf; but gradually, why I know not, it gave her no further concern, and I was permitted to leave the room, and do as I pleased without being subjected to any remarks.

Such was the state of affairs when the Paris season drew near. Madame Bathurst had been induced to remain in Brittany, and was continually with us. She had often asked me to come over to England and pass a few weeks with them, and I had jokingly replied that I would. One morning Madame d'Albret said to me,—

"My dear Valerie, Madame Bathurst has again requested me to allow you to go to England with her. Now if you think that you would like to pass a short time with her, instead of remaining at Paris during the season, I really have no objection, if it would give you pleasure."

"My dear madam, I was only joking when I said so."

"Well, you have made Madame Bathurst think you were in earnest, my dear," replied she; "and I thought so too, and have this morning promised that you shall go with her. I thought you would perfect yourself in English, and it would be a good opportunity of relieving you for a short time of your constant attendance upon me; so, my dear Valerie, I advise you to go. It will amuse you, and a little change will do you good: besides, my dear, I perceive that the attentions of Monsieur de G—— are not agreeable to you, and it is as well to break it off by a short absence."

"I shall not dispute your wishes, madam," replied I, mournfully, for my heart misgave me, why I knew not, "but if I do go, it will be to oblige you, and not because I really wish it."

"My dear Valerie, I think it will be for the best, and therefore you will oblige me. I have promised for you, and I should be sorry to have to recall my promise—so consent, my dear, and I will write to Madame Bathurst, that she may be prepared to receive you."

"Certainly, madam," replied I, "your wishes will ever be a law to me:" and so saying, I left the room, and going to my own chamber, I threw myself down on the bed, and wept bitterly, without knowing why.

About ten days after this, Madame Bathurst called for me to take me to the chateau of Monsieur de G——'s father, where I was to remain till the next morning, when we were to post to Paris. It was with great pain that I quitted Madame d'Albret; but her kindness to me appeared to have increased rather than diminished, after the proposal of our short separation. "God bless you, my dear Valerie," she said, "you must write to me twice a week; I shall be most impatient for your return." I parted from her with many tears, and did not leave off weeping till we arrived at the chateau at which Madame Bathurst resided.

I was received with formal politeness by the old gentleman, and Monsieur de G——, who was also at home, and in an excessive gay humour. "Alas, mademoiselle," cried he, "what a desert you will leave behind you! It is too cruel, this travelling mania on your part. We never shall see you again."

There was so much irony in his face as he said this, that I hardly knew what to make of it; but it made me feel anxious and dissatisfied. I would have given much to have abandoned the journey, but Madame d'Albret's wishes were a law to me. To avoid reflection, which was painful, I talked with Caroline, the niece of Madame Bathurst, and as we were to set off at daylight, we retired early. The following morning we set off, and in due time arrived at Paris, where we remained but one day, and then proceeded to Boulogne, where we embarked.

It was now November, and half-way across the Channel we were enveloped in a fog, and it was with difficulty that we made the harbour. We set off for London, the fog continued during the whole day, and on our arrival at the suburbs it was thicker than ever, and the horses were led through the streets by people carrying flambeaux. I had heard that England was a *triste pays,* and I thought it so indeed. At last I observed to Madame Bathurst, "*Est-ce qu'il n'y a jamais de soleil dans ce pays, madame?*"

"Oh, yes," replied she, laughing, "and a very beautiful sun too."

The next day we set off for Madame Bathurst's country seat, to pass the Christmas. Before we were three miles out of London, the fog had disappeared, the sun shone out brilliantly, and the branches of the leafless trees covered with rhime, glittered like diamond wands as we flew past them. What with the change in the weather, and the rapid motion produced by the four English post-horses, I thought England beautiful; but I must say that the first two days were a trial, the more so as I was very despondent from having quitted Madame d'Albret. I was delighted with Madame Bathurst's country seat, the well-arranged gardens, the conservatories, the neatness displayed in everything, so different from France, the cleanness of the house and furniture; the London carpets over the whole of the rooms and staircases, were, in my opinion, great improvements; but I cared little for the society, which I found not only dull, but it appeared to me to be selfish. I found a lively companion in Caroline, and we sat up in a little boudoir, where we were never interrupted. Here I practised my music, and at Madame Bathurst's request, spoke alternately English and French with my little companion, for our mutual improvement.

I had written twice to Madame d'Albret, and had received one very kind answer; but no mention was made of my return, although it was at first arranged that my visit was to be three weeks or a month. A fortnight after my arrival at Fairfield, I received a second letter from Madame d'Albret, kind as usual, but stating, to my great grief, that she was not well, having had an attack on her chest from having taken a violent cold. I answered the letter immediately, requesting that I might be permitted to return home and nurse her, for I felt very uneasy. For three weeks, during which I had no reply, I was in a state of great anxiety and distress, as I imagined that Madame d'Albret must have been too ill to write, and I was in a fever of suspense. At last I received a letter from her, stating that she had been very ill, and that she had been recommended by the physicians to go to the south of France for the winter. At the same time, as she could not put off her departure, she wrote to Madame Bathurst, requesting, if not inconvenient, that she would allow my visit to be extended till the spring, at which season she expected to return to Paris. Madame Bathurst read her letter to me, and stated how happy she should be for me to remain. I could do no otherwise but thank her, although I was truly miserable. I wrote to Madame d'Albret, and stated what my feelings were; but as she had, by what was said in her letter, already left for the south of France, I knew that my letter would arrive too late to enable her to alter her determination. All I requested was, that she would give me continual intelligence of her health.

I was, however, much consoled in my distress by the kindness of Madame Bathurst, and affectionate manners of her niece Caroline, who was my constant companion. There was a great deal of company not only visiting, but staying in the house; but although there was much company, there was very little society. Horses, dogs, guns, were the amusements of the gentlemen during the day; in the evening we saw little of them, as they seldom left the dinner-table before Caroline and I had retired to our rooms; and the ladies appeared to me to be all afraid of each other, and to be constantly on the reserve.

Christmas had passed, and I had not heard again from Madame d'Albret, which was a source of great vexation and many bitter tears. I fancied her dying in the south of France, without any one to take care of her. I often spoke to Madame Bathurst on the subject, who offered all the excuses that she could devise; but I thought at the same time appeared to be very grave, and unwilling to continue the conversation. At last I thought of Madame Paon, and I wrote to her, inquiring whether she knew how Madame d'Albret was, detailing to her how I had come to England, and how Madame d'Albret had been seriously indisposed, stating my fears from not having received any reply to my last letters. The day after I had written to Madame Paon, Caroline, who was sitting with me in the boudoir, observed, "I heard Mrs. Corbet say to my aunt that she had seen Madame d'Albret at Paris about ten days ago."

"Impossible!" replied I; "she is in the south of France."

"So I understood," replied Caroline; "but she did say so, and my aunt immediately sent me out of the room on a message. I am sure it was to get rid of me, that she might talk to Mrs. Corbet."

"What can this mean?" exclaimed I. "Oh, my heart forebodes evil! Excuse me, Caroline, but I feel very miserable;" and I laid my face down on the table, covering it with my hands, and tears trickled fast through my fingers.

"Speak to my aunt," said Caroline, consolingly; "do not cry, Valerie, it may be all a mistake."

"I will at once speak to Madame Bathurst," said I, raising my head, "it will be the best plan."

I went into my room, bathed my eyes, and then sought Madame Bathurst, whom I found in the conservatory, giving directions to the gardener. After a time she took my arm, and we walked down the terrace.

"Madame Bathurst," said I, "I have been made very miserable by Caroline stating that Mrs. Corbet had told you that she met Madame d'Albret at Paris. How can this be?"

"I cannot imagine more than yourself, my dear Valerie," replied Madame Bathurst, "except that Mrs. Corbet was mistaken."

"Do you think it was madame?"

"I cannot say, Valerie; but I have written to Paris to ascertain the fact, which is to me incomprehensible. A few days will let us into the truth; I cannot believe it—indeed, if it were true, I shall consider that Madame d'Albret has treated me ill; for much as I am pleased to have you here, she has not been candid with me in proposing that you should remain the winter, upon the plea of her being obliged to go to the south, when she is still at Paris. I cannot understand it, and until confirmed, I will not believe it. Mrs. Corbet is not an acquaintance of hers, and may, therefore, be mistaken."

"She must be, madam," replied I; "still it is strange that I do not hear from her. I am fearful something is wrong, and what it can be I cannot surmise."

"Let us talk no more about it, my dear Valerie. A few days will decide the point."

A few days did decide the point, for I received an answer from Madame Paon, in which she said:—

"My dear Mademoiselle Chatenœuf,—

"You may imagine my surprise at receiving your letter, and I fear you must prepare yourself for unpleasant intelligence. Madame d'Albret is in Paris, and has never been in the south of France that I have heard. When she first called, I inquired after you. The reply was, that you were on a visit to a lady in England; that you had left her; that you had a *manie pour l'Angleterre:* and so saying, she shrugged up her shoulders. I was about to inquire more particularly, but she cut the conversation short by asking to see a new pelisse, and I perceived at once that there was something wrong, but what I could not comprehend. I did not see her till four or five weeks afterwards, when she called, accompanied by a Monsieur de G——, a person well known in Paris, where he bears a very indifferent character, as a desperate gambler, and a man of very bad disposition, concealed under a very polished exterior; but his character is better known in England, which country, I am told, he was obliged to quit in consequence of some gaming transaction, anything but honourable. I again made inquiries after you, and this time the reply was given by Monsieur de G——, who replied that your were an *ingrate,* and your name must not be in future mentioned by any one to Madame d'Albret.

"The handsome face of Monsieur de G—— was changed to that of a demon when he made this remark, and fully proved to me the truth of the report that he was a person of very bad disposition. Madame d'Albret made no remark, except that she should be careful how she ever engaged a *demoiselle de compagnie* again. I was struck at this remark from her, as I always considered that you were (and, indeed, I know you were at one time) viewed in a very different light, and I was quite mystified. About a fortnight afterwards Madame d'Albret called upon me, and announced her intended marriage to Monsieur de G——, and requested me to make her wedding dresses. Here the whole mystery was out; but why, because she marries Monsieur de G——, you should lose her protection, and why Monsieur de G—— should be so inveterate against you, is more than I can tell. I have now, my dear mademoiselle, given you a detail of all I know, and shall be most happy to hear from you if you will please to write to me, &c. &c. "EMILE PAON, *née* MERCE."

Here was a solution of the whole mystery. I read the letter, and fell back on the sofa, gasping for breath. It was some time before I could recover myself. I was alone in my bedroom, my head and eyes swimming; but I staggered to the washing-stand, and obtained some water. It was half an hour before I could recall my astonished senses, and then everything appeared as clear to me as if it had been revealed. Monsieur de G——'s double attentions; his spiteful look at my refusal; his occupying himself wholly with Madame d'Albret after I refused him; her wishing to get rid of me by sending me to England with Madame Bathurst, and her subsequent false and evasive conduct. Monsieur de G—— had had his revenge, and gained his point at the same time. He had obtained the wealth of Madame d'Albret to squander at the gaming-table, and had contrived, by some means or another, to ruin me in her good opinion. I perceived at once that all was lost, and when I considered the awkwardness of my position, I was almost in despair.

CHAPTER VI.

As I continued for more than an hour on the sofa, gloomily passing in review my short career, my present position, and occasionally venturing a surmise upon the future, a feeling which I had not had before—one which had hitherto been latent—pride, gradually was awakened in my bosom, and as it was aroused, it sustained me. I have before observed, that fear had been my predominating feeling till I had quitted my parents; love and gratitude had succeeded them; but now, smarting under injustice, pride, and, with pride, many less worthy passions were summoned up, and I appeared in the course of two short hours to be another being. I felt confidence in myself, my eyes were opened all at once, as it were, to the heartlessness of the world; the more I considered the almost hopeless condition in which I was, the more my energy was roused. I sat down on the sofa a confiding, clinging girl; I rose up a resolute, clear-sighted woman.

I reflected, and had made up my mind that Madame d'Albret would never forgive one whom she had injured as she had me. She had induced me to break off all family and parental ties (such as they were); she had made me wholly dependent upon her, and had now cast me off in a cruel and heartless manner. She had used deceit, because she knew that she could not justify her conduct. She had raised calumnies against me, accusing me of ingratitude, as an excuse for her own conduct. Anything like a reconciliation, therefore, was impossible, and any assistance from her I was determined not to accept. Besides, was she not married to Monsieur de G——, whom pique at my refusal had made my enemy, and who had, in all probability, as he pressed his own suit, perceived the necessity, independent of the gratification it afforded him to be my ruin, of removing me as a serious obstacle to Madame d'Albret's contracting a new alliance? From that quarter, therefore, there was nothing to be expected or hoped for, even if it were desired. And what was my position with Madame Bathurst? On a visit. At the termination of which I was houseless.

That Madame Bathurst would probably offer me a temporary asylum, for she would hardly turn me out of doors, I felt convinced; but my new-born pride revolted at the idea of dependence upon one on whom I had no claim whatever. What, then, was to be done? I examined my capital. I was handsome, but that was of no use to me; the insidious conduct of Monsieur de G—— had raised to positive dislike the indifference that I felt for his sex, and I had no inclination to make a market of my personal advantages. I could sing and play well. I spoke French and English, and understood Italian. I could embroider and work well with my needle. Such were my capabilities, my stock-in-trade, with which to commence the world; I was therefore competent, to a certain degree, to give lessons in music and in French, or to take a governess's place, or to become a *modiste*.

I thought of Madame Paon; but when I reflected in what manner I had visited her, the respect and homage, I may say, which had been offered up to me, and how different my reception and treatment would be if I entered the establishment as one of themselves, the reflection was too mortifying, and I determined, that if I were driven to such an employment for my livelihood, it should be where I was not known. After much consideration, I decided that I would see Madame Bathurst, make known to her my intentions, and ask her assistance and recommendation to procure me a situation. I arranged my hair, removed all traces of my late agitation, and went down to her. I found her alone, and asking her whether she could spare me a few minutes of her time, I handed to her the letter which I had received from Madame Paon, and then made her acquainted with that portion of my history with which she had been unacquainted. As I spoke, my courage revived, and my voice became firm—I felt that I was no longer a girl.

"Madame Bathurst, I have confided this to you, because you will agree with me that there can be nothing more between Madame d'Albret and me; for even if she made an offer, I would never accept it. I am now in a very false position, owing to her conduct. I am here on a visit, supposed by you to be the *protégée* of that lady, and a person of some consequence. Her protection has been taken away from me, and I am now a beggar, with nothing but my talents for my future support. I explain this to you frankly, because I cannot think of remaining as your visitor; and if I do not ask too much, all that I wish ot your friendship is, that you will give me such a recommendation as you think I deserve, by which I may obtain the means of future livelihood."

"My dear Valerie," replied Madame Bathurst, "I will not hurt your feelings. It is a heavy blow, and I am glad to perceive, that instead of being crushed by it, you appear to rise. I have heard of Madame d'Albret's marriage, and the deceit which she has been practising evidently to get rid of you. Not many days ago I wrote to her, pointing out the variance between what she stated in her letters, and her actual position, and requesting to know what was to be done relative to you. Her answer I have received this day. She states that you have cruelly deceived her; that at the very time that you professed the utmost gratitude and affection, you were slandering her, and laughing at her behind her back, particularly to Monsieur de G——, to whom she is now married; and that, however she might be inclined to forgive and overlook your conduct herself, that Monsieur de G—— is resolute, and determined that you never shall come again under his roof. She has, therefore, transmitted a billet of 500 francs to enable you to return to your father's house."

"Then," replied I, "it is as I suspected; Monsieur de G—— is the cause of all."

"Why did you trust him, Valerie, or rather why were you so imprudent, and I must add, ungrateful, to speak of Madame d'Albret as you did?"

"And you believe it, Madame Bathurst, you believe that I did so? I can only say, that if such is your belief, the sooner we part the better."

I then told her what I had omitted in my narrative, how I had refused Monsieur de G——, and, explaining his character, showed that he had acted thus out of interest and revenge.

"I believe it all now, Valerie, and I must beg your pardon for having supposed that you had been ungrateful. This explanation relieves me, and enables me to make you the offer which I had thought of doing, had I not been checked by this calumny against you. I say, therefore, for the present, my dear Valerie, remain here. You are quite equal to be governess to Caroline, but I prefer you should remain with me more as a friend than as a governess. I say this, because I fear you will be too proud to remain as a dependant, without making yourself useful. You know that I did intend to take a governess for Caroline as soon as we went to London. I will now take you, if you will consent, and shall feel the obligation on my side, as I shall not only have retained a capable person, but shall also not lose a dear young friend."

"I thank you for the offer, my dear madam," replied I, rising and courtesying; "I trust, however, that you will allow me a little time for reflection before I decide. You must admit that this is a most critical epoch in my life, and I must not make one false step if it is possible to prevent it."

"Certainly," replied Madame Bathurst, "certainly. You are right, Valerie, in reflecting well before you decide; but I must say that you are rather haughty in your manner towards me."

"I may have been, my dear Madame Bathurst, but if so, take my excuses. Recollect, the Valerie of yesterday, who was your visitor and young friend, is not the Valerie of to-day!" and with these words I took up the cheque for 500 francs which Madame Bathurst had laid on the table, left the room, and returned to my own apartment.

I returned to my room, and was glad to be once more alone; for although I bore up well under the circumstances, still the compressed excitement was wearying to the frame. I had resolved to accept the offer of Madame Bathurst at the time that she made it, but I did not choose to appear to jump at it, as she probably expected that I would. I felt no confidence in any one but my own self, after the treatment of Madame d'Albret, and I considered that Madame Bathurst would probably dismiss me, as soon as my services were no longer required, with as little ceremony as had Madame d'Albret. That I was capable of taking charge of and instructing Caroline, I knew well, and that Madame Bathurst would not easily procure a governess so capable in singing and music as myself. There would be consequently no obligation, and I resolved that I would reject her terms if they were not favourable. I had some money, for I had spent but a small portion of twenty sovereigns which Madame d'Albret had given me in a purse when I quitted her. I had, therefore, the means of subsistence for some little time, should I not come to terms with Madame Bathurst.

After an hour's reflection, I sat down and wrote a letter

to Madame Paon, stating what had occurred, and my determination to obtain my own livelihood, and adding, that as I was not sure whether I should accept of Madame Bathurst's offer, I wished her to give me a letter of introduction to some French acquaintance of hers in London, as I was an utter stranger to everything, and without advice, should probably be cheated in every way. As soon this letter was finished, I commenced another to Madame d'Albret, which was in the following words:—

"My dear Madam,—

Yes, I will still say my dear madam; for although you will never hear of me again, you are still dear to me, more dear perhaps than you were, when I considered you my patroness and my more than mother. And why so?—Because when those we love are in misfortune, when those who have benefited us are likely to soon want succour themselves, it is then the time that we should pour out our gratitude and love. I do not consider it your fault, my dear Madame d'Albret, that you have been deceived by a base hypocrite, who wears so captivating a mask; I do not blame you that you have been persuaded by him that I have slandered and behaved ungratefully to you. You have been blinded by your own feelings towards him and by his consummate art. I am also to blame for not having communicated to you that *he* made me a proposal of marriage but a short time previous to my departure, and which I indignantly rejected, because he had taken such an unusual step without any previous communication with you on the subject—not that I would have accepted him, even if you had wished it, for I knew how false and unworthy he was considered to be. I should have told you, my dear madam, of this offer of marriage on his part, but he requested me as a favour not to mention it to you, and I did not then know that he was a ruined man, a desperate gambler, and that he had been obliged to quit this country for dishonourable practices at the gaming-table, as you may easily discover to be true; for even Madame Paon can give you all the necessary information. And into this man's hands have you fallen, my dear Madame d'Albret. Alas, how you are to be pitied! my heart bleeds for you, and I fear that a few months will suffice to prove to you the truth of what I now write. That I am a sufferer by the conduct of Monsieur de G—— is true. I have lost a kind patroness, an indulgent mother, and am now left to obtain my own livelihood how I can. All my visions, all my dreams of happiness with you, all my wishes of proving my gratitude and love for your kindness have vanished, and here I am, young, alone, and unprotected. But I think not of myself; at all events I am free —I am not chained to such a person as Monsieur de G——; and it is of you, and all that you will have to suffer, that my thoughts and heart are full. I return you the cheque for 500 francs—I cannot take the money. You are married to Monsieur de G——, and I can accept nothing from one who has made you believe that Valerie could be calumnious and ungrateful. Adieu, my dear madam; I shall pray for you, and weep over your misfortunes. "Yours ever gratefully,

"VALERIE DE CHATENŒUF."

That there was a mixed feeling in this letter I confess. As I said in it, I really pitied Madame d'Albret and forgave her her unkindness; but I sought revenge upon Monsieur de G——, and in seeking that, I planted daggers into the heart of Madame d'Albret; but I did not at the time that I wrote reflect upon this. What I wished to do was to vindicate myself, and that I could not do without exposing Monsieur de G——, and exposing him in his true colours was, of course, awakening Madame d'Albret to her position sooner than she would have been, and filling her mind with doubts and jealousy. That this was not kind, I felt when I perused what I had written previous to folding the letter; but I felt no inclination to alter it, probably because I had not quite so wholly forgiven Madame d'Albret as I thought that I had. Be it as it may, the letter was sealed and despatched by that night's post, as well as that written to Madame Paon.

I had now only to arrange with Madame Bathurst, and I went down into the drawing-room, where I found her alone. "I have considered, my dear Madame Bathurst," said I, "your kind proposal. I certainly have had a little struggle to get over, as you must admit that it is not pleasant to sink from a visitor in a family into a dependant, as I must in future be if I remain with you; but the advantages of being with a person whom I respect as much as I do you, and of having charge of a young person to whom

I am so attached as I am to Caroline, have decided me on accepting your offer. May I know then, what may be the terms upon which I am received as governess?"

"Valerie, I feel that this is all pride," replied Madame Bathurst, "but still it is not disreputable pride, and though I shall yield to it, I would have made no terms, but retained you as a dear friend, my purse and everything in the house at your command, and I hoped that you would have allowed me so to do, but as you will not, I have only to say that I should have expected to pay any governess whom I might have retained for Caroline a salary of £100 per annum, and that I offer you the same."

"It is more than sufficient, my dear madam," replied I, "and I accept your offer if you will take me on trial for six months."

"Valerie, you make me laugh, and make me angry at the same time; but I can bear much from you now, for you have had a heavy blow, my poor child. Now let's say no more on the subject; all is settled, and the arrangement will remain a secret, unless you publish it yourself."

"I certainly shall make no secret of it, Madame Bathurst; I should be sorry to show false colours, and be supposed by your friends to be otherwise than what I really am. I have done nothing that I ought to be ashamed of, and I abhor deceit. Whatever may be my position in life, I trust that I shall never disgrace the name that I bear, and I am not the first of a noble name who has had a reverse in fortune."

How strange that I now, for the first time in my life, began to feel pride in my family name. I presume because when we have lost almost everything, we cherish more that which remains to us. From the time that Madame Bathurst had first known me till the last twenty-four hours, not a symptom of pride had ever been discovered in me. As the *protégée* and adopted daughter of Madame d'Albret, with brilliant prospects, I was all humility—now a dependant, with a salary of £100 per annum, Valerie was as proud as Lucifer himself. Madame Bathurst perceived this, and I must do her the justice to say, that she was very guarded in her conduct towards me. She felt sympathy for me, and treated me with more kindness, and I may say with more respect, than she did when I was her visitor and her equal.

The next day I informed Caroline of the change in my prospects, and of my having accepted the office of governess; that was to say, on a six months' trial. I pointed out to her that it would now be my duty to see that she did not neglect her studies, and that I was determined to do justice to Madame Bathurst's confidence reposed in me. Caroline, who was of a very amiable and sweet disposition, replied, "That she should always look upon me as her friend and companion, and from her love for me, would do everything I wished," and she kept her word.

The reader will agree with me, that it was impossible for any one to have been lowered down in position more gently than I was in this instance. The servants never knew that I had accepted the offer of governess, for I was invariably called Valerie by Madame Bathurst and her niece, and was treated as I was before when a visitor to the house. I bestowed much time upon Caroline, and taught myself daily, that I might be more able to teach her. I went back to the elements in everything, that I might be more capable of instructing, and Caroline made rapid progress in music, and promised to have, in a few years, a very fine voice. We went to town for the season, but I avoided company as much as possible—so much so, that Madame Bathurst complained of it.

"Valerie, you do wrong not to make your appearance. You retire in such a way that people naturally put questions to me, and ask if you are the governess, or what you are."

"I wish them to do so, my dear madam, and I want you to reply frankly. I am the governess, and do not like anything like concealment."

"But I cannot admit that you are what may be called a governess, Valerie. You are a young friend staying with me, who instructs my niece."

"That is what a governess ought to be," replied I, "a young friend who instructs your children."

"I grant it," replied Madame Bathurst; "but I fear if you were to take the situation in another family, you would find that a governess is not generally so considered or so treated. I do not know any class of people who are more to be pitied than these young people who enter families as governesses; not considered good enough for the drawing-room, they are too good for the kitchen; they are treated with *hauteur* by the master and mistress, and only admitted, or suffered for a time to be in their company; by the servants they are considered as not having claims to those attentions and civilities, for which they are paid and fed; because receiving salaries, or 'wages like themselves,' as they assert, they are not entitled in their opinion to be attended upon. Thus are they, in most houses, neglected by all parties. Unhappy themselves, they cause ill-will and dissension, and more servants are dismissed, or give warning, on account of the governesses, than from any other cause. In the drawing-room they are a check upon conversation; in the schoolroom, if they do their duty, they are the cause of discontent, pouting, and tears; like the bat, they are neither bird nor beast, and they flit about the house like ill omens; they lose the light-heartedness and spring of youth; become sour from continual vexation and annoyance, and their lives are miserable, tedious, and full of repining. I tell you this candidly; it is a harsh picture, but I fear too true a one. With me I trust you will be happy, but you will run a great risk if you were to change and go into another family."

"I have heard as much before, my dear madam," replied I; "but your considerate kindness has made me forget it. I can only say that it will be a melancholy day when I am forced to quit your roof."

Visitors announced, interrupted the conversation. I have before mentioned the talent I had for dress, and the kindness of Madame Bathurst induced me to exert all that I possessed in her favour. Every one was pleased, and expressed admiration at the peculiar elegance of her attire, and asked who was the *modiste* she employed, and Madame Bathurst never failed to ascribe all the merit to me.

Time passed on rapidly, and the season was nearly over. Madame Bathurst had explained to her most intimate friends the alteration which had taken place in my prospects, and that I remained with her more as a companion than in any other capacity. This procured me consideration and respect, and I very often had invitations to parties; but I invariably refused; except, occasionally, accepting a seat in the box at the opera and French plays, I was content to remain quiet.

Madame Paon had, as I requested, sent me a letter of introduction to a friend of hers, a Monsieur Gironac, who lived in Leicester-square. He was a married man, without family. He obtained his livelihood by giving lessons on the flute, on the guitar, and in teaching French during the day, and at night was engaged as second violin in the orchestra of the Opera-house; so that he had many strings to his bow, besides those of his fiddle. His wife, a pretty little lively woman, taught young ladies to make flowers in wax, and mended lace in the evenings. They were a very amiable and amusing couple, always at good-natured warfare with each other, and sparring all day long, from the time they met until they parted. Their battles were the most comical and amusing I ever witnessed, and generally ended in roars of laughter. They received me with the greatest kindness and consideration, treating me with great respect, until our extreme intimacy no longer required it, and our friendship increased more than it could have done from Caroline expressing a wish to learn to model flowers, and becoming the pupil of Madame Gironac. Such were the state of affairs when the London season was over, and we once more returned to the country.

The time flew away rapidly. Madame Bathurst treated me with kindness and respect, Caroline with affection, and I was again quite happy and contented. I was earnest in my endeavours to improve Caroline, and moreover had the satisfaction to feel and hear it acknowledged that my attempts were not thrown away. I looked forward to remaining at least till Caroline's education was complete, which it could not be under two or three years; and feeling security for such a period, I gave myself little thought of the future, when a circumstance occurred which put an end to all my calculations.

I have stated that Caroline was the niece of Madame Bathurst; she was the daughter of a younger sister who had contracted an unfortunate marriage, having eloped with a young man who had not a shilling that he could call his own, and whose whole dependence was upon an uncle without a family. This imprudent match had, however, raised the indignation of his relative, who from that moment told him he was to expect nothing from him either before or after his death. The consequence was, that Madame Bathurst's sister and husband were in a state of great distress, until Madame Bathurst, by exerting herself in his behalf, procured for him a situation of £300 per annum in the Excise. Upon this sum, and the occasional presents of Madame Bathurst, they contrived to live, but having two boys and a girl to educate, Madame Bathurst took charge of the latter, who was Caroline, promising that she would either establish her in life, or leave her a sufficiency at her death. Madame Bathurst had a very large jointure, and could well afford to save up every year for Caroline, which she had done ever since she had taken charge of her, at seven years old. At the time that I have been speaking of, it appeared that the uncle of the father of Caroline died, and notwithstanding his threat bequeathed to his nephew the whole of his large property, by which he became even more wealthy than Madame Bathurst. The consequence was, that Madame Bathurst received a letter announcing this intelligence, and winding up with a notification that Caroline was to be immediately taken back to her father's house. In the letter—which I read, for Madame Bathurst, who was in great distress, handed it to me, observing at the time, "This concerns you as well as me and Caroline"—there were not any expressions of gratitude for the great kindness which they had received from her hands; it was an unkind, unfeeling letter, and I was disgusted when I had gone through it.

"Is this all the return that you receive for what you have done for your sister and her husband?" observed I; "the more I see of this world, the more I hate it."

"It is indeed most selfish and unfeeling," replied Madame Bathurst: "Caroline has been so long with me, that I have looked upon her as my own child, and now she is to be torn from me, without the least consideration of my feelings. It is very cruel and very ungrateful."

Madame Bathurst, after this remark, rose and left the room. As I afterwards discovered, she replied to the letter, pointing out how long she had had charge of Caroline, and now considered her as her daughter, and requesting her parents to allow her to return to her after she paid them a visit; pointing out how unkind and ungrateful it was of them to take her away, now that their circumstances were altered, and how very painful it would be for her if they did so. To this appeal on her part she received a most insulting answer, in which she was requested to make out an account of the expenses incurred for the education and maintenance of her niece, that they might be reimbursed forthwith. On this occasion, for the first time, I saw Madame Bathurst really angry, and certainly not without good cause. She sent for Caroline, who as yet had only been informed that her father and mother had succeeded to a large inheritance, and put the letter into her hands with a copy of her own, requesting that she would read them, watching her countenance with the severest scrutiny as she complied with the injunction, as if to discover if she inherited the ingratitude of her parents. Such was not the case, for poor Caroline sunk, covered her face with her hands, and then rushing to Madame Bathurst, fell on her knees before her, and burying her face in her aunt's lap, cried as if her heart would break. After a few minutes, Madame Bathurst raised up her niece, and kissed her, saying,

"I am satisfied, my dear Caroline at least is not ungrateful. Now, my child, you must do your duty, and obey your parents—as we must part, the sooner we part the better. Valerie, will you see that everything is ready for Caroline's going away to-morrow morning?"

Saying this, Madame Bathurst disengaged herself from Caroline, and quitted the room. It was a long while before I could reason the poor girl into anything like composure. I could not help agreeing with her, that the conduct of her parents was most ungracious towards Madame Bathurst; but at the same time I pointed out to her how natural it was, that having but one daughter, her parents should wish for her return to their own care; that the resigning her to Madame Bathurst must have been a severe trial to them, and that it could only be from consulting her advantage that they could have consented to it; but, notwithstanding all that I could urge, Caroline's indignation against her parents, of whom she knew but little, was very great, and her dislike to return home as strong. However, there was no help for it, as Madame Bathurst had decided that she was to go, and I persuaded her to come with me and prepare her clothes ready for packing up. We did not meet at dinner that day, Madame Bathurst sending an excuse that she was too much out of spirits to leave her room: Caroline and I were equally so, and we remained where we were. In the evening, Madame Bathurst sent for me; I found her in bed, and looking very ill.

"Valerie," said she, "I wish Caroline to start early to-morrow morning, that, as you accompany her, you may be able to return here before night. I shall not be able to see her to-morrow morning. I must, therefore, bid her farewell this night; bring her here, and the sooner it is over the better."

I went for Caroline, and a bitter parting it was. I hardly know which of the three cried the most, but after half an hour Madame Bathurst signed to me to take Caroline away, which I did, and afterwards put her into bed as soon as I could. Having remained with her till she had sobbed herself to sleep, I went down to the servants, and gave Madame Bathurst's directions for the next morning, and then retired myself. Worn out as I was with such a day of anxiety and distress, I could not close my eyes for some time, reflecting upon what might be the issue of this breaking up of the connection to myself. I had been engaged as governess to Caroline, and I could not well expect that Madame Bathurst would wish to retain me now that Caroline was removed from her care; neither, indeed, would my pride permit me to accept such an offer if made, as I should become a mere dependant on her bounty, with no services to offer in return. That I must leave Madame Bathurst, was certain, and that I must look out for some other situation. I took it for granted that Madame Bathurst would not permit me to leave immediately, but allow me a short time to look out for a suitable situation; but whether I should decide upon taking the situation of a governess after what Madame Bathurst had told me, or what situation I should seek, was the cause of much thought and indecision. At last I could make no mind up, and decided that I would trust to Providence, and having so far come to a conclusion, I fell asleep.

After an early breakfast, I set off in the carriage with Caroline in charge, and before noon, we arrived at her father's house. The servants, dressed in very gaudy liveries, ushered us into the library, where we found her father and mother waiting to receive her. A first glance satisfied me that they were swelled with pride at the change in their fortunes. Caroline was not received with great cordiality. There was a stiffness on the part of her parents which would have checked any feelings of affection on her part, had she been inclined to show them, which I was sorry to perceive she did not; indeed, her feelings appeared rather those of resentment for the conduct they had shown to her aunt. After the salutation of meeting, Caroline sat down on a sofa, opposite to her father and mother. I remained standing, and when the pause took place, I said,

"I was deputed by Madame Bathurst to convey your daughter safe to you, and as soon as the horses are baited, I am to return home."

"Who may this person be, Caroline?" demanded her mother.

"I must apologize to Mademoiselle de Chatenœuf for not having introduced her," replied Caroline, blushing with annoyance. "She is a very dear friend of mine and my aunt's."

"Latterly I have been the governess of your daughter, madam," said I.

"Oh!" said the lady. "Will somebody ring the bell?"

I presumed by this somebody, it was intended to convey to me that I was to perform that office; but as they had not had the common civility to ask me to take a chair, I took no notice.

"Will you ring the bell, my dear?" said the lady to her husband.

The gentleman complied; and when the servant entered, the lady said, "Show the governess into the small breakfast-room, and tell the coachman to put up his horses and bait them. He must be round again in an hour."

The man stood with the door in his hand, waiting for me to follow him. Not a little indignant, I turned to Caroline, and said to her, "I had better wish you good-bye now."

"Yes, indeed, Valerie, you had," replied Caroline, rising from the sofa, "for I am ashamed to look you in the face, after such treatment as you have received. Will you," continued she, with great spirit, "accept my apology for the behaviour of my parents towards one who is of a much higher family, and much higher breeding than they can boast of."

"Hush! Caroline," said I; "recollect—"

"I do recollect, and shall continue to recollect, the insults to my dear aunt in the first place, and now the insult to you, my dear Valerie," retorted Caroline, who then put her arms round my neck, and kissed me several times; having so done, she darted from me, threw herself on the sofa, and burst into tears, while I hastened to follow the servant, to escape from such an unpleasant scene.

I was shown into a small room, where I remained some little time, thinking how true were Madame Bathurst's observations as to what I might expect in the position of a governess, when a servant came in, and in a condescending manner, asked if I did not wish to have some lunch. I replied in the negative.

"You can have a glass of wine if you choose," continued he.

"You may leave the room," I replied, calmly; "I wish for nothing."

The man went out, slamming the door, and I was again alone. I reflected upon the scene I had just been witness to, and I own that I was surprised at Caroline's conduct, who had always appeared so mild and amiable; but the fact appeared to me to be, that when parents give up their children to the care of another, they surrender at the same time all those feelings which should exist between parent and child to the party who undertakes the charge of them. The respect and love which by nature belonged to them were now transferred to her aunt, to whom Caroline was always obedient and attached. The insult to me was resented by Caroline as if it had been offered by perfect strangers to her; Caroline not feeling herself at all checked by filial duty. There appeared to be little prospect of any addition to the happiness of either of the parties by the return of Caroline to her father's house; and how it would end I could not surmise.

At last my reverie was interrupted by the servant coming in and telling me that the carriage was at the door. I immediately followed him, and set off on my return, during which I resolved that I would not leave my own expectations any longer in doubt, but come immediately to an understanding with Madame Bathurst.

As it was late when I arrived, I did not see Madame Bathurst that evening, but she came down to breakfast the next morning, when I informed her of all that had occurred at her sister's, and the unceremonious manner in which I had been treated; and having done so, I then observed, that of course I did not expect to remain with her now that Caroline was gone, and begged she would give me her advice and assistance in procuring another situation.

"At all events, do not be in a hurry, Valerie," replied Madame Bathurst; "I trust you will not refuse to be my visitor until you are suited to your liking. I will not ask you to stay with me, as I know you will refuse, and I do not pay unnecessary compliments. And yet, why should you not? I know you well, and am attached to you. I shall feel the loss of Caroline severely. Why not remain?"

"Many thanks, my dear madam," replied I, "for your kind wishes and expressions, but you know my resolution has been made to earn my own livelihood."

"I know that; but a resolution may be altered when circumstances demand it. Madame d'Albret was no more related to you than I am, and yet you accepted her offer."

"I did, madam," replied I, bitterly, "and you know the result. I would have staked my life upon her sincerity and affection, and yet how was I cast away? With every feeling of gratitude, my dear madam, I cannot accept your offer, for I never will put myself in a similar position a second time."

"You do not pay me a very great compliment by that remark, Valerie," said Madame Bathurst, somewhat harshly.

"Indeed, my dear madam, I should be sorry if anything I have said should annoy one who has been so kind and considerate to me as you have been; but I know that I should be miserable and unhappy if not independent, and I never can risk a second shock, like that I received from the conduct of Madame d'Albret. I entreat as a favour that you will not continue the subject."

"Well, Valerie, I will not; perhaps had I been treated as you have been, I might feel the same. What then do you propose to seek? Is it the situation of a governess?"

"Anything in preference, my dear madam; I was sufficiently humiliated yesterday. I should prefer that of a lady's maid, although I hope not to descend quite so low."

"There are so few situations for a person educated as you have been. There is a companion for a lady, which I believe is anything but pleasant: there is that of amanuensis, but it is seldom required. You might certainly go out and give lessons in music, and singing, and in the French language; but there are so many French masters and mistresses, and for music and singing a master is always preferred, why, I do not exactly know. However, I think something may be done when we go to town, but till then all that we can do is to talk the matter over. Perhaps something may turn up when we least expect it. I will, however, now that I know your decision, make every inquiry, and give you all the assistance in my power."

I expressed my thanks and gratitude, and the conversation ended.

I did not, however, trust altogether to Madame Bathurst. I wrote a letter to my acquaintance Madame Gironac, in Leicester-square, stating what had occurred, and what my ideas and intentions were, requesting her to give me her advice and opinion as to the best plan I could follow. In a few days I received from her the following reply, which I insert as characteristic of the party.

"My dear Mademoiselle,—

"Your letter gave great pain to me; and as for my husband, he was quite furious, and declared that he would not live a minute longer in such an abominable world. However, to oblige me, he has not yet made away with himself. It really is dreadful to see a young lady like you in such an awkward position from the weakness and follies of others; but we must submit to what the *bon Dieu* disposes, and when things come to the worst, hope that a change will take place, as any change must then be for the better. I have consulted my husband about what you propose, but he negatives everything. He says you are too good for a governess; would be thrown away as a companion to a lady; that you must not be seen in a cab, going about giving lessons—in fact, he will listen to nothing except that you must come and live with us. I can only say, my dear mademoiselle, that I join in the latter request, and that it would make me perfectly happy, and that the honour and pleasure of your company would be more than a compensation. Still, it is but a poor home to offer to you, but at all events one that you might condescend to take advantage of rather than remain to be mortified by those who think, as they do in this country, that money is everything. Do, pray, then come to us, if you feel inclined, and then we ean talk over things quietly, and wait upon Providence. My husband has now hardly time to eat his dinner, he has so many pupils of one kind and the other; and I am happy to say that I have also most of my time occupied; and if it pleases God to continue us in good health, we hope to be able to put by a little money for a rainy day, as they say in this country, where it is always raining. Assure yourself, my dear mademoiselle, of our love, respect, consideration.

"Annette Gironac."

We went to town earlier than usual, Madame Bathurst feeling lonely in the country after the departure of Caroline, from whom she had not received a line since her quitting her. This of course was to be ascribed to her parents, who thus returned all Madame Bathurst's kindness as soon as they no longer required her assistanee. I know not how it was, but gradually a sort of coolness had arisen between Madame Bathurst and me. Whether it was that she was displeased at my refusing her offer to remain with her, or thought proper to wean herself from one who was so soon to quit her, I know not. I did nothing to give offence: I was more quiet and subdued, perhaps, than before, because I had become more reflective; but I could not accuse myself of any fault or error, that I was aware of.

We had been about a week in London, when an old acquaintance of Madame Bathurst's, who had just returned from Italy, where she had resided for two years, called upon her. Her name was Lady R——: she was the widow of a baronet, not in very opulent circumstances, although with a sufficiency to hire, if not keep a carriage. She was, moreover, an author, having written two or three novels, not very good I was told, but still, emanating from the pen of a lady, they were well paid. She was very eccentric, and rather amusing. When a woman says everything that comes into her head, out of a great deal of chaff there will drop some few grains of wheat; and so sometimes, more by accident than otherwise, she said what is called a good thing. Now, a good thing is repeated, while all the nonsense is forgotten; and Lady R—— was considered a wit as well as an author. She was a tall woman; I should think very near, if not past, fifty years of age, with the remains of beauty in her countenance: apparently, she was strong and healthy, as she walked with a spring, and was lively and quick in all her motions.

"*Cara mia,*" exclaimed she, as she was announced, running up to Madame Bathurst, "and how have you been all this while—my biennial absence in the land of poetry—in which I have laid up such stores of beauteous images and ideas in my mind, that I shall make them last me during my life. Have you read my last? It's surprising, every one says, and proves the effect of climate upon composition—quite new—an Italian story of thrilling interest. And you have something new here, I perceive," continued she, turning to me; "not only new, but beautiful—introduce me: I am an enthusiast in the sublime and beautiful. Is she any relation? No relation!—Mademoiselle de Chatenœuf!—what a pretty name for a novel. I should like to borrow it, and paint the original from nature. Will you sit for your likeness?"

That Lady R—— allowed no one to talk but herself was evident. Madame Bathurst, who knew her well, allowed her to run on; and I, not much valuing the dose of flattery so unceremoniously bestowed upon me, took an opportunity, when Lady R—— turned round to whisper something to Madame Bathurst, to make my escape from the room. The following morning, Madame Bathurst said to me,

"Valerie, Lady R—— was very much pleased with your appearance when she made her visit yesterday; and as she told me, after you had left the room, that she wanted just such a person as yourself as a companion and amanuensis, I thought it right to say that you were looking out for something of the kind, and that you were remaining under my protection until you could procure it. We had more conversation on the subject, and she said, before she left, that she would write to me on the subject. Her note has just been put into my hands; you can read it. She offers you a salary of one hundred pounds per annum; all your expenses paid except your dress. As far as salary goes, I think her terms liberal. And now, as to

Lady R——. My opinion of her is in a few words. You saw her yesterday, and I never knew her otherwise; never more or less rational. She is an oddity; but she is goodnatured; and, I am told, more liberal and charitable than many others who can afford it better. Now you know all I can tell you about her, and you must decide for yourself. Here is her note; you need not give me an answer till to-morrow morning."

I made one or two observations and then left the room. The note was very kind, certainly, but it was as flighty as her manners. I hastened to my own bedchamber, and sat down to reflect. I felt that I was not exactly comfortable with Madame Bathurst, and certainly was anxious to be independent; but still, I could not exactly make up my mind to accept the offer of Lady R——. She was so different from those I had been accustomed to live with. I was still deliberating, when Madame Bathurst's maid came into my room, telling me it was time to change my dress for dinner. As she was assisting me, she said,

"And so, Miss Chatenœuf, you are about to quit us, I find. I am so sorry—first, Miss Caroline—now you. I hoped you would stay with us, and I should soon have become an expert milliner under your directions."

"Who told you, Mason, that I was going to leave you?"

"Mrs. Bathurst told me so, and not a quarter of an hour ago," replied the woman.

"Well," replied I, "she told you truly, Mason; such is the case;" for this information of Mason's decided me upon accepting the offer of Lady R——; for Madame Bathurst, it appeared to me, had certainly decided it for me by making such a premature communication to her servant.

The reader may suppose, that when I made this discovery, I felt little pain at the idea of parting with Madame Bathurst; and the following morning I coolly announced my intention of accepting the offer of Lady R——. Madame Bathurst looked at me very hard, as if surprised at not hearing from me any regrets at leaving her, and expressions of gratitude for all favours; but I could not express what I really did not feel at the time. Afterwards, I thought that I had been wrong, as, to a certain degree, I was under obligations to her; not that I think, had she been ever so inclined to get rid of me, she could have well turned me out of the house, although I had been foisted upon her in such a way by Madame d'Albret. Still I was under obligations to her, and should have expressed myself so, if it had not been for the communication made to me by the maid, which proved that her expressions to me were not sincere.

"Well, then," replied Madame Bathurst, at last, "I will write to Lady R—— immediately. I presume I may say that you are at her commands as soon as she can receive you?"

"Yes, madam, at an hour's notice," replied I.

"You really appear as if you were anxious to quit me, mademoiselle," said Madame Bathurst, biting her lip.

"I certainly am," replied I. "You informed Mason that I was to go, previous to having my decision; and therefore I gladly withdraw myself from the company of those who have made up their minds to get rid of me."

"I certainly did tell Mason that there was a prospect of your quitting me," replied Madame Bathurst, colouring up; "but—however, it's no use entering into an investigation of what I really said, or catechizing my maid: one thing is clear, we have been mutually disappointed with each other, and therefore it perhaps is better that we should part. I believe that I am in your debt, Mademoiselle de Chatenœuf. Have you reckoned how long you have been with me?"

"I have reckoned the time that I instructed Caroline."

"*Miss* Caroline, if you please, Mademoiselle de Chatenœuf."

"Well, then, madam, Miss Caroline, since you wish it; it is five months and two weeks," replied I, rising from my chair.

"You may sit down, mademoiselle, while I make the calculation," said Madame Bathurst.

"It is too great an honour for a Chatenœuf to sit in your presence," replied I, quietly, remaining on my feet.

Madame Bathurst made no reply, but calculating the sum of money due to me on a sheet of note-paper, handed it to me and begged me to see if it was correct.

"I have no doubt of it, madam," replied I, looking at it and then laying it down on the desk before her.

Madame Bathurst put the sum in bank notes and

sovereigns down before me, and said, "Do me the favour to count it, and see if it is correct;" and then rising, said, "Your wishes will be complied with by my servants as usual, mademoiselle, as long as you remain under my roof. I wish you farewell."

The last words were accompanied with a low courtesy, and she then quitted the room.

I replied with a salute as formal as her own, and mortified at the treatment I had received, I sat down, and a few tears escaped, but my pride came to my assistance, and I soon recovered myself.

This scene was, however, another proof to me of what I must in future expect; and it had the effect of hardening me, and blunting my feelings. "*Miss* Caroline!" said I to myself, "when the *protégée* of Madame d'Albret, and the visitor of Madame Bathurst, it was Caroline, and dear Valerie. She might have allowed me to quit her without pointing out to me, in so marked a manner, how our relative positions have been changed. However, I thank you, Madame Bathurst; what obligations I may have been under to you are now cancelled, and I need not regret the weight of them as I might have done. Ah! Madame d'Albret, you took me from my home, that I might not be buffeted by my mother, and now you have abandoned me to be buffeted by the whole world. Well, be it so, I will fight my way, nevertheless;" and as I left the room to pack up my trunks, I felt my courage rise from this very attempt on the part of Madame Bathurst to humiliate me.

The letter of Madame Bathurst to Lady R—— brought the latter to the house that afternoon. I was up in my room when I was informed by the servants that she waited below to see me. When I entered, she was alone, Madame Bathurst having gone out in her carriage, and as soon as she saw me, she rushed into my arms almost, taking me by both hands, and saying how happy she was that she had acquired such a treasure as a friend and companion; wished to know whether I could not come with her immediately, as her carriage was at the door, and went on for nearly ten minutes without a check, asking fifty questions, and not permitting me to answer one. At last I was able to reply to the most important, which was, that I would be happy to come to her on the following morning, if she would send for me. She insisted that I should come to breakfast, and I acceded to her request, as Madame Bathurst, who was not an early riser, would not be down at the hour mentioned, and I wished to leave the house without seeing her again, after our formal adieu. Having arranged this, she appeared to be in a great hurry to be off, and skipped out of the room before I could ring the bell to order the carriage.

I completed my preparations for departure, and had some dinner brought into my own room, sending down an excuse for not joining Madame Bathurst, stating that I had a bad headache, which was true enough. The next morning, long before Madame Bathurst was up, I was driven to Baker-street, Portman-square, where Lady R—— resided. I found her ladyship in her *robe de chambre.*

"Well," said she, "this is delightful. My wishes are crowned at last. I have passed a night of uncertainty, rolling about between hopes and fears, as people always do when they have so much at stake. Let me show you your room."

I found a very well-furnished apartment prepared for me, looking out upon the street.

"See, you have a front view," she said, "not extensive, but still you can rise early and moralize. You can see London wake up. First, the drowsy policeman; the tired cabman, and more tired horse, after a night of motion, seeking the stable and repose; the housemaid, half-awake, dragging on her clothes; the kitchen-wench washing from the steps the dirt of yesterday; the milkmaid's falsetto, and the dustman's bass; the bakers' boys, the early post-delivery, and thus from units to tens, and from tens to tens of thousands, and London stirs again. There is poetry in that, and now let us down to breakfast. I always breakfast in my *robe de chambre;* you must do the same, that is, if you like the fashion. Where's the page?"

Lady R—— rang the bell of the sitting-room, which she called a boudoir, and a lad of fourteen, in a blue blouse and leather belt, made his appearance.

"Lionel, breakfast in a moment. Vanish, before the leviathan can swim a league—bring up hot rolls and butter."

"Yes, my lady," replied the lad, pertly, "I'll be up again before the chap can swim a hundred yards;" and he shot out of the room in a second.

"There's virtue in that boy; he has wit enough for a prime minister, or a clown at Astley's. I picked him up by a mere chance; he is one of my models."

What her ladyship meant by models I could not imagine, but I soon found out. The return of the lad with breakfast put an end to her talking for the time being. When we had finished, the page was again summoned.

"Now then, Lionel, do your spiriting gently."

"I know," said the boy; "I'm not to smash the cups and saucers as I did yesterday."

The lad collected the breakfast things on a tray, with great rapidity, and disappeared with such a sudden turn round, that I fully anticipated he would add to yesterday's damage before he was down the stairs.

As soon as he was gone, Lady R—— coming up to me, said,

"And now let me have a good look at you, and then I shall be content for some time. Yes, I was not mistaken, you are a perfect model, and must be my future heroine. Yours is just the beauty that I required. There, that will do, now sit down and let us converse. I often have wanted a companion. As for an amanuensis, that is only a nominal task; I write as fast as most people, and I cannot follow my ideas, let me scribble for life, as I may say; and as for my writing being illegible, that's the compositor's concern, not mine. It's his business to make it out, and therefore I never have mine copied. But I wanted a beautiful companion and friend—I wouldn't have an ugly one for the world, she would do me as much harm as you will do me service."

"I am sure I hardly know how I am to do you service, Lady R——, if I do not write for you."

"I dare say not; but when I tell you that I am more than repaid by looking at you when I feel inclined, you will acknowledge that you do me service; but we will not enter into metaphysics, or psychological questions just now, it shall all be explained by-and-by. And now the first service I ask of you is, at once to leap over the dull fortnight of gradual approaching, which at last ends in intimacy. I have ever held it to be a proof of the suspiciousness of our natures, and unworthy. You must allow me to call you Valerie at once, and I must entreat of you to call me Sempronia. Your name is delightful, fit for a first-class heroine. My real baptismal name is one that I have abjured, and if my godfathers and godmothers did give it to me, I throw it back to them with contempt. What do you think it was?—Barbara. Barbara, indeed! 'My mother had a *maid* called Barbara,' Shakspeare says, and such a name should be associated with brooms and yellow soap. Call me Sempronia from this time forward, and you confer a favour on me. And now I must write a little, so take a book and a seat on the sofa, for, at the opening of this chapter my heroine is exactly in that position, 'in maiden meditation, fancy free.'"

CHAPTER VII.

Lady R—— sat down before her writing materials, and I took my seat on the sofa, as she had requested, and was soon occupied with my reading. I perceived that, as she wrote, her ladyship continually took her eyes off her paper, and fixed them upon me. I presumed that she was describing me, and I was correct in my idea, for, in about half an hour, she threw down her pen, and cried,

"There, I am indebted to you for the best picture of a heroine that I ever drew! Listen."

And her ladyship read to me a most flattering description of my sweet person, couched in very high-flown language.

"I think, Lady R——," said I, when she had finished, "that you are more indebted to your own imagination than to reality in drawing my portrait."

"Not so, not so, my dear Valerie. I may have done you justice, but certainly not more. There is nothing like having the living subject to write from. It is the same as painting or drawing, it only can be true when drawn from nature; in fact, what is writing but painting with the pen?"

As she concluded her sentence, the page, Lionel, came in with a letter on a waiter, and hearing her observation, as he handed the letter, he impudently observed:

"Here's somebody been painting your name on the outside of this paper; and as there's sevenpence to pay, I think it's rather dear for such a smudge."

"You must not judge from outside appearance, Lionel,"

replied Lady R——: "the contents may be worth pounds. It is not prepossessing, I grant, in its superscription, but may, like the toad, ugly and venomous, wear a precious jewel in its head. That was a vulgar error of former days, Lionel, which Shakspeare has taken advantage of."

"Yes, that chap painted with a pen at a fine rate," replied the boy, as Lady R—— opened the letter and read it.

"You may go, Lionel," said she, putting the letter down.

"I just wanted to know, now that you've opened your toad, if you have found the jewel, or whether it's a vulgar error?"

"It's a vulgar letter, at all events, Lionel," replied her ladyship, "and concerns you; it is from the shoemaker at Brighton, who requests me to pay him eighteen shillings for a pair of boots ordered by you, and not paid for."

"Well, my lady, I do owe for the boots, true enough; but it's impossible for me always to recollect my own affairs, I am so busy with looking after yours."

"Well, but now you are reminded of them, Lionel, you had better give me the money, and I will send it to him."

At this moment Lady R—— stooped from her chair to pick up her handkerchief. There were some sovereigns lying on the desk, and the lad, winking his eye at me, took one up, and, as Lady R—— rose up, held it out to her in silence.

"That's right, Lionel," said Lady R——; "I like honesty."

"Yes, madam," replied the impudent rogue, very demurely; "like most people who tell their own stories, I was born of honest, but poor parents."

"I believe your parents were honest; and now, Lionel, to reward you, I shall pay for your boots, and you may keep your sovereign."

"Thank your ladyship," replied the lad. "I forgot to say that the cook is outside for orders."

Lady R—— rose, and went out of the room; and Mr. Lionel, laughing at me, put the sovereign down with the others.

"Now, I call that real honesty You saw me borrow it, and now you see me pay it."

"Yes; but suppose her ladyship had not given you the sovereign, how would it have been then?" said I.

"I should have paid her very honestly," replied he. "If I wished to cheat her, or rob her, I might do so all day long. She leaves her money about everywhere, and never knows what she has; besides, if I wanted to steal, I should not do so with those bright eyes of yours looking at me all the time."

"You are a very saucy boy," replied I, more amused than angry.

"It's all from reading, and it's not my fault; for her ladyship makes me read, and I never yet read any book about old times in which the pages were not saucy; but I've no time to talk just now—my spoons are not clean yet;" so saying, he quitted the room.

I did not know whether I ought to inform her ladyship of this freak of her page's; but as the money was returned, I thought I had better say nothing for the present. I soon found out that the lad was correct in asserting that she was careless of her money, and that, if he chose, he might pilfer without chance of discovery; and moreover, that he really was a good and honest lad, only full of mischief and very impudent; owing, however, to Lady R——'s treatment of him; for she rather encouraged his impudence than otherwise. He was certainly a very clever, witty boy, and a very quick servant; so quick, indeed, at his work, that it almost appeared as if he never had anything to do, and he had plenty of time for reading, which he was very fond of.

Lady R—— returned, and resumed her writing.

"You sing, do you not? I think Mrs. Bathurst told me you were very harmonious. Now, Valerie, do me a favour: I want to hear a voice carolling some melodious ditty. I shall describe it so much better, if I really heard you sing. I do like reality; of course, you must sing without music, for my country-girl cannot be crossing the mead with a piano in one hand, and a pail of water in the other."

"I should think not," replied I, laughing; "but am not I too near?"

"Yes, rather; I should prefer it on the stairs, or on the first floor landing; but I could not be so rude as to send you out of the room."

"But I will go without sending," replied I; and I did so, and having arrived at my station, I sang a little French refrain, which I thought would answer her ladyship's purpose. On my return her ladyship was writing furiously, and did not appear to notice my entrance. I took my seat quietly, and in about ten minutes she again threw down the pen, exclaiming:

"I never wrote so effective a chapter! Valerie, you are more precious to me than fine gold; and as Shylock said of his ring, 'I would not change thee for a wilderness of monkeys.' I make the quotation as expressive of your value. It was so kind-hearted of you to comply with my wish. You don't know an author's feelings. You have no idea how our self-love is flattered by success, and that we value a good passage in our works more than anything else in existence. Now, you have so kindly administered to my ruling passion twice in one morning, that I love you exceedingly. I dare say you think me very odd, and people say that I am so; I may ask you to do many odd things for me, but I shall never ask you to do what a lady may not do, or what would be incorrect for you to do, or for me to propose; that you may depend upon, Valerie: and now I close my manuscript for the present, being well satisfied with the day's work."

Lady R—— rang the bell, and on Lionel making his appearance, she desired him to take away her writing materials, put her money into her purse—if he knew where the purse was—and then asked him what were her engagements for the evening.

"I know *we* have an engagement," replied the boy; "I can't recollect it, but I shall find it in the drawing-room."

He went out, and in a minute returned.

"I have found it, my lady," said he. "Here's the ticket; Mrs. Allwood at home, nine o'clock."

"Mrs. Allwood, my dear Valerie, is a literary lady, and her parties are very agreeable."

The page looked at me from behind Lady R——'s chair, and shook his head in dissent.

"Shall *we* go?" continued Lady R——.

"If you please, madam," replied I.

"Well, then, we will take a drive before dinner, and the evening after dinner shall be dedicated to the feast of reason and the flow of soul. Dear me, how I have inked my fingers, I must go upstairs and wash them."

As soon as Lady R—— left the room, Master Lionel began,

"Feast of reason and flow of soul; I don't like such entertainment. Give me a good supper and plenty of champagne."

"Why, what matter can it make to you?" said I, laughing.

"It matters a good deal. I object to literary parties," replied he. "In the first place, for one respectable carriage driving up to the door, there are twenty cabs and jarveys, so that the company isn't so good; and then at parties, when there is a good supper, I get my share of it in the kitchen. You don't think we are idle down below. I have been to Mrs. Allwood's twice, and there's no supper, nothing but feast of reason, which remains upstairs, and they're welcome to my share of it. As for the drink, its negus and cherry-water; nothing else, and if the flow of soul is not better than such stuff, they may have my share of that also. No music, no dancing, nothing but buzz, buzz, buzz. Won't you feel it stupid!"

"Why, one would think you had been upstairs instead of down, Lionel."

"Of course I am. They press all who have liveries into the service, and I hand the cakes about rather than kick for hours at the legs of the kitchen-table. I hear all that's said just as well as the company, and I've often thought I could have given a better answer than I've heard some of your great literaries. When I hand the cakes to-night, take them I point out to you: they'll be the best."

"Why, how can you tell?"

"Because I try them all before I come in the room."

"You ought to be ashamed to acknowledge it."

"All comes of reading, miss," replied he. "I read that in former times great people, kings and princes and so on, always had their victuals tasted first, lest there should be poison in them: so I taste upon that principle, and I have been half-poisoned sometimes at these cheap parties; but I'm getting cunning, and when I meet a suspicious-looking piece of pastry, I leave it for the company; but I can't wait to talk any longer, miss, I must give coachman his orders."

"I never asked you to talk, Mr. Lionel," said I.

"No, you didn't; but still I know you like to hear me: you can't deny that. Now, to use my lady's style, I am to tell the coachman to put a girdle round the park in forty minutes;" so saying, the lad vanished, as he usually did, in a second.

The lad was certainly right when he said that I did like to hear him talk, for he amused me so much, that I forgave his impudence and familiarity. Shortly afterwards, we went out in the carriage, and having driven two or three times round the park, returned home to dinner. At ten o'clock, we went to Mrs. Allwood's party. I was introduced to a great many literary stars, whom I had never before heard of; but the person who attracted the most attention was a Russian count, who had had his ears and nose cut off by the Turks. It certainly did not add to his beauty, however it might have to his interest. However, Lionel was right. It was a very stupid party to me; all talking at once and constantly on the move to find fresh listeners; it *was* all buzz, buzz, buzz, and I was glad when the carriage was announced. Such were the events of the first day which I passed under the roof of Lady R——.

Indeed, this first day may be taken as a sample of most others, and a month passed rapidly away. Each day, however, was marked with some peculiar eccentricity on her part; but these diverted me. I was often requested to do strange things in my position as a model; but with all her oddities Lady R—— was a gentlewoman in manner and in feeling; and what I should certainly have refused to any one else, I did for her without reluctance. I now called her Sempronia, as she requested, and, moreover, I became very intimate with Master Lionel, who would be intimate, whether or no, and who, like Lady R——, was a source of great amusement. At times, when I was alone and communed with myself, I could not help surveying my peculiar position. I was engaged at a large salary—for what? to look handsome, to put myself in attitudes, and to do nothing. This was not flattering to my talents (such as I had), but still I was treated with kindness and confidence; was the companion of her ladyship; was introduced and taken to all the parties to which she was asked, and never made to feel my dependence. I had already imbibed a strong friendship for Lady R——, and I was therefore content to remain. One morning she said to me,

"My dear Valerie, do me the favour to tighten the laces of my stays."

"She was, as usual, writing in her dressing-gown.

"Oh, tighter yet; as tight as you can draw them. That will do nicely."

"Why you can hardly breathe, Sempronia."

"But I can write, my dear child, and, as I before observed, the mind and the body influence each other. I am about to write a strictly moral dialogue, and I never could do it unless I am strait-laced. Now I feel fit for the wife of Cato and of Rome."

A few days afterwards she amused me still more. After writing about half an hour, she threw down her pen—

"I never can do it; come upstairs, my dear Valerie, and help me off with my stays. I must be *à l'abandon.*"

I followed her, and having removed these impediments, we returned to the boudoir.

"There," said she, sitting down, "I think I shall manage it now: I feel as if I could."

"Manage what?" inquired I.

"My dear, I am about to write a love-scene, very warm and impassioned, and I could not do it, confined as I was. Now that I am loose, I can give loose to the reins of my imagination, and delineate with the arrow of Cupid's self. My heroine is reclining, with her hand on her cheek; put yourself in that attitude, my dear, dear Valerie, as if you were meditating upon the prolonged absence of one dear to you. Exactly—beautiful—true to nature—but I forgot, a page enters—don't move, I'll ring the bell."

Lionel answered quickly, as usual.

"Here, Lionel, I want you to play the page."

"I've no time for play, my lady; I'm page in earnest. There's all the knives to clean."

"Never mind the knives just now. Observe, Lionel, you are supposed to be sent a message to that lovely girl, who is sitting absorbed in a soft reverie. You enter her presence unperceived, and are struck with her beauty; you lean against a tree, in a careless but graceful attitude, with your eyes fixed upon her lovely features. Now lean against the door, as I have described, and then I shall be able to write."

I could not help smiling at the absurdity of this scene, the more so as Lionel, just passing his fingers through his hair, and then pulling up his shirt collar, took his position, saying,

"Now, Miss Valerie, we'll see who performs best: I think you will be sooner tired of sitting than I shall be of looking at you."

"Excellent, Lionel! — exactly the position that I wished," said Lady R——, scribbling as fast as she could; "that stare of yours is true to nature — Cymon and Iphigenia—a perfect tableau!—don't move, I beg; I only require ten minutes."

I looked up at Master Lionel, and he made such a grimace, that I could hardly keep my countenance, and I did not exactly feel satisfied at thus performing, as it were, with a servant; but still, that servant was Lionel, who was very unlike other servants. In ten minutes, as promised, we were released, much to my satisfaction. Lionel went off to clean his knives, and I took up my book, and really when I perceived the delight of Lady R——, at what she called her success, I no longer felt anything like annoyance at having complied with her wishes.

One morning, when Lady R—— had walked out, and the page, Lionel, was in the room, I entered into conversation with him, and asked how it was that he had been so much better educated than were lads in his position in general.

"That's a question that I often ask myself, Miss Valerie," replied he, "as they say in some autobiographies. The first recollection I have of myself was finding myself, walking two-and-two, in a suit of pepper-and-salt, along with about twenty other very little boys, at a cheap preparatory school, kept by the Misses Wiggins. There I remained—nobody came to see me: other boys talked of their papas and mammas—I had none to talk about: they went home at the holidays, and brought back toys and plumcakes; I enjoyed my holidays alone, scraping holes in the gravel, for want of better employment, between my meals, and perhaps not opening my mouth, or hearing the sound of my own voice, more than three or four times in the twenty-four hours. As I had plenty of time for reflection during the vacations, as I grew bigger, I began to imagine that somehow or another I must have had a father and mother, like the other boys, and began to make very impertinent (as I was told) inquiries about them. The Misses Wiggins gave me a good wigging, as they call it, for my unwarranted curiosity, pointing out the indelicacy of entering upon such subjects; and thus was my mouth stopped.

At last I grew up too big for the school, and was not to be managed by two old maids, and I presume it was through their representations that I was at last honoured by a visit from an old housekeeper, a woman above fifty, whom I never saw before. I ventured to put the forbidden questions to her, and she replied that I had neither father nor mother; that they were both dead, and that I was educated by the kindness of a great lady, whose dependants they had been, and that the great lady would call and see me perhaps, or if she did not, would send for me, and do something for me. Well, about four years ago (I was then twelve years old, I was told, but my idea is that I am older than they say), I was sent for by Lady R——, and at first I was dressed in a turban and red jacket, and sat on the floor. I was told that I was to be her page, and I liked it very much, as I did nothing but run messages and read books, which I was very fond of; and Lady R—— took some pains with me; but as I grew bigger, so did I fall off from my high estate, and by degrees descended from the drawing-room to the kitchen.

"My finery was not renewed; at first I had a plain suit, and did my work under the footman; and two years ago, when the footman was sent away, rather than be under the orders of another, I volunteered to do the work, which I have done ever since, and now receive high wages, and wear sugar-loaf buttons, as you perceive. Now, Miss Valerie, that's all I know of myself; but I suspect that Lady R—— knows more; still it may be, that what the old woman told me was correct, and that I was the child of one of her favourite dependants, and was educated by her in the manner that I was, for you know how many odd things she does."

"What is your other name, Lionel?"

"Bedingfield, I am told, is my name," replied he.

"Have you ever spoken to Lady R——," inquired I, "relative to your parents?"

"I once did; but she said they were Sir Richard's people, not hers (that is, her father's, the late baronet's), and that she knew nothing about them, except that my father was a steward or bailiff to him in the country, and that he had left directions that she should do something for me. Her ladyship did not appear to be inclined to talk about them much, and sent me away as soon as she had told me what I now repeat to you; however, I have found out something since that—but there's her ladyship's knock;" so saying, Lionel vanished.

Soon after her ladyship's return, Madame Gironac, who had called upon me two or three times, was announced. I went out of the room, and when I met her in the dining-parlour, she told me that she had brought some of her imitations of flowers on wax, to show them to her ladyship. I immediately went up, and asked Lady R—— if she would like to see them; to which proposal she assented. When Madame Gironac displayed her performances, which were very natural and beautiful, her ladyship was delighted, and purchased several of them, after which I again went down stairs, and had a long conversation with my warm-hearted little friend.

"I don't like this situation of yours, mademoiselle," said she, "nor does my husband. Now I was thinking, Mademoiselle de Chatenœuf, that it would not be a bad plan if you were to learn how to make those flowers. I will teach you for nothing; and I will teach you what I never teach my pupils, which is, how to prepare the wax, and a great many other little secrets which are worth knowing."

"I shall be very glad to learn, my dear madam," replied I; "but I can afford to pay you for your time and trouble, and must insist upon doing so; if not, I will not be your pupil."

"Well, well, we must not quarrel about that. I know that no one likes to be under an obligation, especially one like you—but learn you must—so let us arrange for the lessons."

I did so; and from that day until I quitted Lady R——, I applied myself so assiduously to the art, that, with the unreserved communciations of Madame Gironac, I became a proficient, and could equal her own performances—Madame Gironac declared that I excelled her, because I had more taste.—But to return.

After I had parted with Madame Gironac, I went up-stairs, and found Lady R—— sitting at the table, looking at the purchases she had made.

"My dear Valerie," cried she, "you don't know how you have obliged me by introducing that little woman and her flowers. What a delightful and elegant employment for a heroine to undertake—so ladylike! I have determined that mine shall support herself by imitating flowers in wax. I am just at the point of placing her in embarrassed circumstances, and did not well know how she was to gain her livelihood, but, thanks to you, that is selected, and in a most charming and satisfactory manner. It is so hard to associate poverty with clean hands."

About a fortnight afterwards, after some other conversation, Lady R—— said,

"My dear Valerie, I have a surprise for you. The season is nearly over, and, what is more important, my third volume will be complete in a fortnight. Last night, as I was wooing Somnus in vain, an idea came into my head. I proposed going to pass the autumn at Brighton, as you know, but last night I made up my mind that we would go over the water; but whether it is to be Havre, or Dieppe, or Paris, or anywhere else, I cannot say; but certainly La Belle France. How do you like the idea? I think of making a sort of sentimental journey. We will seek adventures. Shall we go like Rosamond and Celia? I with 'gallant curtal axe,' dressed as a youth. Shall we be mad, Valerie? What say you?"

I hardly knew what to say. Lady R—— appeared to have a most unusual freak in her head, and to be a little more odd than usual. Now I had no wish to go to France, as I might fall in with people whom I did not wish to see; and, moreover, from what I had heard of her ladyship's adventures in Italy, I was convinced that she was one of many, I may say, who fancy that they may do as they please out of their own country, and I certainly did not wish to figure in her train; I therefore replied,

"I know my own country well, Lady R——, and there cannot be a less eligible one for a masquerade. We should meet with too many *désagrémens,* if unprotected by male society, and our journey would be anything but sentimental. But if you do go to France, does Lionel accompany you?"

"Well I do not know, but I should like him to learn the language. I think I shall take him. He is a clever boy."

"Very," replied I; "where did you pick him up?"

"He is a son of my late father's—('a son of' exclaimed I)—tenant, or something, I was going to say," continued Lady R——, colouring; "but I could not recollect exactly what the man was. Bailiff, I think. I know nothing about his father, but he was recommended to me by Sir Richard before he died."

"Recommended as a servant?" replied I; "he appears to me to be too good for so menial a position."

"I have made him above his position, Valerie; not that he was recommended as a servant, but recommended to my care. Perhaps some day I may be able to do more for him. You know that we are to go to Lady G——'s ball to-night. It will be a very brilliant affair. She gives but one during the season, and she always does the thing in good style. Bless me, how late it is! The carriage will be round in two minutes; I've a round of visits to pay."

"Will you excuse me? I have promised to take a lesson of Madame Gironac."

"Very true: then I must enter upon my melancholy task alone. What can be so absurd as a rational and immortal soul going about distributing pasteboard!"

We went to Lady G——'s ball, which was very splendid. I had been dancing, for although I was not considered, probably, good enough among the young aristocrats to be made a partner for life, as a partner in a waltz or quadrille I was rather in request; for the odium of governess had not yet been attached to my name, having never figured in that capacity in the metropolis, where I was unknown. I had but a short time taken my seat by Lady R——, when the latter sprang off in a great hurry, after what I could not tell, and her place was immediately occupied by a lady, who I immediately recognised as a Lady M——, who had, with her daughters, composed a portion of the company at Madame Bathurst's country seat.

"Have you forgotten me, Mademoiselle de Chateneuf?" said Lady M——, extending her hand.

"No, my lady, I am glad to see you looking so well. I hope your daughters are also quite well?"

"Thank you; they look very well in the evening, but rather pale in the morning. It is a terrible thing a London season, very trying to the constitution; but what can we do? We must be out and be seen everywhere, or we lose caste—so many balls and parties every night. The fact is, that if girls are not married during the three first seasons after they come out, their chance is almost hopeless, for all the freshness and charm of youth, which are so appetizing to the other sex, are almost gone. No constitution can withstand the fatigue. I've often compared our young ladies to the carriage-horses—they are both worked to death during the season, and then turned out to grass in the country to recover themselves, and come up fresh for the next winter. It really is a horrible life; but girls must be got off. I wish mine were, for what with fatigue and anxiety I'm worn to a shadow. Come, Mademoiselle de Chatenœuf, let us go into the next room. It is cooler, and we shall be more quiet; take my arm: perhaps we shall meet the girls."

I accepted her ladyship's invitation, and we went into the next room, and took a seat upon a sofa in a recess.

"Here we can talk without being overheard," said Lady M——; "and now, my dear young lady, I know that you have left Madame Bathurst, but why I did not know. Is it a secret?"

"No, my lady; when Caroline went away, I was of no further use, and therefore I did not wish to remain. You may perhaps know that I went to Madame Bathurst's on a visit, and that an unforeseen change of circumstances induced me to remain for some time as instructress to her niece."

"I heard something of that sort, a kind of friendly arrangement, at which Madame Bathurst had good cause to be content. I'm sure I should have been, had I been so fortunate; and now you are residing with Lady R——: may I inquire, without presuming too much, in what capacity you are with Lady R——?"

"I went there as an amanuensis, but I have never written a line. Lady R—— is pleased to consider me as a companion, and I must say that she has behaved to me with great kindness and consideration."

"I have no doubt of it," replied Lady M——; "but still it appears to me (excuse the liberty I take, or ascribe it to a feeling of good-will), that your position with Lady R—— is not quite what those who have an interest in you would wish. Every one knows how odd she is, to say the least of it, and you may not be perhaps aware, that occasionally her tongue outruns her discretion. In your presence she of course is on her guard, for she is really good-natured, and would not willingly offend any one or hurt their feelings; but when led away by her desire to shine in company, she is very indiscreet. I have been told that at Mrs. W——'s dinner-party the other day, to which you were not invited, on your name being brought up, she called you her charming model, I think was the phrase; and on an explanation being demanded of the term, she said you stood for her heroines, putting yourself in postures and positions while she drew from nature, as she termed it; and that, moreover, on being complimented on the idea, and some of the young men offering, or rather intimating, that they would be delighted to stand or kneel at your feet, as the hero of the tale, she replied that she had no occasion for their services, as she had a page or footman, I forget which, who did that portion of the work. Surely this cannot be true, my dear Mademoiselle de Chatenœuf?"

Oh! how my blood boiled when I heard this.

How far it was true, the reader already knows; but the manner in which it was conveyed by Lady M—— quite horrified me. I coloured up to the temples, and replied,

"Lady M——, that Lady R—— has very often, when I have been sitting, and she has been writing, told me that she was taking me as a model for her heroine, is very true; but I have considered it as a mere whim of hers, knowing how very eccentric she is. I little thought from my having good naturedly yielded to her caprice, that I should have been so mortified as I have been by what you have communicated to me. That she must have been indiscreet is certain, for it was known only to herself and me."

"And the footman."

"Footman, my lady? There is a boy—a sort of page, there."

"Exactly; a lad of fifteen or sixteen, a precocious, pert

boy, who is much indulged by Lady R——, and if report says true, is nearer related to her than she is willing to acknowledge. Did you never observe that there is a strong likeness?"

"Good heavens, my lady, you surprise me."

"And, I fear, have also annoyed you; but," continued Lady M—— laying her hand on mine, "I thought it kinder to let you know your peculiar position than to sneer and ridicule, as others do, behind your back. This is a sad world in one respect; if there is any scandal or false report spread against us, it is known to every one but ourselves. We cannot find, but rarely, a friend who is so really our friend as to tell us of it. The poison is allowed to circulate without the power being given to us of applying an antidote—so hollow is friendship in this world. My dear mademoiselle, I have done otherwise; whether you thank me for it or not, I cannot tell; perhaps not, for those who communicate unpleasant intelligence, are seldom looked kindly upon."

"Lady M——," replied I, "I do thank you most heartily. I do consider that you have acted a friendly part. That I have been dreadfully shocked and mortified, I admit," continued I, wiping away the tears that forced their passage; "but I shall not give an opportunity for future unjust insinuations or remarks, as I have made up my mind that I shall leave Lady R—— as soon as possible."

"My dear mademoiselle, I did not venture to make you acquainted with what I knew would, to a person of your sensitive mind, be the cause of your quitting the protection of Lady R—— without having considered whether an equivalent could not be offered to you; and I am happy to say that I can offer you a home, and I trust comfort and consideration, if you will accept of them. The fact is, that had I known that you had any idea of quitting Madame Bathurst, I should have made the offer then—now I do so with all sincerity;—but at present you are agitated and annoyed, and I will say no more. If I send the carriage for you to-morrow at two o'clock, will you do me the favour to come and see me? I would call upon you, but of course the presence of Lady R—— would be a check to our free converse. Say, my dear, will you come?"

I replied in the affirmative, and Lady M—— then rose, and giving me her arm, we walked back to the bench which I had left, where I found Lady R—— in a hot dispute with a member of parliament. I sat down by her unnoticed, and Lady M—— having smiled an adieu, I was left to my own reflections, which were anything but agreeable. My head ached dreadfully, and I looked so ill that Lady R——'s warm antagonist perceived it, and pointed it out to her, saying,

"Your *protégée* is not well, I fear, Lady R——."

I replied to Lady R——, "that I had a violent headache, and wished to get home, if it were possible."

She immediately consented, and showed great concern. As soon as we were home, I need hardly say, that I hastened to my room.

I sat down and pressed my forehead with my hands: my knowledge of the world was increasing too fast. I began to hate it—hate men, and women even more than men. What lessons had I learnt within the last year. First Madame d'Albret, then Madame Bathurst, and now Lady R——. Was there no such thing as friendship in the world—no such thing as generosity? In my excited state it appeared to me that there was not. All was false and hollow. Self was the idol of mankind, and all worshipped at its altar. After a time I became more composed; I thought of little Madame Gironac, and the recollection of her disinterested kindness put me in a better frame of mind. Mortified as I was, I could not help feeling that it was only the vanity of Lady R——, and her desire to shine, to which I had been made a sacrifice, and that she had no intention of wounding my feelings. Still, to remain with her after what had been told to me by Lady M—— was impossible. And then I reflected upon what steps I should take. I did not like to tell Lady R—— the real grounds of my leaving her. I thought it would be prudent to make some excuse and part good friends. At last it occurred to me that her intention of going to France would be a good excuse. I could tell her that I was afraid of meeting my relatives.

Having decided upon this point, I then canvassed the words of Lady M——. What could she offer me in her house? She had three daughters, but they were all out, as the phrase is, and their education supposed to be completed. This was a mystery I could not solve, and I was obliged to give up thinking about it, and at last I fell asleep. The next morning I woke up, jaded in mind, and with a bad headache, but I dressed and went down to breakfast. Lady R—— asked after my health, and then said,

"I observed you talking very confidently with Lady M——. I was not aware that you knew her. Between ourselves, Valerie, she is one of my models."

"Indeed," replied I, "I do not think that her ladyship is aware of the honour conferred upon her."

"Very likely not; but in the last work she was portrayed to the life. Lady M—— is a schemer, always plotting; her great object now is to get her three daughters well married."

"I believe that most mothers wish that, Lady R——."

"I grant it, and perhaps manœuvre as much, but with more skill than she does, for every one sees the game that she is playing, and the consequence is, that the young men shy off, which they probably would not if she were quiet, for they are really clever, unaffected, and natural girls, very obliging, and without any pride; but how came you to be so intimate with Lady M——?"

"Lady M—— and her eldest daughter were staying for some time with Madame Bathurst in the country when I was there."

"Oh, I understand, that accounts for it."

"I am going to call upon Lady M——, if she sends her carriage for me," replied I. "She told me that she would, if she could, at two o'clock. She has proposed my paying her a visit; I presume it will be after she leaves town."

"But that you will not be able to do, Valerie; you forget our trip to France."

"I did not think that you were serious," replied I; "you mentioned it as the resolution of a night, and I did not know that you might not think differently upon further consideration."

"Oh no, my resolutions are hastily formed, but not often given up. Go to Paris we certainly shall."

"If you are determined upon going, Lady R——, I am afraid that I cannot accompany you."

"Indeed!" exclaimed her ladyship, in surprise. "May I ask why not?"

"Simply because I might meet those I am most anxious to avoid; there is a portion of my history that you are not acquainted with, Lady R——, which I will now make known to you."

I then told her as much as I thought necessary relative to my parents, and stated my determination not to run the risk of meeting them. Lady R—— argued, persuaded, coaxed, and scolded, but it was all in vain; at last she became seriously angry, and left the room. Lionel soon afterwards made his appearance, and said to me, in his usual familiar way,

"What's the matter, Miss Valerie? The governess is in a rage about something; she gave me a box on the ear."

"I suppose you deserved it, Lionel," replied I.

"Well, there may be differences of opinion about that," replied the boy. "She went on scolding me at such a rate that I was quite astonished, and all about nothing. She blew up cook—didn't she—blew her half up the chimney—and then she was at me again. At last I could bear it no longer, and I said, 'Don't flare up, my lady.'"

"'Don't my lady me,' cried she, 'or I'll box your ears.'"

"Well, then, as she is always angry if you call her my lady, I thought she was angry with me for the same reason, so I said, 'Sempronia, keep your temper,'—and didn't I get a box on the ear."

I could not help laughing at this recital of his cool impudence, the more so as he narrated it with such an air of injured innocence.

"Indeed, Lionel," said I at last, "you well deserved the box on the ear. If you ever quit the service of Lady R——, you will find that you must behave with proper respect to those above you; if not, you will not remain an hour in any other house. Lady R—— is very odd and very good-tempered, and permits more liberties than any other person would. I will, however, tell you why Lady R—— is displeased. It is because she wishes me to go to France with her, and I have refused."

"Then you are going to leave us?" inquired Lionel, mournfully.

"I suppose so," replied I.

"Then I shall go, too," said the boy. "I'm tired of it."

"But why should you go, Lionel? You may not find another situation half so comfortable."

"I shall not seek one. I have only stayed here with the hope that I may find out from her ladyship who and what my parents were, and she will not tell me. I shall live by my wits, never fear; 'the world 's my oyster,' as Shakspeare says, and I think I've wit enough to open it."

I had not forgotten the observations of Lady M—— relative to Lionel, and what the lad now said made me surmise that there was some mystery, and, on examination of his countenance, there *was* a family likeness to Lady R——. I also called to mind her unwillingness to enter upon the subject when I brought it up.

"But, Lionel," said I, after a pause, "what is it that makes you suppose that Lady R—— conceals who were your parents—when we last talked on the subject, you said you had found out something—she told me that your father was a bailiff, or steward to Sir Richard."

"Which I have proved to be false. She told me that my father was Sir Richard's butler; that I have also discovered to be false; for one day the old housekeeper, who called upon me at school, came here, and was closeted with Lady R—— for half an hour. When she went away, I called a hackney coach for her, and getting behind it, went home with her to her lodgings. When I found out where she lived, I hastened back immediately, that I might not be missed, intending to have made a call upon her. The next day Lady R—— gave me a letter to put in the twopenny-post; it was directed to a Mrs. Green, to the very house where the hackney-coach had stopped, so I knew it was for the old housekeeper. Instead of putting the letter in the post, I kept it till the evening, and then took it myself.

"'Mrs. Green,' said I, for I found her at home with another old woman, sitting over their tea, 'I have brought you a letter from Lady R——.' This is about a year ago, Miss Valerie.

"'Mercy on me,' said she, 'how strange that Lady R—— should send you here.'

"'Not strange that she should send a letter by a servant,' said I, 'only strange that I should be a servant.'

"I said this, Miss Valerie, as a random throw, just to see what answer she would make.

"'Why, who has been telling you anything?' said she, looking at me through her spectacles.

"'Ah,' replied I, 'that's what I must keep to myself, for I'm under a promise of secrecy.'

"'Mercy on me, it couldn't be—no, that's impossible,' muttered the old woman, as she opened the letter and took out a bank-note, which she crumpled up in her hand. She then commenced reading the letter; I walked a little way from her, and stood between her and the window. Every now and then she held the letter up to the candle, and when the light was strong upon it, I could read a line from where I stood, for I have been used to her ladyship's writing, as you know. One line I read was, 'remains still at Culverwood Hall;' another was, 'the only person now left in Essex.' I also saw the words 'secrecy' and 'ignorant' at the bottom of the page. The old woman finished the letter at last, but it took her a good while to get through it.

"'Well,' says she, 'have you anything more to say?'

"'No,' says I; 'you are well paid for your secrecy, Mrs. Green.'

"'What do you mean?' said she.

"'Oh, I'm not quite so ignorant as you suppose,' replied I.

"'Ignorant,' said she, confused, 'ignorant of what?'

"'When were you last in Essex?' said I.

"'When, why? what's that to you, you impudent boy?'

"'Nay, then I'll put another question to you. How long is it since you were at Culverwood Hall?'

"'Culverwood Hall! What do you know about Culverwood Hall? the boy's mad, I believe; go away, you've done your message; if you don't, I'll tell her ladyship.'

"'Certainly, Mrs. Green,' said I. 'I wish you a good night.'

"I left the room, slamming the door, but not allowing the catch to fall in, so that I held it a little ajar, and then I heard Mrs. Green say to the other woman,

"'Somebody's been with that boy; I wonder who it can be? He's put me in such a flurry. Well, these things will out.'

"'Yes, yes, it's like murder,' replied the other; 'not

that I know what it's all about, only I see there's a secret—perhaps you'll tell me, Mrs. Green?'

"'All I dare tell you is that there is a secret,' replied Mrs. Green, 'and the boy has got an inkling of it somehow or another. I must see my lady—no, I had better not,' added she; 'for she is so queer that she'll swear that I've told him. Now there's only one besides myself and her ladyship who knows anything, and I'll swear that he could not have been with the boy, for he's bedridden. I'm all of a puzzle, and that's the truth. What a wind there is; why the boy has left the door open. Boys never shut doors.'

"Mrs. Green got up and slammed the door to, and I walked off; and now, Miss Valerie, that's all that I know of the matter; but why I should be sent to a good school and wear pepper-and-salt, and to be taken away to be made first a page, and now a footman, I can't tell; but you must acknowledge that there is some mystery, after what I have told you."

"It certainly is strange, Lionel," replied I, "but my advice is, that you remain patiently till you can find it out, which by leaving Lady R—— you are not likely to do."

"I don't know that, Miss Valerie; let me get down to Culverwood Hall, and I think I would find out something, or my wits were given me to no purpose. But I hear her ladyship coming up-stairs: so good-bye, Miss Valerie."

And Lionel made a hasty retreat.

Lady R—— slowly ascended the stairs, and came into the room. Her violence had been exhausted, but she looked sullen and moody, and I could hardly recognise her; for I must do her the justice to say, that I had never before seen her out of temper. She sat down in her chair, and I asked her whether I should bring her her writing materials.

"A pretty state I am in to write," replied she, leaning her elbows on the table, and pressing her hands to her eyes. "You don't know what a rage I have been in, and how I have been venting it upon innocent people. I struck that poor boy—shame on me! Alas! I was born with violent passions, and they have been my curse through life. I had hoped that years had somewhat subdued them, but they will occasionally master me. What would I not give to have had your placid temper, Valerie! How much unhappiness I should have been spared! How much error should I have avoided! I was going to say, how much crime."

Lady R—— was evidently more talking to herself than to me when she said the last words, and I therefore made no reply. A silence of more than a quarter of an hour followed, which was broken by Lionel coming in, and announcing the carriage of Lady M——.

"That woman is the cause of all this," said Lady R——; "I am sure that she is. Pray do not wait, Valerie. Go and see her. I shall be better company when you come back."

I made no reply, but left the room, and putting on my bonnet, was driven to Lady M——'s. She received me with great cordiality, and so did her daughters, who were in the room; but they were dismissed by their mother, who then said, "I told you last night, my dear Mademoiselle de Chatenœuf, that I wished you to reside with me. You may say in what capacity, and I acknowledge that I hardly know what answer to give. Not as governess, certainly, for I consider it an odious position, and one that I could not offer you; indeed, my girls do not require teaching, as they have finished their studies; in only one thing you could be of advantage to them in that respect, which is in music and singing. But I wish you to come as their companion, as I am convinced that they will gain much by your so doing. I wish you, therefore, to be considered by others as a visitor at the house, but at the same time I must insist, that from the advantages my girls will derive from your assisting them in music and singing, you will accept the same salary per annum which you have from Lady R——. Do you understand me? I wish you to remain with me, not as a model after the idea of Lady R——, but as a model for my girls to take pattern by. I shall leave it to yourself to act as you please. I am sure my girls like you already, and will like you better. I do not think that I can say more, except that I trust you will not refuse my offer."

There was a delicacy and kindness in this proposal on the part of Lady M—— which I felt gratefully; but it appeared to me, that after all it was only an excuse to offer me an asylum without any remuneration on my part. and I stated my feeling on that point.

"Do not think so," replied Lady M——. "I avoided saying so, because I would not have you styled a music-mistress; but on that one point alone you will more than earn your salary, as I will prove to you, by showing you the annual payments to professors for lessons; but you will be of great value to me in other points, I have no doubt. May I, therefore, consider it as an *affaire arrangée?*"

After a little more conversation, I acquiesced, and having agreed that I would come as soon as Lady R—— went to the continent, or at all events, in three weeks, when Lady M—— quitted London, I took my leave, and was conveyed back to Lady R—— in the carriage which had been sent for me.

On my return, I found Lady R—— seated where I had left her.

"Well," said she, "so you have had your audience; and I have no doubt but that you were most graciously received. Oh! I know the woman; and I have been reflecting upon it during your absence, and I have discoverd what she wants you for; but this she has not mentioned, not even hinted at. She knows better; but when once in her house, you will submit to it, rather than be again in search of a home."

"I really do not know what you mean, Lady R——," said I.

"Has not Lady M—— asked you to come as a visitor, without specifying any particular employment?"

"No, she has not. She has proposed my staying in the house to give lessons to her daughters in music, and to be their companion; but there is nothing stated as to a fixed residence with her."

"Well, Valerie, I know that I am odd; but you will soon find out whether you have gained by the change."

"Lady R——, I really do not consider you should be so sarcastic or unkind towards me. I do not like to go to France with you, for reasons which I have fully explained, at the expense of disclosing family affairs, which I had much rather not have mentioned. You leave me by myself, and I must seek protection somewhere. It is kindly offered by Lady M——, and in my unfortunate position I have not to choose. Be just and be generous."

"Well, well, I will," said Lady R——, the tears starting in her eyes; "but you do not know how much I am annoyed at your leaving me. I had hoped, with all my faults, that I had created in you a feeling of attachment to me—God knows, that I *have tried.* If you knew all my history, Valerie, you would not be surprised at my being strange. That occurred when I was of your age, which would have driven some people to despair or suicide. As it is, it has alienated me from all my relations,—not that I have many. My brother, I never see or hear from, and have not for years. I have refused all his invitations to go down to see him, and he is now offended with me; but there are causes for it, and years cannot wipe away the memory of what did occur."

"I assure you, Lady R——, I have been very sensible of your kindness to me," replied I, "and shall always remember it with gratitude; and if you think I have no regard for you, you are mistaken; but the subject has become painful—pray let us say no more."

"Well, Valerie, be it so; perhaps it is the wisest plan."

To change the conversation, I said—"Is not your brother the present baronet?"

"Yes," replied Lady R——.

"And where does he reside?"

"In Essex, at Culverwood Hall, the seat of all my misfortunes."

I started a little at the mention of the place, as it was the one which the reader may remember was spoken of by Lionel. I then turned the conversation to other matters, and by dinner-time Lady R—— had recovered herself, and was as amiable as ever.

From that day until Lady R—— set off for Paris, there was not a word said relative to Lady M——. She was kind and polite, but not so warm and friendly as she had been before, and in her subdued bearing towards me, was more agreeable. Her time was now employed in making preparations for her tour. Lionel was the only one who was to accompany her except her own maid. At last she fixed the day of her departure, and I wrote to Lady M——, who returned an answer that it suited her exactly, as she would go to the country the day after. The evening before Lady R——was to start, was passed very gloomily. I felt great sorrow at our separation, more than I could have imagined; but when you have been associated with a person who is good-tempered and kind, you soon feel more for them than you would suppose, until you are about to quit them.

Lady R—— was very much dispirited, and said to me, "Valerie, I have a presentiment that we never shall meet again, and yet I am anything but superstitious. I can truly say that you are the only person to whom I have felt real attachment since my youth, and I feel more than I can describe. Something whispers to me, 'Do not go to France,' and yet something impels me to go. Valerie, if I do come back, I trust that you will consider my house your home, if at any time you cannot place yourself more to your satisfaction; I will not say more, as I know that I am not exactly a lovable person, and my ways are odd; but do pray look upon me as your sincere friend, who will always be ready to serve you. I have to thank you for a few happy months, and that is saying much. God bless you, my dear Valerie."

I was moved to tears by what Lady R—— said, and I thanked her with a faltering voice.

"Come now," said she, "I shall be off too early in the morning to see you: let us take our farewell."

Lady R—— put a small packet into my hand, kissed me on the forehead, and then hastened up to her own room.

That people love change is certain; but still there is a mournfulness connected with it, even in a change of residence; the packing up, the litter attending it, the corded trunks and packages, give a forlorn appearance to the house itself. To me it was peculiarly distressing; I had changed so often within the last year, and had such a precarious footing wherever I went; I felt myself to be the sport of fortune, and a football to the whims and caprices of others. I was sitting in my bedroom, my trunks packed but not yet closed down, thinking of Lady R——'s last conversation, and very *triste*. The packet was lying on the table before me, unopened, when I was roused by a knock at the door. I thought it was Lady R——'s maid, and I said, "Come in."

The door opened, and Lionel made his appearance.

"Is it you, Lionel? What do you want?"

"I knew that you were up, and I recollected, as we

leave before you do to-morrow, that you would have no one to cord your luggage, so I thought I would come up and do it for you to-night, Miss Valerie, if it is ready."

"Thank you, Lionel, it is very considerate of you. I will lock the trunks up, and you can cord them outside."

Lionel took out the trunks and corded them in the passage. When he had finished he said to me,

"Good-bye, Miss Valerie, you will see me again very soon."

"See you very soon, Lionel! I am afraid there is no chance of that, for Lady R—— intends to stay abroad for six months."

"I do not," replied he.

"Why, Lionel, it would be very foolish for you to give up such a good situation. You have such unusual wages: twenty pounds a year, is it not?"

"Yes, Miss Valerie. I should not get half that in another situation, but that is one reason why I am going to leave. Why should she give me twenty pounds a year? I must find out why, and find out I will, as I said to you before. She don't give me twenty pounds for my beauty, although she might give you a great deal more, and yet not pay you half enough."

"Well, Lionel, I think you have been here long enough. It is too late to sit up to pay compliments. Fare you well."

I shut my door upon him gently, and then went to bed. As usual after excitement, I slept long and soundly. When I awoke the next morning, I found it was broad day, and nearly ten o'clock. I rang the bell, and it was answered by the cook, who told me that she and I were the only people in the house. I rose, and as I passed by my table, I perceived another package lying by the side of the one which Lady R—— had given me. It was addressed to me, and I opened it. It contained a miniature of Lady R—— when she was about my age, and very beautiful she must have been. It was labelled "Sempronia at eighteen. Keep it for my sake, dear Valerie, and do not open the paper accompanying it until you have my permission, or you hear of my being no more."

I laid the miniature down and opened the first packet given me by Lady R——. It contained bank notes to the amount of one hundred pounds, nearly double the salary due to me. The contents of both these packets only made me feel more melancholy, and I sighed heavily as I put them in my dressing-case; but time ran on, and I had agreed to be at Lady M——'s at one o'clock, when the carriage would be sent for me. I therefore hastened my toilet, closed the remainder of my luggage, and went down to the breakfast which the cook had prepared for me. While I was at breakfast, a letter was brought by the post. It had been directed to Madame Bathurst, and was re-directed to Lady R——'s address. It was from Madame Paon, and as follows:—

"My dear Madlle. de Chatenœuf,—

"As I take it for granted that you do not see the French papers, I write to tell you that your predictions relative to Monsieur G—— have all proved correct. A month after the marriage, he neglected Madame, and spent his whole time at the gaming-table, only returning home to obtain fresh supplies from her. These were at last refused, and in his rage he struck her. A suit for separation of person and property was brought into court last week, and terminated in favour of Madame d'Albret, who retains all her fortune, and is rid of a monster. She came to me yesterday morning, and showed me the letter which you had written to her, asking me whether I did not correspond with you, and whether I thought, that after her conduct, you could be prevailed upon to return to her. Of course I could not give any opinion; but I am convinced that if you only say that you forgive her, that she will write to you and make the request. I really do not well see how you can do otherwise, after the letter which you wrote to her, but of course you will decide for yourself. I trust, Mademoiselle, you will favour me with a speedy answer, as Madame d'Albret is here every day, and is evidently very impatient.

"I am, my dear Mademoiselle, yours,

"Emile Paon, *née* Merce."

To this letter I sent the following reply by that day's post:—

"My dear Madame Paon,—

"That I sincerely forgive Madame d'Albret is true; I do so from my heart; but although I forgive her, I cannot listen to any proposal to resume the position I once held. Recollect that she has driven all over Paris, and accused me among all her friends of ingratitude and slander. How then, after having been discarded for such conduct, could I again make my appearance in her company? Either I have done as she has stated, and if so, am unworthy of her patronage, or I have not done so, and therefore have been cruelly used: made to feel my dependence in the bitterest way, having been dismissed and thrown upon the world with loss of character. Could I ever feel secure or comfortable with her after such injustice? or could she feel at her ease on again presenting one as her *protégée* whom she had so ill treated? Would she not have to blush every time that she met with any of our former mutual friends and acquaintances? It would be a series of humiliations to us both. Assure her of my forgiveness and goodwill, and my wishes for her happiness; but to return to her is impossible. I would rather starve. If she knew what I have suffered in consequence of her hasty conduct towards me, she would pity me more than she may do now; but what is done is done. There is no remedy for it. Adieu, Madame Paon. Many thanks for your kindness to one so fallen as I am.

"Yours truly and sincerely,

"VALERIE."

I wrote the above under great depression of spirits, and it was with a heavy heart that I afterwards alighted at Lady M——'s residence in St. James's Square. If smiles, however, and cordial congratulations, and shakes of the hand, could have consoled me, they were not wanting on the part of Lady M—— and her daughters. I was shown all the rooms below, then Lady M——'s room, the young ladies' rooms, and lastly my own, and was truly glad when I was at last left alone to unpack and arrange my things.

The room alloted to me was very comfortable, and better furnished than those in which the young ladies slept, and, as far as appearances went, I was in all respects treated as a visitor, and not as a governess. The maid who attended me was very civil, and as she assisted and laid my dresses in the wardrobe, made no attempt to be familiar. I ought to have informed the reader that Lady M—— was a widow, Lord M—— having died about two years before. Her eldest son, the present Lord M——, was on the continent. Dinner was announced; there were only two visitors, and I was treated as one of the company. In fact, nothing could be more gratifying than the manner in which I was treated. In the evening, I played and sang. The young ladies did the same; their voices were good, but they wanted expression in their singing, and I perceived that I could be useful.

Lady M—— asked me, when we were not overheard, "what I thought of her daughters' singing?"

I told her frankly.

"It is impossible to doubt the truth of what you say, my dear Mademoiselle de Chatenœuf, after having heard your performance. I knew that you were considered a good performer, but I had no idea of the perfection which you have arrived at."

"If your daughters are really fond of music, they would soon do as well, my lady," replied I.

"Impossible," exclaimed her ladyship; "but still they must gain something from listening to you. You look fatigued. Do you wish to go to bed? Augusta will go up with you."

"I have a nervous headache," replied I, "and I will accept your ladyship's considerate proposal."

Augusta, the eldest daughter, lighted a chamber-candle, and went up with me into my room. After a little conversation, she wished me good night, and thus passed the first day in St. James's Square.

CHAPTER VIII.

As arranged by Lady M——, the next day we went to Harking Castle, the family seat, in Dorsetshire, and I was not sorry to be again quiet, after the noise and bustle of a London season. As Lady M—— had observed, the young ladies were sadly jaded with continual late hours and hot rooms, but they had not been a week in the country before they were improved in appearance and complexion. They certainly were amiable, nice girls; clever, and without pride, and I soon became attached to them. I attended to their music, and they made great progress. I also taught them the art of making flowers in wax, which I had so lately learnt myself. This was all I could do, except mildly remonstrating with them when I saw what did not appear to me to be quite correct in their conduct and deportment. Lady M—— appeared quite satisfied, and treated me with great consideration, and I was in a short time very happy in my new position.

For the first month, there were no visitors in the house; after that, invitations were sent out. Lady M—— had said that she would have a month's quiet to recover herself from the fatigues of the season, and I had no doubt but that she also thought her daughters would be much benefited, as they really were, by a similar retirement. It was on the Monday that company was expected, and on Friday Lady M—— desired Augusta, the eldest daughter, to put on a new dress which had just been made by the two lady's-maids, and come down in it that she might see it on. When Augusta made her appearance, and her mother had surveyed the dress, she said,

"I do not quite like it, Augusta, and yet I do not exactly know where it's wrong; but something requires to be altered: it does not hang gracefully."

As she said this, I was reading a book, and I naturally looked up, and immediately perceived the alteration which the dress required. I pointed it out, and with a few pins made the dress sit well.

"Why this is a new talent, my dear Mademoiselle de Chatenœuf, one that I had no idea that you possessed; although I admit that no one dresses more elegantly than you do," said Lady M——. "How much I am obliged to you for taking so much trouble."

"I am most happy to be of any service Lady M——, and you may always command me," replied I. "I have the credit of being a very good milliner."

"I believe you can do anything," replied Lady M——. "Augusta, go up to Benson and show her the alterations that are required, and tell her to make them directly. After all," continued Lady M——, to me, "it is bad economy making dresses at home; but I really cannot afford to pay the extravagant prices charged by Madame Desbelli. My bills are monstrous, and my poverty, but not my will, consents. Still it does make such a difference in the appearance, being well dressed, that if I could, I never would have a dress made at home; but the saving is astonishing—nearly two-thirds, I assure you."

"If you will allow me to interfere a little, my lady," replied I, "I think you can have them as well made at home as by Madame Desbelli. I think I can be useful."

"You are very kind, Mademoiselle de Chatenœuf, but it will be taxing you too much."

"Not at all, Lady M—— if I have your sanction."

"You shall do just as you please, my dear," replied Lady M——; "I give you full authority over the whole household, if you wish it; but, indeed, I think Benson will be much obliged to you for any slight hint that you may give her, and I am sure that I shall; but the carriage is at the door—do you drive to-day?"

"Not to-day, I thank you, Lady M——," replied I.

"Well, then, I will take Hortense and Amy with me, and leave Augusta with you."

After Lady M——'s departure, I went up to the room where the maids were at work. I altered the arrangement of Augusta's dress so as to suit her figure, and cut out the two others for Hortense and Amy. Wishing to please Lady M——, I worked myself at Augusta's dress, and had it completed before Lady M—— had returned from her drive. It certainly was now a very different affair, and Augusta looked remarkably well in it. She was delighted herself, and hastened down to her mother to show it to her. When I came down to dinner, Lady M—— was profuse in her acknowledgments; the two other dresses, when finished, gave equal satisfaction, and from that time till the period of my quitting Lady M——, all the dresses, not only of the young ladies, but those of Lady M——, were made at home, and my taste and judgment invariably appealed to, and most cheerfully given. I felt it my duty to be of all the use that I could be, and perhaps was not a little gratified by the compliments I received upon my exquisite taste. Time passed on; during the shooting season, Augusta, the eldest daughter, received a very good offer, which was accepted; and at the Christmas festivities, Hortense, the second girl, accepted another proposal, which was also very favourable. Lady M—— was delighted at such success.

"Is it not strange, my dear Mademoiselle de Chatenœuf, that I have been fagging two seasons, night and day, to get husbands for those girls, and now alone here, in solitude and retirement almost, they have both obtained excellent establishments. I do really declare that I believe it is all owing to you, and the delightful manner in which you have dressed them."

"I should rather think that it is owing, in the first place, to their having so much improved in personal appearance since they have been down in the country," replied I; "and further, to the gentlemen having now an opportunity of discovering their truly estimable qualities, which they were not likely to do at Almack's or other parties during a London season."

"You may think so," replied Lady M——, "but it is my conviction that all is owing to their being so tastefully dressed. Why, every one admires the elegance of their costume, and requests patterns. Well, now I have only Amy on my hands, and I think that her sisters' high connections will assist in getting her off."

"She is a sweet girl, Amy," replied I, "and were I you, Lady M——, I should be in no hurry to part with her."

"Indeed, but I am," replied Lady M——, "you don't know the expense of girls, and my jointure is not so very large; however, I must not complain. Don't you think Amy looks better in lilac than any other colour?"

"She looks well in almost any colour," replied I.

"Yes, with your taste, I grant," replied Lady M——. "Are you aware that we go to town in a fortnight? We must look after the *trousseaux*. It was arranged last night that both marriages shall take place in February. Amy will of course be one of the bridemaids, and I trust to you, my dear Mademoiselle de Chatenœuf, to invent something very *distingué* for her on that occasion. Who knows but that it may get her off? but it's late, so good night."

I could not admire Lady M——'s apparent hurry to get rid of her daughters; but it certainly was the one thing needful which had occupied all her thoughts and attention during the time that I had been with her. That it was natural she should wish that her children were well established, I granted; but all that she appeared to consider was good connection, and the means of living in good style; every other point as to the character of the husbands being totally overlooked.

A fortnight after Christmas we all went to London, and were, as Lady M—— had observed, very busy with the *trousseaux*, when one day the butler came to say that a young gentleman wished to see me, and was waiting in the breakfast parlour below. I went down, wondering who it could be, when to my surprise, I found Lionel, the page of Lady R——, dressed in plain clothes, and certainly looking very much like a gentleman. He bowed very respectfully to me when he entered, much more so than he had ever done when he was a page with Lady R——, and said,

"Miss Valerie, I have ventured to call upon you, as I thought when we parted, that you did me the honour to feel some little interest about me, and I thought you would like to know what has taken place. I have been in England now four months, and have not been idle during that time."

"I am certainly glad to see you, Lionel, although I am sorry you have left Lady R——, and I hope you have been satisfied with the result of your inquiries."

"It is rather a long story, Miss Valerie, and if you wish to hear it, you will oblige me by sitting down while I narrate it to you."

"I hope it will not be too long, Lionel, as I shall be wanted in an hour or so, to go out with Lady M——, but I am ready to hear you," continued I, sitting down as he requested.

Lionel stood by me, and then commenced:—"We arrived at Dover the evening of the day that we left, Miss Valerie; and Lady R——, who had been in a state of great agitation during the journey, was so unwell, that she remained there four or five days. As soon as she was better, I thought it was advisable that she should settle my book, and pay me my wages before we left England, and I brought it to her, stating my wish, as the sum was then very large.

"'And what do you want money for?' said she, rather angrily.

"'I want to place it in safety, my lady,' replied I.

"'That's as much as to say that it is not safe with me.'

"'No, my lady,' replied I. 'But suppose any accident were to happen to you abroad, would your executors ever believe that you owed more than £25, besides a year's wages, to a page like me? They would say that it could not be, and would not pay me my money; neither would they believe that you gave me such wages.'

" 'Well,' she replied, ' there is some truth in that, and it will, perhaps, be better that I do pay you at once; but where will you put the money, Lionel?'

" 'I will keep the check, my lady, if you please.'

" 'Then I will write it to order, and not to bearer, replied she, ' and then if you lose it, it will not be paid, for it will require your own signature.'

" 'Thank you, my lady,' replied I.

" Having examined my accounts and my wages due, she gave me a check for the full amount. The next morning, the packet was to sail at nine o'clock. We were in good time, and as soon as Lady R—— was on board, she went down into the cabin. Her maid asked me for the bottle of salts which I had purposely left under the sofa-pillow at the Ship Hotel. I told her that I had left it, and as there was plenty of time would run and fetch it. I did so, but contrived not to be back until the steamer had moved away from the pier, and her paddles were in motion. I called out, ' Stop, stop,' knowing of course that they would not, although they were not twenty yards away. I saw Lady R——'s maid run to the captain and speak to him, but it was of no use, and thus I was left behind, without Lady R—— having any suspicion that it was intentional on my part.

" I waited at the pier till the packet was about two miles off, and then walked away from the crowd of people who were bothering me with advice how to proceed, so that I might join my mistress at Calais. I returned to the hotel for a portion of my clothes which I had not sent on board of the packet, but had left in charge of the boots, and then sat down in the tap to reflect upon what I should do. My first object was to get rid of my sugar-loaf buttons, for I hated livery, Miss Valerie; perhaps it was pride, but I could not help it. I walked out till I came to a slop-seller's, as they call them at seaports, and went in; there was nothing hanging up but seamen's clothes, and on reflection, I thought I could not do better than to dress as a sailor; so I told the man that I wanted a suit of sailor's clothes.

" 'You want to go to sea, I suppose,' said the man, not guessing exactly right, considering that I just refused to embark.

" However, I bargained first for a complete suit, and

then sold him my liveries, exchanging my dress in the back parlour. I then returned to the tap, obtained my other clothes, and as soon as the coach started, got outside and arrived in London. I called upon you at this house, and found that you were in the country, and then I resolved that I would go down to Culverwood Hall."

"And now you must leave off, Lionel, for the present," said I, "for I must go out with Lady M——. Come to-morrow, early, and I shall have leisure to hear the rest of your story."

The following morning Lionel returned, and resumed his history.

"Miss Valerie, little things often give you more trouble than greater; and I had more difficulty to find out where Culverwood Hall was than you may imagine. I asked many at the inn where I put up, but no one could tell me, and at such places I was not likely to find any book which I could refer to. I went to the coach-offices and asked what coaches started for Essex, and the reply was, 'Where did I want to go?' and, when I said Culverwood Hall, no one could tell me by which coach I was to go, or which town it was near. At last, I did find out from the porter of the Saracen's Head, who had taken in parcels with that address, and who went to the coachman, who said that his coach passed within a mile of Sir Alexander Moystyn's, who lived there. I never knew her ladyship's maiden name before. I took my place by the coach, for I had gone to the banker's in Fleet-street, and received the money for my check, and started the next morning at three o'clock.

"I was put down at a village called West-gate, at an inn called the Moystyn Arms. I kept to the dress of a sailor, and when the people spoke to me on the coach, kept up the character as well as I could, which is very easy to do when you have to do with people who know nothing about it. I shivered my timbers, and all that sort of thing, and hitched up my trousers, as they do at the theatres. The coachman told me that the inn was the nearest place I could stop at, if I wanted to go to the hall, and taking my bundle, I got down and he drove off. A sailor-boy is a sort of curiosity in a country villlage, Miss Valerie, and I had many questions put to me; but I answered them by putting others. I said that my friends were formerly living at the hall in the old baronet's time, but that I knew little about them, as it was a long while ago; and I asked if there were any of the old servants still living at the place. The woman who kept the inn told me that there was one, old Roberts, who still lived in the village, and had been *bedridden* for some years. This of course was the person I wanted; and I inquired what had become of his family. The reply was, that his daughter, who had married Green, was somewhere in London, and his son, who had married Kitty Wilson, of the village, had gone to reside as gamekeeper somewhere near Portsmouth, and had a large family of children.

"'You're right enough,' replied I, laughing, 'we are a large family.'

"'What, are you old Roberts's grandson?' exclaimed the women. 'Well, we did hear that one of them, Harry, I think, did go to sea.'

"'Well, now, perhaps you'll tell me where I am to find the old gentleman?' replied I.

"'Come with me,' said she, 'he lives hard by, and glad enough he'll be, poor man, to have any one to talk with him a bit, for it's a lonesome life he leads in bed there.'

"I followed the woman, and when about a hundred yards from the inn, she stopped at the door of a small house, and called to Mrs. Meshin, to 'go up and tell old Roberts that one of his grandsons is here.' A snuffy old woman made her appearance, peered at me through her spectacles, and then stumped up a pair of stairs which faced the door. Shortly afterwards I was desired to come up, and did so. I found an old man with silver hair lying in bed, and the said Mrs. Meshin, with her spectacles, smoothing down the bedclothes, and making the place tidy.

"'What cheer, old boy?' said I, after T. P. Cooke's style.

"'What do you say? I'm hard of hearing, rather,' replied the old man.

"'How do you find yourself, sir?' said I.

"'Oh, pretty well for an old man; and so you're my grandson Harry; glad to see you. You may go, Mrs. Meshin, and shut the door; and, do you hear, don't listen at the keyhole.'

"The stately lady, Mrs. Meshin, growled, and then left the room, slamming the door.

"'She is very cross, grandson,' said the old man, 'and I see nobody but her. It's a sad thing to be bedridden this way, and not to get out in the fresh air, and sadder still to be tended by a cross old woman, who won't talk when I want her, and won't hold her tongue when I want her. I'm glad to see you, boy. I hope you won't go away directly, as your brother Tom did. I want somebody to talk to me, sadly; and how do you like being at sea?'

"'I like the shore, better, sir.'

"'Ay, so all sailors say, I believe; and yet I would rather go to sea than lie here all day long. It's all owing to my being out as I used to do, night after night, watching for poachers. I had too little bed then, and now I've too much of it. But the sea must be grand. As the Bible says,' 'They who go upon the great waters, they see the wonders of the deep.'

"I was glad to find that the old man was so perfect in all his mental faculties, and after having listened to, rather than replied to, observations about his son and my supposed brothers and sisters, by which I obtained a pretty accurate knowledge of them, I wished him good-bye, and promised to call and have a long talk in the morning.

"On my return to the inn, I was able to reply to all the interrogatories which were put to me relative to my supposed relations, thanks to the garrulity of old Roberts, and put many questions relative to the family residing at the hall, which were freely answered. As the evening advanced, many people came in, and the noise and smoking was so disagreeable to me, that I asked for a bed, and retired. The next morning I repaired to old Roberts, who appeared delighted to see me.

"'You are a good boy,' said he, 'to come and see a poor bedridden old man, who has not a soul that comes near him perhaps in a week. And now tell me what took place during your last voyage.'

"'The last vessel I was on board of,' replied I, 'was a packet from Dover to Calais.'

"'Well, that must be pleasant; so many passengers.'

"'Yes, sir; and who do you think I saw on board of the packet the other day—somebody that you know.'

"'Ay, who?'

"'Why Lady R——,' replied I, 'and that young gentleman who, I heard say, once lived with her as her servant.'

"'Ay!' said the old man, 'indeed! then she has done justice at last. I'm glad on it, Harry, glad on it, for it's a relief to my mind. I was bound to the secret, and have kept it; but when a man is on the brink of the grave, he does not like to have a secret like that upon his mind, and I've more than once talked to my daughter about—'

"'What, Aunt Green?'

"'Yes, your Aunt Green; but she would never listen to me. We both took our oath, and she said it was binding; besides, we were paid for it. Well, well, I thank God, for it's a great load off my mind.'

"'Yes, sir,' replied I, 'you need not keep the secret any longer now.'

"'And how has he grown up?' said the old man; 'is he good-looking?'

"'Very much so, sir,' replied I, 'and looks very much like a gentleman.'"

I could not help laughing at this part of Lionel's story, although I could not but admit the truth. Lionel observed it, and said,

"You cannot be surprised at my giving myself a good character, Miss Valerie, for, as they say in the kitchen, it's all that a poor servant has to depend upon."

"Go on," replied I.

"'He was a very fine child while he lived with us; but he was taken away at six years old, and I have never seen him since.'

"'Some people say that he is very like Lady R——.'

"'Well, why should he not be? ay, she was once a very beautiful young person.'

"'Well, grandfather, I have never heard the rights of that story,' said I, 'and now that you are at liberty to tell it, perhaps you will let me have the whole history.'

"'Well,' said the old man, 'as there is no longer a secret, I do not know but that I may. Your aunt Green, you know, was nurse to Lady R——, and remained in the family for years afterwards; for old Sir Alexander Moystyn was confined to his room for years with gout and other complaints, and your aunt Green attended him. It was just as Sir Alexander had recovered from a very bad fit, that Miss Ellen, who was Lady R——'s sister, and years younger than she was, made her runaway match with Colonel Dempster, a very fashionable, gay young man, who had come down here to shoot with the present baronet. Every one was much surprised at this, for all the talk was that the match would be with the eldest sister, Lady R——, and not the youngest. They went off somewhere abroad. Old Sir Alexander was in a terrible huff about it, and was taken ill again; and Lady R——, who was then Miss Barbara, appeared also much distressed at her sister's conduct. Well, a year or more passed away, when, one day, Miss Barbara told your aunt Green that she wished her to go with her on a journey, and she set off in the evening with four post-horses, and travelled all night till she arrived at Southampton. There she stopped at a lodging, and got out, spoke to the landlady, and calling my daughter out of the chaise, desired her to remain below while she went upstairs. My daughter was tired of staying so long, for she remained there for five hours, and Miss Barbara did not make her appearance; but they appeared to be very busy in the house, running up and down stairs. At last a grave person, who appeared to be a doctor, came into the parlour, followed by the landlady—in the parlour in which my daughter was sitting.

"'‘It's all over, Mrs. Wilson,' said he, ‘nothing could save her; but the child will do well, I have no doubt.'

"'‘What's to be done, sir?'

"'‘Oh,' replied the doctor, ‘the lady above-stairs told me that she was her sister, so of course we must look to her for all future arrangements.'

"'After giving a few directions about the infant, the doctor left the house, and soon after that Miss Barbara came down stairs.

"'‘I'm quite worn out, Martha,' said she, ‘let us go to the hotel as fast as we can. You sent away the carriage, of course. I would it had remained, for I shall hardly be able to walk so far.'

"'She took her arm, and as the landlady opened the door, she said,

"'‘I will call to-morrow, and give directions about the infant, and everything which is necessary. I never went through such a trying scene,' said Miss Barbara; ‘she was an old schoolfellow of mine, who entreated me to come to her in her distress. She died giving birth to her infant, and it was, I presume, with that presentiment, that she sent for me, and entreated me, on her death-bed, to protect the unfortunate child, for she has been cast away by her relations in consequence of her misconduct. You have never had the small-pox, Martha, have you?'

"'No, miss,' she replied, 'you know I never have.'

"'Well, it was having the small-pox at the same time that she was confined, that has caused her death, and that was the reason why I did not send for you to come up and assist.'

"'My daughter made no answer, for Miss Barbara was of a haughty temper, and she was afraid of her; but she did not forget that the doctor had told the landlady that Miss Barbara had stated the lady to be her sister. My daughter had thought it very odd that Miss Barbara had not told her, during their journey, where she was going, and whom she was going to see, for Miss Barbara had wrapped herself up in her cloak, and pretended to be asleep during the whole time, only waking up to pay the post-boys; but Miss Barbara was of a very violent temper, and had, since her sister's marriage, been much worse than before; indeed, some said that she was a little mad, and used to walk at moonlights.

"'When they arrived at the hotel, Miss Barbara went to bed, and insisted upon her sleeping in the same room, as she was afraid of being alone in an hotel. My daughter thought over the business as she lay in bed, and at last resolved to ascertain the truth; so she got up early the next morning, and walked to the lodging-house, and when the door was opened by the landlady, pretended to come from her mistress to inquire how the infant was. The reply was, that it was doing well; and then a conversation took place, in which my daughter found out that the lady did not die of the small-pox, as Miss Barbara had stated. The landlady asked my daughter if she would not like to come up and look at the corpse. My daughter consented, as it was what she was about to request, and when she went up, sure enough it was poor Mrs. Dempster, Miss Ellen that was, who had run away with the colonel.

"'An't [illegible] pity, ma'am,' said the landlady, 'her husband died [illegible] two months ago, and they say he was so handsome a man; indeed he must have been, for here's his picture, which the poor lady wore round her neck.'

"'When your aunt had satisfied herself, and cried a little over the body, for she was very fond of Miss Ellen, she went back to the hotel as fast as she could, and getting a jug of warm water from the kitchen, she went into Miss Barbara's room, and had just time to throw off her bonnet and shawl, when Miss Barbara woke up, and asked who was there.

"'"It's me, miss,' replied my daughter, 'I've just gone down for some warm water for you, for it's past nine o'clock, and I thought you would like to be up early.'

"'"Yes, I must get up, Martha, for I intend to return home to-day. It's no use waiting here. I will have breakfast, and then walk to the lodgings, and give directions. You may pack up in the mean time, for I suppose you do not wish to go with me.'

"'"Oh no, miss,' replied your aunt, 'I am frightened out of my wits at having been in the house already, now that I know that the lady died of the small-pox.'

"'Well, Miss Barbara went away after breakfast, and remained for two or three hours, when she returned, a servant bringing the baby with her. My daughter had packed up everything, and in half an hour they were on the road back, the baby with them, in my daughter's arms. Now, you see, if it had not been for the accidental remark of the doctor in your aunt's presence, she would have been completely deceived by Miss Barbara, and never would have known whose child it was; but your aunt kept her own counsel; indeed, she was afraid to do otherwise.

"'As they went home, Miss Barbara talked a great deal to your aunt, telling her that this Mrs. Bedingfield was a great friend of hers, with whom she had corresponded for years after they had left school; that her husband had been killed in a duel a short time before, that he was a gambler, and a man of very bad character, nevertheless she had promised Mrs. Bedingfield before she died, that she would take care of the child, and that she would do so. She then said, 'Martha, I should like your mother to take charge of it; do you think that she would? but it must be a secret, for my father would be very angry with me, and besides, there might be unpleasant reports.' Your aunt replied, 'that she thought that her mother would,' and then Miss Barbara's proposal that your aunt should get out of the chaise when they stopped to change horses at the last stage, when it was dark, and no one could perceive it, and walk with the infant until she could find some conveyance to my house.

"'This was done, the child was brought to your grandmother, who is now in heaven, and then your aunt made known to us what she had discovered, and whose child it was. I was very angry, and if I had not been laid up at the time with the rheumatism, would have gone right into Sir Alexander's room, and told him who the infant was; but I was overruled by your grandmother and your aunt, who then went away and walked to the hall. So we agreed that we would say exactly what Miss Barbara said to us when she came over to us on the next day.'"

"Well, then, Lionel, I have to congratulate you on being the son of a gentleman, and the nephew of Lady R——. I wish you joy with all my heart," said I, extending my hand.

"Thank you, Miss Valerie. It is true that I am so, but proofs are still to be given; but of that hereafter."

"Lionel, you have been standing all this while. I think it would be most uncourteous if I did not request you to take a chair." Lionel did so, and then proceeded with the old man's narrative.

"'About a month after this, Sir Richard R—— came down, and after three weeks was accepted by Miss Barbara. It was a hasty match every one thought, especially as the news of Mrs. Dempster's death had, as it was reported, been received by letter, and all the family had gone into mourning. Poor old Sir Alexander never held up his head afterwards, and in two months more he was carried to the family vault. Your aunt then came home to us, and as you have heard, married poor Green, who was killed in a poaching business about three months after his marriage. Then came your poor grandmother's death of a quinsy, and so I was left alone with your aunt Green, who then took charge of the child, who had been christened by the name of Lionel Bedingfield. There was some talk about the child, and some wonders whose it could be; but after the death of Sir Alexander, and Miss Barbara had gone away with her husband, nothing more was thought or said about it. And now, boy, I've talked enough for to-day, to-morrow I'll tell you the rest of the history.'

"Perhaps, Miss Valerie, you think the same of me, and am tired with listening," observed Lionel.

"Not at all; and I have leisure now, which I may not have another time; besides, your visits, if so frequent, may cause inquiries, and I shall not know what to say."

"Well, then, I'll finish my story this morning, Miss Valerie. The next day, old Roberts continued: 'It was about three months after Sir Alexander's death, when her brother, the new baronet, came down to Culverwood Hall, that Miss Barbara made her appearance again as Lady R——. Your grandmother was just buried, and poor Green had not been dead more than a month. Your aunt, who was much afflicted at the loss of her husband, and was of course very grave and serious, began to agree with me that it would be very wicked of us, knowing whose child it was, to keep the secret. Moreover, your aunt had become very fond of the infant, for it in a manner consoled her for the loss of her husband. Lady R—— came to the cottage to see us, and we then both told her that we did not like to keep secret the child's parentage, as it was doing a great injustice, if injustice had not been done already. Lady R—— was very much frightened at what we said, and begged very hard that we would not expose her. She would be ruined, she said, in the opinion of her husband, and also of her own relations. She begged and prayed so hard, and made a solemn promise to us that she would do justice to the child as soon as she could with prudence, that she overcame our scruples, and we agreed to say nothing at present. She also put a bank-note for £50 into my daughter's hands to defray expenses and pay for trouble, and told her that the same amount would be paid every year until the child was taken away.

"'I believe this did more to satisfy our scruples than anything else. It ought not to have done so, but we were poor, and money is a great temptation. At all events, we were satisfied with Lady R——'s promise, and with her liberality; and from that time till the child was seven years old we received the money, and had charge of the boy. He was then taken away and sent to school, but where we did not know for some time. Lady R—— was still very liberal to us, always stating her intention of acknowledging the child to be her nephew. At last my daughter was summoned to London, and sent to the school for the boy; Lady R—— stating it to be her intention of keeping him at her own house, now that her husband was dead. This rejoiced us very much; but we had no idea that it was as a servant that he was to be employed, as your aunt afterwards found out, when she went up to London and called unexpectedly upon Lady R——. However, Lady R—— said that what she was doing was for the best, and was more liberal than usual; and that stopped our tongues.

"'Three years back your aunt left this place to find employment in London, and has resided there ever since as a clear-starcher and getter-up of lace; but she often sends me down money, quite sufficient to pay for all the few comforts and expenses required by a bedridden old man. There, Harry, now I've told you the whole story; and I am glad that I am able to do so, and that at last she has done justice to the lad, and there is no further a load upon my conscience, which often caused me to lay down my Bible, when I was reading, and sigh.'

"'But,' said I, 'are you sure that she has acknowledged him as her nephew?"

"'Am I sure! Why, did not you say so?'

"'No; I only said that he was with her, travelling in her company.'

"'Well, but—I understood you that it was all right.'

"'It may be all right,' replied I, 'but how can I tell? I only saw them together. Lady R—— may still keep her secret, for all I can say to the contrary. I don't wonder at its being a load on your mind. I shouldn't be able to sleep at nights; and as for my reading my Bible, I should think it wicked to do so, with the recollection always before me, that I had been a party in defrauding a poor boy of his name, and perhaps fortune.'

"'Dear me! dear me! I've often thought as much, Harry.'

"'Yes, grandfather, and, as you say, on the brink of the grave. Who knows but you may be called away this very night?'

"'Yes, yes, who knows, boy,' replied the old man, looking rather terrified; 'but what shall I do?'

"'I know what I would do,' replied I. 'I'd make a clean breast of it at once. I'd send for the minister and a magistrate, and state the whole story upon affidavit. Then you will feel happy again, and ease your mind, and not before.'

"'Well, boy, I believe you are right; I'll think about it. Leave me now.'

"'Think about your own soul, sir—think of your own danger, and do not mind Lady R——. There can be but a bad reason for doing such an act of injustice. I will come again in an hour, sir, and then you will let me know your decision. Think about what the Bible says about those who defraud the widow and *orphan*. Good-bye for the present.'

"'No, stop, boy, I've made up my mind. You may go to Mr. Sewell, the clergyman,—he often calls to see me, and I can speak to him. I'll tell him.'

"I did not wait for the old man to alter his mind, but hastened as fast as I could to the parsonage-house, which was not four hundred yards distant. I went to the door, and asked for Mr. Sewell, who came out to me. I told him that old Roberts wanted to see him immediately, as he had an important confession to make.

"'Is the old man going, then? I did not hear that he was any way dangerously ill?'

"'No, sir, he is in his usual health, but he has something very heavy on his conscience, and he begs your presence immediately, that he may reveal an important secret.'

"'Well, my lad, go back to him and say that I will be there in two hours. You are his grandson, I believe?'

"'I will go and tell him, sir,' replied I, evading the last question.

"I returned to old Roberts, and informed him that the clergyman would be with him in an hour or two; but I found the old man already hesitating and doubting again.

"'You didn't tell him what it was for, did you? for perhaps——'

"'Yes, I did. I told him you had an important secret to communicate that lay heavy on your conscience.'

"'I'm sadly puzzled,' said the old man, musing.

"'Well,' replied I, 'I'm not puzzled; and if you don't confess, I must. I won't have my conscience loaded, poor fellow that I am; and if you choose to die with the sin upon you of depriving the orphan, I will not.'

"'I'll tell—tell it all—it's the best way,' replied old Roberts, after a pause.

"'There now,' said I, 'the best thing to be done is for me to get paper and pen, and write it all down for Mr. Sewell to read when he comes; then you need not have to repeat it all again.'

"'Yes, that will be best, for I couldn't face the clergyman.'

"'Then how can you expect to face the Almighty?' replied I.

"'True—very true: get the paper,' said he.

"I went to the inn and procured writing materials, and then returned and took down his confession of what I have now told you, Miss Valerie. When Mr. Sewell came, I had just finished it, and I then told him that I had written it down, and handed it to him to read. Mr. Sewell was much surprised and shocked, and said to Roberts, 'You have done right to make this confession, Roberts, for it may be most important; but you must now swear to it in the presence of a magistrate and me. Of course you have no objection?'

"'No, sir; I'm ready to swear to the truth of every word.'

"'Well, then, let me see. Why, there is no magistrate near us just now but Sir Thomas Moystyn; and as it concerns his own nephew, there cannot be a more proper person. I will go up to the hall immediately, and ask him to come with me to-morrow morning.'

"Mr. Sewell did so; and the next day he and Sir Thomas Moystyn came down in a phaeton, and went up to old Roberts. I rather turned away, that my uncle, as he now proves to be, might not, when I was regularly introduced to him, as I hope to be, as his nephew, recognise me as the sailor lad who passed off as the grandson of old Roberts."

"Then you admit that you have been playing a very deceitful game?"

"Yes, Miss Valerie. I have a conscience; and I admit that I have been playing what may be called an unworthy game; but when it is considered how much I have at stake, and how long I have been defrauded of my rights by the duplicity of others, I think I may be excused if I have beat them at their own weapons."

"I admit that there is great truth in your observations, Lionel; and that is all the answer I shall give."

"I remained outside the door while old Roberts signed the paper, and the oath was administered. Sir Thomas put many questions afterwards. He inquired the residence of his daughter, Mrs. Green, and then they both went away. As soon as they were gone, I went in to old Roberts, and said,

"'Well now, sir, do you not feel happier that you have made the confession?'

"'Yes,' replied he, 'I do, boy; but still I am scared when I think of Lady R—— and your aunt Green; they'll be so angry.'

"'I've been thinking that I had better go up to Mrs. Green,' I said, 'and prepare her for it. I can pacify her, I'm sure, when I explain matters. I must have gone away the day after to-morrow, and I'll go up to London to-morrow.'

"'Well, perhaps it will be as well,' replied old Roberts; 'and yet I wish you could stay and talk to me—I've no one to talk to me now.'

"Thinks I, I have made you talk to some purpose, and have no inclination to sit by your bedside any longer; however, I kept up the appearance to the last, and the next morning set off for London. I arrived three days before I saw you first, which gave me time to change my sailor's dress for the suit I now wear. I have not yet been to Mrs. Green, for I thought I would just see you, and ask your advice. And now, Miss Valerie, you have my whole history."

"I once more congratulate you, with all my heart," replied I, offering my hand to Lionel. He kissed it respectfully, and as he was in the act, one of the maids opened the door, and told me that Lady M—— had been some time waiting to see me. I believe I coloured up, although I had no cause for blushing; and wishing Lionel good-bye, I desired him to call on Sunday afternoon, and I would remain at home to see him.

It was on Thursday that this interview took place with Lionel, and on the Saturday I received a letter from Lady R——'s solicitor, by which I was shocked by the information of her ladyship having died at Caudebec, a small town on the river Seine; and begging to know whether I could receive him that afternoon, as he was anxious to communicate with me. I answered by the person who brought the letter, that I would receive him at three o'clock; and he made his appearance at the hour appointed. He informed me that Lady R—— had left Havre in a fishing-boat, with the resolution of going up to Paris by that strange conveyance; that having no protection from the weather, she had been wet for a whole day, without changing her clothes; and on her arrival at Caudebec, had been taken with a fever, which, from the ignorance of the faculty in that sequestered place, had proved fatal. Her maid had just written the intelligence, inclosing the documents from the authorities substantiating the fact.

"You are not, perhaps, aware, Miss, that you are left her executrix?"

"I her executrix!" exclaimed I, with astonishment.

"Yes," replied Mr. Selwin. "Before she left town she made an alteration in her will; and stated to me that you would be able to find the party most interested in it, and that you had a document in your hands which would explain everything."

"I have a sealed paper which she inclosed to me, desiring I would not open it, unless I heard of her death, or had her permission."

"It must be that to which she refers, I presume," replied he. "I have the will in my pocket: it will be as well to read it to you, as you are her executrix."

Mr. Selwin then produced the will, by which Lionel Dempster, her nephew, was left her sole heir; and by a codicil, she had, for the love she bore me, as she stated in her own handwriting, left me £500 as her executrix, and all her jewels and wearing apparel.

"I congratulate you on your legacy, Miss de Chateneuf," said he; "and now, perhaps, you can tell me where I can find this nephew; for I must say it is the first that I ever heard of him."

"I believe that I can point him out, sir," replied I; "but the most important proofs, I suspect, are to be found in the paper which I have not yet read."

"I will then, if you please, no longer trespass on you," said Mr. Selwin, "when you wish me to call again, you will oblige me by sending word, or writing by post."

The departure of Mr. Selwin was quite a relief to me

I longed to be alone, that I might be left to my own reflections, and also that I might peruse the document which had been confided to me by poor Lady R——. I could not help feeling much shocked at her death—more so, when I considered her liberality towards me, and the confidence she reposed in one with whom she had but a short acquaintance. It was like her, nevertheless; who but Lady R—— would ever have thought of making a young person so unprotected and so unacquainted as I was with business—a foreigner to boot—the executrix of her will; and her death occasioned by such a mad freak—and Lionel now restored to his position and his fortune—altogether it was overwhelming, and after a time I relieved myself with tears. I was still with my handkerchief to my eyes, when Lady M—— came into the room.

"Crying, Miss Chatenœuf," said her ladyship, "it is at the departure of a very dear friend."

There was a sort of sneer on her face as she said this; and I replied—

"Yes, my lady, it is for the departure of a dear friend, for Lady R—— is dead."

"Mercy, you don't say so; and what are these gentlemen who have been calling upon you?"

"One is her solicitor, madam," replied I, "and the other is a relative of hers."

"A relation; but what has the solicitor called upon you for? if it is not an intrusive question."

"No, my lady; Lady R—— has appointed me her executrix."

"Executrix! well I now do believe that Lady R—— was mad!" exclaimed Lady M——. "I wanted you to come up to my boudoir to consult you about the pink satin dress, but I fear your important avocation will not allow you at present, so I will leave you till you are a little recovered."

"I thank you, my lady," said I, "I will be more myself to-morrow, and will then be at your disposal."

Her ladyship then left the room. I was not pleased at her manner, which was very different from her usual courtesy towards me; but I was not in a state of mind to weigh well all that she said, or how she said it. I hastened to my room to look for the paper which Lady R——

had inclosed to me previous to her departure. I will give the whole contents to my readers.

"MY DEAR VALERIE,—

"I will not attempt to account for the extreme predilection which I, an old woman in comparison, immediately imbibed for you before we had been an hour in company. Some feelings are unaccountable and inexplicable, but I felt a sympathy, a mesmeric attraction, if I may use the term, which was uncontrollable at our first meeting, and which increased every day during our residence together. It was not the feeling of a mother towards a child—at least I think not, for it was mingled with a certain degree of awe and presentiment of evil if ever we parted again. I felt as if you were my *fate*, and never has this feeling departed from me. On the contrary, now that we separate, it has become stronger than ever. How little do we know of the mysteries of the mind, as well as of the body! We know that we are fearfully and wonderfully made, and that is all. That there are influences and attractions uncontrollable and unexplained, I feel certain. Often have I reflected and wondered on this as I have lain in bed and meditated 'even to madness,' but have been unable to remove the veil. [Alas, poor Lady R——, thought I, I doubt it not, you were madder than I thought you were.] Imagine, then, my grief and horror when I found that you had determined to leave me, dear Valerie. It was to me as the sentence of death; but I felt that I could not resist; it was my fate, and who can oppose its decrees? It would indeed have pained your young and generous heart if you knew how I suffered, and still suffer from your desertion; but I considered it as a judgment on me—a visitation upon me for the crimes of my early years, and which I am now about to confide to you, as the only person in whom I feel confidence, and that justice may be done to one whom I have greatly injured. I would not die without reparation, and that reparation I intrust to you, as from my own pen I can explain that without which, with all my good intentions towards the party, reparation might be difficult. But I must first make you acquainted with the cause of crime; and to do this you must hear the events of my early life.

"My father, Sir Alexander Moystyn, had four children.

two sons and two daughters. I was the first-born, then my two brothers, and afterwards, at an interval, my sister; so that there was a difference of eight years between me and my sister Ellen. Our mother died in giving birth to Ellen; we grew up; my brothers went to Eton and college. I remained the sole mistress of my father's establishment. Haughty by nature, and my position, the power it gave me, the respect I received—and if you will look at the miniature I inclose with this, I may, without vanity, add, my beauty, made me imperious and tyrannical. I had many advantageous offers, which I rejected, before I was twenty years of age. My power with my father was unbounded; his infirmities kept him for a long time a prisoner in his room, and my word was law to him, as well as to the whole household. My sister Ellen, still a child, I treated with harshness—first, I believe, because she promised to rival me in good looks; and secondly, because my father showed greater affection towards her than I liked. She was meek in temper, and never complained. Time passed—I refused many offers of marriage. I did not like to resign my position for the authority of a husband, and I had reached my twenty-fifth year, and my sister Ellen was a lovely girl of seventeen, when it was fated that all should be changed.

"A Colonel Dempster came down with my eldest brother, who was a captain in the same regiment of guards—a more prepossessing person I never beheld, and for the first time I felt that I would with pleasure give up being at the head of my father's establishment to follow the fortunes of another man. If my predilection was so strong, I had no reason to complain of want of attention on his part. He courted me in the most obsequious manner, the style more suited to my haughty disposition, and I at once gave way to the feelings with which he had inspired me. I became fervently in love with him, and valued one of his smiles more than an earthly crown. Two months passed, his original invitation had been for one week, and he still remained. The affair was considered as arranged, not only by myself, but by everybody else. My father, satisfied that he was a gentleman by birth, and being able to support himself by his own means in so expensive a regiment, made no inquiries leaving the matter to take its own course. But although two months had passed away, and his attentions to me were unremitting, Colonel Dempster had made no proposal, which I ascribed to his awe of me, and his diffidence as to his success. This rather pleased me than otherwise; but my own feelings now made me wish for the affair to be decided, and I gave him every opportunity that modesty and discretion would permit. I saw little of him during the mornings, as he went out with his gun with the other gentlemen; but in the evenings he was my constant and devoted attendant. I received many congratulations from female acquaintances (friends I had none) upon my having conquered one who was supposed to be invulnerable to the charms of our sex, and made no disclaimer when spoken to on the subject. Every hour I expected the declaration to be made, when, imagine my indignation and astonishment, at being informed one morning when I arose, that Colonel Dempster and my sister Ellen had disappeared, and it was reported that they had been seen in a carriage driving at furious speed.

"It was but too true. It appeared that Colonel Dempster, who had been informed by my brother of my temper and disposition, and who was aware that without paying court to me, his visit would not be extended, and who had fallen in love with Ellen almost as soon as he saw her, had practised this dissimulation towards me to enable him, without my knowledge, to gain my sister's affections; that his mornings were not spent in shooting with my brother, as was supposed, but in my sister Ellen's company; my brother, to whom he had acknowledged his attachment, conniving with him to deceive me. A letter from the colonel to my father, excusing himself for the step he had taken, and requesting him to pardon his daughter, was brought in the same morning and read by me. 'Very foolish of him,' said my father; 'what is the use of stealing what you may have for asking. He might have had Ellen if he had spoken to me; but I always thought that he was courting you, Barbara.'

"This letter, proving the truth of the report, was too much for me. I fell down at my father's feet in a violent fit, and was carried to my bed. The next I day was seized with a brain fever, and it was doubtful if ever my reason would return. But it did gradually, and, after a confinement to my room of three months, I recovered both health and reason, partially, I may say, for I doubt not but that the shock I then received has had a lasting effect upon me, and that it has caused me to be the unsettled, restless, wandering thing that I now am, only content when in motion, and using my pen to create an artificial excitement. I believe most people are a little cracked before they begin to write. I will not assert that it is a proof of madness, but it is a proof that a very little more would make them mad. Shakspeare says, 'the lover, the lunatic, and the poet, are of an imagination all compact.' It matters little whether it is prose or poetry; there is often more imagination and more poetry in prose than in rhyme. But to proceed—

"I arose with but one feeling—that of revenge; I say but one feeling, alas! I had forgotten to mention hatred, the parent of that revenge. I felt myself mortified and humiliated, cruelly deceived and mocked. My love for him was now turned to abhorrence, and my sister was an aversion. I felt that I never could forgive her. My father had not replied to the colonel's letter; indeed, the gout in his hand prevented him, or he would probably have done so long before I left my room. Now that I was once more at his side, he said to me,

"'Barbara, I think it is high time to forgive and forget. I would have answered the colonel's letter before, but I could not. Now we must write and ask them to come and pay us a visit.'

"I sat down and wrote the letter, not according to his dictation, which was all kindness, but stating that my father would never forgive him or my sister, and requested all correspondence might cease, as it would be useless.

"'Read what you have said, Barbara.'

"I read the letter as if it was written according to his wishes.

"'That will do, dearest—they'll come back fast enough. I long to have Ellen in my arms again—she was very precious to me, that child, for she cost the life of your dear mother. I want to ask her why she ran away. I really believe that it was more from fear of your anger than of mine, Barbara.'

"I made no reply, but folded the letter and sealed it. As I always opened the post-bag, I prevented my father from ever receiving the many letters written by my poor sister, imploring his forgiveness, and did all I could to excite his anger against her. At last I found out from her letters, that they had gone to the continent. Months passed. My poor father fretted sadly at the silence of Ellen, and the supposed rejection of his kind overtures. His unhappy state of mind had evidently an effect upon his body; he grew weaker and more querulous every day. At last a letter arrived from Ellen, which I now blush to say gave me inexpressible joy. It announced the death of her husband—a trifling wound on the thumb having terminated in lock-jaw and death.

"'He is dead, then,' thought I; 'if I lost him, she has no longer possession of him.'

"Alas! what a demon had taken possession of me! The letter further said, that she was coming over directly, and that she expected to be shortly confined. This letter was addressed to me, and not to my father. The death of her husband did not diminish my hatred against my sister; on the contrary, I felt as if I had her now in my power, and that my revenge upon her was about to be accomplished. After meditating upon what course I should pursue, I determined to write to her. I did so, stating that my father's anger was not to be appeased; that I had tried all I could to soften his wrath, but in vain; that he was growing weaker every day, and I thought her rash conduct had been the cause of it; that I did not think that he could last much longer, and I would make another appeal to him in her favour, which the death of her husband would probably occasion to be more successful.

"In a fortnight I had a reply, in which my poor sister invoked blessings on my head for my supposed kindness, and told me that she was in England, and expected every hour to be confined; that she was ill in body and in spirits, and did not think that she could get over it. She begged me, by the remembrance of our mother, who died giving her birth, that I would come to her. Surely I might have forgotten my enmity after all that the poor girl had suffered; but my heart was steeled.

"On consideration, I now thought proper to tell my father that Colonel Dempster was dead, and my sister returned to England, adding her request that I would attend her in her confinement, and my willingness so to do. My poor father was much shocked, and begged me in a tremulous voice to set off immediately. I promised so to do, but requested that he would not say a word to any one as to the cause of my absence until he heard from me, as it would occasion much talk among the servants, and perhaps ill-natured remarks might be made. He promised, and I departed, with a maid who had been my nurse, and upon whose secrecy I thought I could rely. What my intentions were, I can hardly say; all I knew was, that my revenge was not satiated, and I would leave no opportunity of wreaking it that offered.

"I found my sister in the very pangs of labour, heartbroken at the supposed resentment of my father, and his refusal of his forgiveness. I did not alleviate her misery by telling her the truth, which I might have done. I was indeed a demon, or possessed by one.

"She died giving birth to a boy. I then felt sorrow, until I looked at the child, and saw that it was the image of the colonel—the man who had caused me such misery. Again my passions were roused, and I vowed that the child should never know his father. I made my maid believe that the lady I visited was an old schoolfellow, and never mentioned my sister's name, at least I thought so at the time, but I afterwards found that I had not deceived her. I persuaded her to take the child to her father's, saying that I had promised my friend on her deathbed that I would take care of it, but that it must be a secret, or invidious remarks would be made. I then returned to Culverwood Hall, dropping my nurse and the child on my way, and reported to my father my sister's death, of course concealing that the child was living. Sir Alexander was much affected, and wept bitterly; indeed, from that day he rapidly declined.

"I had now satiated my revenge, and was sorry when I had done so. Until then I had been kept up by excitement, now all excitement was over, and I had time for reflection. I was miserable, and in a state of constant warfare with my conscience, but in vain; the more I reflected, the more I was dissatisfied with myself, and would have given worlds that I could recall what I had done.

"At this time Sir Richard R—— came down on a visit. He admired me, proposed, and was accepted, chiefly that I might remove from the hall, than for any other cause. I thought that new scenes and change of place would make me forget, but I was sadly mistaken. I went away with my husband, and as soon as I was away, I was in a constant fright lest my nurse should betray me to my father, and begged Sir Richard to shorten his intended tour and allow me to return to the hall, as the accounts of my father's health were alarming. My husband consented, and I had not been at the hall more than a fortnight when my father's death relieved me from further anxiety on that score.

"Another fear now possessed me; I saw by my father's will that he had left £5,000 to me and also to my sister; in case of one dying, the survivor to have both sums; but the same cause of alarm was in my great aunt's will. My great aunt had left £10,000 to me and £10,000 to my sister Ellen, to be settled upon us at our marriage, and in case of either dying without issue, the survivor to be legatee. Thus in two instances, by concealing the birth of the child, I was depriving it of its property, and obtaining it for myself. That I was ignorant of these points is certain, and unfortunate it was that it was so, for had I known it, I would not have dared to conceal the birth of the child, lest I should have been accused of having done so for pecuniary considerations, and I well knew, that if betrayed by my nurse, such would be the accusation made against me. I would willingly, even now, have acknowledged the child as my nephew, but knew not how to do so, as my husband had possession of the money, and I dared not confess the crime that I had been guilty of. If ever retribution fell upon any one, it fell upon me. My life was one of perfect misery, and when I found that my nurse and her father objected to keeping the secret any longer, I thought I should have gone distracted. I pointed out to them the ruin they would entail upon me, and gave my solemn promise that I would see justice done to the child. This satisfied them. For several years I lived an unhappy life with my husband, until I was at last relieved by his death. You may ask how it was that I did not acknowledge the child at his death; the fact was, that I was afraid. I had put him to school, and he was then twelve or thirteen years old. I removed him to my own house, with the intention of so doing, and because my nurse and her father reminded me of my promise; but when he was in my house, I could not see my way, or how I could tell the story without acknowledging my guilt; and this pride prevented.

"I remained thus irresolute, every day putting off the confession, till the boy, from first being allowed to remain in the drawing-room, sank down into the kitchen. Yes, Valerie, Lionel, the page, the lacquey, is Lionel Dempster, my nephew. I said that I could not bear to make the avowal, and such is the case. At last I satisfied myself that what I did was for the boy's good. Alas! how easy we satisfy ourselves when it suits our views. I had left him my property, I had educated him, and I said, by being brought up in an humble position, he will be cured of pride, and will make a better man. Bad reasoning, I acknowledge.

"Valerie, I have left you my executrix, for even after my death, I would as much as possible avoid exposure. I would not be the tale of the town, even for a fortnight, and it certainly will not help Lionel, when it is known to all the world that he has served as a footman. My solicitor knows not who my nephew is, but is referred to you to produce him. In a small tin box in the closet of my bedroom, you will find all the papers necessary for his identification, and also the names and residence of the parties who have been my accomplices in this deed; also all the intercepted letters of my poor sister's. You must be aware that Lionel is not only entitled to the property I have left him, but also to his father's property, which, in default of heirs, passed away to others. Consult with my solicitor to take such steps as are requisite, without inculpating me more than is necessary; but if required, let all be known to my shame, rather than the lad should not be put in possession of his rights.

"You will, I am afraid, hate my memory after this sad disclosure; but in my extenuation recall to mind how madly I loved, how cruelly I was deceived. Remember, also, that if not insane, I was little better at the time I was so criminal; and may it prove to you a lesson how difficult it is, when once you have stepped aside into the path of error, ever to recover the right track.

"You now know all my sufferings, all my crimes. You now know why I have been, not without truth, considered as a person eccentric to folly, and occasionally on the verge of madness. Forgive me and pity me, for I have indeed been sufficiently punished by an ever-torturing conscience! "BARBARA R——."

CHAPTER IX.

I PUT the papers down on the table as soon as I had finished them, and for a long while was absorbed in meditation.

"Is it possible," thought I, "that love disappointed can turn to such fury—can so harden the heart to all better feelings—induce a woman to shorten the days of her parent—to allow a sister to remain in painful error on her death-bed, and wreak vengeance upon an innocent being, regardless of all justice? Grant, then, that I may never yield to such a passion! Who would have ever imagined, that the careless, eccentric Lady R—— had such a load of crime weighing her down, and daily and hourly reminded of it by the presence of the injured party? How callous she must have become by habit, to still delay doing an act of justice—how strange that the fear of the world and its opinion should be greater than the fear of God!"

This last remark proved how little I yet knew of the world, and then my thoughts went into another direction. As I have already said, I had been brought up as a Catholic; but, after my grandmother's death, I had little encouragement or example shown me in religious duties. Now, having been more than two years in England, and continually with Protestants, I had gone to the established Protestant church with those I resided with at first; because I considered it better to go to that church, although I knew it to be somewhat at variance with my own, rather than go to no church at all, and by habit I was gradually inclining to Protestantism; but now the idea came across my mind, if Lady R—— had confessed as we Catholics do, this secret could not have been kept so long; and, if she withheld herself from the confessional, had her agents been Catholics, the secret would have been divulged to the priest by them, and justice would have been done to Lionel; and, having made this reflection, I felt as it were, that I was again a sincere Catholic.

After a little more reflection I put away the papers,

wrote a letter to Mr. Selwyn, the solicitor, requesting that he would call upon me the following morning, and then went down to Lady M——.

"I suppose that we shall not have much of the pleasure of your company, Miss de Chatenœuf," said her ladyship, "now that you have such a novel occupation?"

"It is a very distressing one," replied I, "and I wish Lady R—— had not paid me such a compliment. Might I trespass upon your ladyship's kindness to request the loan of the carriage for half an hour to obtain some papers from Lady R——'s house in Baker-street?"

"Oh, certainly," replied her ladyship. "Pray, have you seen Lady R——'s will?"

"Yes, madam."

"And how has she disposed of her property?"

"She has left it all to her nephew, Lady M——."

"Nephew! I never heard her speak of a nephew before. Sir Richard had no nephews or nieces, for he was an only son, and the title has now gone into the Vivian branch, and I never heard of her having a nephew. And what has she left you, mademoiselle, if it is not asking too much?"

"Lady R—— has left me £500, my lady."

"Indeed, well then, she pays you for your trouble. But really, Miss de Chatenœuf, I do wish you could put off this business until after the marriages. I am so hurried and worried that I really do not know which way to turn, and really I have felt your loss these last two days more than you can imagine. You are so clever, and have so much taste, that we cannot get on without you. It's all your own fault," continued her ladyship, playfully, "you are so goodnatured, and have made us so dependent upon you, that we cannot let you off now. Nothing in the *trousseaux* is approved of unless stamped by the taste of Mademoiselle Valerie de Chatenœuf. Now, a week cannot make a great difference, and lawyers love delay: will you oblige me, therefore, by leaving Lady R——'s affairs for the present?"

"Certainly, Lady M——," replied I. "I will stop a letter I was about to send to her solicitor, and write another to the effect you wish, and I will not repeat my request for the carriage until after the marriages have taken place."

"Many thanks," replied her ladyship, and I went out, took my letter from the hall table, and wrote another to Mr. Selwyn, stating that I could not enter into any business until the following week, when I should be prepared to receive him.

I wrote another to the same effect to Lionel, requesting him not to call again, but that I would write and let him know where to meet me as soon as I was more at leisure. Indeed, I was glad that Lady M—— had made the request, as the trouble, and chattering, and happy faces, which were surrounding the *trousseaux*, and the constant employment and appeals made to me, drove away the melancholy which Lady R——'s affairs had occasioned me. I succeeded to a great degree in recovering my spirits, and exerted myself to my utmost, so that everything was complete and satisfactory to all parties two days before the wedding was to take place.

At last the morning came. The brides were dressed, and went down into the drawing-room, frightened and perplexed, but their tears had been shed above. The procession of carriages moved on to Hanover-square; there was a bishop of course, and the church was filled with gay and tastefully-dressed women. The ceremony was performed, and the brides were led into the vestry-room to recover, and receive kisses and congratulations. Then came the banquet, which nobody hardly tasted except the bishop, who had joined too many couples in his lifetime to have his appetite at all affected by the ceremony, and some two or three others who were old stagers on the road of life, and who cared little whether it was a wedding-breakfast, or refreshments after a funeral.

At last, after a most silent entertainment, the brides retired to change their dresses, and, when they reappeared, they were handed into the carriages of their respective bridegrooms as soon as they could be torn away from the kisses and tears of Lady M——, who played the part of a bereaved mother to perfection. No one to have seen her then, raving like another Niobe, would have imagined that all her thoughts, and endeavours, and manœuvres, for the last three years, had been devoted to the sole view of getting them off; but Lady M—— was a perfect actress, and this last scene was well got up.

As her daughters were led down to the carriages, I thought that she was going to faint; but it appeared, on second thoughts, that she wished first to see the girls depart in their gay equipages; she therefore tottered to the window, saw them get in, looked at Newman's grays and gay postilions—at the white and silver favours—the dandy valet and smart lady's-maid in each rumble. She saw them start at a rattling pace, watched them till they turned the corner of the square, and then—and not till then—fell senseless in my arms, and was carried by the attendants into her own room.

After all, the poor woman must have been very much worn out, for she had been for the last six weeks in a continual worry lest any *contre-temps* should happen, which might have stopped or delayed the happy consummation.

The next morning her ladyship did not leave her room, but sent word down that the carriage was at my service; but I was fatigued and worn out, and declined it for that day. I wrote to Lionel and to Mr. Selwyn, desiring them to meet me in Baker-street at two o'clock the next day; and then passed the day quietly, in company with Amy, the third daughter of Lady M——, whom I have before mentioned. She was a very sweet, unaffected girl; and I was more partial to her than to her sisters, who had been just married. I had paid great attention to her, for she had a fine voice, and did credit to my teaching, and there was a great intimacy between us, arising on my part from my admiration of her ingenuous and amiable disposition, which even her mother's example to the contrary could not spoil.

After some conversation relative to her sisters and their husbands, she said,

"I hardly know what to do, Valerie. I love you too well to be a party to your being ill-treated, and yet I fear that you will be pained if I tell you what I have heard about you. I know also that you will not stay, if I do tell you, and that will give me great pain; but *that* is a selfish feeling which I could overcome. What I do not like is hurting your feelings. Now, tell me candidly, ought I to tell you, or not?"

"I will give you my opinion candidly," replied I. "You have said too little or too much. You speak of my being ill-treated; certainly, I should wish to guard against that, although I cannot imagine who is my enemy."

"Had I not heard it, I could not have believed it either," replied she. "I thought that you had come here on a visit as a friend; but what makes me think that I ought to tell you is, that there will be something said against your character, which I am sure must be false."

"Now, indeed, I must request that you will tell me everything, and soften nothing down, but tell me the whole truth. Who is it that intends to attack my character?"

"I am sorry—very sorry to say, it is mamma," replied she, wiping away a tear.

"Lady M——!" exclaimed I.

"Yes," replied she; "but now you must listen to all I have to say. I am sure that I am doing right in telling you, and therefore nothing shall prevent me. I love my mother—what a sad thing it is that I cannot respect her! I was in the dressing-room, when my mother was lying on the sofa in her bedroom this morning, when her great friend, Mrs. Germane, came up. She sat talking with my mother for some time, and they appeared either to forget or not to care if I heard them, for at last your name was mentioned.

"'Well, she does dress you and your girls beautifully, I must say,' said Mrs. Germane. 'Who is she? They say that she is of a good family; and how came she to live with you as a milliner?'

"'My dear Mrs. Germane, that she does live with me as a milliner is true, and it was for that reason only I invited her to the house; but she is not aware that I retain her in that capacity. She is, I understand from Mrs. Bathurst, of a noble family in France, thrown upon the world by circumstances, very talented, and very proud. Her extreme taste in dress I discovered when she was living with Mrs. Bathurst; and when I found that she was about, through my management, to leave Lady R——, I invited her here as a sort of friend, and to stay with my daughters—not a word did I mention about millinery; I had too much tact for that. Even when her services were required, I made it appear as her own offer, and expressed my thanks for her condescension, and since that, by flattery and management, she has continued to dress my daughters for me; and, I must say, that I do believe it has been owing to her exquisite taste that my daughters have gone off so well.'

"'Well, you have managed admirably,' replied Mrs. Germane; 'but, my dear Lady M——, what will you do with her now?'

"'Oh,' replied Lady M——, 'as Amy will now come out, I shall retain her in my employ until she is disposed of; and then——'

"'Yes, then will be the difficulty,' replied Mrs. Germane; 'after having allowed her to live so long with you as a visitor, I may say, how will you get rid of her?'

"'Why, I was puzzling myself about that, and partly decided that it should be done by mortifying her, and wounding her feelings, for she is very proud; but, fortunately, I have found out something which I shall keep to myself, until the time comes, and then I can dismiss her at a moment's warning.'

"'Indeed!' said Mrs. Germane, 'what could you have found out?'

"'Well, I will tell you; but you must not mention it again. My maid entered the room the other day, when mademoiselle was receiving a young man who called upon her, and she found them kissing.'

"'You don't say so!'

"'Yes, a kiss was given, and my maid saw it. Now, I can easily make it appear that my maid never mentioned it to me till the time that it may be convenient to make use of it, and then I can send her away; and if any questions are asked, hint at a little impropriety of conduct.'

"'And very properly too,' replied Mrs. Germane. 'Had I not better hint a little beforehand to prepare people?'

"'Why, it may be as well, perhaps; but be cautious, very cautious, my dear Mrs. Germane.'

"Mademoiselle de Chatenœuf, I am sorry that I am obliged, in doing my duty to you, to expose mamma," said Amy, rising up from her chair; "but I am sure that you could not be guilty of any impropriety, and I will not allow you to be accused of it, if it is to be prevented."

"Many thanks," replied I. "My dear Amy, you have behaved like a kind friend. I have only, in duty to myself, to clear up the charge against me, of impropriety.

You must not imagine me guilty of that. It is true that your mother's maid did come in when a young lad of seventeen, who was grateful to me for the interest I took in his welfare, and who was taking leave of me at the time, did raise my hand to his lips and kiss it, and had he done so before your mother, I should not have prevented it. This was the kiss which, as your mother asserts, passed between us, and this is the only impropriety that took place. Oh, what a sad, treacherous, selfish, wicked world this is!" cried I, throwing myself on the sofa, and bursting into tears.

Amy was making every attempt to console me, and blaming herself for having made the communication, when Lady M—— came down stairs into the room.

"What is all this? what a scene!" exclaimed she. "Mademoiselle de Chatenœuf, have you had any bad news?"

"Yes, my lady," replied I, "so bad that I am under the necessity of leaving you directly."

"Indeed! may I inquire what has happened?"

"No, my lady, it is not in my power to tell you. I have only to repeat, that I must, with your permission, leave this house to-morrow morning."

"Well, mademoiselle," replied her ladyship, "I do not want to pry into your secrets, but this I must say, that where there is concealment, there must be wrong; but I have lately discovered so much, that I do not wonder at concealment—nor am I, indeed, surprised at your wish to leave me."

"Lady M——," replied I, haughtily, "I have never done anything during the time that I have been under your roof which I have to blush for—nor indeed anything that requires concealment. This I can proudly say. If I conceal now, it is to spare others, and, I may add, to spare you. Do not oblige me to say more in presence of your daughter. It will be sufficient for me to hint to you, that I am now aware why I was invited to your house, and what are your plans for dismissing me when it suits you."

"Eaves-dropping, then, is a portion of your character, mademoiselle," cried Lady M——, colouring up to the temples.

"No, madam, such is not the case, and that is all the answer I shall give; it is sufficient for you that you are exposed, and I do not envy your present feelings. I have only to repeat, that I shall leave this house to-morrow morning, and I will not further trouble your ladyship with my company."

I then walked out of the room, and as I passed Lady M——, and observed her confusion and vexation, I felt that it was she who was humiliated, and not me. I went up to my room and commenced my preparations for immediate departure, and had been more than an hour busy in packing up, when Amy came into my room.

"Oh Valerie, how sorry I am—but you have behaved just as I think that you ought to have done; and how very kind of you not to say that I told you. My mother was so angry after you left; said that the maids must have been listening, and declares she will give them all warning; but I know that she will not do that. She spoke about your meeting a young man, and kissing going on; but you have already explained all that."

"Amy," replied I, "after I am gone, take an opportunity of saying to Lady M——, that you mentioned this to me, and tell her that my reply was, if Lady M—— knew who that young man was, how he is connected, and how large a fortune he will inherit, she would be very glad to see him kiss one of her daughter's hands with a different feeling from that which induced him to kiss mine."

"I will, depend upon it," said Amy; "and then mamma will think that she has lost a good husband for me."

"She will meet him some of these days," replied I; "and what is more, he will defend me from any attack made on that score."

"I will tell her that, also," said Amy, "it will make her careful of what she says."

One of the servants then knocked at the door, and said, that Lady M—— wished to see Miss Amy.

"Wish me good-bye now," said I, "for you may not be permitted to see me again."

The dear girl embraced me cordially, and with tears in her eyes, left the room. I remained till I had finished packing, and then sat down. Shortly afterwards her ladyship's maid came in, and delivered me an envelope from her ladyship, enclosing the salary due to me, with Lady M——'s compliments written outside.

I saw no more of Lady M—— or her daughter that

evening. I went to bed, and, as in my former changes, I reflected what steps I should take. As for the treatment I had received, I was now to a certain degree hardened to it, and my feelings certainly were not so acute as when, the first time, I had received a lesson of what I might expect through life from the heartlessness and selfishness of the world; but in the present case there was a difficulty which did not exist in the former—I was going away without knowing where I was to go. After a little thought, I determined that I would seek Madame Gironac, and ascertain whether she could not receive me until I had decided upon my future plans.

My thoughts then recurred to other points. I recollected that I had to meet Mr. Selwyn and Lionel, in Baker-street, and I resolved that I would go there with my effects early the next morning, and leave them in charge of the cook, who was taking care of the house. I calculated also the money that I had in possession and in prospect. I had such a good stock of clothes when I came to England with Madame Bathurst, that I had no occasion, during the two years and more that I had now been in England, to make any purchases of consequence— indeed, I had not expended more than the twenty pounds I had brought with me. I had received some few presents from Lady M—— and Madame Bathurst, and a great many from Lady R——. Altogether, I calculated that I had about two hundred and sixty pounds in my desk, for Lady R—— had given me one hundred pounds for only a portion of the year; then there was the five hundred pounds which she had left me, besides her wearing apparel and trinkets, which last I knew to be of value. It was a little fortune to one in my position, and I resolved to consult Mr. Selwyn as to the best way of disposing of it. Having wound up my meditations with the most agreeable portion of them, I fell asleep, and in the morning woke up refreshed.

Lady M——'s maid, who had always been partial to me, for I had taught her many things valuable to a lady's-maid, came in early, and said that she knew that I was going away, which she regretted very much. I replied that I should leave as soon as possible, but I wanted some breakfast. This she brought up to my room.

I had not finished when Amy came in the room and

said, "I have permission to come and wish you good-bye, Valerie. I told mamma what you said about the person who was seen to kiss your hand. She acknowledges now that it was your hand that was kissed, and she was so astonished, for she knows that you never tell stories; and, what do you think, she desired me to find out what was the young gentleman's name that had so large a fortune. I said I would if I could, and so I will, by asking you outright, not by any other means. I don't want to know his name," continued she, laughing, "but I'm sure mamma has in her mind fixed upon him for a husband for me, and would now give the world that you were not going away, that through you he might be introduced to her."

"I cannot tell you, my dear," replied I. "I am not at liberty to mention it at present, otherwise I would with pleasure. I am going now. May God bless you, my dearest, and may you always continue to be the same frank and amiable creature that you are now! I leave you with regret, and I pray earnestly for your happiness. You have made me very happy by telling me that your mamma acknowledges that it was my hand that was kissed; after that, she will hardly attempt to injure me, as she proposed.

"Oh no, Valerie, I think she is afraid to do so now. This young man of fortune has made her think differently. He would, of course, protect you from slander, and expose her if she attempted it. Then, good-bye."

We embraced, and then I ordered a hackney coach to be called, and drove with my luggage to Baker-street. The cook welcomed me, saying that she expected my coming, as Mr. Selwyn had called to tell her of Lady R——'s death, and that when she asked to whom she was to look for her wages, he had told her that I was the person who was to settle all her ladyship's affairs, as everything was left on my hands. She showed me a letter from Martha, Lady R——'s maid, by which I found that they would probably arrive in Baker-street that very day, with all her ladyship's effects.

"I suppose you will sleep here, miss?" said the cook. "I have aired your bed, and your room is all ready."

I replied that I wished to do so for a night or two, at all events, as I had a good deal to attend to, but that Mr.

Selwyn would call at one o'clock, and that I would speak to him on the subject.

I had requested Lionel to call at twelve, an hour previous to Mr. Selwyn, that I might make him acquainted with the contents of Lady R——'s papers addressed to me. He was punctual to the time, and I shook hands with him, saying, "Lionel, I congratulate you, at now having proofs of your being the nephew of Lady R——, and also at her having left you considerable property. You will be surprised to hear that she has appointed me her executrix."

"I am not at all surprised," replied Lionel; "I am sure she has done a wise thing at last."

"That is more than I am," replied I; "but I appreciate the compliment. But, Lionel, there is no time to be lost, as Mr. Selwyn, the lawyer, is coming here at one o'clock, and before he comes I wish you to read over Lady R——'s confession, if I may so call it, which will explain the motives of her conduct towards you. I am afraid that it will not extenuate her conduct; but recollect that she has now made all the reparation in her power, and that we must forgive as we hope to be forgiven. Sit down and read these papers, while I unpack one or two of my boxes upstairs."

"The last time that we were here, I corded them up for you, Miss Valerie; I hope that you will allow me to assist you again."

"Thank you, but you will have no time to read what Lady R—— has said, and the cook and I can manage without you."

I then left the room and went upstairs. I was still busy in my room when a knock at the street door announced the arrival of Mr. Selwyn, and I went down into the drawing-room to meet him. I asked Lionel, who was walking up and down the room, whether he had finished the papers, and he replied by a nod of the head. The poor lad appeared very miserable, but Mr. Selwyn entered, and I could not say more to him.

"I hope I have not kept you waiting, Mademoiselle de Chatenœuf," said he.

"No, indeed. I came here at ten o'clock, for I have left Lady M——, and I may as well ask at once whether there is any objection to my taking a bed in this house for a few nights?"

"Objection! Why, mademoiselle, you are sole executrix, and everything is at present yours, in fact, for the time. You have, therefore, a right to take possession until he appears, and the will is proved."

"The hero is before you, Mr. Selwyn. Allow me to introduce you to Mr. Lionel Dempster, the nephew of Lady R——."

Mr. Selwyn bowed to Lionel, and congratulated him upon his accession to the property.

Lionel returned the salute, and then said, "Mademoiselle Chatenœuf, I am convinced that in this case Mr. Selwyn must be made a party to all that has occurred. The reading of these papers has rather disturbed me, and it would be painful to me to hear everything repeated in my presence. With your permission, I will walk out for an hour, and leave you to explain everything to Mr. Selwyn, for I am sure that I shall need his advice. Here is the confession of old Roberts, which I shall leave for his perusal. Good morning, then, for the present."

So saying, Lionel took up his hat and quitted the room.

"He is a very prepossessing young man," observed Mr. Selwyn. "What a fine eye he has!"

"Yes," replied I; "and now that he has so large a property, others will find out that he is a prepossessing young man with fine eyes; but sit down, Mr. Selwyn, for you have to listen to a very strange narrative."

When he had finished it, he laid it down on the table, saying, "This is perhaps the strangest history that has ever come to my knowledge during thirty years of practice. And so she brought him up as a footman. I now recognise him again as the lad who has so often opened the door for me; but I confess I never should have done so if I had not heard what you have now communicated."

"He was always much above his position," replied I. "He is very clever and very amusing; at least I found him so when he served me in his menial capacity, and certainly was much more intimate with him than I ever thought I could be with a servant. At all events, his education has not been neglected."

"Strange! very strange!" observed Mr. Selwyn, "this is a curious world; but I fear that his history cannot be kept altogether a secret; for you must recollect, mademoiselle, that his father's property must be claimed, and no doubt it will be disputed. I must go to Doctors' Commons and search out the will, at once, of Colonel Dempster; he intends, as I presume he does by what he said just now, to employ me. After all, it will, if known, be but a nine days' wonder, and do him no harm; for he proves his birth by his appearance, and his breeding is so innate as to have conquered all his disadvantages."

"When I knew him as a servant, I thought him an intelligent and witty lad, but I never could have believed that he would have become so improved in such a short time: not only his manners, but his language is so different."

"It was *in* him," replied Mr. Selwyn; "as a domestic, the manners and language of a gentleman would have been out of place, and he did not attempt them; now that he knows his position, he has called them forth. We must find out this Mrs. Green, and have her testimony as soon as possible. Of course, after the deposition of old Roberts, Sir Thomas Moystyn will not be surprised when I communicate to him the confession of Lady R——; and the disposition of her property. In fact, the only difficulty will be in the recovery of the property of his father, Colonel Dempster, and—"

A knock at the street door announced the return of Lionel. When he entered the room, Mr. Selwyn said,

"Mr. Dempster, that you are the nephew of Lady R——, to whom she has bequeathed her property, and what was your own, is sufficiently established in my opinion. I will therefore, with your permission, read her ladyship's will."

Lionel took a seat, and the will was read. When it was finished, Mr. Selwyn said,

"Having been Lady R——'s legal adviser for many years, I am able to tell you, within a trifle, what property you will receive. There are £57,000 three per cents; this house and furniture, which I purchased the lease of for her, and which is only saddled with a ground-rent for the next forty years; and I find a balance of £1,200 at the banker's. Your father's property, Mr. Dempster, of course, I know nothing about, but will ascertain this to-morrow by going to Doctors' Commons. I think I may venture to assure the executrix that she will run no risk in allowing you to take any sum of money you may require from the balance in the bank, as soon as the will is proved, which had better be done to-morrow, if it suits Mademoiselle de Chatenœuf."

"Certainly," replied I; "I am anxious to get rid of my trust as soon as possible, and give Mr. Dempster possession. There is a tin box of papers, Mr. Selwyn, which I cannot get at till the return of Lady R——'s maid, as the keys are with Lady R——'s effects, which she is bringing home with her."

"Yes, they will no doubt be important," replied Mr. Selwyn: "and now, Mr. Dempster, if you are in want of any ready cash, I shall be your banker with pleasure till you can have possession of your own."

"I thank you, sir, I am not in want of any," replied Lionel, "for the present; but, as soon as I may be permitted to have money from the bank, I shall be glad, as it is not my intention to remain in England."

"Indeed!" exclaimed I.

"No, Mademoiselle Valerie," said Lionel. "I am but too well aware of many deficiencies which must arise from the position I have been so long in, not to wish to remedy them as soon as possible; and, before I appear as the heir of Lady R——, it is my intention, as soon as I can, to go to Paris, and remain there for two years, or perhaps, until I am of age; and I think in that time to improve myself, and make myself more what the son of Colonel Dempster should be. I am young yet, and capable of instruction."

"You propose a very proper step, Mr. Dempster," said Mr. Selwyn; "and during your absence all legal proceedings will be over, and, if the whole affair is made public, it will be forgotten again by the time that you propose to return. I am sure that the executrix will be most happy to forward such very judicious arrangements. I will now take my leave, and beg Mademoiselle de Chatenœuf to meet me at Doctors' Commons at three o'clock to-morrow; that will give me time to look for Colonel Dempster's will. Good morning, mademoiselle; good morning, Mr. Dempster."

Mr. Selwyn went out, and left us alone.

"May I ask, Miss Valerie, whether you have left Lady M——?"

"Yes," replied I; and I told him what had passed,

adding, "I stay here for a night or two, and shall go then to Madame Gironac's."

"Why not stay here altogether? I hope you will. I shall go abroad as soon as possible."

"Yes, and you are right in so doing; but, Lionel, you forget that my duty as executrix will be to make the best of the estate for you until you are of age, and this house must be let furnished; Mr. Selwyn told me so while you were away; besides, I am not a young lady of fortune, but one most unfortunately dependent upon the caprices of others, and I must submit to my fate."

Lionel made no reply for some little while, and then he said,

"I am very glad that Lady R—— has shown the high opinion she had of you; but I cannot forgive her treatment of my mother. It was too cruel; but I had better not talk any more about it; and I am sure, Miss Valerie, you must be anxious to be alone. Good afternoon, Miss Valerie."

"Good-bye, Lionel, for the present," replied I. "By the bye, did the cook recognise you?"

"Yes; and I told her that I had given up going out to service."

"I think that you had better not come here, Lionel, till I have dismissed Lady R——'s maid, which I shall do the day after her arrival. I will meet you at Mr. Selwyn's office—it will be better."

To this Lionel agreed, and we parted.

The next day the will was proved, and Mr. Selwyn then informed us that he had found the will of the late Colonel Dempster, which had left his property to his child unborn, as might be supposed, with a jointure on the estate, which was entailed. The will, in consequence of the supposed non-existence of Lionel, had been proved by the next of kin, a gentleman of large property, and of whom report spoke highly. It was the intention of Mr. Selwyn to communicate with him directly. The probate duty, &c., had required a large portion of the £1,200 left in the bank, but there was still enough to meet all Lionel's wants for a year, if he wished to go abroad immediately; and another dividend would be due in a month, so that there could be no difficulty. Mr. Selwyn explained all this as we drove to his chambers, where I signed some papers a:

his request, and Lionel received a cheque on the bank, and I sent, by Mr. Selwyn, instructions to meet his drafts for the future.

This affair being arranged, Lionel stated his intention of quitting immediately for Paris. He said that he would go for his passport that afternoon, as there was time enough left for him to give in his name at the office; and that he would call to-morrow afternoon to bid me farewell. He then took his leave, and left me with Mr. Selwyn, with whom I had a long conversation, during which I stated to him that I had some money of my own, as well as what had been left me by Lady R——, which I wished to put in safety. He recommended that I should lodge what I then had at a banker's, and, as soon as had received the rest, he would look out for a good mortgage for me. He then handed me into a coach, and bade me farewell, stating that he would call on the day after the morrow, at three o'clock, as by that time Lady R——'s maid must have arrived, and I should have obtained possession of the key of the tin box, the papers in which he was anxious to examine.

On my return to Baker-street, I found that Lady R——'s maid had arrived, and I of course immediately took possession of everything. I then paid her her wages, and dismissed her, giving her permission to remain and sleep in the house, and promising her a character. It appeared very summary to dismiss her so soon, but I was anxious she should not see Lionel, and I told her that, as executrix, I was not warranted in keeping her a day longer than was necessary, as I was answerable for all expenses. Having now the keys, I was able to examine everything. I first found the tin box, with various papers in it; among others, a packet, on which was written, "Papers relative to my sister Ellen and her child." I thought I would not open them till Mr. Selwyn was present, as it might appear as if I was curious; so I laid them aside. I then despatched the cook with a note to Madame Gironac, requesting that she would come and spend the evening with me, as I had much to communicate to her. Indeed, I felt dull alone in such a large house, and I also felt the want of a sincere friend to talk with.

Having nothing better to do, I opened the various drawers and cupboards which contained the apparel, &c.,

of Lady R——, and found such a mass of things that I was astonished. In her whimsical way, she had at times purchased silks and various jewels, which she had never made use of, but thrown on one side. There were more stuffs for making up dresses than dresses made up,—I should say nearly double. I found one large bundle of point-lace, some of it of great beauty, which I presume had belonged to her mother, and of other laces there was a great quantity. The jewels which she had taken abroad with her were very few, and such as she wore in common; her diamonds, and all that was of value, I knew she had sent to her banker's a day or two previous to her departure, and I thought I would wait till I had seen Mr. Selwyn again before I claimed them.

Madame Gironac came as requested, and I then communicated to her all that had taken place. She was delighted at my good fortune, and said she hoped that I would now come and live with them, as I had the means of living, without being subject to the caprices of others; but I could give no answer till I knew what my property might amount to. All I could promise was, to go to her as soon as I had finished my business in Baker-street, and then I would afterwards decide what steps it would be advisable for me to take.

After a long conversation, during which Madame Gironac was as lively as ever, we separated, Madame Gironac promising to come and pass the next day with me, and assist me in looking over Lady R——'s wardrobe. During the afternoon, I had selected a good many of Lady R——'s dresses, and some which did not please my taste, or had been much worn, I gave to her maid, on the following morning, before her departure. This pleased her very much, as she knew that her mistress's wardrobe had been bequeathed to me, and did not expect to obtain any portion of it; but the drawers and closets were so loaded, that I could well afford to be generous. Madame Gironac came to breakfast the next morning, accompanied by her husband, who was delighted to see me, and having as usual quarrelled, after their fashion, he bounced out of the room, declaring that he never would see that odious little woman any more.

"Oh, Monsieur Gironac, you forget you promised to come and dine here."

"Well, well, so I did; but, Mademoiselle Valerie, that promise has prevented a separation."

"It is very unlucky that you asked him, Mademoiselle Valerie," replied his wife, "all my hopes are destroyed Good-bye, Monsieur Gironac, and be grateful that you have been prevented from committing a folly; now go, we are to be very busy, and don't want you."

"I will go, madam; and hear me," said Monsieur Gironac, with mock solemnity; "as I live, I will not return—till dinner-time."

He then bounced out of the room. We then proceeded to sort and arrange. Madame Gironac, who was a good judge, stated the laces to be worth at least £200, and the other articles, such as silks, &c., with the dresses and lace, at about £100 more. The laces and silks not made up she proposed selling for me, which she said that she could to various customers, and the dresses and lace she said could be disposed of to a person she knew, who gained her livelihood by remaking up such things.

We were thus employed, when Lionel called. He had obtained his passport, and had come to wish me good-bye. When he rose to say farewell, he said,

"Miss Valerie, I can hardly say what my feelings are towards you. Your kindness to me when I was a supposed footman, and the interest you always took in anything concerning me, have deeply impressed me with gratitude; but I feel more. You are much too young for my mother, but I feel the reverence of a son, and if I did dare to use the expression, I feel towards you, what I think are the feelings that a brother should have towards a sister."

"I am flattered by your saying so, Lionel," replied I. "You are now in a much higher position, or rather soon will be, than I shall ever obtain in this world, and that you have such feelings towards me for any little kindness I have shown to you, is highly creditable to your heart. Have you any letters of introduction to any one in Paris? but now I think of it, you cannot well have."

"No," replied he; "I may have by-and-by, but how could I possibly obtain one at present?"

A thought struck me.

"Well, Lionel, you do not know my history; but I was once very intimate with a lady at Paris, and although we parted bad friends, she has since written kindly to me, and I believe her to have been sincere in so doing. I will give you a letter of introduction to her; but do not blame me if I have been deceived in her a second time."

I went to the table and wrote the following short note:—

"My dear Madame D'Albret,—

"This letter will be presented to you by a Mr. Lionel Dempster, a young Englishman of fortune, and a great friend of mine. He is going to reside at Paris, to improve himself, until he comes of age; and I give him this introduction to you for two reasons; the first, because I want to prove to you that, although my feelings would not permit me to accept your last kind offer, I have long forgotten and forgiven any little injustice you did me: and the second, because I feel convinced that in your society, and that which you keep, he will gain more advantage than perhaps in any other in Paris.

"Yours, with esteem,

"Valerie de Chatenœuf."

"There, Lionel, this may be of use to you; if not, write and let me know. You will, of course, let me hear from you occasionally?"

"May heaven preserve you, Miss Valerie!" replied Lionel. "I only hope the time may arrive when I may be able to prove my gratitude."

Lionel kissed my hand, and the tears rolled down his cheeks as he quitted the room.

"He is a charming young man," said Madame Gironac, as soon as the door was shut.

"He is a very superior young man, in my opinion," replied I; "and I am most anxious that he should do well. I did not think it possible that I ever could have written again to Madame d'Albret, but my good-will towards him induced me. There is Monsieur Gironac's knock; so now for a quarrel, or a reconciliation, which is it to be?"

"Oh, we must reconcile first, and then have a quarrel afterwards: that is the established rule."

Monsieur Gironac soon joined us. We passed a very lively evening, and it was arranged that I should in three days take up my quarters at their house.

The next day Mr. Selwyn called at the time appointed, and I made over to him the box and papers. He told me that he had seen Mrs. Green, and had had her full confession of what took place, in corroboration of all that was stated by Lady R—— and old Roberts, and that he had written to Mr. Armiger Dempster, who had succeeded to the property of Lionel's father.

I then told him that I wished to go with him to the bank, to lodge the money I then had, and to obtain Lady R——'s jewel-case which was deposited there.

"Nothing like the time present," said Mr. Selwyn; "my carriage is at the door. I will have the pleasure of taking you there and then returning with you. But I have another appointment, and must be so impolite as to request that you will hurry your toilet as much as possible."

This was done, and in an hour I had lodged my money and obtained the jewel-case.

Mr. Selwyn took me back again, and, having put the tin box into the carriage, wished me farewell.

I told him that I was about to take up my residence with the Gironacs, gave him their address, and then we parted.

That evening I opened the jewel-case, and found it well stocked. The value of its contents I could not possibly be acquainted with; but that so many diamonds and other stones were of value I knew well. I placed the other caskets of Lady R—— in the case, and then proceeded to make up my packages ready for transportation to Madame Gironac's, for there were a great many trunks full. I occupied myself with this for the remainder of the time that I was in Baker-street, and when Monsieur Gironac and his wife called, according to promise, to take me to their home, it required two coaches, and well loaded, to take all the luggage; a third conveyed Monsieur and Madame Gironac, myself, and the jewel-case. I found a very cheerful room prepared for me, and I had the pleasant feeling, as we sat down to our small dinner, that I had a home.

Madame Gironac was indefatigable in her exertions, and soon disposed of all the laces and wardrobe that I had decided upon parting with, and I paid the sum that they realized, viz. £310, into the banker's. The disposal of the jewels was a more difficult affair, but they were valued by a friend of Monsieur Gironac's, who had once been in the trade, at £630. After many attempts to dispose of them more favourably, I succeeded in obtaining for them the sum of £570.

Mr. Selwyn had called upon me once or twice, and I had received my legacy with interest; deducting the legacy-duty of £50, it came to £458. I had, therefore, the following sums in all: £230 of my savings; £310 for the wardrobe and laces, £570 for the jewels, and £458 for the legacy; amounting in all to £1,568. Who would have imagined, three months before, that I should ever have possessed such a sum? I did not, certainly.

Mr. Selwyn, as soon as he knew what sum I had to dispose of, viz. £1,500, for I retained the £68 for my expenses, procured me a mortgage at five per cent. on excellent landed security; and thus did the poor forlorn Valerie possess an income of £75 per annum.

As soon as this was all arranged, I felt a tranquillity I had not known before. I was now independent. I could work, it is true, if I felt inclined, and had an opportunity. I could, however, do without work. The Gironacs, finding that I insisted upon paying for my board, and knowing that I could now afford it, agreed to receive forty pounds per annum—more they would not listen to. Oh! what a balm to the feelings is the consciousness of independence, especially to one who had been treated as I had been. There were two situations to which I had taken a violent abhorrence—that of a governess, and now that of a milliner; and I thanked Heaven that I was no longer under any fear of being driven into either of those unfortunate employments. For the first month that I remained with the Gironacs, I absolutely did nothing but enjoy my emancipation; after that, I began to talk over matters with Monsieur Gironac, who pointed out to me, that now that I could live upon my own means, I should endeavour to increase them, so as to be still more at my ease.

"What do you propose that I should do, then, monsieur?" replied I.

"I should propose that you establish yourself as a music-mistress, and give lessons on the pianoforte and singing. By degrees you will get a connection, and you will still be your own mistress."

"And when you have nothing else to do, mademoiselle, you must make flowers in wax," said Madame Gironac. "You make them so well, that I can always sell yours when I cannot my own."

"I must not interfere with you, Elise," said I; "that would be very ungrateful on my part."

"Pooh—nonsense—there are customers enough for us both."

"I thought this advice to be very good, and made up my mind to follow it. I had not money sufficient to purchase a piano just then, as it would be five months before the half-year's interest of the mortgáge would be due; so I hired one from a dealer with whom Monsieur Gironac was intimate, and practised several hours every day. Fortune appeared inclined to favour me, for I obtained employment from four different channels.

The first and most important was this: I went every Sunday to the Catholic Chapel with Madame Gironac, and of course I joined in the singing. On the third Sunday, as I was going out, I was touched on the arm by one of the priests, who requested to speak with me in the vestry. Madame Gironac and I followed him, and he requested us to sit down.

"Who have I the pleasure of addressing?" said he to me.

"Mademoiselle de Chatenœuf, sir," replied I.

"I am not aware of your circumstances, mademoiselle," said he, "but the name is one well known in France. Still those who hold our best names are very often not in affluent circumstances in this country. I trust, let it be as it may, that you will not be offended, but the fact is, your singing has been much admired, and we would wish for your service, gratuitous, if you are in good circumstances, but well paid for, if you are not, in the choir."

"Mademoiselle de Chatenœuf is not, I am sorry to say, in good circumstances, monsieur," replied Madame Gironac.

"Then I will promise that she shall be well rewarded for her exertions, if she will consent to sing in the chapel—but do you consent?"

"I have no objection, sir," replied I.

"Allow me, then, to call the gentleman who presides over the choir," said the priest, going out.

"Accept by all means, Mademoiselle Valerie. It will be an introduction for you as a music-mistress, and very advantageous."

"I agree with you," replied I, "and I like singing sacred music."

The priest returned with a gentleman, who told me that he had listened with great pleasure to my singing, and begged, as a favour, that I would sing him a solo, which he had brought with him.

As I could sing at sight, I did so. He was satisfied, and it was agreed that I should come on Saturday, at twelve, to practise with the rest of the choir. The following Sunday, I sang with them, and also sang the solos. After the service was over, I received three guineas for my performance, and was informed that a similar sum would be given to me every Sunday on which I sang. My voice was much admired; and when it was known that I gave lessons, I very soon had engagements from many Catholic families. My charges to them were moderate,—five shillings a lesson of one hour.

The next channel was through Monsieur and Madame Gironac. He recommended me to a gentleman whom he taught, as a music-mistress for his sisters and daughters, and she to all her various customers and employers. I soon obtained several pupils by her exertions. The third was from an intimacy I had formed with an acquaintance of Madame Gironac, with a Mademoiselle Adèle Chabot, who was of a good French family, but earning her livelihood as a French teacher in one of the most fashionable schools at Kensington.

Through her recommendation, I obtained the teaching of the young ladies at the school,—but of her more hereafter. The fourth channel was through the kindness of Mr. Selwyn, the lawyer, to whom I shall now again revert. I had several visits from Mr. Selwyn after I had left Baker-street, and on one of these he informed me, that upon the proofs of Lionel Dempster's identity being examined by the legal advisers of Mr. Dempster, of Yorkshire, they were considered so positive, that the aforenamed gentleman immediately came to terms, agreeing to give up the property to Lionel, provided, in consequence of the great improvements he had made, he was not come upon for arrears of income arising from it. That Mr. Selwyn advised this offer to be accepted, as it would prevent any exposure of Lady R——, and the circumstances under which Lionel had been brought up, from being made public. Lionel had written to say that he was anxious that any sacrifice should be made rather than the affair should be exposed; and the terms were consented to, and Lionel came into possession of further property to the amount of £900 per annum. As we became more intimate, Mr. Selwyn asked me many particulars relative to myself, and, by his habit of cross-examining, soon gained the best portion of my history; only one point I did not mention to him,—that my family supposed that I was dead.

CHAPTER X.

One day he came, accompanied by Mrs. Selwyn, who joined him very earnestly in requesting me to pass a day or two with them at their country house at Kew. I accepted the invitation, and they called for me in their carriage on their way down. It was summer time, and I was very glad to be out of London for a day or two. I found a charming family of two sons and three daughters, grown up, and who appeared very accomplished. Mr. Selwyn then, for the first time, asked me whether I was settled or not.

I told him no,—that I was giving lessons in music—that I sang at the chapel, and that I was laying by money.

He said I was right, and that he hoped to be able to procure me pupils; "But now," said he, "as I did not know that you had a voice, I must be permitted to hear it, as otherwise I shall not be able to make my report."

I sat down immediately and sang, and he and Mrs. Selwyn, as well as the daughters, were highly pleased with my performance. During my stay, Mr. Selwyn treated me in, I may say, almost a parental manner, and extracted something more from me relative to my previous life, and he told me that he thought I had done wisely in remaining independent, and not again trusting to Lady M—— or Madame d'Albret. I went afterwards several times to their town house, being invited to evening parties, and the people who were there and heard my singing, sent for me to teach their daughters.

In six months after I had taken up my residence with the Gironacs, I was in flourishing circumstances. I had twenty-eight pupils, ten at five shillings per lesson, and eight at seven shillings, and they took lessons twice a week. I had also a school, for which I received about five guineas per week, and the singing at the chapel, for which I received three. In fact, I was receiving about eighteen pounds a week during the winter season; but it must be confessed that I worked hard for it, and expended two or three pounds a week in coach-hire. Nevertheless, although I now spent more money on my appearance, and had purchased a piano, before the year was over, I had paid £250 into Mr. Selwyn's hands to take care of for me. When I thought of what might have still been my position had it not been for the kindness of poor Lady R——; when I reflected how I had been cast upon the world, young and friendless, by Madame d'Albret, and that I was now making money rapidly by my own exertions, and that at such an early age (for I was but little past twenty years old), had I not reason to be grateful? I was so, and most truly so, and, moreover, I was happy, truly happy. All my former mirth and vivacity, which had been checked during my sojourn in England, returned. I improved every day in good looks, at least so every body told me but Mr. Selwyn; and I gained that, which to a certain degree my figure required, more roundness and expansion. And this was the poor Valerie, supposed to have been drowned in the river Seine!

I forgot to say, that about three weeks after Lionel went to Paris, I received a letter from Madame d'Albret, in which she thanked me warmly for my having introduced the young Englishman to her, as she took it as a proof of my really having forgiven her what she never should forgive herself. She still indulged the hope that she might one day embrace me. With respect to Lionel, she said that he appeared a modest, unassuming young lad, and that it should not be her fault if he did not turn out an accomplished gentleman; that he had already the best fencing and music-masters, and was working very hard at the language. As soon as he could speak French tolerably, he was to commence German and Italian. She had procured him a *pension* in an excellent French family, and he appeared to be very happy.

I could not help reflecting, as I read the contents of this letter, upon the change which had taken place in Lionel Dempster, as soon as he found himself established in his rights. From an impudent, talkative page, he at once became a modest, respectful, and silent young man. What could have caused this change? Was it because, when a page, he felt himself above his condition; and now that he had gained a name and fortune, that he felt himself beneath it? I decided, when I remembered how anxious he was to improve himself, that such was the case; and I further inferred that it showed a noble, generous, and sensitive mind. And I now felt very glad that I had written to Madame d'Albret, and all my objections to seeing her again were removed. Why so? because I was independent. It was my dependence that made me so proud and unforgiving. In fact, I was on better terms with the world, now that I had somewhat raised myself in it. I was one day talking over my life with Mr. Selwyn, and after pointing out how I had been taken in by my ignorance and confidence; how much wiser I had become already from experience, and my hopes that I should one day cease to be a dupe, he replied,

"My dear Miss Valerie, do not say so. To have been a dupe is to have lived; we are dupes when we are full of the hope and warmth of youth. I am an old man; my profession has given me great knowledge of the world; knowledge of the world has made me cautious and indifferent; but this has not added to my happiness, although it may have saved my pocket. No, no; when we arrive at that point, when we warm before no affection, doubting its truth; when we have gained this age-bought experience, which has left our hearts as dry as the remainder biscuits after a long voyage—there is no happiness in this, Valerie. Better to be deceived and trust again. I almost wish that I could now be the dupe of a woman or a false friend, for I should then feel as if I were young again."

"But, sir," replied I, "your conduct is at variance with your language; why else such kindness shown to me, a perfect stranger, and one without claims upon you?"

"You over-rate my little attention, my dear Valerie; but that proves that you have a grateful heart. I speak of myself as when in contact with the world. You forget that I have domestic ties to which the heart is ever fresh. Were it not for home and the natural affections, we men would be brutes indeed. The heart, when in conflict with the world, may be compared to a plant scorched by the heat of the sun; but, in the shade of domestic repose, it again recovers its freshness for the time."

I have stated that, through the recommendation and influence of a Mademoiselle Adèle Chabot, I taught music at an establishment for young ladies at Kensington. It was what is called a finishing-school. The terms were very high, and the young ladies did not always sit down to boiled mutton; but, from what I learned from Adèle, in other points it was not better than schools in general; but it had a reputation, and that was sufficient.

One day, I was informed by Mrs. Bradshaw, the proprietress of the establishment, that I was to have a new pupil the next quarter, which was very near; and when it did arrive, and the young lady was brought in, who should it be but Caroline, my former companion and pupil at Madame Bathurst's?

"Valerie!" exclaimed she, rushing into my arms.

"My dear Caroline, this is an unexpected pleasure," said I; "but how came you here?"

"I will tell you some day," replied Caroline, not wishing to talk about her family while the teacher, who came in with her, was present.

"I hope Madame Bathurst is well?" inquired I.

"Quite well, when I saw her last," said Caroline.

"Well, my dear, we must work, and not talk, for my time is valuable," said I; "so sit down, and let me hear whether you have improved since I last gave you a lesson."

The teacher then left the room, and Caroline, having run over a few bars, stopped, and said, "I never can play till I have talked to you, Valerie. You asked me how I came here. At my own request; or, if a girl may use such language, because I insisted upon it. I was so uncomfortable at home, that I could bear it no longer. I must speak against my father and mother—I cannot help it; for it is impossible to be blind; they are so strange, so conceited, so spoiled by prosperity, so haughty and imperious, and so rude and uncouth to any whom they consider beneath them, that it is painful to be in their company. Servants will not remain a month in the house—there is nothing but exchange, and everything is uncomfortable. After having lived with my aunt Bathurst, who you will acknowledge to be a lady in every respect, I really thought I was in a *Hôpital de Fous*. Such assumption, such pretension, such absurdities, to all which they wished to make me a party. I have had a wilderness of governesses, but not one would or could submit to the humiliations which they were loaded with. At last, by rebelling in every way, I gained my point, and have escaped to school. I feel that I ought not to speak disparagingly of my parents; but still I must speak the truth to you, although I would say nothing to others; so do not be angry with me, Valerie."

"I am more sorry that it is so, than that you should tell me of it, Caroline; but from what I saw during my short visit, I can fully give credit to all you have said."

"But is it not a hard case, Valerie, when you cannot respect your parents?" replied Caroline, putting her handkerchief to her eyes.

"It is, my dear; but still, on the whole, it is perhaps for the best. You were taken from your parents, and were well brought up; you return to them, and find them many degrees below you in the scale of refinement, and therefore you cannot respect them. Now, if you had never left them, you would of course have remained down at their level, and would have respected them, having imbibed the same opinions, and perceiving nothing wrong in their conduct. Now, which of the two would you prefer, if you had the power to choose?"

"Most certainly to be as I am," replied Caroline; "but I cannot but grieve that my parents should not have been like my aunt Bathurst."

"I agree with you in that feeling; but what is—is, and we must make the best of it. You must excuse your parents' faults as much as you can, since your education will not permit you to be blind to them, and you must treat them with respect from a sense of duty."

"That I have always done," replied Caroline; "but it too often happens that I have to decide between the respect I would show to my parents, and a sense of justice, or a love of truth opposed to it—that is the greatest difficulty."

"Very true," replied I, "and in such cases you must act according to the dictates of your own conscience."

"Well," replied Caroline, "I think I have done wise in getting away altogether. I have seen little of my aunt Bathurst since you took me to my father's house; for, although some advances were made towards a reconciliation, as soon as my aunt was told that my father and mother had stated that I had been most improperly brought up by her, she was so angry at the false accusation, that all intercourse is broken off, I fear, for ever. Oh, how I have longed to be with my aunt again! But, Valerie, I never heard why you left her. Some one did say that you had gone, but why was not known."

"I went away, Caroline, because I was no longer of any use in the house after you had been removed, and I did not choose to be an incumbrance to your aunt. I preferred gaining my livelihood by my own exertions, as I am now doing, and to which resolution on my part, I am indebted for the pleasure of our again meeting."

"Ah, Valerie, I never loved you so much as I did after I had lost you," said Caroline.

"That is generally the case, my dear," replied I; "but now if you please, we will try this sonata. We shall have plenty of time for talking, as we shall meet twice a week."

Caroline played the sonata, and then dropping her fingers on the keys, said, "Now, Valerie, do you know what was one of my wild dreams which assisted in inducing me to come here? I'll tell you. I know that I shall never find a husband at my father's house. All well-bred people, if they once go there, do not go a second time, and, whatever may be the merits of the daughter, they have no time to find them out, and leave the house, with the supposition that she, having been educated in so bad a school, must be unworthy of notice. Now I mean, if I can, to elope from school, that is if I can find a gentleman to my fancy—not to Gretna Green, but as soon as I am married, to go to my aunt Bathurst direct, and you know that once under a husband's protection, my father and mother have no control over me. Will you assist my views, Valerie? It's the only chance I have of happiness."

"A very pretty confession for a young lady, not yet eighteen," replied I; "and a very pretty question to put to me, who have been your governess, Caroline. I am afraid that you must not look to me for assistance, but consider it, as you termed it at first, a wild dream."

"Nevertheless, dreams come true sometimes," replied Caroline, laughing; "and all I require is birth and character: you know that I must have plenty of money."

"But, my dear Caroline, it is not people of birth and character who prowl round boarding-schools in search of heiresses."

"I know that; and that was why I asked you to help me. At all events, I'll not leave this place till I am married, or going to be married, that's certain, if I stay here till I'm twenty-five."

"Well, do not make rash resolutions; but surely, Caroline, you have not reason to complain of your parents' treatment; they are kind and affectionate towards you."

"Indeed they are not, nor were they from the time that I returned to them with you. They try by force to make me espouse their own incorrect notions of right and wrong, and it is one scene of daily altercation. They abuse and laugh at aunt Bathurst, I believe, on purpose to vex me; and, having never lived with them from my infancy, of course, when I met them, I had to learn to love them. I was willing so to do, notwithstanding their unkindness to my aunt, whom I love so dearly, but they would not let me; and now I really believe that they care little about me, and would care nothing, if I were not their only daughter, for you know, perhaps, that both my brothers are now dead?"

"I knew that one was," replied I.

"The other, William, died last year," replied Caroline; "his death was a release, poor fellow, as he had a complaint in the spine for many years. Do you know what I mean to do? I shall write to aunt Bathurst to come and see me."

"Well, I think you will be right in so doing; but will not your father and mother come to you?"

"No, for they are very angry, and say, that until I come to my senses, and learn the difference between people who are somebodies, and people who are nobodies, they will take no notice of me; and that I may remain here till I am tired; which they think I shall soon be, and write to come back again. The last words of my father, when he brought me here and left me, were,—'I leave you here to come to your senses.' He was white with anger: but I do not wish to talk any more about them."

"And your time is up, Caroline; so you must go and make room for another pupil. Miss Greaves is the next."

Shortly after my meeting with Caroline, I received a letter from Lionel, stating that it was his intention to come over to England for a fortnight, and asking whether he could execute any commissions for me in Paris, previous to his departure. He also informed me that he had received a very kind letter from his uncle, the baronet, who had had several interviews with Mr. Selwyn, and who was fully satisfied with his identity, and acknowledged him as his nephew. This gave me great pleasure. I replied to his letter, stating that I should be most happy to see him, but that as for commissions, I was too poor to give him any. Madame d'Albret had sent her kind souvenirs to me in Lionel's letter, and I returned them in my reply. Indeed, now that I was earning a livelihood, and by my own exertions, I felt that I was every day adding to my means and future independence, a great change, I may safely say for the better, took place in me. My pride was lessened, that is, my worst pride was superseded by a more honest one. I had a strange revulsion in feeling towards Madame d'Albret, Madame Bathurst, and Lady M——, and I felt that I could forgive them all. I was no longer brooding over my dependent position, fancying, perhaps, insults never intended, or irritated by real slights. Everything was *couleur de rose* with me, and that *couleur* was reflected upon everything.

"Ah, Mademoiselle Valerie," said Madame Gironac to me one day, "I had no idea when I first made your acquaintance that you were so witty. My husband and all the gentlemen say that you have *plus d'esprit* than any woman they ever conversed with."

"When I first knew you, Annette, I was not happy; now I am happy, almost too happy, and that is the reason I am so gay."

"And I don't think you hate the men so much as you did," continued she.

"I am in a humour to hate nobody," replied I.

"That is true; and, Mademoiselle Valerie, you will marry one of these days; mind," continued she, putting up her finger, "I tell you so."

"And I tell you, no," replied I. "I think there is only one excuse for a woman marrying, which is, when she requires some one to support her; that is not my case, for I thank Heaven I can support myself."

"*Nous verrons*," replied Madame Gironac.

Caroline did, however, find the restraint of a school rather irksome, and wished very much to go out with me. When the holidays arrived, and the other young ladies had gone home, I spoke to Mrs. Bradshaw, and as she was very partial to me, and knew my former relations with Caroline, she gave her consent. Shortly afterwards, Mrs. Bradshaw accepted an invitation to pass three weeks with some friends, and I then proposed that Caroline should pass the remainder of the holidays with me, to which Mrs. Bradshaw also consented, much to Caroline's delight. Madame Gironac had made up a bed for her in my room, and we were a very merry party.

A few days after Caroline came to the house, Lionel made his appearance. I should hardly have believed it possible that he could have so improved in appearance in so short a time. He brought me a very kind letter from Madame d'Albret, in which she begged, as a proof of my having forgiven her, that I would not refuse a few presents she had sent by Lionel. They were very beautiful and expensive, and, when I had had some conversation with Lionel, I made up my mind that I would not return them, which certainly I at first felt more inclined to do than to keep them. When Lionel took leave, promising to come to dinner, Caroline asked me who that gentlemanly young man was. I replied, that it was a Mr. Lionel Dempster, the nephew of Lady R——; but further conversation was interrupted by the arrival of young Mr. Selwyn, who came with a message from his father inviting me to Kew. I declined the invitation, on the plea of Caroline being with me. Mr. Selwyn remained some time conversing with me, and at last inquired if I should like to go to the next meeting at the Horticultural Gardens, at the same time offering me two tickets. As I was anxious to see the gardens, I accepted them. He told me that his father would call for us, and his mother and sisters were to be there, and then he took leave.

"Who is Mr. Selwyn?" inquired Caroline.

I told her.

"Well," said she, "I have seen two nice young men this morning; I don't know which I like best, but I think Mr. Selwyn is the more manly of the two."

"I should think so, too, Caroline," replied I; "Mr. Selwyn is twenty-four years old, I believe, and Mr. Dempster is younger, I think, than you are."

"I did not think he was so young; but, Valerie, are we not to go to the National Gallery?"

"Yes, when Monsieur Gironac comes home to escort us; we may as well put on our bonnets, for he will be here in a few minutes."

"Oh, Valerie, how fortunate it was that I came to Mrs. Bradshaw's," said Caroline, "and that I met you! I should have been moped, that is certain, if I had not; but now I'm so happy—that's Monsieur Gironac's knock, I'm sure."

But Caroline was wrong, for it was Mademoiselle Chabot, of whom I have before spoken, who made her appearance. Mademoiselle Chabot was an acquaintance of Madame Gironac, and it was through my having become intimate with her, that I obtained the teaching at Mrs. Bradshaw's. Adèle Chabot was a very pretty person, thoroughly French, and dressed with great taste. She was the resident French teacher in Mrs. Bradshaw's establishment; and, although twenty-five years old, did not look more than eighteen; she was very amusing and rather wild, although she looked very demure. I never thought that there was anything wrong in Adèle, but, at the same time, I did not consider that Caroline would derive any good from her company, as Caroline required to be held in check as it was. But, as is usually the case, the more I attempted to check any intimacy between them, the more intimate they became. Adèle was of a good family; her father had fallen at Montmartre, when the allies entered Paris after the battle of Waterloo: but the property left was very small to be divided among a large family, and consequently Adèle had first gone out as a governess at Paris, and ultimately accepted the situation she now held. She spoke English remarkably well, indeed, better than I ever heard it spoken by a French-woman; and everybody said so as well as me.

"Well, Adèle, I thought you were at Brighton," said Caroline.

"I was yesterday, and I am here to-day; I am come to dine with you," replied Adèle, taking off her bonnet and shawl, and smoothing her hair before the glass. "Where's Madame Gironac?"

"Gone out to give a lesson in flower-making," replied I.

"Yes, she is like the little busy bees, always on the wing, and, as the hymn says, 'How neat she spreads her wax!' and Monsieur, where is he?"

"Gone out to give a lesson, also," replied I.

"Yes, he's like the wind, always blowing, one hour the flute, another the French horn, then the bassoon or the bugle, always blowing and always shifting from one point to the other; never a calm with him, for when he comes home there's a breeze with his wife, *à l'aimable*, to be sure."

"Yes," replied Caroline, "always blowing, but never coming to blows."

"You are witty, Mademoiselle Caroline," said Adèle, "with your paradox. Do you know that I had an adventure at Brighton, and I am taken for you, by a very fashionable young man?"

"How can you have been taken for me?" said Caroline.

"The gentleman wished to find out who I was, and I would not tell him. He inquired of the chambermaid of the lodging-house, and bribed her, I presume, for the next day she came up to my room and asked me for my card, that her mistress might write my name down correctly in the book. I knew that the mistress had not sent her, as I had, by her request, entered my own name in the book three days before, and I was therefore certain that it was to find out who I was for the gentleman who followed me everywhere. I recollected that I had a card of yours in my case, and I gave it to her very quietly, and she walked off with it. The next day, when I was at the library, the gentleman addressed me by your name; I told him that it was not my name, and requested that he would not address me again. When I left Brighton yesterday, I discovered the chambermaid copying the addresses I had put on my trunks, which was your name, at

Mrs. Bradshaw's; so now I think we shall have some fun."

"But, my dear Adèle, you have not been prudent; you may compromise Caroline very much," said I; "recollect that men talk, and something unpleasant may occur from this want of discretion on your part."

"Be not afraid, Valerie; I conducted myself with such prudery that an angel's character could not suffer."

"I do not mean to hint otherwise, Adèle; but still you must acknowledge that you have done an imprudent thing."

"Well, I do confess it; but, Valerie, every one has not your discretion and good sense. At all events, if I see or hear any more of the gentleman, I can undo it again,—but that is not very likely."

"We have had two gentlemen here to-day, Adèle," said Caroline, "and one dines with us."

"Indeed; well, I'm in *demi-toilette*, and must remain so, for I cannot go all the way back to Mrs. Bradshaw's to dress."

"He is a very handsome young man, is he not, Valerie?"

"Yes," replied I, "and of large fortune, too."

"Well, I shall not have a fair chance, then," said Adèle, "for go back I cannot."

"Now, Adèle, you know how much more becoming the *demi-toilette* is to you than the evening dress," replied Caroline, "so don't pretend to deny it."

"I deny nothing, and I admit nothing," replied Adèle, laughing, "except that I am a woman, and now draw your own inferences and conclusions—*ce m'est égal*."

We had a very pleasant dinner-party. Adèle tried to flirt with Lionel, but it was in vain. He had no attentions to throw away, except upon me; once he whispered, "I should not feel strange at being seated with others, but to be by *your* side does make me awkward. Old habits are strong, and every now and then I find myself jumping up to change your plate."

"It's a great pleasure to me, Lionel, to find you in the position you are entitled to from your birth. You will soon sit down with people of more consequence than Valerie de Chatenœuf."

"But never with any one that I shall esteem or respect so much, be they who they may," replied Lionel.

During dinner, I mentioned that Mr. Selwyn had called and engaged Caroline and me to go to the horticultural fête.

"I wish Madame Gironac was going," continued I, "she is so fond of flowers."

"Never mind, my dear Valerie; I will stay at home and earn some money."

"Madam," cried Monsieur Gironac, pretending to be very angry, and striking with his fist on the table so as to make all the wine-glasses ring, "you shall do no such thing. You shall not always oppose my wishes. You shall not stay at home and earn some money. You shall go out and spend money. Yes, madam, I will be obeyed; you shall go to the horticultural fête, and I invite Monsieur Lionel and Mademoiselle Adèle to come with us, that they may witness that I am the master. Yes, madam, resistance is useless. You shall go in a *remise de ver*, or glass-coach, as round as a pumpkin; but you shall not go in glass slippers, like Cinderella, because they are not pleasant to walk in. How Cinderella danced in them has always been a puzzle to me, ever since I was a child, and of what kind of glass they were made."

"Perhaps isinglass," said Lionel.

"No, sir, not isinglass; it must have been fairy glass; but never mind. I ask you, Madame Gironac, whether you intend to be an obedient wife, or intend to resist my commands?"

"*Barbare*," replied Madame Gironac, "am I then to be forced to go to a fête! Ah, cruel man, you'll break my heart; but I submit to my unhappy destiny. Yes, I will go in the *remise de ver*: pity me, my good friends, but you don't know that man."

"I am satisfied with your obedience, madam, and now I permit you to embrace me."

Madame Gironac, who was delighted at the idea of going to the fête, ran to her husband, and kissed him over and over again. Adèle and Lionel accepted Monsieur Gironac's invitation, and thus was the affair settled in Monsieur Gironac's queer way.

The day of the horticultural fête arrived. It was a lovely morning. We were all dressed and the glass-coach was at the door, when Mr. Selwyn arrived in his carriage, and Caroline and I stepped in. I introduced Caroline, who was remarkably well dressed, and very pretty. Mr. Selwyn had before told me that he was acquainted with Madame Bathurst, having met two or three times, and sat by her at a dinner-party. He appeared much pleased with Caroline, but could not make out how she was in my company. Of course, he asked no questions before her.

On our arrival at the gardens, we found young Mr. Selwyn waiting at the entrance to take us to Mrs. Selwyn and his sisters, who had come from their house at Kew. About half an hour afterwards, we fell in with Monsieur Gironac, madame, Adèle, and Lionel. Mr. Selwyn greeted Lionel warmly, introducing him to his family; and on my presenting the Gironacs and Adèle, was very polite and friendly, for he knew from me how kind they had been. Adèle Chabot never looked so well; her costume was most becoming; she had put on her *air mutiné*, and was admired by all that passed us. We were all grouped together close to the band, when, who should appear right in front of us but Madame Bathurst. At that time Caroline was on the one arm of Mr. Selwyn, and I on the other.

"Caroline!" exclaimed Madame Bathurst, "and you here!" turning to me.

While she remained in astonishment, Caroline ran up and kissed her.

"You recollect Mr. Selwyn, aunt, do you not?"

"Yes," said Madame Bathurst, returning the salute of Mr. Selwyn, "but still I am surprised."

"Come with me, aunt, and I will tell you all about it."

Caroline then walked to a seat at a little distance, sat down, and entered into conversation with Madame Bathurst. In a few minutes, Madame Bathurst rose, and came up to our party, with Caroline on her arm.

She first thanked Mr. Selwyn for his kindness in bringing her niece to the fête, and then turning to me, said with some emotion, as she offered her hand, "Valerie, I hope we are friends. We have mistaken each other."

I felt all my resentment gone, and took her offered hand.

She then led me aside, and said, "I must beg your pardon, Valerie, I did not——"

"Nay," replied I, interrupting her, "I was too hasty and too proud."

"You are a good, kind-hearted girl, Valerie—but let us say no more about it. Now introduce me to your friends."

I did so. Madame Bathurst was most gracious, and appeared very much struck with Adèle Chabot, and entered into conversation with her, and certainly Adèle would not have been taken for a French teacher by her appearance. There was something very aristocratic about her. While they were in converse, a very gentlemanlike man raised his hat to Madame Bathurst, as I thought, and passed on. Adèle coloured up, I observed, as if she knew him, but did not return the salute, which Madame Bathurst did.

"Do you know that gentleman, Mademoiselle Chabot?" inquired Caroline. "I thought he bowed to you, and not to aunt."

"I have seen him before," replied Adèle, carelessly "but I forget his name."

"Then I can tell you," added Madame Bathurst; "it is Colonel Jervis, a very fashionable man, but not a very great favourite of mine; not that I have anything to accuse him of particularly, except that he is said to be a very worldly man."

"Is he of good family?" inquired Adèle.

"Oh yes, unexceptionable on that point; but it is time for me to go. There is my party coming down the walk. Caroline, dear, I will call upon you to-morrow at three o'clock, and then we will make our arrangements."

Madame Bathurst then bade adieu to Mr. Selwyn and the rest, saying to me, "*Au revoir*, Valerie."

Shortly afterwards we agreed to leave. As Mr. Selwyn was returning to Kew, I would not accept the offer of his carriage to take Caroline and me to London, the glass-coach, round as a pumpkin, would hold six, and we all went away together.

I was very much pleased at thus meeting with Madame Bathurst, and our reconciliation, and quite as much so for Caroline's sake; for although she had at first said that she would write to her aunt, she had put it off continually, for reasons which she had never expressed to me. I rather think that she feared her aunt might prove a check on her, and I was, therefore, very glad that they had met, as now Madame Bathurst would look after her.

During the evening, I observed that Adèle and Caroline

had a long conversation *sotto voce*. I suspected that the gentleman, at whose appearance she had coloured up, was the subject of it. The next day Madame Bathurst called, and heard a detailed account of all that had passed from Caroline and from me since we had parted. She said, that as Caroline was put to the school by her father, of course she could not remove her, but that she would call and see her as often as she could. She congratulated me upon my little independence, and trusted that we should ever be on friendly terms, and that I would come and visit her whenever my avocations would permit me. As there were still three weeks of the holidays remaining, she proposed that we should come and pass a portion of the time with her at a villa which she had upon the banks of the Thames.

She said that Caroline's father and mother were down at Brighton, giving very gay parties. Having arranged the time that the carriage should come for us on the following day, she kissed us both affectionately, and went away.

The next day we were at Richmond, in a delightful cottage *ornée;* and there we remained for more than a fortnight. To me it was a time of much happiness, for it was like the renewal of old times, and I was sorry when the visit was over.

On my return, I found a pressing invitation for Caroline and me to go to Kew, and remain two or three days; and as we had still time to pay the visit, it was accepted; but, before we went, Adèle came to see us, and, after a little general conversation, requested that she might speak to me in my own room.

"Valerie," said Adèle, as soon as we were seated, "I know that you think me a wild girl, and perhaps I am so; but I am not quite so wild as I thought myself; for now that I am in a critical position, I come to you for advice, and for advice against my own feelings, for I tell you frankly, that I am very much in love—and moreover—which you may *well* suppose, most anxious to be relieved from the detestable position of a French teacher in a boarding-school. I now have the opportunity, and yet I dread to avail myself of it, and I therefore come to you, who are so prudent and so sage, to request, after you have heard what I have to impart, you will give me your real opinion as to what I ought to do. You recollect I told you that a gentleman had followed me at Brighton, and how for mere frolic I had led him to suppose that I was Caroline Stanhope, I certainly did not expect to see him again, but I did three days after I came up from Brighton. The girl had evidently copied the address on my trunk for him, and he followed me up, and he accosted me as I was walking home. He told me that he had never slept since he had first seen me, and that he was honourably in love with me. I replied that he was mistaken in supposing that I was Caroline Stanhope; that my name was Adèle Chabot, and that now that I had stated the truth to him, he would alter his sentiments. He declared that he should not, pressed me to allow him to call, which I refused, and such was our first interview.

I did not see him again until at the horticultural fête, when I was talking to Madame Bathurst. He had told me that he was an officer in the army, but he did not mention his name. You recollect what Madame Bathurst said about him, and who he was. Since you have been at Richmond, he has contrived to see me every day, and I will confess that latterly I have not been unwilling to meet him, for every day I have been more pleased with him. On our first meeting after the fête, I told him that he still supposed me to be Caroline Stanhope, and that seeing me walking with Caroline's aunt had confirmed him in his idea; but I assured him that I was Adèle Chabot, a girl without fortune, and not, as he supposed, a great heiress. His answer was, that any acquaintance of Madame Bathurst's must be a lady, and that he had never inquired or thought about my fortune. That my having none would prove the disinterestedness of his affection for me, and that he required me and nothing more. I have seen him every day almost since then; he has given me his name, and made proposals to me, notwithstanding my reiterated assertions that I am Adèle Chabot, and not Caroline Stanhope. One thing is certain, that I am very much attached to him, and if I do not marry him, I shall be very miserable for a long time:" and here Adèle burst into tears.

"But why do you grieve, Adèle?" said I; "you like him, and he offers to marry you. My advice is very simple,—marry him."

"Yes," replied Adèle, "if all was as it seems. I agree with you that my course is clear; but, notwithstanding his repeated assertions that he loves me as Adèle Chabot, I am convinced in my own mind that he still believes me to be Caroline Stanhope. Perhaps he thinks that I am a romantic young lady who is determined to be married *pour ses beaux yeux* alone, and conceals her being an heiress on that account, and he therefore humours me by pretending to believe that I am a poor girl without a shilling. Now, Valerie, here is my difficulty. If I were to marry him, as he proposes, when he comes to find out that he has been deceiving himself, and that I am not the heiress, will he not be angry, and perhaps disgusted with me—will he not blame me instead of himself, as people always do, and will he not ill-treat me? If he did, it would break my heart, for I love him—love him dearly. Then, on the other hand, I may be wrong, and he may be, as he says, in love with Adèle Chabot; so that I shall have thrown away my chance of happiness from an erroneous idea. What shall I do, Valerie? Do advise me."

"Much will depend on the character of the man, Adèle. You have some insight into people's characters, what idea have you formed of his?"

"I hardly can say; for when men profess to be in love, they are such deceivers. Their faults are concealed, and they assume virtues which they do not possess. On my first meeting with him, I thought that he was a proud man—perhaps I might say a vain man—but, since I have seen more of him, I think I was wrong."

"No, Adèle, depend upon it you were right; at that time you were not blinded as you are now. Do you think him a good-tempered man?"

"Yes, I firmly believe that he is. I made a remark at Brighton: a child that had its fingers very dirty ran out to him, and as it stumbled printed the marks of its fingers upon his white trousers, so that he was obliged to return home and change them. Instead of pushing the child away, he saved it from falling, saying, 'Well, my little man, it's better that I should change my dress than that you should have broken your head on the pavement.'"

"Well, Adèle, I agree with you that it is a proof of great good temper."

"Well, then, Valerie, what do you think?"

"I think that it is a lottery; but all marriages are lotteries, with more blanks than prizes. You have done all you can to undeceive him, if he still deceives himself. You can do no more. I will assume that he does deceive himself, and that disappointment and irritation will be the consequence of his discovery, that you have been telling the truth. If he is a vain man, he will not like to acknowledge to the world that he has been his own dupe. If he is a good-hearted man, he will not long continue angry; but, Adèle, much depends upon yourself. You must forbear all recrimination—you must exert all your talents of pleasing to reconcile him to his disappointment; and, if you act wisely, you will probably succeed: indeed, unless the man is a bad-hearted man, you must eventually succeed. You best know your own powers, and must decide for yourself."

"It is that feeling—that almost certain feeling that I shall be able to console him for his disappointment, that impels me on. Valerie, I will make him love me, I am determined."

"And when a woman is determined on that point, she invariably succeeds in the end, Adèle. This is supposing that he is deceiving himself, which may not be the case, Adèle; for I do think you have sufficient attractions to make a man love you for yourself alone; and recollect that such may be the case in the present instance. It may be that at first he followed you as an heiress, and has since found out that if not an heiress, you are a very charming woman, and has in consequence been unable to resist your influence. However, there is only one to whom the secrets of the heart are known. I consider that you have acted honourably, and if you choose to risk the hazard of the die, no one can attach blame to you."

"Thank you, Valerie; you have taken a great load off my heart. If you think I am not doing wrong, I will risk everything."

"Well, Adèle, let you decide how you may, I hope you will prosper. For my part, I would not cross the street for the best man that ever was created. As friends, they are all very well; as advisers, in some cases. they are useful; but when you talk of marrying one, and becoming his slave, that is quite another affair. What were you and Caroline talking about so earnestly in the corner?"

"I will confess the truth, it was of love and marriage, with an episode about Mr. Charles Selwyn, of whom Caroline appears to have a very good opinion."

"Well, Adèle, I must go down again now. If you wish any advice at any future time, such as it is, it is at your service. You are making 'A Bold Stroke for a Husband,' that's certain. However, the title of another play is 'All's Well that Ends Well.'"

"Well, I will follow out your playing upon plays, Valerie, by saying that with you 'Love's Labour's Lost.'"

"Exactly," replied I, "because I consider it 'Much Ado About Nothing.'"

The next day, Lionel came to bid me farewell, as he was returning to Paris. During our sojourn at Madame Bathurst's, he had been down to see his uncle, and had been very kindly received. I wrote to Madame d'Albret, thanking her for her presents, which, valuable as they were, I would not return after what she had said, and confided to Lionel a box of the flowers in wax that I was so successful in imitating, and which I requested her to put on her side-table in remembrance of me. Mr. Selwyn sent the carriage at the time appointed, and we went down to Kew, where I was as kindly received as before.

What Adèle told me of the conversation between Caroline and her made me watchful, and before our visit was out, I had made up my mind that there was a mutual feeling between her and young Mr. Selwyn. When we were going away, this was confirmed, but I took no notice. But although I made no remark, this commencement of an attachment between Caroline and him occupied my mind during the whole of our journey to town.

In Caroline's position, I was not decided if I would encourage it and assist it. Charles Selwyn was a gentleman by birth and profession, a very good-looking and very talented young man. All his family were amiable, and he himself remarkably kind-hearted and well-disposed. That Caroline was not likely to return to her father's house, where I felt assured that she was miserable, was very evident, and that she would soon weary of the monotony of a school at her age was also to be expected. There was, therefore, every probability that she would, if she found an opportunity, run away, as she stated to me she would, and it was ten chances to one that in so doing she would make an unfortunate match, either becoming the prey of some fortune-hunter, or connecting herself with some thoughtless young man.

Could she do better than marry Mr. Selwyn? Certainly not. That her father and mother, who thought only of dukes and earls, would give their consent, was not very likely. Should I acquaint Madame Bathurst? That would be of little use, as she would not interfere. Should I tell Mr. Selwyn's father? No. If a match at all, it must be a runaway match, and Mr. Selwyn, senior, would never sanction anything of the kind. I resolved, therefore, to let the affair ripen as it might. It would occupy Caroline, and prevent her doing a more foolish thing, even if it were to be ultimately broken off by unforeseen circumstances. Caroline was as much absorbed by her own thoughts as I was during the ride, and not a syllable was exchanged between us till we were roused by the rattling over the stones.

"My dear Caroline, what a reverie you have been in," said I.

"And you, Valerie."

"Why, I have been thinking; certainly, when I cannot have a more agreeable companion, I amuse myself with my own thoughts."

"Will you tell me what you have been thinking about?"

"Yes, Caroline, provided you will be equally confiding."

"I will, I assure you."

"Well, then, I was thinking of a gentleman."

"And so was I," replied Caroline.

"Mine was a very handsome, clever young man."

"And so was mine," replied she.

"But I am not smitten with him," continued I.

"I cannot answer that question," replied Caroline, "because I do not know who you were thinking about."

"You must answer the question as to the gentleman you were thinking of, Caroline. I repeat that I am not smitten with him, and that his name is Mr. Charles Selwyn."

"I was also thinking of Mr. Charles Selwyn," replied Caroline.

"And you are not smitten with him any more than I

am, or he is with you?" continued I, smiling, and looking her full in the face.

Caroline coloured, and said,

"I like him very much from what I have seen of him, Valerie; but, recollect, our acquaintance has been very short."

"A very proper answer, my dear Caroline, and given with due maidenly decorum—but here we are; and there is Madame Gironac nodding to us from the window."

The next day Caroline went back to Mrs. Bradshaw's, and I did not see her till the music-lesson of Wednesday afterwards. Caroline, who had been watching for me, met me at the door.

"Oh! Valerie, I have a great deal to tell. In the first place, the establishment is in an uproar at the disappearance of Adèle Chabot, who has removed her clothes, and gone off without beat of drum. One of the maids states that she has several times seen her walking and talking with a tall gentleman, and Mrs. Bradshaw thinks that the reputation of her school is ruined by Adèle's flight. She has drunk at least two bottles of Eau-de-Cologne and water to keep off the hysterics, and is now lying on the sofa, talking in a very incoherent way. Miss Phipps says she thinks her head is affected."

"I should think it was," replied I. "Well, is that all?"

"All! why, Valerie, you appear to think nothing of an elopement. All! why, is it not horrible?"

"I do not not think it very horrible, Caroline; but I am glad to find that you have such correct ideas on that point, as it satisfies me that nothing would induce you to take such a step."

"Well," replied Caroline, quickly, "what I had also to communicate is, that I have seen my father, who informed me that on their return from Brighton in October, they expect that I will come home. He said that it was high time that I was settled in life, and that I could not expect to be married if I remained at a boarding-school."

"Well, and what did you say?"

"I said that I did not expect to be married, and I did not wish it; that I thought my education was far from complete, and that I wished to improve myself."

"Well?"

"Then he said that he should submit to my caprices no longer, and that I should go back in October, as he had decided."

"Well?"

"Well, I said no more, and he went away."

Having received all this intelligence, I went upstairs. I found Mrs. Bradshaw crying bitterly, and she threw herself into my arms.

"Oh, Mademoiselle Chatenœuf!—the disgrace!—the ruin!—I shall never get over it," exclaimed she.

"I see no disgrace or ruin, Mrs. Bradshaw. Adèle has told me that a gentleman had proposed marriage to her, and asked my advice."

"Indeed!" exclaimed Mrs. Bradshaw.

"Yes."

"Well, that alters the case; but still, why did she leave in this strange way?"

"I presume the gentleman did not think it right that she should marry out of a young ladies' establishment, madam."

"Very true: I did not think of that."

"After all, what is it? Your French teacher is married—surely that will not injure your establishment?"

"No, certainly—why should it?—but the news came upon me so abruptly, that it quite upset me. I will lie down a little, and my head will soon be better."

Time went on; so did the school. Miss Adèle, that was, sent no wedding-cake, much to the astonishment of the young ladies; and it was not till nearly three weeks afterwards that I had a letter from Adèle Chabot, now Mrs. Jervis. But, before I give the letter to my readers, I must state, that Mr. Selwyn, junior, had called upon me the day before Caroline went to school, and had had a long conversation with her, while I went out to speak with Madame Gironac on business: further, that Mr. Selwyn, junior, called upon me a few days afterwards, and after a little common-place conversation, *à l'anglaise*, about the weather, he asked after Miss Caroline Stanhope, and then asked many questions. As I knew what he wished, I made to him a full statement of her position, and the unpleasant predicament in which she was placed. I also stated my conviction that she was not likely to make a happy match, if her husband were selected by her father and mother; and how much I regretted it, as she was a very amiable, kind-hearted girl, who would make an excellent wife to any one deserving of her. He thought so too, and professed great admiration of her; and having, as he thought, pumped me sufficiently, he took his leave.

A few days afterwards, he came upon some pretended message from his father, and then I told him that she was to be removed in October. This appeared to distress him; but he did not forget to pull out of his pocket a piece of music, sealed up, telling me that, by mistake, Caroline had left two pieces of music at Kew, and had taken away one belonging to his sister Mary; that he returned one, but the other was mislaid, and would be returned as soon as it was found; and would I oblige him so far as to request Miss Stanhope to send him the piece of music belonging to his sister, if she could lay her hand upon it?

"Well, I will do your bidding, Mr. Selwyn," replied I; "it is a very proper message for a music-mistress to take; and I will also bring back your sister's music, when Caroline gives it me, and you can call here for it. If I am out, you can ask Madame Gironac to give it to you." Upon which, with many thanks and much gratitude for my kindness, Mr. Selwyn withdrew.

Having made all this known to the reader, he shall now have the contents of Adèle's letter.

CHAPTER XI.

We must now read Adèle's letter.

"My dear Valerie,—

"The die is cast, and I have now a most difficult game to play. I have risked all upon it, and the happiness of my future life is at stake. But let me narrate what has passed since I made you my confidante. Of course, you must know the day on which I was missing. On that day I walked out with him, and we were in a few minutes joined by a friend of his, whom he introduced as Major Argat. After proceeding about one hundred yards farther we arrived at a chapel, the doors of which were open, and the verger looking out, evidently expecting somebody.

"'My dear angel,' said the colonel, 'I have the license in my pocket; I have requested the clergyman to attend, he is now in the chapel, and all is ready. My friend will be a witness, and there are others in attendance. You have said that you love me, trust yourself to me. Prove now that you are sincere, and consent at once that our hands as well as our hearts be united.'

"Oh! how I trembled. I could not speak. The words died away upon my lips. I looked at him imploringly. He led me gently, for my resistance was more in manner than in effect, and I found myself within the chapel, the verger bowing as he preceded us, and the clergyman waiting at the altar. To retreat appeared impossible; indeed I hardly felt as if I wished it, but my feelings were so excited that I burst into tears. What the clergyman may have thought of my conduct, and my being dressed so little like a bride, I know not; but the colonel handed the license to his friend, who took it to the clergyman while I was recovering myself. At last we went up to the altar, my head swam, and I hardly knew what was said, but I repeated the responses, and I was—a wife. When the ceremony was over, and I was attempting to rise from my knees, I fell, and was carried by the colonel into the vestry, where I remained on a chair trembling with fear. After a time, the colonel asked me if I was well enough to sign my name to the marriage register, and he put the pen in my hand. I could not see where to sign, my eyes were swimming with tears. The clergyman guided my hand to the place, and I wrote Adèle Chabot. The knowledge what the effect of this signature might possibly have upon my husband quite overcame me, and I sank my head down upon my hands upon the table.

"'I will send for a glass of water, sir,' said the clergyman, leaving the vestry to call the verger, or clerk; 'the lady is fainting.'

"After he went out, I heard the colonel and his friend speaking in low tones apart. Probably they thought that I was not in a condition to pay attention to them,—but I had too much at stake.

"'Yes' replied the colonel, 'she has signed, as you

say, but she hardly knows what she is about. Depend upon it, it is as I told you.'

"I did not hear the major's reply, but I did what the colonel said.

"'It's all the better; the marriage will not be legal, and I can bring the parents to my own terms.'

"All doubt was now at an end. He had married me convinced, and still convinced that I was Caroline Stanhope, and not Adèle Chabot, and he had married me supposing that I was an heiress. My blood ran cold, and in a few seconds I was senseless, and should have fallen under the table, had they not perceived that I was sinking, and ran to my support. The arrival of the clergyman with the water recovered me. My husband whispered to me that it was time to go, and that a carriage was at the door. I do not recollect how I left the church; the motion of the carriage first roused me up, and a flood of tears came to my relief. How strange it is, Valerie, that we should be so courageous and such cowards at the same time. Would you believe, when I had collected myself, with a certain knowledge that my husband had deceived himself—a full conviction of the danger of my position when he found out his mistake, and that my future happiness was at stake—I felt glad that the deed was done, and would not have been unmarried again for the universe. As I became more composed, I felt that it was time to act. I wiped away my tears and said, as I smiled upon my husband, who held my hand in his, 'I know that I have behaved very ill, and very foolishly, but I was so taken by surprise.'

"'Do you think that I love you the less for showing so much feeling, my dearest?' he replied; 'no, no, it only makes you still more dear to me, as it convinces me what a sacrifice you have made for my sake.'

"Now, Valerie, could there be a prettier speech, or one so apparently sincere, from a newly-married man to his bride, and yet recollect what he said to his friend not a quarter of an hour before, about having my parents in his power by the marriage not being legal? I really am inclined to believe that we have two souls, a good and an evil one, continually striving for the mastery; one for this world, and the other for the next, and that the evil one will permit the good one to have its influence, provided that at the same time it has its own or an equal share in the direction of us. For instance, I believe the colonel was sincere in what he said, and really does love me, supposing me to be Caroline Stanhope, with the mundane advantages to be gained by the marriage, and that these better feelings of humanity are allowed to be exercised, and not interfered with by the adverse party, who is satisfied with its own Mammon share. But the struggle is to come when the evil spirit finds itself defrauded of its portion, and then attempts to destroy the influence of the good. He does love me now, and will continue to love me, if disappointment shall not tear up his still slightly-rooted affections. Now comes my task to cherish and protect it, till it has taken firm root, and all that woman can do shall be done. I felt that all that I required was time.

"'Where are we going?' said I.

"'About twenty miles from London,' replied my husband, 'after which, that is to-morrow, you shall decide upon our future plans.'

"'I care not where,' replied I; 'with you, place is indifferent, only do not refuse me the first favour that I request of you.'

"'Depend upon it I will not,' replied he.

"'It is this, dearest, take me where you will, but let it be three months before we return or come near London. You must feel my reason for making this request.'

"'I grant it with pleasure,' replied he; 'for three months I am yours, and yours only. We will live for one another.'

"'Yes, and never let us mention anything about future prospects, but devote the three months to each other.'

"'I understand you,' replied the colonel, 'and I promise you it shall be so. I will have no correspondence even—there shall be nothing to annoy you or vex you in any way.'

"'For three months,' said I, extending my hand.

"'Agreed,' said he; 'and to tell you the truth, it would have been my own feeling, had it not been yours. When you strike iron, you should do it when it is hot, but when you have to handle it, you had better wait till it is cool; you understand me, and now the subject is dropped.

"My husband has adhered most religiously to his word up to the present time, as you will see by the date of this letter. We are now visiting the lakes of Cumberland. Never could a spot be better situated for the furtherance of my wishes. The calm repose and silent beauty of these waters must be reflected upon the mind of any one of feeling, which the colonel certainly does not want; and when you consider that I am exerting all the art which poor woman has to please, I do hope and pray to heaven that I may succeed in entwining myself round his heart before his worldly views are destroyed by disappointment. Pray for me, dear Valerie—pray for one who loves you dearly, and who feels that the whole happiness of her life is at stake. "Yours, "Adèle."

"So far all goes well, my dear Adèle," thought I; "but we have yet to see the end. I will pray for you with all my heart, for you deserve to be happy, and none can be more fascinating than you, when you exert yourself. What is it in women that I do not feel which makes them so mad after the other sex? Instinct, certainly; for reason is against it. Well, I have no objection to help others to commit the folly, provided that I am not led into it myself." Such were my reflections as I closed the letter from Adèle.

A few days afterwards I received a note from Mr. Selwyn, junior, informing me that his father had been made a puisne judge. What that was I did not know, except that he was a judge on the bench of some kind. He also stated his intention of calling upon me on the next day.

"Yes," thought I, "to receive the music from Caroline. Of course she will return it to me when I give her a lesson to-day."

I was right in my supposition. Caroline brought me a piece of music with a note, saying, "Here is the music belonging to Miss Selwyn, Valerie; will you take an opportunity of returning it to her? Any time will do; I presume she is in no hurry;" and Caroline coloured up when her eyes met mine.

To punish her, I replied, "Oh, no, there can be no hurry; I shall be down at Kew in a fortnight or three weeks, I will take it with me then."

"But my note, thanking Mr. Selwyn, will be of very long date," replied Caroline, "and I want the other piece of music belonging to me which I left at Kew."

"Well, Caroline, you cannot expect me to be carrying your messages, and going to the chambers of a handsome young Chancery barrister. By the bye, I had a note from him this morning, telling me that his father is advanced to the bench. What does that mean?"

"That his father is made a judge. Is that all he said?" replied Caroline, carelessly.

"Why, now I think of it, he said that he would call upon me to-morrow, so I can give him this music when he calls."

At this intelligence, Caroline's face brightened up, and she went away. Mr. Selwyn called the next day, and I delivered the music and the note. He informed me that he had now all his father's private as well as Chancery business, and wished to know whether he was to consider himself my legal adviser. I replied,

"Certainly; but that he could not expect the business of a teacher of music to be very profitable."

"No, nor do I intend that it shall be, but it will be a great pleasure," replied he, very gallantly. "I hope you have some money to put by."

"Yes," replied I, "I have some, but not quite enough; by the end of the year I hope to have £500."

"I am glad that you have told me, as a profitable investment may occur before that time, and I will secure it for you."

He asked permission to read Caroline's note, and then said that he would find the other piece of music, and leave it at Monsieur Gironac's in the course of a day or two—after which he took his leave. I received that evening a letter from Lionel, which had a great effect upon me. In it he stated, that at the fencing-school he had made acquaintance with a young officer, a Monsieur Auguste de Chatenœuf,—that he had mentioned to him that he knew a lady of his name in England; that the officer had asked him what the age of the lady might be, and he had replied.

"Strange," said the officer; "I had a very dear sister, who was supposed to be drowned, although the body was never found. Can you tell me the baptismal name of the lady you mention?"

"It then occurred to me," continued Lionel, "that I might be imprudent if I answered, and I therefore said that I did not know, but I thought you had been called by your friends Annette."

"'Then it cannot be she,' replied he, 'for my sister's name was Valerie. But she may have changed her name —describe to me her face and figure.'

"As I at once felt certain that you were the party, and was aware, that the early portion of your life was never referred to by you, I thought it advisable to put him off the scent, until I had made this communication. I therefore replied, 'That (excuse me) you were very plain, with a pug nose, and very short and fat.'

"'Then it must be somebody else,' replied the officer. 'You made my heart beat when you first spoke about her, for I loved my sister dearly, and have never ceased to lament her loss.'

"He then talked a great deal of you, and gave me some history of your former life. I took the opportunity to ask whether your unnatural mother was alive, and he said, 'Yes, and that your father was also alive and well.'

"I did not dare to ask more. Have I done right or wrong, my dear Mademoiselle Chatenœuf? If wrong, I can easily repair the error. Your brother, for such I presume he is, I admire very much. He is very different from the officers of the French army in general, quite subdued, and very courteous, and there is a kind spirit in all he says, which makes me like him more. You have no idea of the feeling he showed, when he talked about you—that is, if it is you—which I cannot but feel almost certain that it is. One observation of his, I think it right to make known to you, which is, that he told me that since your supposed death, your father had never held up his head; indeed, he said that he had never seen him smile since."

The above extract from Lionel's letter created such a revulsion, that I was obliged to retire to my chamber to conceal my agitated feelings from Madame Gironac. I wept bitterly for some time. I thought of what my poor father must have suffered, and the regrets of poor Auguste at my supposed death; and I doubted whether I was justified in the act I had committed, by the treatment I had received from my mother. If she had caused me so much pain, was I right in having given so much to others who loved me? My poor father, he had never smiled since! Should I permit him to wear out his days in sorrowing for my loss—oh, no! I no longer felt any animosity against others who had ill-treated me. Surely, I could forgive even my mother, if not for love of her, at all events for love of my father and my brother. Yes, I would do so, I was now independent of my mother and all the family. I had nothing to fear from her; I could assist my family if they required it.

Such were my first feelings—but then came doubts and fears. Could not my mother claim me? insist upon my living with her? prevent my earning my livelihood? or if I did employ myself, could she not take from me all my earnings? Yes, by the law of France, I thought she could. Then again, would she forgive me the three years of remorse? the three years during which she had been under the stigma of having, by her barbarity, caused her child to commit self-destruction; the three years of reproach which she must have experienced from my father's clouded brow? Would she ever forgive me for having obtained my independence by the very talents which she would not allow me to cultivate? No, never, unless her heart was changed.

After many hours of reflection, I resolved that I would make known my existence to Auguste, and permit him to acquaint my father, under a promise of secrecy, but that I would not trust myself in France, or allow my mother to be aware of my existence, until I could ascertain what her power might be over me. But before I decided upon anything, I made up my mind that I would make a confidant, and obtain the opinion of Judge Selwyn. By the evening's post I wrote a note to him, requesting that he would let me know when I might have an interview.

An answer arrived the next day, stating, that Judge Selwyn would call and take me down with him to Kew, where I should sleep, and return to town with him on the following morning. This suited me very well, and as soon as the carriage was off the stones, I said that I was now about to confide to him that portion of my life with which he was unacquainted, and ask his advice how I ought to proceed, in consequence of some intelligence lately communicated by Lionel. I then went into the whole detail, until I arrived at my being taken away from the barracks by Madame d'Albret; the remainder of my life he knew sufficient of, and I then gave him Lionel's letter to read, and when he had done so, I stated to him what my wishes and what my fears were, and begged him to decide for me what was best to be done.

"This is an eventful history, Valerie," said the old gentleman. "I agree with you on the propriety of making your existence known to your brother, and also to your father, who has been sufficiently punished for his cowardice. Whether your father will be able to contain his secret, I doubt very much; and from what you have told me of your mother, I should certainly not trust myself in France. I am not very well informed of the laws of the country, but it is my impression that children are there under the control of their parents until they are married. Go to France I therefore would not, unless it were as a married woman: then you will be safe. When does Lionel come over?"

"He will come at any time, if I say I wish it."

"Then let him come over, and invite your brother to come with him, then you can arrange with him. I really wish you were married, Valerie, and I wish also that my son was married; I should like to be a grandfather before I die."

"With respect to my marrying, sir, I see little chance of that; I dislike the idea, and, in fact, it would be better to be with my mother at once; for I prefer an old tyranny to a new one."

"It does not follow, my dear Valerie; depend upon it, there are many happy marriages. Am I a tyrant in my own house? Does my wife appear to be a slave?"

"There are many happy exceptions, my dear sir," replied I. "With respect to your son's marrying, I think you need not despair of that; for it is my opinion that he very soon will be—but this is a secret, and I must say no more."

"Indeed," replied the judge. "I know of no one, and he would hardly marry without consulting me."

"Yes, sir, I think that he will, and I shall advise him so to do—as it is necessary that nothing should be known till it is over. Trust to me, sir, that if it does take place, you will be quite satisfied with the choice which he makes; but I must have your pledge not to say one word about it. You might spoil all."

The old judge fell back in his carriage in a reverie, which lasted some little while, and then said,

"Valerie, I believe that I understand you now. If it is as I guess, I certainly agree with you that I will ask no more questions, as I should for many reasons not wish it to appear that I know anything about it."

Soon afterwards we arrived at Kew, and, after a pleasant visit, on the following morning early, I returned to town with the judge. I then wrote to Lionel, making known to him as much as was necessary, under pledge of secrecy, and stating my wish that he should follow up my brother's acquaintance, and the next time that he came over, persuade him to accompany him; but that he was not to say anything to him relative to my being his sister, on any account whatever.

Young Selwyn called the same day that I came from Kew, with the piece of music which was missing. I made no remarks upon the fact, that the music might have been delivered to me by his sister, because I felt assured that it contained a note more musical than any in the score; I gave it to Caroline, and a few days afterwards, observing that she was pale and restless, I obtained permission for her to go out with me for the day. Mr. Selwyn happened to call a few minutes after our arrival at Madame Gironac's, and that frequently occurred for nearly two months, when the time arrived that she was to be removed from the school.

The reader will, of course, perceive that I was assisting this affair as much as I could. I admit it; and I did so out of gratitude to Mr. Selwyn's father, for his kindness to me. I knew Caroline to be a good girl, and well suited to Mr. Selwyn; I knew that she must eventually have a very large fortune; and, provided that her father and mother would not be reconciled to their daughter after the marriage, that Mr. Selwyn had the means, by his practice, of supporting her comfortably without their assistance. I considered that I did a kindness to Caroline and to Mr. Selwyn, and therefore did not hesitate; besides, I had other ideas on the subject, which eventually turned out as I expected, and proved that I was right.

On the last day of September, Caroline slipped out, and followed me to Madame Gironac's; Mr. Selwyn was ready with the license. We walked to church, the ceremony was performed, and Mr. Selwyn took his bride down to his father's house at Kew. The old judge was somewhat prepared for the event, and received her very graciously. Mrs. Selwyn and his sisters were partial to Caroline, and followed the example of the judge. Nothing could pass off more quietly or more pleasantly. For reasons which I did not explain, I requested Mr. Selwyn, for the present, not to make known his marriage to Caroline's parents, as I considered it would be attended with great and certain advantage; and he promised me that he would not only be silent upon the subject, but that all his family should be equally so.

If Mrs. Bradshaw required two bottles of Eau-de-Cologne and water to support her when she heard of the elopement of Adèle Chabot, I leave the reader to imagine how many she required when an heiress intrusted to her charge had been guilty of a similar act.

As Caroline had not left with me, I was not implicated, and the affair was most inscrutable. She had never been seen walking, or known to correspond with any young man. I suggested to Mrs. Bradshaw that it was the fear of her father removing her from her protection which had induced her to run away, and that most probably she had gone to her aunt Bathurst's. Upon this hint, she wrote to Mr. Stanhope, acquainting him with his daughter's disappearance, and giving it as her opinion that she had gone to her aunt's, being very unwilling to return home. Mr. Stanhope was furious; he immediately drove to Madame Bathurst's, whom he had not seen for a long time, and demanded his daughter. Madame Bathurst declared that she knew nothing about her. Mr. Stanhope expressed his disbelief, and they parted in high words.

A few days afterwards, the colonel and Adèle came to town, the three months acceded to her wishes having expired; and now I must relate what I did not know till some days afterwards, when I saw Adèle, and who had the narrative from her husband.

It appeared, that as soon as the colonel arrived in London, still persuaded that he had married Caroline Stanhope, and not Adèle Chabot, without stating his intention to her, he went to Grosvenor-square, and requested to see Mr. Stanhope. This was about a fortnight after Caroline's elopement with Mr. Selwyn. He was admitted, and found Mr. and Mrs. Stanhope in the drawing-room. He had sent up his card, and Mr. Stanhope received him with great hauteur.

"What may your pleasure be with me, sir? [Looking at the card.] Colonel Jervis, I think you call yourself?"

Now, Colonel Jervis was a man well known about town, and, in his own opinion, not to know him argued yourself unknown; he was therefore not a little angry at this reception, and being a really well-bred man, was also much startled with the vulgarity of both parties.

"My name, Mr. Stanhope, as you are pleased to observe," said the colonel, with hauteur, "is Jervis, and my business with you is relative to your daughter."

"My daughter, sir?"

"Our daughter! Why, you don't mean to tell us that *you* have run away with our daughter?" screamed Mrs. Stanhope.

"Yes, madam, such is the fact; she is now my wife, and I trust that she is not married beneath herself."

"A colonel!—a paltry colonel!—a match for my daughter! Why, with her fortune she might have married a duke," screamed Mrs. Stanhope. "I'll never speak to the wretch again. A colonel, indeed! I suppose a militia-colonel. I dare say you are only a captain, after all. Well, take her to barracks, and to barracks yourself. You may leave the house. Not a penny—no, not a penny do you get. Does he, Stanhope?"

"Not one half a farthing," replied Mr. Stanhope, pompously. "Go, sir; Mrs. Stanhope's sentiments are mine."

The colonel, who was in a towering passion at the treatment he received, now started up, and said, "Sir and madam, you appear to me not to understand the usages of good society, and I positively declare, that had I been aware of the insufferable vulgarity of her parents, nothing would have induced me to marry the daughter. I tell you this, because I care nothing for you. You are on the stilts at present, but I shall soon bring you to your senses; for know, sir and madam, although I did elope with and married your daughter, the marriage is not legal, as she was married under a false name, and that was her own act—not mine. You may therefore prepare to receive your daughter back, when I think fit to send her—disgraced and dishonoured; and then try if you can match her with a duke. I leave you to digest this piece of information, and now wish you good morning. You have my address, when you feel inclined to apologize, and do me the justice which I shall expect before a legal marriage takes place."

So saying, the colonel left the house; and it would be difficult to say which of the three parties was in the greatest rage.

The colonel, who had become sincerely attached to Adèle, who had well profited by the time which she had gained, returned home in no very pleasant humour. Throwing himself down on the sofa, he said to her in a moody way,

"I'll be candid with you, my dear; if I had seen your father and mother before I married you, nothing would have persuaded me to have made you my wife. When a man marries, I consider connexion and fortune to be the two greatest points to be obtained; but such animals as your father and mother I never beheld. Good Heaven! that I should be allied to such people!"

"May I ask you, dearest, to whom you refer, and what is the meaning of all this? My father and mother! Why, colonel, my father was killed at the attack of Montmartre, and my mother died before him."

"Then who and what are you," cried the colonel, jumping up; "are you not Caroline Stanhope?"

"I thank Heaven, I am not. I have always told you that I was Adèle Chabot, and no other person. You must admit that. My father and mother were no vulgar people, dearest husband, and my family is as good as most in France. Come over with me to Paris, and you will then see who my relatives and connections are. I am poor, I grant; but recollect that the revolution exiled many wealthy families, and mine among the rest, although we were permitted eventually to return to France. What can have induced you to fall into this error, and still persist (notwithstanding my assertions to the contrary), that I am the daughter of those vulgar upstarts, who are proverbial for their want of manners, and who are not admitted into hardly any society, rich as they are supposed to be?"

The colonel looked all amazement.

"I'm sorry you are disappointed, dearest," continued Adèle, "if you are so. I am sorry that I'm not Caroline Stanhope with a large fortune; but if I do not bring you a fortune, by economy I will save you one. Let me only see that you are not deprived of your usual pleasures and luxuries, and I care not what I do, or how I live. You will find no exacting wife in me, dearest, troubling you for expenses you cannot afford. I will live but to please you, and if I do not succeed, I will die—if you wish to be rid of me."

Adèle resumed her caresses with the tears running down her cheeks, for she loved her husband dearly, and felt what she said.

The colonel could not resist her: he put his arms round her and said, "Do not cry, Adèle; I believe you, and moreover, I feel that I love you. I am thankful that I have not married Caroline Stanhope, for I presume she cannot be very different from her parents. I admit that I have been deceiving myself, and that I have deceived myself into a better little wife than I deserve, perhaps. I really am glad of my escape. I would not have been connected with those people for the universe. We will do as you say: we will go to France for a short time, and you shall introduce me to your relations."

Before the next morning, Adèle had gained the victory. The colonel felt that he had deceived himself, that he might be laughed at, and that the best that could be done was to go to Paris and announce from thence his marriage in the papers. He had a sufficiency to live upon, to command luxury as well as comforts, and on the whole he was now satisfied, that a handsome and strongly-attached wife, who brought him no fortune, was preferable to a marriage of mere interest. I may as well here observe, that Adèle played her cards so well, that the colonel was a happy and contented man. She kept her promise, and he found with her management that he had more money than a married man required, and he blessed the day in which he had married by mistake. And now to return to the Stanhopes.

Although they were too angry at the time to pay much heed to the colonel's parting threats, yet when they had cooled, and had time for reflection, Mr. and Mrs. Stanhope were much distressed at the intelligence that their daughter was not legally married. For some days they remained quiet; at last they thought it advisable to come to terms, to save their daughter's honour. But during this delay on their part, Adèle had called upon me, and introduced her husband and made me acquainted with all that had passed. They stated their intention of proceeding to Paris immediately, and although I knew that Adèle's relations were of good family, yet I thought an introduction to Madame d'Albret would be of service to her. I therefore gave her one, and it proved most serviceable; for the colonel found himself in the first society in Paris, and his wife was well received and much admired. When, therefore, Mr. Stanhope made up his mind to call upon the colonel at the address of the hotel where they had put up, he found they had left, and nobody knew where they had gone. This was a severe blow, and Mr. and Mrs. Stanhope were in a state of the utmost uncertainty and suspense. Now was the time for Mr. Selwyn to come forward, and I despatched a note to him, requesting him to come to town. I put him in possession of Adèle's history, her marriage with the colonel, and all the particulars with which the reader is acquainted, and I pointed out to him how he should act when he called upon Mr. Stanhope, which I advised him to do immediately. He followed my advice, and thus described what passed on his return.

"I sent up my card to Mr. and Mrs. Stanhope, and was received almost as politely as the colonel. I made no remark, but taking a chair, which was not offered to me, I said, 'You have my card, Mr. Stanhope; I must, in addition to my name, inform you that I am a barrister, and that my father is Judge Selwyn, who now sits on the King's Bench. You probably have met him in the circles in which you visit, although you are not acquainted with him. Your sister, Madame Bathurst we have the pleasure of knowing.'

"This introduction made them look more civil; for a judge was with them somebody.

"'My object in coming here is to speak to you relative to your daughter.'

"'Do you come from the colonel, then?' said Mrs. Stanhope, sharply.

"'No, madam. I have no acquaintance with the colonel.'

"'Then how do you know my daughter, sir?'

"'I had the pleasure of meeting her at my father's.

She stayed a short time with my family at our country seat at Kew.'

"'Indeed!' exclaimed Mrs. Stanhope; 'well, I had no idea of that. I'm sure the judge was very kind; but, sir, you know that my daughter has married very unfortunately.'

"'That she has married, madam, I am aware, but I trust not unfortunately.'

"'Why, sir, she has married a colonel,—a fellow who came here and told us it was no marriage at all!'

"'It is to rectify that mistake, madam, which has induced me to call. The colonel, madam, did hear that your daughter was at Mrs. Bradshaw's establishment, and wished to carry her off, supposing that she was a very rich prize; but, madam, he made a slight mistake—instead of your daughter, he has run away and married the French teacher, who has not a sixpence. He has now found out his mistake, and is off to Paris to hide himself from the laughter of the town.'

"This intelligence was the cause of much mirth and glee to Mr. and Mrs. Stanhope; the latter actually cried with delight, and I took care to join heartily in the merriment. As soon as it had subsided, Mrs. Stanhope said,—

"'But, Mr. Selwyn, you said that my daughter was married. How is that?'

"'Why, madam, the fact is, that your daughter's affections were engaged at the time of this elopement of the colonel's, and it was her intention to make known to you that such was the case, presuming that you would not refuse to sanction her marriage; but when the elopement took place, and it was even reported that she had run away, her position became very awkward, and the more so, as some people declared (as the colonel asserted), that she was not legally married. On consulting with the gentleman of her choice, it was argued thus: If Miss Stanhope goes back to her father's house after this report that she is not legally married, it will be supposed that the colonel, finding that he was disappointed in his views, had returned her dishonoured upon her parents' hands, and no subsequent marriage would remove the impression. It was, therefore, considered advisable, both on her parents' account and on her own, that she also should elope, and then it would be easily explained that it was somebody else who had eloped with the colonel, and that Miss Stanhope had married in a secret way. Miss Stanhope, therefore, was properly married in church before respectable witnesses, and conducted immediately afterwards by her husband to his father's house, who approved of what was done, as now no reflection can be made, either upon Miss Stanhope or her respectable parents.

"'Well, let us all know the person to whom she is married.'

"'To myself, madam; and your daughter is now at Judge Selwyn's, where she has been ever since her marriage, with my mother and sisters. My father would have accompanied me, to explain all this; but the fact is, that his lordship is now so much occupied that he could not. He will, however, be happy to see Mr. Stanhope, who is an idle man, either at his town house, or at his country seat. I trust, madam, as I have the honour to be your son-in-law, you will permit me to kiss your hand?'

"'Caroline may have done worse, my dear,' said the lady to her husband, who was still wavering. 'Mr. Selwyn may be a judge himself, or he may be a Lord Chancellor, recollect that. Mr. Selwyn, you are welcome, and I shall be most happy to see his lordship, and my husband shall call upon him when we know when he will be at leisure. Oh! that colonel; but he's rightly served—a French teacher. Ha, ha, ha!' and Mrs. Stanhope's mirth was communicated to her husband, who now held out his hand to me in a most patronizing manner.

"'Well, sir, I give you joy. I believe you have saved my daughter's character; and my dear, added he, very pompously, 'we must do something for the young people.'

"'I trust, sir, I bear your forgiveness to Caroline.'

"'Yes, you do, Mr. Selwyn,' said the lady. 'Bring her here as soon as you please. Oh that colonel! ha, ha, ha! and it is capital. A French teacher. Ha, ha, ha.'"

Such was the winding-up of this second marriage. Had not Mr. and Mrs. Stanhope been much subdued by the intelligence received from the colonel of the marriage being illegal, and had they not also been much gratified at the mistake of the colonel, things might not have gone off so pleasantly. I have only to add, that Mr. Stanhope, who appeared to obey his wife in everything, called upon the judge, and their interview was very amicable. Mr. Stanhope, upon the judge stating that his son had sufficient income, immediately became profuse, and settled £2,000 per annum upon his daughter, during his life, with a promise of much more eventually. Caroline was graciously received by her mother, and presented with some splendid diamonds. The judge told me that he knew the part I had taken in the affair, and shook his finger at me.

Thus ended this affair, and Madame Gironac, when she heard how busy I had been in the two elopements, said,

"Ah, Valerie, you begin by marrying other people. You will end in finding a husband for yourself."

"That is quite another thing, madam," I replied; "I have no objection in assisting other people to their wishes, but it does not follow that therefore I am to seek for myself what I do not wish."

"Valerie, I am a prophetess. You will be married some time next year. Mark my words."

"I will not forget them, and at the end of the year we shall see who is right and who is wrong."

After all this bustle and turmoil, there was a calm, which lasted the whole winter. I followed up my usual avocations. I had as many pupils as I could attend to, and saved money fast. The winter passed away, and in the spring I expected Lionel with my brother Auguste. I looked forward to seeing my brother, with great impatience; not a day that he was out of my thoughts. I was most anxious to hear of my father, my brothers, and sisters, and every particular connected with the family; even my mother was an object of interest, although not of regard; but I had forgiven all others who had ill-treated me, and I felt that I forgave and forgot, if she would behave as a mother towards me. I had received kind letters from Madame d'Albret and Adèle; the letters of the latter were most amusing. Madame Bathurst had called upon me several times. I was at peace with all the world and with myself. At last, I received a letter from Lionel, stating that he was coming over in a few days; that he had great difficulty in persuading my brother to come with him, as he could not afford the expense out of his own means, and did not like to lie under such an obligation. At last he had been overruled, and was coming with him.

"Then I shall see you again, dear Auguste!" thought I; "you who always loved me, always protected me and took my part, and who so lamented my supposed death;" and my thoughts turned to the time when he and I were with my grandmother in the palace, and our early days were passed over in review. "My poor grandmother, how I loved you! and how you deserved to be loved!" And then I calculated what I might have been, had I been left with my grandmother, and had inherited her small property; and, on reflection, I decided that I was better off now than I probably should have been, and that all was for the best. I thought of the future, and whether it was likely I ever should marry, and I decided that I never would, but that if I ever returned to my family, I would assist my sisters, and try to make them happy.

"Yes," thought I, "marry I never will—that is *decided*—nothing shall ever induce me."

My reverie was interrupted by the entrance of a stranger, who, apologizing to me, stated that he had come to seek Monsieur Gironac.

I replied that he was not at home, and probably it would be half an hour before he returned to dinner.

"With your leave, mademoiselle," said he, gracefully bowing, "I will wait till he returns. I will not, however, trespass upon your time, if it is disagreeable; perhaps the servant will accommodate me with a chair elsewhere?"

I requested that he would be seated, as there was no fire in any other room; and he took a chair. He was a Frenchman, speaking good English; but he soon discovered that I was his countrywoman, and the conversation was carried on in French. He informed me that he was the Comte de Chavannes. But I must describe him. He was rather small in stature, but elegantly made; his features were, if anything, effeminate, but very handsome; they would have been handsome in a woman. The effeminacy was, however, relieved by a pair of moustaches, soft, silky, and curling. His manners were peculiarly fascinating, and his conversation lively and full of point. I was much pleased with him during the half-hour that we were together, during which we had kept up the conversation with much spirit. The arrival of Monsieur Gironac put an end to our *tête-à-tête*, and having arranged his business with him, which was relative to some flute-music, which the comte wished to be published, after a few minutes' more conversation, he took his leave.

"Now there's a man that I would select for your husband, Valerie," said Monsieur Gironac, after the comte had left. "Is he not a very agreeable fellow?"

"Yes he is," I replied; "he is very entertaining and very well bred. Who is he "

"His history is told in few words," replied Monsieur Gironac. "His father emigrated with the Bourbons; but, unlike most of those who emigrated, he neither turned music-master, dancing-master, hair-dresser, nor teacher of the French language. He had a little money, and he embarked in commerce. He went as supercargo, and then as travelling partner in a house to America, the Havannah, and the West Indies; and after having crossed the Atlantic about twenty times in the course of the late war, he amassed a fortune of about £40,000. At the restoration, he went to Paris, resumed his title, which he had laid aside during his commercial course, was well received by Louis XVIII., and made a colonel of the Legion of Honour. He returned to this country to settle his affairs, previous to going down to Brittany, and died suddenly, leaving the young man you have just seen, who is his only son and heir, alone on the wide world, and with a good fortune as soon as he came of age. At the time of his father's death, he was still at school. Now he is twenty-four years old, and has been for three years in possession of the property, which is still in the English funds. He appears to like England better than France, for most of his time is passed in London. He is very talented, very musical, composes well, and is altogether a most agreeable young man, and fit for the husband of Mademoiselle Valerie de Chatenœuf. Now you have the whole history; the marriage is yet to take place."

"Your last observation is correct; or rather it is not, for the marriage will never take place."

"*Mais, que voulez-vous*, mademoiselle?" cried Monsieur Gironac; "must we send for the angel Gabriel for you?"

"No," replied I, "he is not a marrying man, any more than I am a marrying woman. Is it not sufficient that I admit your count to be very agreeable?—that won't content you. You want me to marry a man whom I have seen for one half-hour. Are you reasonable, Monsieur Gironac?"

"He has rank, wealth, good looks, talent, and polished

manners; and you admit that you do not dislike him; what would you have more?"

"He is not in love with me, and I am not in love with him."

"Mademoiselle Valerie de Chatenœuf, you are *une enfant*. I will no longer trouble myself with looking out for a husband for you. You shall die a sour old maid;" and Monsieur Gironac left the room, pretending to be in a passion.

A few days after the meeting with Count de Chavannes, Lionel made his appearance. My heart beat quick as I welcomed him.

"He is here," said he, anticipating my question; "but I called just to know when we should come, and whether I was to say anything to him before he came."

"No, no, tell him nothing—bring him here directly—how long will it be before you return?"

"Not half an hour. I am at my old lodgings in Suffolk-street, so good-bye for the present;" and Lionel walked away again.

Monsieur and Madame Gironac were both out, and would not return for an hour or two. I thought the half-hour would never pass; but it did at last, and they knocked at the door. Lionel entered, followed by my brother Auguste. I was surprised at his having grown so tall and handsome.

"Madame Gironac is not at home, mademoiselle," said Lionel.

"No, Monsieur Lionel."

"Allow me to present to you Monsieur Auguste de Chatenœuf, a lieutenant in the service of his majesty the king of the French."

Auguste bowed, and, as I returned the salute, looked earnestly at me and started.

"Excuse me, mademoiselle," said he, coming up to me, and speaking in a tremulous voice; "but—yes, you must be Valerie."

"Yes, dear Auguste," cried I, opening my arms.

He rushed to me and covered me with kisses, and then staggering to a chair, sat down and wept. So did I, and so did Lionel, for sympathy and company.

"Why did you conceal this from me, Lionel?" said he, after a time · "see how you have unmanned me."

"I only obeyed orders, Auguste," replied Lionel; "but, now that I have executed my commission, I will leave you together; for you must have much to say to each other. I will join you at dinner-time."

Lionel went out and left us together; we renewed our embraces, and after we were more composed, entered into explanations. I told him my history in as few words as possible, promising to enter into details afterwards, and then I inquired about the family. Auguste replied:

"I will begin from the time of your disappearance. No one certainly had any suspicion of Madame d'Albret having spirited you away; indeed, she was, as you know, constantly at the barracks till my father left, and expressed her conviction that you had destroyed yourself. The outcry against your mother was universal; she dared not show herself, and your father was in a state to excite compassion. Four or five times a day did he take his melancholy walk down to the Morgue to ascertain if your body was found. He became so melancholy, morose, and irritable, that people were afraid lest he would destroy himself. He never went home to your mother but there was a scene of reproaches on his part, and defence on hers, that was a scandal to the barracks. All her power over him ceased from that time, and has ceased for ever since, and perhaps you know that he has retired?"

'How should I know, Auguste?"

'Yes; he could not bear to look the other officers in the face; he told me that he considered himself, from his weakness and folly, to have been the murderer of his child; that he felt himself despicable, and could not longer remain with the regiment. As soon as the regiment arrived at Lyons, he sent in his retirement, and has ever since been living at Pau, in the south of France, upon his half-pay and the other property which he possesses."

"My poor father!" exclaimed I, bursting into tears.

"As for me, you know that I obtained leave to quit the regiment, and have ever since been in the 51st of the line. I have obtained my grade of lieutenant. I have seen my father but once since I parted with him at Paris. He is much altered, and his hair is gray."

"Is he comfortable where he is, Auguste?"

"Yes, Valerie; I think that he did wisely; for it was ruinous travelling about with so many children. He is comfortable, and, I believe, as happy as he can be. Oh, if he did but know that you were alive, it would add ten years to his life."

"He shall know it, my dear Auguste," exclaimed I, as the tears coursed down my cheeks. "I feel now that I was very selfish in consenting to Madame d'Albert's proposal, but I was hardly in my senses at the time."

"I cannot wonder at your taking the step, nor can I blame you. Your life was one of torture, and it was torture to others to see what you underwent."

"I pity my father, for weak as he was, the punishment has been too severe."

"But you will make him happy now, and he will rejoice in his old days."

"And now, Auguste, tell me about Nicolas—he never liked me, but I forgive him—how is he?"

"He is, I believe, well; but he has left his home."

"Left home?"

"You know how kind your mother was to him—I may say, how she doted upon him. Well, one day he announced his intention of going to Italy, with a friend he had picked up, who belonged to Naples. His mother was frantic at the idea, but he actually laughed at her, and behaved in a very unfeeling manner. Your mother was cut to the heart, and has never got over it; but, Valerie, the children who are spoiled by indulgence, always turn out the most ungrateful."

"Have you heard of him since?"

"Yes; he wrote to me, telling me that he was leading an orchestra in some small town, and advancing rapidly—you know his talent for music—but not one line has he ever written to his mother."

"Ah me!" sighed I, "and that is all the return she has for her indulgence to him. Now tell me about Clara."

"She is well married, and lives at Tours: her husband is an *employé*, but I don't exactly know what."

"And Sophie and Elisée?"

"Are both well, and promise to grow up fine girls, but not so handsome as you are, Valerie. It was the wonderful improvement in your person that made me doubt for a moment when I first saw you."

"And dear little Pierre, that I used to pinch that I might get out of the house, poor fellow?"

"Is a fine boy, and makes his father very melancholy, and his mother very angry, by talking about you."

"And now, Auguste, one more question. On what terms are my father and mother, and how does she conduct herself?"

"My father treats her with ceremony and politeness, but not with affection. She has tried every means to resume her empire over him, but finds it impossible, and she has now turned *dévote.* They sleep in separate rooms, and he is very harsh and severe to her at times, when the fit comes on him. Indeed, Valerie, if you sought revenge, which I know you do not do, you have had sufficient; for her brow is wrinkled with care and mortification."

"But do you think she is sorry for what she has done?"

"I regret to say I do not. I think she is sorry for the consequences, but that her animosity against you would be greater than ever if she knew that you were alive, and if you were again in her power, she would wreak double vengeance. Many things have occurred to confirm me in this belief. You have overthrown her power, which she never will forgive; and as for her religion, I have no faith in that."

"It is then as I feared, Auguste; and if I make known my existence to my father, it must be concealed from my mother."

"I agree with you that it will be best; for there is no saying to what point the vengeance of an unnatural mother may be carried. But let us quit this subject, for the present at least; and now tell me more about yourself."

"I will—but there is Lionel's knock: so I must defer it till another opportunity. Dear Auguste, give me one more kiss, while we are alone."

CHAPTER XII.

In a few minutes after Lionel's return, which he had considerably postponed, until Monsieur Gironac's dinner-hour had all but arrived, my good host first, and then kind, merry little madame, made their appearance, and a little while was consumed in introductions, exclamations, admirations, and congratulations, all tinctured not a little by that national vivacity, which other folks are in the habit of calling extravagance, and which, as my readers well know already, the good Gironacs had by no means got rid of, even in the course of a long *séjour* in the matter-of-fact metropolis of England.

Fortunately, my friends were for the most part *au fait* to the leading circumstances of my life, so that little explanation was needed.

And more fortunately yet, like tide and time, dinner waits for no man; nor have I ever observed, in all my adventurous life, that the sympathy of the most sentimental, the grief of the most woe-begone, or the joy of the happiest, ever induces them to neglect the summons of the dinner-bell, and the calls of the responsive appetite.

In the midst of the delight of madame, at having at last to receive the brother of *cette chère Valerie,* and that brother, too, *si bel homme et brave officier, et d'une ressemblance si parfaite à la charmante sœur,* dinner was luckily announced; and the torrent-tide of madame's hospitality was cut short, by her husband's declaration that we were all, like himself, dying of hunger; and that not a word more must be spoken, touching sympathies or sentiments, until we had partaken of something nutritious, *de quoi soutenir l'épuisement des émotions si déchirantes.*

Madame laughed, declared that he was *un barbare, un malheureux sans grandeur de l'âme,* and taking possession of Auguste, led him away into the dining-room: where, though she told me afterwards that she was *au comble de désespoir* at having to set us down to so every-day a meal, we found an excellent dinner, and spent a very pleasant hour until coffee was served; when, with it, not a little to my surprise, nor very much to my delight, Monsieur de Chavannes made his appearance.

There was a quizzical look on Monsieur Gironac's face, and a roguish twinkle in his eye, which led me to believe that what was really a matter of surprise to me, was none to my worthy host; for the Count de Chavannes had never visited the house before, in the evening; nor, from what I had understood, was he on terms of particular intimacy with the Gironacs.

I was foolish enough to be, at first, a little put out at this; and having manifested some slight embarrassment on his first entrance, which I learned afterwards did not escape his eye, though he was far too well bred to show it, I made the matter worse by calling my pride to my aid, incited thereto by Madame Gironac's glance and smile at my blushing confusion, and certainly in no respect contributed to the gaiety of the evening. Nothing, however, I must admit, could have been more gentlemanly, or in better taste, than the whole demeanour of Monsieur de Chavannes, and I could not help feeling this, and comparing it mentally with the inferior bearing of others I had seen, even in the midst of my fit of *hauteur* and frigidity.

He neither immediately withdrew himself on learning that my brother, whom I had not seen for many years, had but just arrived, as any half-bred person would have done under the like circumstances, with an awkward apology for his presence, tending only to make every one else more awkward yet; nor made set speeches, nor foolish compliments, on a subject too important for such trifling.

He did not trouble me with any attentions, which he perceived would be at that moment distasteful, but exhibited the most marked desire to cultivate the acquaintance of Auguste, to whom he showed a degree of deference, though himself somewhat the senior, as to a military man, that flattered his *esprit de corps*, mingled with a sort of frank cordiality, which except from countryman to countryman in a foreign land, would perhaps have been a little overdone: but, under the actual circumstances, it could not have been improved.

For the short time he remained, he conversed well and wittily; yet with a strain of fancy and feeling, blended with his wit, which rendered it singularly original and attractive; and perfectly succeeded, though I know not whether he intended it or not, in directing the attention of the company from my altered and somewhat unamiable mood.

Among other things, I remember that, in the course of conversation, while tendering some civilities to Auguste, the use of his riding-horses, his cabriolet, or his services in showing him some of the lions of London, he observed that Monsieur de Chatenœuf must not consider such an offer impertinent on his part, since he believed, if our genealogy were properly traced, some sort of cousinship could be established; as more than one of the De Chavannes had intermarried in old times with the Chatenœufs of Gascony, when both the families, like their native provinces, had been acting in alliance with the English Plantagenets against the French kings of the house of Valois.

A few words were said, in connection with this, touching the singularity of the fact, that it would seem as if England had something to do with the associations of the two families; but I do not think the remark was made by De Chavannes, and whatever it was, it was not sufficiently pointed to be in any way offensive or annoying.

On the whole, hurt as I was in some sort by the idea which had taken hold of me, that the Gironacs, through a false and indelicate idea of advancing my welfare, were endeavouring to promote a liking between myself and the count, I cannot deny that the evening, on the whole, was a pleasant one, and that, if at first it had been my impression that De Chavannes was agreeable, entertaining, and well bred, I was now prepared to admit he had excellent taste, and delicate feelings into the bargain.

Still I felt that I did not like him, or perhaps I should rather say his attentions—though in fact he had paid me none,—and was rather relieved when he made his bow and retired.

Shortly afterwards, Auguste observed that I seemed dull and tired, and Madame Gironac followed suit by saying that it was no wonder if the excitement and interest created by the unexpected arrival of so dear a brother had proved too much for my nerves.

Thereupon, after promising to return early in the morning, so that we might have a long talk about the past, and a long consultation about the future, Lionel and Auguste bade us good night also; but not before Lionel had said to me as he was taking leave,

"I think, Mademoiselle, that it will be no more than proper that I should drive down to Kew to-morrow morning, and wait upon Judge Selwyn, who has always been so kind to me—have you any message for him?"

"Oh! yes. I beg you will tell him that Auguste has come, and that I request he will let me know when we may wait on him?"

"And the answer will be, Mademoiselle, his waiting upon you. Is that what you desire?"

"I only desire what I state—to know when and how we may see him, for I know very little of Auguste's heart, if he does not wish to return thanks to one who, except our dear friends here, has been poor Valerie's surest confidant and protector. But you will find the judge's family increased since you saw him. His son has persuaded my pretty little friend Caroline Stanhope to become his wife, and she is living with the judge's family at present."

Lionel expressed his surprise and pleasure at the news; but I thought at the moment that the pleasure was not real, though I have since had reason to believe that the gravity which came over his face as he spoke, was the gravity of thought, rather than that, as I fancied at the time, of disappointment.

Nothing more passed worthy of record, and, after shaking hands with Lionel, and kissing my long-lost brother, I was left alone with the Gironacs, half-expectant of a playful scolding.

"Well, Mademoiselle Valerie de Chatenœuf," began monsieur, as soon as the gentlemen had left us, "is it because you have found out that you have got a handsome brother, that you are determined to drive all other handsome young men *au désespoir?*—or is it that you wish to break the heart, especially, of this *pauvre Monsieur de Chavannes,* that you have treated us all with an air *si hautaine, si hautaine,* that if you had been the queen of France, it could not have been colder?"

"I told you once before, Monsieur Gironac," I replied, "that your Count de Chavannes does not care a straw how I treat him, or with what air; and if he did, I do not. He is simply a civil, agreeable gentleman, who looks upon me as he would upon any other young lady whom he is glad to talk to when she is in the humour to talk; and whom, when she is not, he leaves to herself, as all well-bred men do. But, I repeat, I do not care enough about him to think for one moment whether he is *hautaine* or not. And he feels just the same about me, I am certain."

"What brings him here, then, eh?—where he never came before to-night?—not for the *beaux yeux* of madame, I believe," with a quizzical bow to his wife, "or for the *grand esprit* of myself. I have an eye, I tell you, as well as other people, and I can see one *petit peu.*"

"I have no doubt you can, monsieur," I answered, rather pettishly; "for I suppose you asked him yourself; and if you did so on my account, I must beg you will omit that proof of kindness in future, for I do not wish to see him."

"Oh! Monsieur Gironac, for shame; you have made her very angry with your ridiculous badinage—you have made her angry, really, and I do not wonder. Who ever heard of teasing a young lady about a gentleman she has never seen, only three times, and who has never declared any preference?"

"Madame," replied her husband, in great wrath, either real or simulated, "*vous êtes une ingrate,—une,—une*—words fail me, to express what I think of your enormous and unkind ingratitude. I am *homme incompris,* and Mademoiselle here—Mademoiselle is either *une enfant,* or she does not know her own mind. Shall I give the Comte Chavannes his *congé,* or shall I not? I shall not,—for if she be *une enfant,* it is fit her friends look after her; if she does not know her own mind, it is good she have some one who do!—*voilà tout.* Here is why I shall not go *congédier monsieur le Comte.* Why, rather, I shall request him to dine with me to-morrow, the next day, the day after. If he do not, I swear by my honour, *foi de Gironac,* I will dine at home again never more."

I could not help laughing at this tirade of the kind-hearted little man, on the strength of which he patted me on the head, and said I was *bonne enfant,* if I were not *si diablement entêtée,* and bade me go to bed, and sleep myself into a better humour; a piece of advice which appeared to me so judicious, that I proceeded at once to obey it, and bidding them both a kind good night, betook myself to my own room to ponder rather than to sleep. And, in truth, I felt that I had need of reflection; for with the return of Auguste, a tide of feelings, which had long lain dormant rather than dead within me, had almost overwhelmed me; and the hardness which had its origin in the bitterness of conscious dependence, and which had gained strength from the pride of self-acquired independence, began to thaw in my heart, and to give way to milder and gentler feelings.

The thoughts of home, the desire for my country, the love for my father, who, though weak and almost imbecile, had ever been kind to me in person, the craving affection for my brothers and my sisters, nay, something approaching to pity or regret for the mother who had proved herself but a stepmother towards me, all revived in increased and reinvigorated force.

By-and-by, too, I began to feel that I should be very wretched after the parting with my beloved brother at the end of so brief a renewal of love and intimacy; to be aware of what I had scarcely felt before, in the self-confidence of the position I had won—that it is a sad and lonely thing to be a sojourner in a foreign land, with no natural friends, no kind kindred, on whom to rely in case of sickness or misfortune;—and to consider how dark and grave a thing must be solitary old age, and perhaps a solitary death-bed, far from the home of one's youth, the friends of one's childhood.

Then there arose another thought connected with the preceding, by that extraordinary and inexplicable chain, which seems to run through the whole mind of man, linking together things apparently as far asunder as the poles, which have, however, in reality, a kindred origin. That thought was, wherefore should my life be solitary? Why should I stand apart and alone from my race, relying on myself only, and depriving myself, for the sake of a perhaps imaginary independence, of all the endearments of social life, all the sweet ties of family?

Perhaps the very presence of my brother had opened my eyes to the truth, that there is no such thing in the world as real independence. To realize that possession, most coveted, and most unattainable, one must be a Robinson Crusoe, alone on his desert island,—a sort of independence which no one, I should think, would practically desire to enjoy.

Before sleep came, I believe that I began to muse about Monsieur de Chavannes; but it was only to think that I did not care in the least about him, nor he about me; and that, so far as he was concerned, I had seen no cause to change my *decided* resolution that I would never marry. All this was, perhaps, in reality, the best of proofs that I did already care something about him, and was very likely before long to care something more; for some one has said, and he, by the way, no ordinary judge of human nature, that if he desired to win a woman's fancy or affection, his first step would be to make her *think* about him—even if it were to hate him! anything before the absence of all thought, the blank void of real absolute indifference.

Indeed, I believe it is nearly true, that a woman rarely begins to think *often* of a man, even if it be as she fancies in dislike, but when, however she may deceive herself, she is on the verge of loving him.

Was such the case with me?

At least, if it were so, I was then so far from knowing it, that I did not even ask myself the question. But I remember that when I fell asleep, I dreamed that I was standing at the altar with the Count de Chavannes, when a band of all those who had ever wronged me,—my mother, Madame d'Albret, Madame Bathurst, the Stanhopes, Lady M——,—rushed between us, and tore us forcibly asunder; and I wept so loud that my sorrow awoke me, and it was some time before I was sure it was a dream.

Early the next morning, Auguste came again to see me; and as Monsieur Gironac was abroad, giving lessons on the flute and guitar, while madame either was, or pretended to be, excessively busy with her wax-flowers, we had the whole day to ourselves until luncheon-time, and we profited by it so well, that before we were interrupted, we had little to learn on either side concerning the passages of our lives, and the adventures which both we and all our family had gone through. And if I had been a little inclined to be proud of myself before, and to give their full value to my energy and decision of character, I certainly now stood in no small danger of being spoiled by Auguste's praises.

For now, half-crying at my trials and troubles,—now laughing at Lady R——'s absurdities,—now bursting into vehement invective against my enemies,—he insisted that I was a perfect heroine—the bravest and most accomplished of women, as well as the dearest of sisters.

But when I had finished my own story, which I did not begin until I had extracted from him every particle of information about my family—

"Well, my little Valerie," he said caressingly, as he put his arm about my waist, "you have told me everything—all your little sorrows, and trials, and troubles—all your little pleasures and successes—all your little schemings and manœuvrings in the love-affairs of other people—and all about the great little fortune which you have accumulated—quite a millionaire, upon my word, with your twenty-five hundred *livres de rente*—but not one word have you told me about your own little *affaires de cœur*. I am afraid, little sister mine, you are either a very great hypocrite, or very cold-hearted; which is it, dearest Valerie?"

"Very cold-hearted, I believe, brother. At least I certainly have no *affaires de cœur* to relate. I cannot pretend to say whether it is my fault or that of other people; but certainly no one ever fell in love with me, if it were not that odious Monsieur G——; and most certainly I have never fallen in love with any one at all."

Auguste gazed earnestly in my face for a moment, as if he would have read my heart; but I met his eyes with mine quite steadily and calmly, till at length I burst into a merry laugh, which I could not restrain.

"Quite true, little sister?" he said, at last, after my manner had in some sort convinced him.

"Quite true, Auguste, upon my honour," I replied.

"Well, Valerie, I suppose I must believe that earnest face, and that honest little laugh of yours."

"You may just as well do so, indeed," I replied; "for no one was ever in love with me, I assure you. And I do not think," I added, with a touch of the old pride, "that a De Chatenœuf is likely to give away a heart that is not desired."

"It is all very strange," he added. "And this Monsieur Lionel Dempster?—"

"Is a little older than poor Pierre, whom I used to pinch when I wanted to get out of my mother's reach; and regards me very much as he would a much elder sister—almost, indeed, as a mother."

"A mother, indeed, Valerie!"

"He once told me something of the kind! He is a very fine young man, certainly, full of talent and spirit, and will make you a very good and agreeable friend—but he is no husband for me, I assure you. He would do much better for Sophie, or Elisée, if he ever should see and like either of them."

"Always busy for others, Valerie! And for yourself—when will you think for yourself?"

"I think I *have* thought, and done, too, for myself, pretty well. You forget my twenty-five hundred *livres de rente.*"

"But twenty-five hundred *livres de rente* are not a husband, Valerie."

"I am not so sure about that. I dare say they would buy one at a pinch," I replied, laughing; "at least, in our *poor* country, where every one you meet in society is not a millionaire, like these cold islanders."

"I think you have grown almost as cold yourself, little sister, and as calculating."

"To be sure I have," I made answer; "and to punish me, Monsieur Gironac swears that I shall die a sour old maid."

"And what do you say?"

"An old maid very likely; but not a sour one, at all events. But, hark! there is a carriage at the door—let me see who it is."

And I jumped up, and running to the window, saw the Selwyn liveries, and Lionel, *en cavalier*, beside the carriage window.

In a moment, the steps were let down; and Caroline speedily made her appearance, commissioned, as she said, by her mother-in-law, to take immediate possession both of myself and Auguste, and to bring us down straightway to Kew. Her husband, she said, would certainly have called on Monsieur de Chatenœuf, and the judge also, but that the courts being all in session, they were both so completely occupied, that, except after dinner, they had not an hour of the twenty-four disengaged.

She was commanded, moreover, she added, to invite Monsieur and Madame Gironac to dine at Kew on the following day. Me, moreover, and Auguste, she was to carry down forthwith in the carriage.

"So now," she said, "get you gone, Valerie, and pack up as quickly as possible all that you require to make yourself beautiful for a week, at least."

"And what do you say to all this, messieurs?" said I, laughingly, to my brother and Lionel; "for there is much more necessity to consult you lords of the creation, as you call yourselves, who are in reality vainer by half, and care five times as much about your toilettes as we much-calumniated women—what do you say about this summary packing up and taking flight? can it be accomplished?"

"It *is* accomplished," replied Lionel; "in so far at least that I have promised, on my own part, and for Monsieur Auguste de Chatenœuf in the bargain, to overlook the preparation of his kit as well as my own, and to bring them down in a cabriolet, while you and your brother are rolling smoothly along in the judge's venerable coach."

"All that is arranged, then," said I, "and I will not detain you above ten minutes, during which time I will send Madame Gironac to amuse you, and you can deliver your own message to her."

And then, without waiting for any answer, I hurried upstairs to make my travelling toilette, and to put up things for a week's visit to my good friends.

In the mean time Madame Gironac, who had always been a great favourite of Caroline's, had taken my place; and by the merriment which I could hear going on, I could not doubt that, on the whole, the party had been a gainer by the exchange.

Before I was quite ready to make my reappearance, there came a smart double knock at the door; and then, after a minute or two, I could distinguish a gentleman's footstep ascending the staircase to the dining-room.

My own room looked towards the back of the house, so that I had no means of seeing for myself who the new comer was; and I did not choose to ask any questions of the servant girl, who was bustling in and out of the door with trunks and travelling-cases innumerable.

So I finished my toilette with a heart that beat, I must confess, a little faster than usual, though I should certainly have been puzzled to explain why; put on my hat and shawl, perhaps a little coquettishly, and went downstairs, half-impatient, half-embarrassed, yet fully persuaded in my own mind that I had not the least expectation of seeing anybody in particular.

I found all the company assembled round the luncheon-table when I entered, and busily engaged with the *côtelettes à la Maintenon* and green peas. Among those present was Monsieur le Comte de Chavannes, whom I certainly did not expect to see.

He rose immediately from the table as I entered, and advanced a step or two to meet me, with a graceful inclination, and a few well-chosen words, to the intent that he had called in order to invite Monsieur de Chatenœuf to go out and take a *promenade à cheval* with him, in order to see the parks and the beauty of London.

All this was said with the utmost frankness, and in the most unaffected manner in the world; and assuredly there was nothing either in the words, or in the manner in which they were uttered, which should have thrown me into a confusion of blushes, and rendered me for a moment almost incapable of answering him.

It must be remembered, however, that I had been rallied very much concerning him of late by Monsieur Gironac, and I could scarcely avoid perceiving that this exceeding assiduity in doing the honours to Auguste could not but be attributed to some more potent cause than mere civility to a fellow-countryman.

My confusion produced, for a second or two, a slight similar embarrassment in the count, and the blood mounted highly to his forehead. Our eyes met, too, at the same instant; and though the encounter was but momentary, from that time a sort of secret consciousness was established between us.

This scene passed in less time than it takes to describe it; and, becoming aware that every one's eyes were upon us, I rallied instinctively, replied by a few civil words of thanks, and took a place at the table, which had been left vacant for me, between my brother and Lionel Dempster. This little interruption at an end, the conversation returned to the course it had taken before I came in, and there was a good deal of very agreeable talk; as is sure to be the case whenever four or five pleasant and clever people are thrown together under circumstances which create a sudden and unexpected familiarity, each person desirous of amusing and rendering himself pleasant to his companions of an hour; but not so anxious to make an impression, as to become stiff, stilted, or affected.

Lionel, as I have said long ago, was remarkably witty and clever by nature, and had profited greatly by his opportunities in France; so much so, that I have rarely seen a young man of his age at all comparable to him. The count was likewise a person of superior abilities and breeding, with a touch of English seriousness and soundness engrafted on the stock of French vivacity; and my brother Auguste was a young, ardent soldier, full of gay youth, high hopes, and brilliant aspirations, all kindled up by the excitement of thus visiting a foreign country, and finding himself in the company of a long-lost and much-beloved sister.

Caroline Selwyn was quick, bright, and lively; Madame Gironac was a perfect mine of life and vivacity; and I, desirous of atoning for my folly of the past evening, did my best to be agreeable.

I suppose I was not wholly unsuccessful, for every time I raised my eyes, I was sure to find those of Monsieur de Chavannes riveted on my face with a deep, earnest gaze, which, though it was instantly averted, even before our glances met, showed that he was in some sort interested either in myself, or in my words.

Before luncheon was finished, Monsieur Gironac made his *entrée*, and it was finally arranged that he and madame should join us at Kew on the following evening; and before we set off, Caroline expressed a hope to the Count de Chavannes that he would call upon his friend Monsieur de Chatenœuf while he was staying at the judge's, explaining that it was impossible for Mr. Selwyn or the judge to wait on him for some days, until the courts had done sitting, when she assured him that they would do so without fail.

He promised immediately, without a moment's hesitation, that he would do so; and I believe a riding-party was made up on the spot between himself, Lionel, and Auguste, for the second or third day.

As soon as everything was settled, Caroline hurried us away, saying that her mother-in-law would think she had run off; and a short agreeable drive carried us down to the judge's pleasant villa, where I was received almost as one of the family; and Auguste, rather as an old friend, than as a stranger and a foreigner.

The time passed away pleasantly, for it was the height of the loveliest spring weather; the situation of the villa on the banks of the Thames was in itself charming; and for once the English month of May was what its poets have described it—that is to say, what it is once in every hundred years.

Every one wished to please and to be pleased, and the Selwyns were of that very rare class of people, whom you like the more the more you see of them—the very reverse of the world, in general—nothing could be more delightful than the week which we passed there.

From the judge I had no concealments; and regarding him almost in the light of a second father, while Auguste was prepared to love him for his love to me, we had many long conversations and consultations concerning my affairs, and the propriety of disclosing my existence to my father.

This I was resolved upon, and both the judge and Auguste approving, it was decided that it should be done.

The only question then, which remained to be disposed of, was, how far my disclosures should be carried, and whether it would be practicable, and if practicable, safe, that I should return to France at present, or indeed at all, while in my present condition.

Auguste gave me his opinion, as he had done repeatedly, that my mother never had laid aside, and never would lay aside, her rancour towards me; and that she would grasp at the first opportunity of taking any vengeance upon me which my presence should afford her.

He did not believe, he said, that my father would be able long to preserve from her the secret of my being alive, and of my having raised myself to a condition of comparative affluence; nor did he feel by any means assured that, while labouring under the revulsion of feelings which the happy tidings would work upon his mind, my mother would not recover her ascendancy over him.

Beyond this, he could say nothing; for as a young Frenchman, and more especially a young French soldier, he knew even less about the laws of France, and the rights of parents over children, than did Judge Selwyn; only, like the judge, he was inclined to the opinion that I had better not trust myself within the limits of any jurisdiction which might be called upon to hand me over to the parental authority, until such time as I should be completely my own mistress as regarded them, which probably could only be effected by ceasing to be my own mistress as regarded some one else.

"For be assured, Valerie," he added, "that the possession of your person for the purpose of annoying you, and avenging herself on you for all the sufferings she has undergone in consequence of your supposed suicide, will become the darling object of her life, so sure as she learns that you are in the land of the living; and the fact of your having secured to yourself a little fortune will not act as a check upon her inclinations."

I sighed deeply; for although I felt and knew the truth of all he said, and expected that he would say it, his words seemed to extinguish the last spark of hope in my heart; and it is a bitter and painful thing in any case for a daughter to feel that she shall in all probability never again be permitted to see the authors of her life, or the companions and scenes of her childhood; but it is doubly so when she feels it to be the fault of the wickedness or weakness of those whom she would fain love and esteem, but cannot.

The good judge marked my emotion, and, laying his hand kindly on my shoulder, said, "You must not give way, my dear girl; you have done all that is right and true and honest; and the course which you have taken has been forced upon you. To yield now, and return home to be tortured and despoiled of the little all which your own good sense and your own good conduct have procured you—for, apart from good sense and good conduct, there is no such thing in the world as good fortune—would not only be positive insanity, but positive ingratitude to the Giver of all good. My advice to you, therefore, is to remain altogether passive, to pursue the career which you have chosen, and, without yourself taking any steps to disclose your present situation, to authorize your brother fully to reveal to your father so much of it as shall appear necessary and desirable to him when on the spot. I should not recommend that your place of residence, or exact circumstances, should be communicated even to him, at least for the present; and should he desire to write to you, the letters should pass through your brother's hands, and be forwarded under cover to me, which will prevent the gaining of intelligence through the post-office. The rest we must leave to the effects of time, and of that Providence which has been displayed so singularly in your behalf already, and which never deserts those who believe humbly, and endeavour sincerely to deserve Divine favour. So this," he added with a smile, "is the end and sum total of an old lawyer's counsel, and an old man's sermon. And now, think over what I have said between you; for I believe you will find it the best course, although it may now hardly suit your excited feelings, and in the mean time, let us go on the lawn and join the ladies, who seem to have got some new metal of attraction."

"Indeed, judge," I replied, "I am quite convinced of the wisdom of what you propose, and I thank you sincerely for your advice as for all your other goodness towards me. No father could be kinder to an only daughter than you have been to me; and God will bless you for it; but, to say the truth, I do feel very sad and downcast just at this moment, and am not equal to the joining that gay party. "I will go up to my own room," I added, "for a little while, and come down again so soon as I can conquer this foolish weakness."

"Do not call it foolish, Valerie," returned the old man with a benignant smile. "Nothing that is natural can be foolish—least of all, anything of natural and kindly feeling. But do not yield to it—do not yield to it. The feelings are good slaves, but wretchedly poor masters. Do as you will, my dear child, but come to us again as soon as you can. In the mean time, Monsieur de Chateneuf, let us go and see who are these new comers."

And with these words he turned away, leaning familiarly upon my brother's arm, and left me to collect myself, and recover from the perturbation of my feelings as well and as soon as I could,—which was not perhaps the more quickly that I had easily recognised in the new arrival the person of the Count de Chavannes.

I have entered perhaps more fully into the detail of my sentiments at this period of my life, for two reasons—one, because of an eventful life, this was upon the whole the most eventful moment—the other, that having hitherto recorded facts and actions rather than feelings or principles, I am conscious that I have represented myself as a somewhat harder and more worldly person than I feel myself in truth to be.

But the hardness and the worldliness were produced, if they existed at all, by the hardness of the circumstances into which I was thrown, and the worldliness of the persons with whom I was brought into contact.

Adversity had hardened my character, and perhaps in some sort my heart also. At least, it had aroused my pride to the utmost, had set me as it were upon the defensive, and led me to regard every stranger with suspicion, and to look in him for a future enemy.

Good fortune had, however, altered all this. All who had been my enemies, who had injured, or misrepresented me, were disarmed, or subdued, or repentant. I had forgiven all the world—was at peace with all the world. I had achieved what to me was a little competence; I was loved and esteemed by those whom I could in return love and esteem, and of whose regard I could be honestly proud. I had recovered my brother—I still hoped to be reconciled to my parents—and—and—why should I conceal it—I was beginning to think it by far less improbable that I should one day marry—in a word, I was beginning to like, if not yet to love.

All these things had been by degrees effecting a change in my thoughts and feelings. I had been gradually thawing, and was now completely melted, so that I felt the necessity of being alone—of giving way—of weeping.

I went to my own chamber, threw myself on my bed, and wept long and freely.

But these were not tears of agony such as I shed when I first learned Madame d'Albret's cruel conduct towards me—nor tears of injured pride such as Madame Bathurst had forced from me by her effort to humiliate me in my own eyes—nor yet tears of wrathful indignation such as burst from me when I detected Lady M—— in her base endeavour to destroy my character.

These were tears of affection, of softness, almost of joy. They flowed noiselessly and gently, and they relieved me, for my heart was very full; and, when I was relieved, I bathed my face, and arranged my hair, and descended the staircase, almost merrily, to join the merry company in the garden.

I found on my joining them, that the Count de Chavannes had already completely gained the good graces, not only of Caroline and her young sisters-in-law, but of Mr. Selwyn and the judge also.

He had come down to Kew with the particular purpose of engaging my brother and Lionel to accompany him, on the next day but one, to Wormwood Scrubs, where there was to be a grand review, in honour of some foreign prince or other, of two or three regiments of light cavalry, with horse-artillery and rockets. It was to conclude with a sham fight, and which he thought would interest Auguste as a military man, and especially one who had commenced his service in the hussars, though he had been subsequently transferred into the line.

This plan had been discussed and talked over, until the ladies, having expressed a laughing desire to see the *spectacle*, it was decided that Caroline, the two Miss Selwyns, and myself, escorted by Lionel, in the rumble, should go down to the review in the judge's carriage, Auguste and the count accompanying us *en cavalier;* and that after the order of the day should be concluded, the whole party, including the count, should return to dinner at Kew.

On the day following, as I did not think it either wise or correct to neglect my pupils, my chapel, or Mrs. Bradshaw's school, although I had sent satisfactory reasons for taking one week's leave of absence, we were all to return to town; I to good Monsieur Gironac's, Auguste and Lionel to the lodgings of the latter in Suffolk-street.

Monsieur de Chavannes did not stay long after I made my appearance, not wishing either to be, or to appear, *de trop* on a first visit; nor had he any opportunity of addressing more than a few common-place observations to me, had he desired to do so. Still I observed the same peculiarity in his manner towards me, as distinct as possible from the sort of proud humility, half-badinage, half-earnest, which he put on in talking with other ladies.

To me he observed a tone of serious softness, with something of earnest deference to everything that fell from my lips, however light or casual, for which he seemed to watch with the utmost eagerness.

He never joked with *me*, though he was doing so continually with the others; not that he was in the least degree grave or formal, much less stiff or affected; but rather that he seemed desirous of proving to me that he was not a mere butterfly of society, but had deeper ideas, and higher aspirations than the every-day world around us.

When he was going away, he for the first time put out his hand to me *à l'anglaise*, and as I shook hands with him, our eyes met once more, and I believe I again blushed a little; for though he dropped his gaze instantly, and bowed low, taking off his hat, he pressed my fingers very gently, ere he let them fall, and then turning to take his leave of the judge and Mr. Selwyn, who had just joined us, mounted his horse—a very fine hunter, by the way, which he sat admirably—again bowed low, and cantered off, followed by his groom, as well mounted as himself.

He was not well out of sight before, as usual, he became the topic of general discussion.

"What a charming person," said Caroline: "so full of spirit and vivacity, and yet so evidently a man of mind and good feeling. Where did you pick him up, Valerie?"

"He is an old friend, I told you, of Monsieur Gironac's, and was calling there by accident when he met Auguste, and since that he has been exceedingly kind and civil to him. That is the whole I know about him."

"Well, he is very handsome," said Caroline; "don't you think so, Valerie?"

"Yes," I answered, quite composedly, "very handsome, a little effeminate-looking, perhaps."

"Oh! no, not in the least," said Caroline; "or if he is, so quick and clever and spirited-looking that it quite takes all that away."

"Caroline," said Selwyn, laughing, "you have no right to have eyes to see, or ears to hear, or mind to comprehend, beauty, or wit, or any other good quality, in any one save me, your lord and master."

"You! you monster!" she replied, laughing gaily, "I never thought you one bit handsome, or witty, or dreamed that you had one good quality. I only married you, you know as well as I do, to get away from school, and from the atrocious tyranny of my music-mistress there. You need not look fie! at me, Valerie, for I'm too big to be put in the corner, now, and he won't let you whip me."

"I think he ought to whip you himself, baby," replied the judge, who had grown very fond of her; and, in truth, she was a very loveable little person in her way, and made her husband a very happy man.

"Now, Judge Selwyn," interposed I, "do you remember a conversation we once had together, in which you endeavoured to force me to believe that men in general, and you in particular, were not tyrants to your wives and families, and now do I hear you giving your son such advice as that? Alas! what can make women so insane?"

"Don't you know? Can't you guess, Mademoiselle Valerie?" asked the old judge, smiling slily, and with the least possible wink of his eye, when some of the others were looking at us, and then he added in a lower voice, "perhaps it will be your turn soon. I think you will soon be able to go to France without much fear of your mother's persecution. Come," he continued, offering me his arm, as the others had now moved a little way apart, "come and take a turn with me in the cedar-walk till dinner 's ready; I want to talk to you, for who knows when one will get another opportunity."

I took his arm without reply, though my heart beat very fast, and I felt uncomfortable, knowing as I did perfectly well beforehand what he was going to say to me.

We turned into the cedar-walk, which was a long shadowy aisle, or bower, overhung with magnificent cedars of Lebanon, running parallel with the banks of the noble river, and so still and secluded that no more proper place could be found for a private consultation.

"Well," said the old man, speaking gently, but not looking at me, perhaps for fear of embarrassing me by his eye, "you know I am in some sort, not only your legal adviser, but your self-constituted guardian, and father confessor—so now, without farther preamble, who is he, Valerie?"

"I will not affect to misunderstand you, judge, though, upon my word, you are entirely mistaken in your conjecture."

"Upon your word! entirely mistaken! I think not—I am sure not."

"You are indeed. I have not seen him above four times, nor spoken fifty words to him."

"Never mind, never mind—who is he?"

"An acquaintance of Monsieur Gironac's—Monsieur le Comte de Chavannes. His father emigrated hither during the Revolution, engaged in commerce, and made a fortune of some £40,000. At the restoration, the old count returned to France, and was made by Louis XVIII. a colonel of the Legion of Honour, and died shortly afterwards. There is an estate, I believe, in Brittany, but Monsieur de Chavannes, who was at school here, and has passed all his younger days in this country, is more an Englishman than a Frenchman, and only visits France at rare intervals. That is all I know about him, and that only by accident, Monsieur Gironac having told me, in his lively way, what I should not have dreamed of inquiring."

"Very proper, indeed—and very good so far, but one would like to know something definite about a man before taking him for one's husband."

"I should think so, indeed, judge; but as I am not going to take him for my husband, I am quite contented with knowing what I do know of him."

"And what do you know?—of yourself,—I speak, of your own knowledge? No hearsay evidence in the case."

"Nothing more than that he is lively and agreeable, that he has very good manners, and seems very good-natured—I might say, he has been very good-natured to Auguste, poor fellow."

"Poor fellow! Yes," answered the judge. "But men are very apt to be good-natured to poor fellows who have got nice sisters with whom they are in love."

"I dare say, judge. But to reply in your own phraseology—that is no case in point; for granting that Auguste's sister is *nice*, which I will not be so modest as to gainsay, Monsieur de Chavannes is not the least in love with her."

"Perhaps, not."

"Certainly, not."

"Well, be it so. What else do you know about him?"

"Nothing, Judge Selwyn."

"Nothing of his character, his principles, his morals, or his habits?"

"Really, judge, one would think, to hear you, that I was going to hire a footman—which I am much too poor to do—and that Monsieur de Chavannes had applied for the place. What on earth have I to do with the young gentleman's character or principles? I know that he is very gentlemanlike, and is neither a coxcomb nor a pedant, which is refreshing in these days."

"And, as Caroline says, very handsome, eh?"

"Yes, I think he is handsome," I replied. "But that has nothing to do with it."

"Not much, truly," said the judge, drily. "And this is all you know?"

"Or desire to know. It seems to me quite enough to know of an acquaintance of a few days' standing."

"Well—well," he answered, shaking his head a little. "Well. He *is* all that you say. A very fine young man, he seems. I like him. Well, I will make inquiries."

"Not on my account, I entreat, Judge Selwyn"—said I, interrupting him eagerly.

"Mademoiselle Valerie de Chatenœuf," he said, drily, though half in jest, "my head is an old one, yours a very young one. I know young folks are apt to think old heads good for nothing."

"I do not, I am sure," interrupted I, again. "I do not, indeed."

"Nor I, Valerie,"—he answered, interrupting me in his turn, with a good-natured smile. "So you shall let me have my way in this matter. But, to relieve you, my dear, permit me to observe that I have two daughters of my own, and one young son, besides Charles, who is old enough to take care of himself; and though I am very glad to ask a young man to dine in my house who has, as you observe, very good manners, and is neither a fool nor a coxcomb, I am not at all willing that he should become what you call an *habitué*, until I know something of his character and principles. And now, as the dressing-bell has rung these ten minutes, and it will take you at least half an hour to beautify your little person, I advise you to make the most of your time. And by all means, Valerie, stick to your resolution—never marry, my dear, never marry; for all men are tyrants."

One might be very sure that I profited by this dismissal, and ran across the lawn as fast as I could, glad to escape the far-sighted experience of the shrewd old lawyer.

"He has seen it, then," I thought to myself. "He has observed it even in this little space; even in this one interview; and he has read it, even as I read it. I wonder if he has read my heart, too. No, no," I continued, communing with myself, "that he cannot have done, for I know not yet myself how to interpret it."

Little thought I then, that whenever our feelings are deeply interested, or when strong passions are at work, even in embryo, we are for the most part the last persons who discover the secrets which are transparent enough, Heaven knows, to all persons but ourselves.

I do not know, nor did I inquire, whether the judge pursued his inquiries concerning the count as he had promised to do; much less did I learn what was their result. But I do know that the following morning the young gentleman called again at the gate with a led horse for my brother; but did not ask if we were at home, merely sending his compliments to the ladies, and requesting Monsieur de Chatenœuf to accompany him for a ride.

Lionel was absent in the city on business; so that Auguste and the count rode out alone, and did not return until it was growing dark, when there was scarcely time to dress for dinner, the latter again sending in an apology for detaining my brother so long, and retiring without getting off his horse.

This gave me, I confess, more pleasure than it would have done to see him, though that would have given me pleasure, too; for I saw in it a proof of something more than mere tact, of mental delicacy, I mean; and an anxiety not to obtrude either upon the hospitality of the Selwyns, or upon my feelings.

Auguste, on his return, was in amazing spirits, and did nothing all dinner-time but expatiate upon the companionable and amiable qualities of De Chavannes, whom he already liked, he said, more than any person he had ever seen for so short a time—so clever, so high-spirited, so gallant. Everything, in a word, that a man could desire for a friend, or a lady for a lover.

"Heyday!" said the judge, laughing at this tirade. "This fine count with his black moustaches seems to have made one conquest mighty quickly. I hope it will not run in the company, or we shall have more elopements"—with a sly glance at Caroline. "Mademoiselle Valerie, here," he continued, "is a terrible person for promoting elopements, too. But we must have none from my house."

We continued to be very gay all dinner-time. After dinner we had some music, and the judge was just pressing me to sing, when Lionel's servant came into the room, having hurried down from London, in pursuit of his master, in consequence of the sudden arrival of a large package of letters from Paris, indorsed "Immediate, and to be delivered with all speed."

This incident broke up the party for the moment; and indeed threw a chill over us all for the whole evening, when it appeared that the principal letter was one to my brother from the commandant of Paris, of which city his regiment formed a part of the garrison, reluctantly revoking his leave of absence, in consequence of some expected *émeute*, and intimating that his presence would be expected at head-quarters on or before the third day of June; an order which it was, of course, impossible to think of neglecting or disobeying, while it would leave him at the furthest but a single week to give to us in London.

It was a bitter disappointment to be separated after so brief a communion; but we consoled ourselves by the recollection that the Straits of Dover are not the Pacific Ocean, and that Paris and London are not a thousand leagues asunder.

CHAPTER XIII.

THERE never was a finer morning in the world than that appointed for the review. It was just the end of May, and all the scenery, even in the very suburbs of the great city, was brilliant with all the characteristic beauty of an English landscape.

The fine horse-chesnut trees and the thick hawthorn hedges were all in full bloom, and the air was perfectly scented with perfumes from the innumerable nursery-grounds which hedge in that side of London with a belt of flowers.

The parks and the suburban roads were crowded with neatly-dressed, modest-looking nurses and nursery-maids, leading whole troops of rosy-cheeked, brown-curled, merry boys and girls to enjoy the fresh morning air; and Auguste was never tired, as we drove along, of admiring everything that met his eyes in quick succession.

The trees, the flowery hedges, the gay parterres, the glimpses of the noble Thames white with the sails of innumerable craft, the beautiful villas with their small highly-cultivated pleasure-grounds, the pretty nursery-maids, and happy English children, all came in for a share of his rapturous admiration; and so vivacious and original were his comments on all that he saw, that he in some sort communicated the infection of his merry humour to us also, and we were all as gay and joyous as the season and the scene.

When we came to the ground destined for the review, my brother was silent, and I saw his cheek turn pale for a moment; but his eye brightened and flashed as it ran over the splendid lines of the cavalry, which, at the moment we came upon the ground, were parading past the royal personage in honour of whom the review was given, and who was on horseback, by the side of a somewhat slender elderly gentleman, dressed in the uniform of a *field-marshal*, whose eagle eye and aquiline nose announced him, at a glance, the *vainqueur du vainqueur de la terre.*

"*Magnifique; mais c'est vraiment magnifique,*" muttered my brother to himself, as the superb life-guards swept along, with their polished steel helmets and breastplates glittering like silver in the sunshine, and their plumes and guidons flashing and twinkling in the breeze. "*Dieu de dieu! qu'ils sont géants les cavaliers, qu'ils sont collossaux les chevaux. Et les allures si lestes, si gracieuses, comme s'ils n'étaient que des juments. Mais c'est un spectacle magnifique!*"

A moment afterwards, a regiment of lancers passed at a trot, with their pennons fluttering in the breeze, and their lance-heads glimmering like stars above the clouds of dust which rose from under their horses' hoofs; and these were followed by several squadrons of hussars, with their crimson trousers and their gaily-furred pelisses; and then troop after troop of horse-artillery clattering along, the high-bred horses whirling the heavy guns and caissons behind them as if they had been mere playthings.

It certainly was a beautiful and brilliant pageant, and the splendid military music of the cavalry bands, the clash and clang of the silver cymbals, the ringing roll of the kettle-drums, and the symphonious cadences of the cornets, horns, and trumpets at the same time, delighted and excited me to the utmost.

But, I confess, that to me, the calm old veteran, sitting unmoved amidst all that pomp and clangour, and evidently marking only every smallest minutiæ of the men, the accoutrements, the movements, was a more interesting, a more moving sight, than all the pageantry of uniform, than all the thrill of music.

I thought how he had sat as cool and impassive under the iron hail of battle, with thousands and thousands of the best and bravest falling around him, the fate of nations hanging on a balanced scale in those fights of giants—I thought how he, alone of men, had faced, undaunted and self-confident, that greater than Hannibal, or Alexander, that world-conqueror, Napoleon—I thought how he had quelled the might of my own gallant land, and my blood seemed to thrill coldly in my veins, as it will at the recital of great deeds and noble daring—and I knew not altogether whether it was the shudder of dislike, or the thrill of admiration that so shook me.

Had he looked proud or self-elate, or triumphant, I felt that I could have hated him; but so impassive, and withal now so frail and feeble, yet with an eye so calmly firm, an expression of rectitude so conscious, I could not but perceive that if an enemy of my *Belle France* was before me, it was an enemy who had been made such by duty, not by choice—an enemy who had done nought in hatred,—all in honour.

I acknowledged to myself that I was in the presence of the greatest living man; and though I could neither love nor worship, I felt subdued and awed into a sort of breathless horror, as one might fancy humanity to be in the presence of some superior intelligence, some being of another world.

The girls observed my riveted and almost fascinated eye, as it dwelt on that mighty soldier, and began to whisper to one another with a sort of very natural pride at the evident interest which we took in their favourite hero.

Their tittering attracted my brother's attention, and following their eyes he was not long in discovering what it was that had excited their mirth, and he looked at me for a moment with something like a frown on his forehead. But it cleared away in a moment, and he smiled at his own vehemence, perhaps injustice.

At that moment, the different regiments began wheeling to and fro in long lines, and open columns of troops, and performing an infinity of manœuvres, which, though I of course did not in the least degree comprehend them, were very fine and beautiful to look at, from the rapidity of the movements, the high spirit of the horses, and the gleam and glitter of the arms, half-seen among the dust-clouds. My brother, however, began, as I could see, to be vehemently excited, and his constant comments and exclamations of surprise and admiration, bore testimony to the correctness with which every movement was executed.

Then came the roar of the artillery, as the guns retreated

before the charging horse, and even I could comprehend and appreciate the marvellous celerity with which flash followed flash, and roar echoed roar, from the same piece, so speedily that it was scarcely possible to comprehend how the gun should have been loaded and re-loaded while the horses were at full gallop.

By this time all the gentlemen had become so much interested and excited by the scene, that, Lionel having got upon his horse, which had been led down to the ground by his servant, they asked our permission to leave us for a short time, and ride nearer to the spot where the artillery were manœuvring.

As we had several servants about us in the first place, and as in the second there is not the slightest danger of ladies being treated with incivility by an English crowd, unless through their own fault or indiscretion, of course no objection was made, and our cavaliers galloped away, promising to return within a quarter of an hour.

Scarcely were they out of sight, before I observed a tall, handsome, soldiery man, though in pain clothes, ride past the carriage on a very fine horse, followed by a groom in a plain dark frock, with a cockade in his hat.

It seemed to me, on the instant, that I had seen his face somewhere before, and that I ought to know him; for the features all seemed familiar, although, had it been to save my life, I could not have said where I had met him.

I was torturing my memory on this head in vain—for he was evidently an Englishman, and I had no acquaintance with any English officer—when he rode past a second time, and seemed to be engaged in endeavouring to decipher the arms on our carriage, and his object appeared to be the discovery of who *I* was; at least, I could not but observe that he looked at me from time to time with a furtive glance from under the brim of his hat, as if he, too, fancied that he knew or remembered me. The same thing happened yet a third time; and then he called his servant to his side, and I saw the man ride up a second afterwards to Judge Selwyn's footman, who was standing at a few yards' distance from the carriage, and ask him some question, which he answered by a word or two, when the groom rode away.

The gentleman, on receiving the reply, nodded his head quietly, as if he would have said, "I thought so," and then he looked at me steadily till he caught my eye, when he raised his hat, made a half-military bow, and trotted slowly away

Caroline's quick eye caught this action in an instant, and turning to me suddenly, she cried quickly—

"Ah! Valerie, who is that? that handsome man who bowed to you?—Where have I seen him before?"

"The very question which I was asking myself, Caroline. I am quite sure that I have seen his face, and yet I cannot remember where. It is very strange."

"Very!" replied a strange, sneering voice, close to my ear, with a slightly foreign accent. "Can you say where you have seen mine, *Ingrate?*"

I turned my head as quick as lightning; for in answering Caroline, who sat on the side of the carriage next to the military spectacle, I had leaned a little inward; and there, with his effeminate features actually livid with rage, and writhing with impotent malignity, stood Monsieur G——, the infamous, divorced husband of Madame d'Albret, and the first cause of almost all my misfortunes.

I looked at him steadily, and replied with bitter but calm contempt—

"Perfectly well, Monsieur G——. And very little did I suppose that I should ever see it again. I imagined, sir, that you were in your proper place,—the galleys!"

It was wrong, doubtless, in me so to answer him—unfeminine, perhaps, and too provocative of insult; but the blood of my race is hot, and vehement to repel insult; and when I thought of the sufferings I had endured, the trials I had encountered, and the contumely which I had borne on account of that man, my every vein seemed to overflow with passion.

"Ha!" he replied, grinding his teeth with rage, and becoming crimson from the rush of blood to his head, while he grasped my wrist hard with his hand, and shook it furiously. "Ha! to the galleys yourself—*Chienne! Ingrate! Perfide! Traîtresse! c'est aux galères que j'ai cru te rencontrer—ou plutôt à la——.*"

What further atrocity the ruffian was about to utter, I know not, for while his odious voice was yet hissing in my ear these atrocious epithets, before the footman, who was standing, as I have said, a few yards off at the other side of the carriage, had time to interfere, I heard the sound of a horse at full gallop, and, the next instant, he was dragged forcibly away, and I saw him quivering in the furious grasp of the Count de Chavannes, who had, it seems, been returning to join us, when the assault was committed.

To gallop to my side, to spring to the ground, to collar the ruffian, drag him from the carriage, and lash him with his whole strength with a rough jockey-whip till he fairly screamed for mercy, were but the work of a moment.

And I could not but marvel afterwards to think how much power and nervous energy his indignant spirit had lent to his slight frame and slender limbs; for in size, he was by no means superior to G——, whom he, nevertheless, handled almost as if he had been a child of five years old.

Want of breath at last, rather than want of will, compelled him to pause in his exercise; and then turning towards us with an air as composed and smiling as if he had been merely dancing a quadrille, he took off his hat, saying:—

"I must implore your pardon, ladies, yours more especially, Mademoiselle Valerie, for enacting such a scene in your presence. *Mais c'était plus fort que moi!*" he added, laughing. "I could not contain myself at seeing a lady so infamously insulted."

Caroline and the Misses Selwyn were so much frightened by the whole fracas, that they were really unable to answer, and I was for the moment so much taken by surprise, that I could not find words to reply. At this moment, covered with dust and blood, for the whip had cut his face in several places, without his hat, and with all his gay attire besmeared and rent, G—— again came up towards the carriage.

He was a very pale, nay white, even to the lips; but it was evidently not with terror but with rage, as his first words testified—

"Monsieur le Comte de Chavannes," he said slowly, "car je vous connais, et vous me connaîtrez aussi, je vous le jure; vous m'avez frappé, vous me rendrez satisfaction, n'est-ce pas?"

Oh! no, no," I exclaimed, before he could answer, clasping my hands eagerly together; "oh, no, no! not on my account, I implore you, Monsieur le Comte—no life on my account—above all, not yours!"

He thanked me by one expressive glance, which spoke volumes to my heart, and perhaps read volumes in return in my pale face and trembling lips, then turned with a calm smile to his late antagonist, and answered him in English.

"I do not know in the least, sir, who you are, and I do not suppose that I ever shall know. I chastised you, five minutes since, for insulting this lady most grossly—"

"Lady!" interrupted the ruffian, with a sneer. "Lady. Lady of plea——"

But the count went on without pausing or seeming to hear him—"which I should have done at all events, whether I had known you or not, and which I shall most assuredly do again, should you think fit to proceed further with your infamies. As for satisfaction, if I should be called upon in a proper way, I shall not refuse it to any person worthy to meet me."

"Which this person is not, sir," interposed yet a third voice; and, looking up, I recognised the officer who had bowed to me: "which this person is not, I assure you, and my word is wont to be sufficient in such cases—Lieutenant-Colonel Jervis,"—he added, with a half-bow to me,—"late of his majesty's —— light dragoons. This person is the notorious Monsieur G——, who was detected cheating at *écarté* at the 'Travellers;' was a defaulter on the St. Leger in the St. Patrick's year; has been warned off every race-course in England by the Jockey Club, besides being horsewhipped by half the Legs in England. He can get no gentleman to bring you a message, sir; and if he could, you must not meet him."

Gnashing his teeth with impotent rage, the detected impostor slunk away, while the count, bowing to Colonel Jervis, replied quietly,—

"I thank you very much, colonel. I am Monsieur de Chavannes; and I have no doubt what you say is perfectly correct. No one but a low ruffian could have behaved as this fellow did. It was, I assure you, no small offence which caused me to strike a blow in the presence of ladies."

"I saw it, Monsieur le Comte," answered Jervis, "I saw it from a distance, and was coming up as fast I could make my horse gallop, when you anticipated me. Then, seeing that I was not wanted, I stood looking on with intense satisfaction; for, upon my word, I never saw a thing better done in my life. No offence, count, but by the way you use your hands, I think you ought to have been an Englishman rather than a Frenchman, which I suppose from your name—for you have no French accent —you are—"

"I was at school in England, colonel," answered the count, laughing, "and so learned the use of my hands."

"That accounts for it—that accounts for it—for on my life I never saw a fellow more handsomely horsewhipped —and I have seen a good many too. Did you, Mademoiselle Valerie de Chatenœuf;—for I believe it is you whom I have the honour of addressing?"

"I have been less fortunate than you, Colonel Jervis, for I never saw any one horsewhipped before, and sincerely hope I shall never see another."

"Don't say that, my dear lady, don't say that. I am sure it is a very pretty sight, when it is well and soundly done. Besides, it seems ungrateful to the count."

"I would not be ungrateful for the world," I replied; "and I am sure the count needs no assurance of that fact. I am for ever obliged by his prompt defence of me—but it is nothing more than I should have expected from him."

"What, that he would fight for you, Valerie?" whispered Caroline, maliciously, in a tone which, perhaps, she did not intend to be overheard; but if such was her meaning, she missed it, for all present heard her distinctly.

I replied, however, very coolly—

"Yes, Caroline, that he would fight for me, or you, or any lady who was aggrieved or insulted in his presence."

"*Mille graces* for your good opinions!" said De Chavannes, with a bow, and a glance that was far more eloquent than words.

"A truce to compliments, if you will not think me impertinent, count," said the colonel; "but I wish to ask this fair lady, if she will pardon me one question; had you ever a friend called ——"

"Adèle Chabot!" I interrupted him; "and I shall be most enchanted to hear of her, or better still to see her, as Mrs. Jervis."

"You have anticipated me; that is what I was about to

say. We arrived in town last night; and she commissioned me at once to make out your whereabouts for her. The Gironacs told me that you were staying at Kew——"

"Yes, at Judge Selwyn's. By the way," I added, a little mischievously, I confess, "allow me to make known to one another, Mrs. Charles Selwyn, *once* Caroline Stanhope, and Colonel Jervis."

Jervis bowed low, but his cheek and brow burned a little, and he looked sharply at me out of the corner of his eye; but I preserved such a demure face, that he did not quite know whether I was *au fait* or not.

Caroline, to do her justice, behaved exceedingly well. Her character, indeed, which had been quite unformed before her marriage, had gained solidity, and her mind, judgment, as well as tone, since her introduction to a family so superior as that of the Selwyns. And she now neither blushed nor tittered, nor, indeed, showed any signs of consciousness, although she gave me a sly pinch, while she was inquiring in her sweetest voice and serenest manner after Adèle, whom she said she had always loved very much, and longed to see her sincerely in her new station, which she was so admirably qualified to fill. "I hear she was vastly admired in Paris, colonel; and no wonder, for I really think she was the very prettiest creature I ever saw in my life. You are a fortunate man, Colonel Jervis."

"I am, indeed," said he, laughing. "Adèle is a very good little creature, and the people were so good-natured as to be very civil to her in Paris, especially your friend Madame d'Albret, Mademoiselle de Chatenœuf. Nothing could exceed her attentions to us. We are very much indebted to you for her acquaintance. By the way, Adèle has no end of letters, and presents of all sorts, for you from her. When can you come and see Adèle?"

"Where are you staying, Colonel Jervis?"

"At Thomas's Hotel, in Berkeley-square, at present, until we can find a furnished house for the season. In August we are going down to a little cottage of mine, in the Highlands. And I believe Adèle has some plan for inducing you to come down and bear her company, while I am slaughtering grouse and black cock."

"Thanks, colonel, both to you and Adèle. But I do not know how that will be. August is two whole months distant yet, and one never knows what may happen in the course of two months. Do you know I was half thinking of paying a visit to France myself, when my brother, who is on visit to me now, returns to join his regiment."

"Were you, indeed?" asked De Chavannes, more earnestly than the subject seemed to warrant. "I had not heard of that scheme before. Is it likely to be carried into effect, mademoiselle?"

"I hardly know. As yet it is little more than a distant dream."

"But you have not yet answered my question, Mademoiselle de Chatenœuf," said the colonel. "You have not yet told me when you will come and see Adèle."

"Oh! pardon me, colonel. I return to town to-morrow, and I will not lose a moment. Suppose I say at one o'clock to-morrow, or two will be better. Caroline, the judge was so good as to say that he would let his carriage take me home; I dare say it can drop me at Thomas's, can it not?"

"Certainly *not*, Valerie! There, don't stare now, or look indignant or surprised. It served you perfectly right; what did you expect me to say? Or why do you ask such silly questions? Of course, it can take you wherever you please, precisely as if it were your own."

"Then at two o'clock, I will be at Thomas's to-morrow, colonel; in the mean time, pray give Adèle my best love."

"I will, indeed. And now I will intrude upon you no longer, ladies," he added, raising his hat. "In fact, I owe you many apologies for the liberty I have taken in introducing myself. I hope you will believe that I would not have done so under any other circumstances."

We bowed, and, without any further remarks, he put spurs to his horse and cantered away.

"A very gentlemanly person," said Caroline; "I think Adèle has done very well for herself."

"You had better not let Mr. Charles Selwyn hear you say so, under all circumstances, or I think that very likely the whipping we were talking about in fun, yesterday, will become real, *cara mia!*"

"Nonsense! for shame, you mischievous thing!" said Caroline, blushing a little, but not painfully.

"Who is this Colonel Jervis?" asked the Count de

Chavannes. "I was a little puzzled, or rather *not* a little: for at first none of you seemed to know him; and, after a little while, you all appeared to know him quite well. Pray explain the mystery."

"He is a very gentlemanly person, count, as Mrs. Selwyn justly observes, and, as you can perceive, a very handsome man. Further than that, he was colonel of one his majesty's *crack* regiments, as they call them, and is now on half-pay. He is, moreover, a man of high fashion, and of the first standing in society. And, last of all, which is the secret of the whole, he is the husband of a very charming little Frenchwoman, a particular friend of Caroline's and mine, one of the prettiest and nicest persons on earth, with whom he ran away some six months since, fancying her to be—"

"Valerie!" exclaimed Caroline, blushing fiery red.

"Caroline!" replied I, quietly.

"What *were* you going to say?"

"Fancying her to be a very great heiress," I continued; "but finding her to be a far better thing, a delightful, beautiful, and excellent wife."

"Happy man!" said De Chavannes, with a half-sigh.

"Why do you say so, count?"

"To have married one for whom you vouch so strongly. Is that any common fortune?"

"It is rather common, count, just of late I mean," said Caroline, laughing. "You do not know that among Valerie's other accomplishments she is the greatest little match-maker in existence. She marries off all her friends as fast—oh! you cannot think how fast."

"I *hope*,—I mean to say I *think*," he corrected himself, not without some little confusion, "that she is not quite so bad as you make her out. She has not yet made any match for herself, I believe. No, no. I don't believe she is quite so bad."

"I would not be too sure, count, were I you," she answered, desirous of paying me off a little for some of the badinage with which I had treated her. "These ladies, with so many strings to their bow—"

It was now my time to exclaim "Caroline!" and I did so not without giving some little emphasis of severity to my tone; for I really thought she was going beyond the limits of propriety, if not of *persiflage;* and I will do her the justice to say that she felt it herself, for she blushed very much as I spoke, and was at once silent.

The awkwardness of this pause was fortunately broken by the return of Auguste and Lionel, at a sharp canter; for the review was now entirely at an end, and they had now for the first moment remembered that, having promised to return in a quarter of an hour, they had suffered two hours or more to elapse, and that we were probably all alone.

Caroline immediately began to rally Lionel and Auguste; the former, with whom she was very intimate, pretty severely, for their want of gallantry in leaving us all alone and unprotected in such a crowd.

"Not the least danger—not the least!" replied Lionel hastily. "Had we not known that, we should have returned long ago."

"In proof of which *no* danger, we have been all frightened nearly to death; Mademoiselle Valerie de Chatenœuf has been grievously affronted, and I am not sure but she would have been beaten by a French *Chevalier d'Industrie,* had it not been for the gallantry of the Count de Chavannes."

And thereupon out came the whole history of Monsieur G——, his horsewhipping, the opportune appearance of Colonel Jervis, and all the curious circumstances of the scene.

I never in my life saw any one so fearfully excited as Auguste. He turned white as ashes, even to his very lips, while his eyes literally flashed fire, and his frame shivered as if he had been in an ague fit. "*Il me le paiera!*" he muttered between his hard-set teeth. "*Il me le paiera, le scélérat! Ma pauvre sœur—ma pauvre petite Valerie!*"

And then he shook the hand of Chavannes with the heartiest and warmest emotion. "I shall never forget this," he said, in a thick, low voice; "never, never! From this time forth, De Chavannes, we are friends for ever. But I shall never, never, be able to repay you."

"Nonsense, *mon cher,* nonsense," replied Chavannes. "I did nothing—positively nothing at all. I should not have been a man, had I done otherwise."

This had, however, no effect at all in stopping Auguste's exclamations and professions of eternal gratitude; nor did he cease until Monsieur de Chavannes said quietly, "Well, well, if you will have it so, say no more about it; and one day or other I will ask a favour of you, which, if granted, will leave me your debtor."

"*If* granted!—it *is* granted," exclaimed Auguste, impetuously. "What is it?—name it—I say it *is* granted."

"Don't be rash, *mon cher*," replied the count, laughing; "it is no slight boon which I shall ask."

"Do not be foolish, Auguste," I interposed; "you are letting your feelings get the better of you, strangely; and, Caroline, if you do not tell the people to drive home, you will keep the judge waiting dinner—a proceeding to which you know he is by no means partial."

"You are right, as usual, Valerie; always thoughtful for other people. So we will go home."

But, just as we were on the point of starting, the groom with the cockade, whom we had seen following Colonel Jervis, trotted up, and touching his hat, asked,

"I beg your pardon, gentlemen, but is any one of you the Count de Chavannes?"

"I am," replied the count; "what do you want with me, sir?"

"From Colonel Jervis, sir," replied the man, handing him a visiting card. "The colonel's compliments, count, and he begs you will do him the favour, in case you hear anything more from that fellow, as you horsewhipped, count, to let him know at Thomas's at once; for you must not treat him as a gentleman, no how, the colonel says; and if so be he gives you any trouble, the colonel can get his flint fixed—the colonel can!"

"Thank you, my man," replied the count; "give my compliments to your master, and I am much obliged for his interest. I shall do myself the honour of waiting on the colonel to-morrow. Be so good as to tell him so."

"I will, sir," said the man; and rode away without another word.

"You see, Monsieur de Chatenœuf, you must not dream of noticing the fellow as a gentleman," said the count.

"Impossible!" Lionel chimed in, almost in the same

breath; and all the ladies followed suit with their absolute "Impossible!"

A rapid drive brought us to the judge's house at Kew, where we found dinner nearly ready, though not waiting: and the events of the day were the topic, and the count the hero, of the evening.

The next morning we returned to town—Auguste and myself, I mean; Monsieur de Chavannes having driven up from Kew in his own cabriolet after dinner.

I called, according to my promise, and found Adèle alone, and delighted to see me, and in the highest possible spirits. She was the happiest of women, she said; and Colonel Jervis was everything that she could wish—the kindest, most affectionate of husbands; and all that she now desired, as she declared, was to see me established suitably.

"You had better let matters take their course, Adèle," I answered. "Though not much of a fatalist, I believe that when a person's time is to come, it comes. It avails nothing to hurry—nothing to endeavour to retard it. I shall fare, I doubt not, as my friends before me, dear Adèle; and if I can consult as well for myself as I seem to have done for my friends, I shall do very well. Caroline, by the way, is quite as happy as you declare yourself to be, and I doubt not are; for I like your colonel amazingly."

"I am delighted to hear it. He also is charmed with you. But who is the Count de Chavannes, of whom he is so full just now? He says he is the only Frenchman he ever saw worthy to be an Englishman—which, though *we* may not regard it exactly as a compliment, he considers the greatest thing he can say in any one's favour. Who is this Count de Chavannes, Valerie?"

I told her, in reply, all that I knew, and that you know, gentle reader, about the Count de Chavannes.

"*Et puis?—Et puis?*" asked Adèle, laughing.

"*Et puis*, nothing at all," I answered.

"No secrets among friends, Valerie," said Adèle, looking me earnestly in the face; "I had none with you, and you helped me with your advice. Be as frank, at least, with me, if you love me."

"I do love you dearly, Adèle; and I have no secrets. There is nothing concerning which to have a secret."

"Nothing?—not this gay and gallant count?"

"Not even he."

"And you are not about to become Madame la Comtesse?"

"I am not, indeed."

"Indeed—in very deed?"

"In very—very deed."

"Well, I do not understand it. By what Jervis told me, I presumed it was a settled thing."

"The colonel was mistaken. There is no thing, settled or unsettled."

"And do you, really, not like him?"

"I really *do* like him, Adèle, as a very pleasant companion for an hour or two, and as a very perfect gentleman."

"Yes, he told me all that. But if you like him so well, why not like him better? Why not love him?"

"I will be plain and true with you, Adèle. I do not choose to consider at all, whether I could, or could *not*, love him. He has never asked me, has never spoken of love to me; and putting it out of the question that it is unmaidenly to love unasked, I am sure it is unwise."

"I understand, I understand. But he *will* ask you, that is certain; and, when he does ask, what shall you say?"

"It will be time enough to consider when that time shall come."

"Another way of saying, 'I shall say *yes!*' But come, Valerie, you must promise me that if you need my assistance, you will call upon me for it. You *know* that anything I can do for you will be done without a thought, but how I best may serve you; and Jervis will do likewise, since he, as I do, considers that under Heaven, we owe our happiness to you."

"I promise it."

"Enough; I will ask no more. Now come up to my room, and I will give you Madame d'Albret's letters, and some pretty presents she has sent you. Do you know, Valerie, nothing could exceed her kindness to us. I believe she repents bitterly her unkindness to you. I cannot repeat the terms of praise and admiration which she applied to you."

"And do you know, Adèle, that it was her infamous

and miserable husband, Monsieur G——, whom the count horsewhipped this very day for insulting me?"

"Indeed? was it indeed? That man's enmity to you will never cease so long as he has life. No, Jervis did not tell me who it was, thinking, I fancy, that neither you nor I would have so much as known his name. But never care about the wretch. Here is madame's letter."

It was as kind a letter as could be written, full of thanks for the favour I had shown her in introducing my friends to her, and of hopes that we should one day meet again, when all the past should be forgotten, and I should resume my own place and station in the society of my own land. She begged my acceptance of the pretty dresses she sent, which she said she had selected, not for their value, but because they were pretty; and, in her postscript, she added what of course outweighed all the rest of her letter, both in interest and importance, that she had recently been informed through a strange channel, and, as it were, by accident, that my mother's health was failing, seriously, and that, although not attacked by any regular disorder, nor in any immediate danger, it was not thought probable that she could live much longer. "In that case, Valerie," she continued, "for, although no one could be so unnatural as to *wish* for a mother's death, how cruel and unmotherly she might be soever, it cannot be expected that you should regard her decease with more than decent observation, and a proper seriousness, I shall look to see you dwelling again among us, and spending the little fortune, which I understand you have so bravely earned, in the midst of your friends, and in your own country."

"That I shall never do," I said, speaking aloud, though in answer partly to her letter, partly to my own words; "that I shall never do. Visit France I may, once and again; but in England I shall dwell. France banished and repudiated me like a stepmother—England received me, kinder than my own, like a mother. In England I shall dwell."

"Wait till you see the lord of your destinies; and learn where he shall dwell. You will have to say, like the rest of us, 'Your country shall be my country, and your God my God,'"—observed Adèle interrupting my musings.

"The first perhaps—the last never! never! Catholic I

was born, Catholic I will die. I do *not* say that I will never marry any but a Catholic, but I *do* say that I will never marry but one who will approve my adoring my own God, according to my own conscience."

"Is the Count de Chavannes a Catholic?"

"Indeed, I know not. But he is a Breton, and the Bretons are a loyal race, both to their king and their God."

I now turned to finish my reading, which had been for the moment interrupted.

"Indeed, my dear Valerie," she concluded her letter, "I have long felt that although we were certainly justified by the circumstances of your situation in taking the steps we did at that time, we have been hardly pardonable in persisting so long in the maintenance of a falsehood, which has certainly been the cause of great pain and suffering to both your parents, the innocent no less than the guilty. I know that your mother can never forgive me for aiding you in your escape from her authority; but for my part, I am willing to bear her enmity, rather than persist in further concealment, so that you need not in any degree consider me in any steps which you may think it wise or right to take towards revelation and reconciliation. Indeed I think, Valerie, that if it can be done with due regard to your own safety and happiness, you ought to discover yourself to both your parents, and, if possible, even to visit the most unhappy, because the guiltier of the two, before her dissolution, which I really believe to be now very near at hand. Every one knows so well what you have undergone, that no blame will attach to you in the least degree. Allow me to add, that should you return to France, as I hope you will do, I shall never forgive you if you do not make my house your home."

This postscript, as will readily be believed, gave me more cause for thought than all the letter beside, and rendered me exceedingly uneasy. If I had felt ill-satisfied before with my condition and my concealment, much more was I now discontented with myself, and unhappy. I was almost resolved to return at all hazards with Auguste; and, indeed, when I consulted with Adèle, she leaned very much toward the same opinion. I would not, however, do anything rashly, but determined to consult not only with my brother, but with the judge, in whose wisdom I had no less confidence than I had in his friendship and integrity.

Things, however, were destined to occur, which in some degree altered and hastened all my proceedings; for that very evening when the Gironacs had retired, on my beginning to consult Auguste, "Listen to me a moment, before you tell me about your letters from France, or anything about returning, and I entreat you answer me truly, and let no false modesty, or little missish delicacy, prevent your doing so. Many a life has been rendered miserable by such foolishness, I have heard say; and being, as it were, almost alone in the world, as if an only brother with an only sister, to whom, if not to one another, should we speak freely?"

"You need not have made so long a preamble, dear Auguste," I replied with a smile; "of course I will answer you; and, when I say that, of course I will answer truly."

"Well, then, Valerie, do you like this Count de Chavannes?"

"It is an odd question, but—Yes. I do like him."

"Do you love him, Valerie?"

"Oh! Auguste—that is not fair. Besides, he has never spoken to me of love. He has never—I do not know whether he loves me—I have no reason to believe that he does."

"No reason!" he exclaimed, half-surprised, half-indignant—"no reason! I should think—but never mind—answer me this; if he did love you, do you love him, or like him enough to take him for your husband?"

"He has spoken to you, Auguste—he has spoken to you!" I exclaimed, blushing very deeply, but unable to conceal my gratification.

"I am answered, Valerie, by the sparkle of those bright eyes. Yes, he has spoken to me, dearest sister; and asked my influence with you, and my permission to address you."

"And you replied——?"

"And I replied, that my permission was a matter of no consequence, for that you were entirely your own mistress, and that my influence would be exerted only to induce you to follow your own judgment and inclinations, and to consult for your own happiness"

"Answered like a good and wise brother. And then he——?"

"Asked, whether I could form any opinion of the state of your feelings. To which I replied, that I could only say that I had reason to suppose that your hand and heart were neither of them engaged, and that the field was open to him if he chose to make a trial. But that I had no opportunity of judging how you felt toward him. I also said, that I thought you knew very little of each other, and that his attachment must have grown up too rapidly to have taken a very strong root. But there I found I was mistaken. For he assured me that it was from esteem of your character, and admiration of your energy, courage, and constancy under adversity, not from the mere prettiness of your face, or niceness of your manners, that he first began to love you. And I since ascertained that there is scarce an incident of your life with which he has not made himself acquainted, and that in the most delicate and guarded manner. I confess, Valerie, that it has raised him greatly in my estimation, to find that he looks upon marriage as a thing so serious and solemn, and does not rush into it from mere fancy for a pretty face and lady-like accomplishments."

"I think so too, Auguste," I replied. "But I wish we knew a little more about him. His character and principles, I mean."

Auguste looked at me for a moment, in great surprise. "What an exceedingly matter-of-fact girl you are, Valerie; I never knew any one in the least like you. Do you know I am afraid you are a little ——" and he paused a moment, as if he hardly knew how to proceed.

"A little hard and cold, is it not, dear Auguste?" said I, throwing my arms about him. "No, no, indeed I am not; but I have been cast so long on my own sole resources, and obliged to rely only on my own energy and clear-sightedness, that I always try to look at both sides of the question, and not to let my feelings overpower me, until I have proved that it is good and wise to do so. Consider, too, Auguste, that on this step depends the whole happiness or misery of a girl's existence."

"You are right, Valerie, and I am wrong. But tell me, do you love him?"

"I do, Auguste. I like him better than any man I have ever seen. He is the only man of whom I could think as a husband—and I have for some time past been fearful of liking him—loving him, too much, not knowing, though I did believe and hope, that he reciprocated my feelings. And now, if I knew but a little more of his principles and character, I would not hesitate."

"Then you need not hesitate, dearest Valerie; for, as if to obviate this objection, he showed me, in the most delicate manner, private letters from his oldest and most intimate friends, and especially from Mr. ——, a most respectable clergyman, who lives at Hendon, by whom he was educated, and with whom he has maintained constant intercourse and correspondence ever since. This alone speaks very highly in his favour; and the terms in which he writes to his pupil, are such as prove them both to be men of the highest character for worth, integrity, and virtue. He has proposed, moreover, that I should ride down with him to-morrow to Hendon, to visit Mr. ——, and to hear from his own lips yet more of his character and conduct, that is to say, if I can give him any hopes of ultimate success."

"Well, Auguste," I replied, "I think with you, that all this speaks very highly in favour of your friend; and I think that the best thing you can do, is to take this ride which he proposes, and see his tutor. In the mean time, I will drive down to Kew, and speak with our good friend Judge Selwyn on the subject. To-morrow evening I will see the count, and hear whatever he desires to say to me."

This was a very matter-of-fact way of dealing with the affair, certainly; but what Auguste had said was in some sort true. I was in truth rather a matter-of-fact girl, and I never found that I suffered by it in the least; for I certainly was not either worldly or selfish, and the feelings do, as certainly, require to be guided and controlled by sober reason.

After coming to this conclusion, I showed Madame d'Albret's letter to Auguste, and we came to the decision, also, that, under the circumstances, Auguste should, immediately on his return, communicate the fact of my being alive and in good circumstances, to my father; leaving it at his discretion to inform my mother of the facts or not, as he might judge expedient.

At a very early hour next morning, I took a glass coach and drove down to Kew, where I arrived, greatly to the astonishment of the whole family, just as they were sitting down to breakfast; and when I stated that I had come to speak on very urgent business with the judge, he desired my carriage to return to town, and proposed to carry me back himself, so that we might kill two birds, as he expressed it, with one stone,—holding a consultation in his carriage, while on his way to court.

As soon as we got into the coach, while I was hesitating how to open the subject, which was certainly a little awkward for a young girl, the judge took up the discourse—

"Well, Valerie," he said, "I suppose you want to know the result of the inquiries which you were so unwilling that I should make about the Count de Chavannes. Is not that true?"

"It is perfectly true, judge—though I do not know how you ever have divined it."

"It is lucky, at least, that I consulted my own judgment, rather than your fancy; for otherwise I should have had no information to give you."

"But as it is, judge?"

"Why as it is, Mademoiselle Valerie, you may marry him as soon as ever he asks you, and think yourself a very lucky young lady into the bargain. He has a character such as not one man in fifty can produce. He is rich, liberal without being extravagant, never plays, is by no means dissipated, and in all respects is a man of honour, ability, and character; such is what I have learned from a quarter where there can be no mistake."

I was a good deal affected for a moment or two, and was very near bursting into tears. The good judge took my hand in his, and spoke soothingly and almost caressingly, bidding me confide in him altogether, and he would advise me, as if he were my own father.

I did so accordingly; and while he approved highly of all that I had done, and of the delicate and gentlemanly manner in which the count had acted, he fully advised me to deal frankly and directly with him. "You like him, I am sure, Valerie; indeed I believe I knew that before you did yourself, and I have no doubt he will make you an admirable husband. Tell him all, show him this letter of your friend Madame d'Albret's, about your mother, and if he desires it, as I dare say he will, marry him at once, and set out together with Auguste, for France, when his leave of absence is expired, and go directly to Paris with your husband. As a married woman, your parents will have no authority of any kind over you, and I think it is your duty to do so."

I agreed with him at once; and when, in the evening, Auguste returned with the count from a visit to his former tutor, which had been in all respects satisfactory, and left me alone with Monsieur de Chavannes, everything was determined without difficulty.

Love-scenes and courtships, though vastly interesting to the actors, are always the dullest things in the world to bystanders; I shall therefore proceed at once to the end, merely stating that the count *was* all, and *did* all, that the most *exigeante* of women could have required—that from the first to the last he was full of delicacy, of tenderness, and honour, and that after twelve years of a happy life with him, I have never had cause to repent for a moment that I consented to give him the hand, which he so ardently desired.

The joy of Madame Gironac can be imagined better than described, as well as the manner in which she bustled about my *trousseau* and my outfit for France, as it was determined that the judge's plan should be adopted to the letter, and that we should start directly from St. George's to Dover and Calais.

Never, perhaps, was a marriage more rapidly organized and completed. The law business was expedited with all speed by Charles Selwyn; Madame Bathurst, the Jervises, the Gironacs, and the Selwyns, were alone present at the wedding, and though we were all dear friends, there was no affectation of tears or lamentable partings; for we knew that, in Heaven's pleasure, we should all meet again within a few months, as, after our wedding tour was ended, Monsieur de Chavannes proposed to take up his abode in England, the land of his choice, as of his education.

There was no bishop to perform the ceremony, nor any *duke* to give away the bride. No long array of liveried servants with favours in their buttons and in their hats—

no pompous paragraph in the morning papers to describe the beauties of the high-bred bride and the dresses of her aristocratic bridemaids—but two hearts were united as well as two hands, and Heaven smiled upon the union.

A quick and pleasant passage carried us to Paris, where I was received with raptures by my good old friend Madame Paon, and with sincere satisfaction by Madame d'Albret, who was proud to recognise her old *protégée* in the new character of the Comtesse de Chavannes, a character which she imagined reflected no small credit on her tuition and patronage.

The threatened *émeute* having passed over, Auguste easily obtained a renewal of his leave of absence, in order to visit his family at Pau, and as he preceded us by three days, and travelled with the utmost diligence, he outstripped us by nearly a week, and we found both my parents prepared to receive us, and both *really* happy at the prosperous tidings.

My poor mother was indeed dying; had we come two days later, we should have been too late, for she died in my arms on the day following our arrival, enraptured to find herself relieved from the heinous crime of which she had so long believed herself guilty, and blessing me with her dying lips.

My father, who had always loved me, and who had erred through weakness of head only, seemed never to weary of sitting beside me, of holding my hand in his, and of gazing in my face. With Monsieur de Chavannes' consent, the whole of my little earnings, amounting now to nearly £3,000, was settled on him for his life, and then on my sisters; and the income arising from it, though a mere trifle in England, in that cheap region sufficed, with what he possessed of his own, to render his old age affluent and happy.

Thus all my trials ended: and if the beginning of my career was painful and disastrous, the cares and sorrows of Valerie de Chatenœuf have been more than compensated by the happiness of Valerie de Chavannes.

I may as well mention here, that a few years afterwards, Lionel Dempster married my second sister, Elisée, a very nice and very handsome girl, and has settled very close to the villa which the count purchased on his return from

France, near Windsor, on the lovely Thames, ministering not a little by their company to the bliss of our happy, peaceful life.

My eldest brother, Auguste, is now a lieutenant-colonel of the line, having greatly distinguished himself in Algeria; Nicholas, who never returned to France, has acquired both renown and riches by his musical abilities, and all the younger branches of the family are happily provided for.

I have three sweet children, one boy and two little girls, and the difficulties and sorrows I experienced, owing to an evil and injudicious course of education, have been so far of use, that they have taught me how to bring up my own children, even more to love and honour than to obey.

Perfect happiness is not allotted to any here below; but few and short have been the latter sorrows, and infinite the blessings, vouchsafed by a kind Providence, to the once poor and houseless, but now rich, and honoured, and, better than all, *loved* Valerie.

THE END.

CPSIA information can be obtained
at www.ICGtesting.com
Printed in the USA
LVHW100515130422
716029LV00002B/121